"Hello. My name is James Highfield Ettinger, vice president of the United States.

Today is the seventeenth of December. By the time anyone views this tape, I will have resigned from office. And by the end of what I have to say here, all of you will understand exactly why I have taken this course of action. I have played a part in a crime. A crime against all that is noble and good and just. A crime against this nation, which I chose to serve. A crime against you, the American public. It is a crime of sickening proportions. I was an unknowing participant in many of the activities which I will describe. But for too long I have withheld the truth from not only my friends and family, but also from the nation I love. I believed it was for the greater good. But I was wrong. All that I share with you now is the truth, and can be verified. So let me begin . . . at the beginning."

THE GREATER GOOD

THE GREATER GOOD

A THRILLER

CASEY MORETON

POCKET STAR BOOKS
New York London Toronto Sydney

The sale of this book without its cover is unauthorized. If you purchased
this book without a cover, you should be aware that it was reported to
the publisher as "unsold and destroyed." Neither the author nor the
publisher has received payment for the sale of this "stripped book."

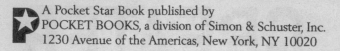 A Pocket Star Book published by
POCKET BOOKS, a division of Simon & Schuster, Inc.
1230 Avenue of the Americas, New York, NY 10020

This book is a work of fiction. Names, characters, places
and incidents are products of the author's imagination or
are used fictitiously. Any resemblance to actual events or
locales or persons, living or dead, is entirely coincidental.

Copyright © 2004 by Casey Moreton

Originally published in hardcover in 2004 by Atria Books

All rights reserved, including the right to reproduce
this book or portions thereof in any form whatsoever.
For information address Atria Books, 1230 Avenue
of the Americas, New York, NY 10020

ISBN-13: 978-0-7434-5658-6
ISBN-10:   0-7434-5658-0

This Pocket Star Books paperback edition May 2006

10 9 8 7 6 5 4 3 2

POCKET STAR BOOKS and colophon are registered
trademarks of Simon & Schuster, Inc.

Cover art and design by James Wang

Manufactured in the United States of America

For information regarding special discounts for bulk
purchases, please contact Simon & Schuster Special Sales
at 1-800-456-6798 or business@simonandschuster.com

To Kari
for believing

Acknowledgments

First and foremost, I would like to thank my editor, Emily Bestler, for giving me a shot and for making the manuscript stronger with each draft. Thanks to both Sarah Branham and Cindy Jackson for their editorial input. And many thanks to Frank Weimann at The Literary Group for performing the miracle of finding the book a home in New York City.

1

IF HE DIDN'T GET OUT NOW, HE'D NEVER forgive himself. He was fifty-five, but after nearly six years in office, fifty-five felt like seventy. He had become a cliché, a caricature of the burned-out politician. In the beginning—before three terms in the Senate, and long before the title of Vice President had soured on him—politics had meant something. Something pure, maybe. Something noble.

If he didn't get out now, he might not have the strength to try again. These days his hairline receded by the minute. A face that had for decades been his calling card, lately only revealed the rigors of this job. His once broad, proud shoulders now felt weak under the burden he'd carried for far too long.

James Ettinger reclined in the soft leather of his reading chair and watched the light of a full moon wash in through his bedroom window at Beagle Run, his vacation lodge in Maine. Miriam, his wife of twenty-seven years, was still asleep beneath the thick quilted comforter on the bed. She looked so peaceful lying there. He stared at her for a long moment, a fond expression on his face. The comforter rose and fell with her breathing. Finally, he got up from his chair with a sigh.

He stood there in his robe, one hand in a deep silk pocket, the other swirling bourbon in a crystal glass. As he gazed out the picture window, he struggled to relax. The activities of the past week had taken him to Asia and Europe and back to the United States in seventy-two hours. It was an exhausting way to live. He hadn't slept for nearly forty-eight hours.

The vice president drained the last of the bourbon and set the glass on the bedside table. Another drink would be nice . . . and then another. Maybe he'd polish off the half-empty bottle he kept tucked away in the study. He stared at the glass on the little mahogany and brass table. It seemed to taunt him. Ettinger shook his head, chastising himself.

The warm dent in the pillow that had been formed by his head was now filled with the plump body of their snooty female Persian, Dolly. Ettinger rested his weight on the edge of the bed, the mattress giving slightly under his two hundred and some–odd pounds. Dolly glared at him with unflinching disdain—her only expression.

"What?" he said at her.

The feline ignored him, wrapping her white puff of a tail down the length of her body. She squinted, likely from a whiff of bourbon on his breath, and worked her paws into the cotton of the pillowcase.

It was 4 A.M. The bourbon had coated his tongue with a wicked aftertaste and made his stomach growl. He lumbered downstairs to the kitchen and foraged through the refrigerator for something—*anything*—sweet. There was strawberry cake with some sort of whipped-cream topping on a glass plate. He sliced off a section and carefully flipped it onto a paper napkin. He found a half-gallon of skim milk in the fridge and filled a green tumbler. He squirted in some Hershey's syrup from a squeeze bottle, stirred it with a butter knife, and carted the feast back to the comfort of the bedroom.

Perched on the edge of his reading chair, he fingered the remote control and flipped channels until he landed on CNN. President Yates was on the screen. The sound was low, and that was fine with Ettinger. He'd heard all that Yates had to say. *The buffoon!* There was a collage of footage of the president doing this and that; speaking to students at a fund-raiser; lighting a Christmas tree at a holiday gathering of constituents; shaking hands with the British prime minister. It all seemed so benign.

He had to hand it to Yates, he'd strutted into office and handled it like a champ for over six years now. But he was really just an ignorant puppet, controlled from afar. They'd managed to pull it off. But the ice was getting thin.

It was definitely time to get out.

But what *then?*

Money wasn't an issue. He'd married money. Of course he loved—*cherished*—Miriam, and could probably have still loved her even without her father's billions. But he hadn't been forced to make that choice. They could slip out of public life and live in luxury. And why not? Any sane man would have fled this circus years ago. Maybe now was his chance. He could buy an island. Waste millions on the biggest boat on Earth and stalk the horizon. Drink till the sun went down; drink when it popped back up. Sail the boat and stay drunk. Grow old and watch his kids grow old. The money was there. Would Miriam go for it? Probably. But that wasn't the issue, was it?

He thumbed the red button on the remote and killed the television. He placed the green tumbler next to the bourbon glass on the bedside table and noticed that Dolly, like Miriam, was now fast asleep. The room was warm, heated by a vent in the floor near his feet. Christmas was closing in. Snow was heavy on the ground and was still blowing in by the truckload. The pines and firs outside the window looked like a postcard.

From the drawer in the bedside table he took a leather-bound book and tucked it under his arm, careful not to make a sound. The book was purchased years before his days as a bond servant to the White House. Printed in gold foil on its spine were the title and the author's name. *Great Expectations*, by Charles Dickens. Ettinger inspected the volume proudly. He had purchased it at a specialty shop in Chicago. It was an impulse purchase. Now though, he fully realized that fate had been his guide on that gray afternoon in Illinois.

Ettinger eased back out the bedroom door, then down the hall and down the stairs toward the kitchen. Just before he reached the kitchen he turned a knob and slipped through a door that hid a narrow flight of stairs to the basement. He locked the door from the inside. A slender chain hung from the ceiling to one side of his head. He gave it a crisp tug. A sixty-watt bulb painted the walls and his feet and the pine board steps with dull yellow light.

The pine boards creaked under his weight. At the bottom of the steps he flicked a switch on the wall. Several banks of fluorescent lamps blinked haphazardly, then pale light pushed away the gloom, allowing him to safely navigate the cold cement slab floor.

The basement was filled mainly with junk collected over a lifetime. A space was cleared toward the center of the big room; arranged on a large oval rug, a metal folding chair faced a video camera. It was an RCA model that required a full-size VHS videotape.

Ettinger picked up the plastic remote control from beneath the chair and sat down. He faced the camera and thumbed a button on the remote. A red light glowed on one side of the camera. He cleared his throat, took a deep breath, and began to speak.

"Hello. My name is James Highfield Ettinger, vice president of the United States. Today is the seventeenth of December. By the time anyone views this tape, I will have resigned from office. And by the end of what I have to say here, all of you will understand exactly why I have taken this course of action. I have played a part in a crime. A crime against all that is noble and good and just. A crime against this nation, which I chose to serve. A crime against you, the American public. It is a crime of sickening proportions."

He stared straight into the camera and spoke with precision and clarity.

"I was an unknowing participant in many of the activities which I will describe. But for too long I have withheld the truth from not only my friends and family, but also from the nation I love. I believed it was for the greater good. But I was wrong. All that I share with you now is the truth, and can be verified. So let me begin . . . at the beginning."

Ninety-seven minutes later, with nothing left to say, James Ettinger wrapped up his confession by hitting the power button on the remote. The red light on the camera went dark. The basement was still; only the groaning from the furnace broke the silence. He remained seated in the folding chair for a few minutes, his mind reacclimating itself to present reality, pushing back the ghosts of those things he'd dredged up this morning for the benefit of the camera.

With the press of a button, the videotape flopped out of the camera. Ettinger pulled the tape out and set it on the folding chair. On the floor beside the chair was the leather-bound edition of *Great Expectations* from the bedroom. He picked it up and flipped open the front cover. Where there should have been pages, there was only a rectangular cutout, an empty compartment cut into the block of wood that had long ago been crafted and painted to look like worn and well-read pages. Over the years he'd stashed a number of rather personal items within this handy novelty piece. The VHS cassette was a perfect fit. He snapped it into place.

In a moment of silent reflection, he held the book with his left hand and gently stroked his right hand down the smooth plastic of the front side of the tape. He thought about what was recorded on it. What it meant. In no uncertain terms, his political career was over. A matter of days and it would all be finished.

So be it. He closed the book.

From amid the clutter that lined the walls, Ettinger withdrew a stack of rubbish. He dodged a pair of Ping-Pong tables that were stored with their aluminum legs tucked beneath the playing surface. There were lawn chairs heaped together, bent and contorted. Broken canoe paddles. Patched life preservers. What a mess.

The stack of rubbish spilled down at an angle to the smooth cement at his feet. He stared at yellowed newspapers, decades old, and magazines with outdated celebrities on their covers. Folded among the heap he found a useless collection of brown paper grocery bags. He chose one without too many water stains and kicked most of the rest of the junk back into a corner, between some croquet mallets and Coleman lanterns.

At a worktable covered with trinkets and gadgets, he ran a pair of scissors up one side of the paper bag and laid it open. He set the false copy of the Dickens classic in the center of the stiff brown paper and wrapped it like a gift, sealing it with heavy packing tape. He plucked a black ballpoint pen from a half-corroded Folgers can and addressed an adhesive shipping label in block lettering, which he then applied to the package. He recapped the pen and toted the small bundle back upstairs.

In the kitchen, he attached several dollars' worth of postage to the top right-hand corner and deposited the parcel into the mail bin that sat at one end of the kitchen counter.

Breakfast with Miriam and the kids and their holiday guests was mainly omelets and sliced fruit. James Ettinger more or less ignored the meal, facing the dining room window in his chair, watching the snow whip from side to side in the morning light, thinking about what he'd done that morning and the repercussions it would bring.

After lunch they played checkers in front of the huge stone fireplace, munched on cookies and chocolates and sipped eggnog and brandy. The satellite dish on the roof could pick up nearly three hundred stations, and they stared at the Weather Channel for hours.

Later, a snowball fight erupted in the front yard. Miriam stood on the porch, laughing, keeping clear of the line of fire. Secret Service agents stood nearby at their posts. It was a familiar sight, and in many ways a very reassuring one, but always intrusive to family life. She ignored them and enjoyed her family.

The snow deepened with the afternoon. Miriam and her sister and their kids piled into the black limousine, headed for Christmas shopping in town. The snowfall continued, but the roads were still navigable. Before leaving, the driver gathered the outgoing mail. While the others shopped, he'd make a quick stop by the post office.

The vice president stayed behind, standing ankle-deep in snow in the yard, talking football with a pair of Secret Service agents who were diehard Redskins fans. The temperature dropped ten degrees in less than three hours. Tonight it might get down below zero. Only the Secret Service cared. They were the ones stuck out here in the elements day and night. After a few minutes, Ettinger dropped the stub of his cigar in the snow and headed back for the warmth of the lodge.

Beagle Run was built about ten years after the Civil War. Miriam's father, E. E. Greeber, bought the rustic lodge and two thousand surrounding acres in the early 1940s, long after his great fortune had blossomed into the realm of excess. At nearly ten thousand square feet, it was enormous, and reeked of money to burn.

The lodge had been a gift to Miriam from her father. Ettinger loved the place. It sat on the coast of Maine, a mile from the water. He fished in the summer and hunted whitetail a week each winter, even though the nature freaks in the media rode him hard. Christmas meant two uninterrupted weeks at Beagle Run. Traditionally, he ate too much, smoked with the Secret Service, slept late, and pondered the vile world of Washington, D.C.

In the game room, he set up an easel with a canvas and toyed with watercolors for forty-five minutes. When he tired of painting he moved on to a paperback he'd worked on all week.

As the hours passed, he became less focused and began to worry. He wondered if he'd done the right thing.

He thought of Nelson, his brother in Montana. Their relationship had fallen off dramatically in the years since he'd taken office. Nelson had a ranch just north of Yellowstone. His tastes and desires were much simpler and less cluttered than the vice president's.

Ettinger settled in behind the laptop computer in his study, taking a moment to fire off a very special email to his older brother, to give him the heads-up regarding the media firestorm they'd face in the coming weeks.

The gang returned bearing gifts of all shapes and sizes, wrapped in expensive designer paper and complexly arranged bows and ribbons. Dinner was quite a feast. Everyone ate until they were sick, except Miriam and her sister, who picked at their plates like sparrows. After a week in the boonies Bradey Ettinger, nineteen, was sick of Beagle Run. He missed the city and his friends and the unrelenting public attention he received as the only son of the vice president. He was a sophomore at Harvard. He'd tired of his fifteen-year-old sister, Jude, within forty-eight hours of this little family holiday. He gnawed on a fat pork rib and glared at her across the table. Jude was picking at the croutons in her salad, totally pleased to be on his nerves.

Miriam's sister, Elaine Greeber-Castel, and her cache of spoiled children carried on like royalty. Elaine was as deep in inherited wealth as Miriam, but her money couldn't buy the kind of prestige that Miriam possessed as the vice president's wife.

After dinner, the big halogen lamps surrounding the pond out front were cranked up, and the kids laced up their skates and hit the ice. The adults lounged in deck chairs and drank cocoa and laughed at the youngsters.

The ice was at least a foot thick, plenty safe for mild recreation, and had been cleared of snow for the evening's recreation. Miriam and Elaine had skated on the big pond when they were girls, and had even taken the sport seriously for a number of years.

Despite the cold, the evening turned into a pleasant family get-together at Beagle Run. Miriam snuggled against her husband, wrapping her arms around his midsection. She nuzzled her face into his shoulder. Her nose glowed pink from the cold. Ettinger enjoyed a hundred-dollar cigar and held his wife tightly to his side. The laughter of the children as they skimmed across the frozen pond rang out like a carol and would have made any father proud. A part of him wished this night could last forever, because the future looked so chaotic and uncertain. Perhaps he'd made a mistake. Perhaps it would have been wiser to simply hold course and let things continue as they had. But it would have eaten him alive. It was too late now, anyway.

After the skating, coats and mittens and rubber boots were shed in the entryway. The fireplace in the game room roared as a fat oak log was thrown on the blaze. Cocoa and hot tea, spiced cider and marshmallow treats were downed by the trayful. Board games came out, along with jigsaw puzzles.

Finally, the vice president kissed his wife on the cheek and let out a yawn.

"I'm going to take a quick shower and read a little before bed," he said, motioning toward the stairs.

In the shower, James Ettinger pressed his hands against the tiled wall and let the soothing hot water spill over his head and face. He toweled off, slipped on some clean boxers, and snatched a robe from the enormous closet across the room from the bed.

He glanced out the window at the full moon,

briefly admiring the look of snow bending the tree limbs. Dolly pawed at the door and he let her in. Moonlight spilled in through the big floor-to-ceiling window behind him. Dolly circled him two or three times, leaning into his legs. Hands on hips, he studied the old cat with a wry smile. He was unaware of the spot of red laser light no bigger than a dime that was moving up his back to his neck. In the instant that it reached the middle of the back of his head, there was a single, quick, crisp sound of chipped window glass, and the upper third of his skull was blown off.

2

THE SHOT, FROM A DISTANCE OF 175 YARDS, had been immaculate. St. John remained in position for a good fifteen seconds after he'd pulled the trigger, watching through the Swiss-made scope on his rifle, making sure his target was down.

St. John was sprawled in the snow on a small rise between a pair of massive firs. In a movement that was precise, fluid, and practiced, he folded the small tripod that had balanced the stock of the rifle on the snow, stood, then shouldered the rifle. He stayed in the shadows.

He was fully camouflaged, dressed in an insulated suit of arctic white from head to toe. Even his weapon was invisible against the snow: the stock, barrel, noise suppressor, scope, strap—all as white as newly fallen powder.

There were no alarms going off, no sudden flurry of Secret Service agents flooding out into the timber to hunt the assassin. Nobody had a clue. The sound of his bullet penetrating the windowpane had been absorbed by the cold night wind, and the noise suppressor on the end of the barrel had reduced the brisk *crack* of the rifle's signature to a tempered cough and eliminated the muzzle flash. The alarm would sound only if the window itself were opened. He would have a wide avenue for a safe escape.

His night-vision goggles turned the world an odd green. He darted along the trailhead forged on his arrival. Dodging branches and large stones hidden by the blanket of powder, he moved with grace, his breathing steady, his heart rate picking up only slightly.

A quarter mile ahead he came to a sudden dip in the terrain. It was a streambed draped in velvety white powder. He turned east, heading downwind. The snow was deeper here, but he didn't have far to go. A massive log had fallen across the old streambed. St. John pulled himself over the trunk of the dead oak, his legs brushing crusted snow and ice from its cold, hard bark.

On the far side of the natural barrier he stopped.

In the center of the streambed was a sizable lump in the snow. He lifted one corner of a flap and yanked the tarpaulin away, revealing his mode of departure. The snowmobile fired up as he thumbed the ignition switch. The headlamp spilled light in front of him. He gunned the throttle and continued eastward. In the darkness the forest was full of ominous hazards; gnarled saplings and low-hanging branches appeared from out of the gloom without warning, taking aim at his head and arms; underbrush scratched at his legs and down the fiberglass shell of his gas-burning horse. Freezing drizzle encrusted the lenses of his ski goggles.

St. John throttled down, slowed to a fraction of his cruising speed, and approached a flatbed farm truck he'd backed against a low embankment. A ramp made of plywood and two-by-four studs slanted from the bed of the truck to the ground at a gentle angle. He bent low, cautiously preparing for impact. The front skids of the snowmobile clapped against the wooden ramp. The machine revved for a moment in a cloud of blue exhaust and then climbed the platform with ease, finally leveling out onto the flat expanse of the bed.

The truck was at least thirty years old, with balding tires and badly rusted fenders. The front half was draped in white camouflage netting; he tugged at it until it fell slack to the ground. There were several heavy straps for securing the snowmobile; St. John cinched them tight, then flung the white camouflage netting over his load, fastening the edges down along the worn planking of the bed of the old Ford.

The county road was clear of traffic. He flipped on the high beams as he tugged the insulated hood from his head. Ten minutes down a two-lane road, he merged onto the interstate and pointed the Ford toward the ocean.

Precisely seventeen minutes after he'd pulled the trigger, St. John stopped the truck on a gravel strip a hundred feet back from a cliff above the Atlantic. He stepped out and unzipped his blizzard suit, revealing a scuba wet suit beneath. He stuffed the blizzard suit behind the seat, cranked the gear column over to neutral, released the emergency brake, and stepped safely out of the way.

The Ford's fat tires crept toward the edge of the cliff, the rubber tread popping on gravel as the old truck gained speed. In less than forty-five seconds, it had rolled to the edge of the cliff, listed for the briefest of moments, tilted downward, then fallen freely into the surf.

St. John turned from the cliff and followed a trail that led around one side of it, down steep, loose, precarious terrain to the edge of the water. There was no beach, just an ultranarrow path that cut in and out through water-blasted boulders. St. John moved carefully but swiftly. He knew the way. The tide crashed against the rocks, sending spray and foam high in the air. The wet suit kept him warm enough.

Around the next bend he spotted the yellow nylon rope that moored his small rubber craft to the shore. He unfastened the heavy cord and gave the raft a hearty push out to sea. He turned, adjusted the choke on the outboard, and gave the starter cord a strong yank. It took four tries. The twenty-horse sputtered then caught and revved. St. John twisted the throttle and glanced at the small compass attached to the wrist of his wet suit. The prow of the craft thumped across whitecaps as he guided it southwest.

His watch read 8:42 P.M. By his estimation, the vice president had been dead for thirty-seven minutes.

3

DEATH DID NOT COME IMMEDIATELY.

Blood was everywhere. James Ettinger lay face-down on the shag carpeting, trying without much success to simply breathe. He was quickly going into shock.

Dolly was pawing at the door, ready to be let out. The impact of Ettinger's body hitting the floor so suddenly had sent her into a frenzy.

He knew that he was going to die. There was no question. And the helplessness he felt was even greater than his fear. He wouldn't even get the chance to say good-bye to Miriam or the children; they'd never make it in time.

Ettinger raised his chin from the floor and tried to look around. Blood covered his face, blurring his vision. Brain matter and bits of skull were on his hands. He struggled to lift himself but simply couldn't. He had no strength. He tried to speak, to scream something, to alert someone nearby. But his voice failed him.

Drawing upon a final reserve of strength, he began to crawl toward the door. Dolly eyed him as he turned her way. Music was playing downstairs. His family was enjoying the holiday, unaware that he was dying no more than a few feet above them. He had barely worked his way into facing the proper direction before the muscles in his neck collapsed, the side of his face slamming to the shag. He closed his eyes, and blackness slipped over him.

Dolly approached with caution, sniffed at the blood on his forehead, then licked at it tentatively with her narrow pink tongue.

The boat was a fishing vessel he'd purchased with cash from a marina a hundred miles from New Orleans. St. John was on deck, looking out over the horizon with a pair of Leupold field glasses. He was standing barefoot, still wearing the wet suit, his hair slicked back. He lowered the binoculars to his chest. A fish rolled at the surface of the dark water to his left. The night was cold. The sea was choppy at the moment but not unbearable.

In the galley he cranked up the propane stove and filled a metal pot with beef stew. As the inboard diesel pushed through choppy waters, he stripped off the wet suit, replacing it with jeans, a heavy sweater, knee-high rubber boots, and a billed cap. Coffee was brewing on the rear burner of the stove. He ripped open a package of saltines and consumed a half dozen in a single breath.

The cabin's pantry was well stocked with groceries. He didn't plan on going hungry.

When the coffee was ready he poured a mugful and drank it black. He needed the caffeine boost. He dined on stew straight from the metal pot, dipping crackers now and then. The stew and the coffee renewed his energy and warmed him from the inside out.

For the next few nights he planned to sleep less than a half hour at a time. Keeping watch was of vital importance. He didn't expect any trouble, but he had a schedule to keep. If he kept his wits about him and played by the numbers, he'd slip away clean as a whistle. He had just earned $5.9 million. Now it was time to collect.

A movie was playing on the big-screen in the family room when Miriam Ettinger asked Jude to run upstairs and see if her father wanted to have pie with them.

The scream could have shattered crystal.

Everyone jumped to their feet and moved in a frantic mob up the stairs. There was total confusion. The Secret Service kept the family out of the room. Orders were shouted. The body was rushed out the back entrance of the lodge and gently hurried onto *Marine Two*, the vice president's helicopter, which was always ready to fly at a moment's notice.

Miriam was in shock. The Secret Service got her on board, and the machine lifted off from the snowy patch of land where it had been perched. The children were in hysterics. Elaine herded them into the lodge and babbled whatever words of comfort she could think of. *Marine Two* cleared the treetops and was gone.

Vice President James Ettinger was officially declared dead at 9:53 P.M., Monday, December 17.

— —

9:53 P.M. in Maine was almost 2 P.M. in Sydney, Australia.

President Clifton Yates had spent the morning hours at a special performance of a local children's choir at the Sydney Opera House. President Yates managed to smile and applaud and offer praise for the mob of sopranos. Later he hit the links with the American ambassador to Australia. By eleven-forty-five Yates was shooting well above par and not a bit happy about it. When the call came, he was in a sand trap, eyeing an orange Titleist golf ball that was all but unplayable.

An aide, still standing back on the fairway, took the call on her digital phone. She pressed it to her ear, facing away from the intrusive sun, bracing her right arm with her left in a very feminine, very professional pose. The aid frowned, then cut her eyes toward the president.

Yates was hissing under his breath at the orange Titleist. The toes of his brown and white Dexters had inched up into position. The open face of the sand wedge was at the ready. His form was atrocious. His breathing grew awkward as his arms tensed. The head of the club lifted up and away from the sand, swinging skyward, then peaked, and began its arc back to earth.

"Sir—"

The word cracked the air surrounding the hazard like static electricity. The swing went wide, digging in a good five inches on the far side of the orange sphere, slinging a hearty scoop of wet sand onto the slick, fresh-cut putting surface of the green.

Everyone within earshot toggled between the red-faced beast in the sand trap and the all-business

THE GREATER GOOD 21

young aide who'd managed to make her way to the edge of the rough.

She held the phone out to him.

"Excuse me, sir. I think you need to take this call."

"Tell me *how*, tell me *when*, tell me *who!*" The president of the United States was sitting in the deep leather chair behind his desk aboard *Air Force One*. His head was cocked back, eyes pinched tight, his left hand bridging his temples. Twenty minutes had passed since he'd taken the call on the golf course. In that time, they'd boarded the plane and were airborne.

"Are you *sure*, Russ?" Yates barked at the phone before he'd gotten answers to his first string of questions.

"Yes, Mr. President," his chief of staff answered from his office inside the White House. "The vice president is dead."

"Good Lord! How could this happen?"

"At this point, sir, I just—"

"Russ!"

"Yes, Mr. President?"

"Where's he at?"

"I, uh, Maine, sir. A private hospital."

"We've got to keep this thing quiet, you understand? At least for a day or two. We're look'n at a brush fire! This'll burn up the airwaves like year-old hay. Good Lord!"

"So far it's been contained," the chief of staff managed to say while the president sucked in a breath. "Only a small group of hospital staff know at this point, and they've all been told to keep quiet about it for reasons of national security."

"When'd it go down?"

"Less than two hours."

"And there's no way somebody's just got their lines crossed on this thing?"

"It's official, Cliff."

The president stared up at the ceiling. *Air Force One* was abuzz with the news of Ettinger's demise. A senior staff member was on a couch to Yates's far left, drumming on the keyboard of a laptop balanced on his knees. He was hammering out a first draft of the speech that the president would give when he addressed the nation at some undetermined point in the days or hours to come.

"What's our time frame before this thing gets out of hand, Russ?"

"Can't say just yet. Twelve hours, a day, two days."

The president unconsciously glanced at his watch. "Twelve hours," he said to no one but the ceiling. He glanced at a second aide in a chair in the corner, scribbling on a legal pad.

"Twelve hours. Is that enough for the boys at the Bureau to get a healthy jump on the investigation?"

"Maybe."

"Maybe." Yates could just see Russ shrugging at his desk in the White House. The president shook his head and took a deep breath, listening to the silence coming from the other end of the line.

Ignoring the other occupants of the office, President Yates plucked a felt tip marker from a slotted brass tray near the phone and scratched down in block lettering the single word that was now playing over and over in his mind like a digital display. When the word was spelled out, he penciled in a box around it, pressing down on the lead until the markings nearly tore at the paper of his desk pad. The word he had written was "Stott."

"Get busy, Russ," the president sighed, unblinking. "Keep this mess away from the media hounds for as long as you can. Once they get wind of it, our boys won't have room to work."

"Already on it, Mr. President."

Clifton Yates slammed the phone in its cradle. Forty-five minutes ago he'd teed off on nine with a Big Bertha driver and watched his Titleist float down the fairway with the grace of a balsa glider. Now he was on his way into the belly of the beast that awaited him in the capital of the free world.

But in his own private world, he felt both a sense of relief, and a new level of anxiety.

Husband and wife were alone in a room.

Miriam Ettinger sat on a chair against a wall in the morgue, knees together, hands together between her thighs. She stared at the floor, then the opposite wall, then the leg of the stainless steel table twelve paces dead ahead, then the gray door that led to an outer corridor. But she saw none of it. Her eyes were glazed over. On the table, under the white sheet, was the corpse of her husband. She had yet to approach and pull back the sheet and comprehend the reality of the moment.

There was activity beyond the door. Miriam ignored it.

Tears blurred her vision.

She rose from the chair and approached the metal table. She took a deep breath, both hands clutching her purse strap.

The shape beneath the sheet looked reasonably lifelike. James could have simply been asleep there, hidden from the intrusion of light. Miriam extended a hand to fold back the sheet so that she could look at him one last time and say good-bye.

She held back, resisting the temptation of a final viewing. He surely would not look like the man she'd loved for more than twenty years. Instead, she slid her hand under the nearest edge of the sheet. His left hand was already cool and stiff. His wedding band glistened in the fluorescent light, the gold dulled slightly by smeared dried blood.

The tears came, coursing down her cheeks, unrestrained. Lifting her late husband's hand above the stainless steel table she pressed her lips to it.

The door to the morgue opened, and a uniformed man stuck his head in. Awkwardness filled his face at the sight of the woman at her dead husband's side.

"Mrs. Ettinger?" he said with as much politeness in his voice as any human could possibly offer.

Miriam did not look up. She spoke with a dry throat. "Yes."

"Whenever you're ready, ma'am," he said, hating himself for having to rush her like this.

She swallowed slowly, never taking her eyes or hand from the cold fingers in her grip. She nodded. "All right."

The guard slipped out and eased the door shut.

Another minute ticked by.

She slipped the wedding band from his ring finger, then tugged the sheet back over the hand.

"I love you, James," she said, and turned to go.

4

London, England

MEGAN DURANT ASKED THE CABDRIVER TO
kindly wait for her while she went inside the cathedral.

"This thing's running, missy," he said, plucking a
cigarette from his lips with a fingerless glove. "It's
your money."

She nodded, then turned to the cathedral. She
was there to pay a quick visit to a dear friend. She
had many errands to attend to before tomorrow's departure for New York, but Sister Catina had been too
important to her life not to stop for at least a brief
hello. When Megan's parents split up, and her mother
essentially abandoned her in London, it was Sister
Catina who helped to salve the wounds in her young
life.

A harsh north wind ushered her up the stone
steps of the cathedral. She wore a long coat that buttoned up the front. A plaid scarf was twirled around
her neck and tucked down the collar. Her dark,
shoulder-length hair danced about with the prodding

of the wind. Both hands, warmed by wool mittens, were tucked inside the deep pockets.

She pushed the enormous door shut behind her as she scuttled in out of the cold, rubber soles squeaking on the expansive marble floor. Megan hesitated where she stood, taking in the solemn atmosphere of all that lay around her, then used one hand to brush a few flakes of snow from her hair.

Megan was slightly startled by the sudden approach of a nun in a white habit.

"I'm Sister Rosalyn. Can I help you, child?"

"Yes," Megan said. "I am here to see Sister Catina."

"Ah, yes." The smile brightened with recognition. "What is your name, please?"

"Megan Durant."

"And is she expecting you?"

"No, no she isn't. I visit Sister Catina every few months. She's a family friend," Megan said.

"I will inform Sister Catina that you've come," the nun said as she turned to go.

Megan had been coming here to visit Sister Catina for as long as she could remember. In the past year, though, the Sister had taken ill, weakening with extreme age. On Megan's last visit, Sister Catina had celebrated her 103rd birthday, an extraordinary feat for anyone, let alone a person who had lived a life of servitude. But the glow of life and abundant joy in her smile and crystalline blue eyes had never been extinguished.

"Sister Catina is asleep," Sister Rosalyn said upon her return. "But you may see her, if you like."

Megan stood and followed close behind down a

long, poorly lit corridor. They passed by tall arched windows that let in filtered light from the courtyard.

The door was ajar. Sister Rosalyn hesitated for a moment with her hand on the coarse wood of the door, then pushed through. Megan trailed behind in the woman's small shadow.

Another nun—much younger, barely out of her teens—sat stiffly in a straight-back chair between the one and only window and the one and only bed, reading quietly aloud from a leather-bound New Testament. She marked her place with a strip of crimson ribbon, smiled shyly, and ducked around Megan and Sister Rosalyn and out of the room.

Sister Catina lay in bed, the top blanket folded down across her shoulders. Her eyes were closed.

Megan thanked Sister Rosalyn for showing her in and found her way to the wooden chair, which was bathed by a pool of light from the window. She looked up as Sister Rosalyn left the room.

"Sister Catina." Megan leaned close, gently touching one of the old woman's wrinkled hands. "It's Megan. I've come to see you for a few minutes, to say hello, to see how you are feeling."

Bells chimed somewhere above them on the roof of the cathedral, ringing in the new hour. It was barely nine in the morning. The nun remained still.

Megan said, "I'm getting married. His name is Olin, he's an American, like myself. Very handsome, and quite wealthy. And I am deeply in love with him. We will marry later this week. I am meeting him in New York. I'm so excited, Sister. Olin makes me so happy. He will love me and take care of me. You would love him, Sister. His heart is made of gold.

Your prayers for me have been answered. God's given me a companion for life."

The wooden slats of the chair creaked as Megan shifted her weight in the seat. "Next time I visit, Olin will come with me. Then the two most important people in my life can be with me at the same time, and you can bless his life the way you've blessed mine."

She stood and tugged the blanket up a fraction until it brushed beneath the nun's chin. She bent low and kissed her gently on the forehead. Megan said, "Sleep well, Sister." She pressed two fingers to her lips, then touched them to the nun's cheek.

The younger nun appeared in the gap at the door and politely thanked Megan for the visit.

Megan found her own way back down along the corridor to the foyer, then out into the cold where the cab was waiting.

At that moment, in the predawn hours at Beagle Run, an FBI tech crew was digging the lead slug from the stained cedar trim that ran around the perimeter of the bathroom door. It was a large-grain bullet, long and slim, built for speed and accuracy.

An army of federal agents pounded the snow outside, hunting for any and every detail that might lead them even one small step in the direction they needed to look.

It was a full eight hours since the vice president had been slain. The trail was cooling by the second. A light dusting of snow had fallen in the meantime, making tracks much more difficult to detect.

They found where the old truck had been

backed to the embankment. A series of measurements were taken between the hole in the window and the bullet's final resting place to determine the angle of entry, which led them to the narrow space between the two massive firs where the shooter had taken aim and let go of a single round. From that point they tracked the shooter's movements by foot, snowmobile, and finally tire tracks. That led to the sloped embankment fifty feet from a gravel road, and a complete dead end.

The agents in charge frowned and argued, looking for answers that weren't there. The director wanted a strong lead by daybreak. He wouldn't be getting it.

5

UNLIKE THE REST OF THE COUNTRY AT THE
moment, the weather in Miami was perfect. Temper-
atures hanging near seventy, and plenty of glorious
sunshine. The water was still a tad cool for a dip in
the ocean, but to be out lying about in the sun, you
couldn't ask for more.

The grandchildren and great-grandchildren were
in the sand just beyond the glass of the patio door.
Anthony Philbrick watched them play. From
where he sat on a wicker deck chair near the wet
bar, he could hear them laughing and screaming.
Mrs. Philbrick had taken off on a walk down the
beach with their two oldest daughters, the twins.
On the arm of his deck chair was his neon blue
drink. He sipped from the drink as he stared at the
horizon.

Speaker of the House Philbrick, who would turn
seventy-nine on New Year's Eve, sipped from the pink
straw and did his very best not to doze. The beach-
front condo in Miami was among his most beloved
investments. The sun coming through the patio door
was warm on his bare toes. Two of his four sons-in-

law had the propane grill fired up on the long deck, and Philbrick could smell the shrimp and steak sizzling on the fire. He caressed the rounded hump of his gut and wondered how much more fatty food his heart would take.

Somewhere in another room, a phone rang. It was the synthetic beep of a cell phone. It rang twice before he heard his personal assistant answer. Twelve seconds later, she was in the room, at his side.

"Mr. Speaker, it's for you." She was holding a tiny, folding cell phone, barely larger than the palm of her hand. Her face was all-business.

"I'm on vacation." His eyes never left the water. A two-man sailboat moved along the horizon in the distance. "Take a message. I'll return it in a month."

"I'm sorry, sir. It's the president."

He put the phone to his ear.

"Mr. President, what a pleasure!" He gave the assistant a look she was used to. It said to disappear.

"Tony, how's the water?"

"Cold and blue, just like my drink."

"Listen, Tony, I hate to interrupt your holiday, but I'm sending a plane to pick you up in forty-five minutes. I need you in D.C. immediately."

"Whatever you say, Mr. President. But this is highly unusual. May I ask why?"

There was the pause. Three or four seconds of dead air. Philbrick watched the children tumble in the sand. The clouds broke, and the sun on his feet and legs and stomach spread across him like a blanket.

"James Ettinger died late last night."

The tingle started at his toes and worked its way

up his spine, to the hairs on the back of his neck. His mouth went dry. His lower jaw fell slack.

"Clifton, I, uh, I . . . I don't know what to say . . ."

"Just be on that plane and get here."

"Of course."

"I need you to be sworn in as the new vice president as soon as possible. I know this is sudden, but it's about to get chaotic around here. I'm asking you to become my second-in-command. Do you understand?"

"Absolutely, Mr. President. You can count on me."

"Your country awaits your service."

Conflicting emotions stirred in Megan as her taxi rounded a corner and she was able to make out in the distance the roofline of the flat. She had been running errands all day and was anxious to spend the last few hours in London with her two roommates. The cab stunk of cheap cigarettes. She would have cracked the window a bit but the choice was to suffocate or freeze. Mercifully, the driver edged up to the curb and barked what the meter read.

It was sad, really. One last night in the flat she'd called home for the past three years. She left the cab and walked along the ancient cement path, past shrubbery and the occasional leafless tree. The apartment building was a long, brick four-story L, topped by wood shingles and draped with ivy.

As was almost always the case, the little things were what she suddenly found herself beginning to miss. The smell of the entryway, a rather musty odor—nothing overbearing or obvious, but distinct all the same. The well-worn oak handrail leading up the four flights of stairs. The slightly bubbled tile at each landing. All of these Megan noticed and clung to as she took her time mounting the steps.

Melancholy swelled in her throat. She rattled her key in the lock and took a deep, sad breath before turning the knob. Many of her best memories belonged to this place, this three-bedroom unit overlooking a busy street in London. Memories she prayed she would not lose with time.

The door creaked, hinges groaning.

Vivian was on the couch, face buried in a magazine.

"Hey, Viv." Megan tossed her keys onto the table in the entryway. She heard a muffled reply, and peeked over the magazine to find a Twinkie stuffed halfway into Vivian's mouth. Vivian turned up her eyes and grinned guiltily.

"Where's Anna?"

"On her way from Darrin's."

"Good. Get dressed, the two of you are treating me to a night on the town."

They hit the club scene fast and furious, the three of them wanting to hold tight to what they'd shared as flatmates. The dance floor was shoulder to shoulder. Music was pulsing from speakers hidden in the walls. Vivian and Megan had a table next to the rail. Vivian had on her famous silk blouse and skirt. Megan toyed with the straw in her drink. The glass looked like a tall beaker.

The trio danced and drank and grew steadily deaf from the music.

They migrated to an even danker hole to eat.

Later, outside the restaurant, Anna said, "Hey, there's a guy from my international finance class—Mitch. He's throwing a little shindig. We could drop by!" A quick glance at her watch. "Starts in an hour. Let's catch a cab!"

"What time is it now?" Megan asked.

Vivian dug at her coat sleeve. "Little after midnight."

"Still early," Anna said, arms crossed. "If I go to bed sober, I'll forever hold this night against you."

The three of them exchanged a conspiratorial look.

The corners of Megan's mouth edged up in a slight grin. "All right, then," she said. "Let's go."

Later, as the sun crawled slowly above the horizon, Anna and Vivian were fast asleep beneath heavy quilts they had piled in the living room. But when the first wedge of light slanted through the window overlooking the street, Megan sensed the warmth on her face and stirred.

She rose, holding a blanket around her, clutching it to her chest and neck.

London was sluggishly coming to life. Delivery trucks moved about on the narrow streets. Megan plugged in the coffeemaker, pulled a straight-back chair from the kitchen, and sat before the window, pale orange light on her face. She understood the imagery very clearly. This was the sunrise of a new life. Last night had been the sunset of an innocent and carefree existence, the only existence she'd known for her twenty-two years. Was she ready? Were her feet fully planted beneath her? Was it too soon? Like smooth flat stones, the questions skipped across the placid surface of her mind.

The aroma of coffee brewing brought about mild stirrings from one of the sleeping lumps beneath the blankets. But it was still early. And with no classes today, there was no reason to rise anytime before noon.

Megan sighed. She loved Olin. The very thought of him forced the doubts into the background. He would make a good husband. She would make a good wife. Together, some years in the distance, they would produce beautiful children. But that was the future. He had unearthed something in her, a patch of spirit she'd been unaware of. The amazing thing was that they really hadn't known each other very long. That fact alone made it seem reasonable to have at least a modicum of hesitancy. But she had fallen madly in love with him at first sight, and he'd done nothing but strengthen her feelings for him since.

Her only desire now was to focus on Olin and their love for each other, and to cast off that nagging voice that produced a wrinkle of uncertainty. Olin was wealthy and successful. Should it matter that she knew so little about him?

By the time the sun was full and bright on her face, a few pedestrians had wandered onto the sidewalks. There was a certain security in knowing that this city would remain her home; though they would marry in the United States, their life would be built in England.

She wished London a good day and went to find her favorite mug.

6

Somewhere in the Atlantic Ocean

ST. JOHN CAME UP ON DECK AS THE FIRST hint of sunlight spread out across the waves. The morning air was cool but pleasant. He wore drab olive green cargo pants and a Michigan State sweatshirt under a hooded rain jacket.

Neither the prevailing currents nor the winds created any sort of problem for the chugging old diesel engine. The prop pushed the boat along at a steady clip.

He stared at the horizon. It was flat and featureless. A bird with broad wings dipped to the water a half a mile to the east, then pounded toward the sky with a finned sea creature dying in the grip of its talons.

He decided that he could easily have been a fisherman, riding the sea to scratch out a living. One of his great-uncles had fished the seas off Portugal. He'd been a hulking man with calloused hands and a hard wind-beaten face. But what a life—away from land for weeks or months at a time, at the mercy of the elements. A life long on punishment and endurance, and short on pleasure or reward.

And here he was, still a young man, barely in his thirties, on his way to a life of his choosing, a life of luxury and bliss. Maybe at the end of this he would buy a *real* boat, with tall sails and fixtures of chrome and brass.

The boat was equipped with reasonably modern navigational technology. He tapped a button and a small red blip that represented his humble little craft sprang onto the digital radar screen. He was right on course. A glance at his watch: nearly 7 A.M.

St. John brushed his teeth, washed his hands, and raised his face to the small round mirror fixed above the tiny sink. The beard had grown in full and curly in the short span of two weeks. It would be a pleasure to take a razor to it. But not just yet.

On deck with the field glasses around his neck he kept watch. Around noon a handful of porpoises rose to the surface, dorsal fins slicing the water. St. John grinned as they spun and dove and crisscrossed in the boat's path.

The three of them—Megan, Vivian, and Anna—rushed into the back of the waiting black cab, slamming its door just as it squealed away from the curb. The drive to Heathrow took forty minutes, during which there was laughter and tears and many hugs. Her companions helped carry her bags as they hurried through the terminal.

She would see them soon, but for some reason this was incredibly emotional, and Megan found herself clinging to them, not wanting to let go. She wore a long coat and her favorite maroon beret. Vivian and Anna each carried one of her bags. They hurried through the crowds and found seats at the British Airways gate. Nineteen minutes later, they hugged and cried again and went their separate ways as she turned and stepped in line for flight 189 from London to New York City.

The first-class seat was like sinking into a warm bath. The deep soft leather drew her in, and for the first time all day she managed to relax and simply enjoy the thought of all that lay ahead for her. The enormous airbus taxied onto the apron and within a few minutes was above the clouds and heading west. Megan ordered pasta and wine, and ate like a bird. She skimmed a magazine from a pouch behind the seat in front of her and eventually managed a nap as they crossed high above the Atlantic. The flight was scheduled to take seven hours and fifty minutes, but the weather might have other ideas in mind. She was in no hurry though. She had several days before she was to meet Olin. Then they would spend a couple of days in New York together before packing up and flying to Las Vegas to tie the knot.

As she slept, the plane thumped along, hammering across pockets of turbulence. Megan was a light sleeper but didn't seem to notice the rough texture of the flight. She was lost in sleep, floating in dreams. Dreams filled with Olin—her sweet Olin. Her prince.

The few months they'd known each other had been a whirlwind. He'd swept her off her feet. From the beginning, she'd been impressed that he had acquired such wealth by such a young age. Megan had never dated anyone with money. He was rich and gorgeous—how could that *not* have influenced her? Such considerations disturbed her, so she simply brushed them aside.

Darkness enveloped the flight. The pilot offered a periodic update. Nobody seemed to listen, or at least to care. Many were napping, or reading, or watching the movie and listening with their headsets. When the city of New York blinked into view through the snow and cloud cover below them, an automatic excitement charged the air. There was bustling and chatter and an increase in movement. The pilot made the announcement, and everyone buckled in. Trays were folded up, books and magazines stowed.

Megan saw the light spread out in the distance. The city was aglow. Her heart pounded with anticipation. It would be an excruciating time waiting for Olin, but she'd make the most of it—shopping, seeing sights, dining out, taking in the galleries and museums. It would be the preamble to the *real* vacation. Dropping into a city the size of New York stirred more than a little trepidation in her chest. After all, she would be alone in the city until he arrived. But she refused to fall prey to these insecurities.

Flight 189 dropped rapidly, banking and circling, steady on its approach. The lights of the landing strip came into view, and then a slight jolt as the landing gear skipped on the pavement. They taxied up alongside the terminal at JFK, and the pilot, in his polished British accent, welcomed his passengers to the Big Apple.

7

THE MAN'S NAME WAS JOEL BENJAMIN. AVERAGE height, average build. 190 pounds, give or take. Dark brown hair and hazel eyes. Forty-seven years old. He was dressed in a rumpled gray suit, his tie loosened around his collar.

Less than ninety seconds earlier, Joel had been on his way to lock himself inside a rest room stall and kill himself. He had been weaving through the throng within the airport, his connecting flight home to St. Louis, Missouri, scheduled to begin boarding at 7:35 P.M. He had his luggage—a folded hanging bag and leather briefcase—with him. He'd made up his mind.

He had glanced at his watch then turned his gaze absently only for the fleetest of moments toward the flow of harried travelers rushing out of JFK.

In that instant, he forgot about his flight, forgot about the rest room, and forgot about the contents of the paper bag inside his briefcase. He had seen a face in the crowd. It had only been a glimpse, but he stopped dead in his tracks, the small hairs on the back of his neck suddenly standing on end. In that moment, he knew where he'd seen that person before.

The face belonged to a young woman. Perhaps early to midtwenties. Beautiful, really. Her hair was jet-black and was cut shoulder-length beneath a maroon beret. She wore a long coat and black shoes.

Joel had seen her for only a fraction of a second. But that was enough. He struggled with his luggage, dodging rudely through the mob. He rushed out through the doors into the cold. She was nowhere to be seen.

Then he spotted the maroon beret fifty feet ahead, at the curb, pulling open the door to a cab. There was a wall of human traffic between them. She was out of reach of both arm and voice. In the next breath she was inside the rear of the taxi, and in the next its taillights swerved into a lane of honking motorists.

Frantically, Joel Benjamin raised one hand in the air, his slim briefcase dangling from his thumb, motioning at a taxi that was plowing ahead through deep ruts in the snow and slush. Miraculously, it stopped. The door handle was slick with ice.

"Drive!" he ordered, slamming the door closed.

And they sped away from the curb.

"The taxi up ahead, four car lengths up, in the right lane, in front of the silver Cadillac . . . don't let it out of your sight! Stay on its bumper until I tell you otherwise!"

The sun had set in New York City. Darkness had fallen hard on the city that never sleeps. It was brutally cold, made all the worse by harsh, unrelenting winds. Snow had first appeared ten days ago, and now the world was white and growing whiter by the minute.

The driver had both hands on the wheel. Traffic was backed up beyond the limits of human vision. Movement went in fits and starts. They crept along for a half a mile, then picked up speed.

The other cab signaled to change lanes, then made a dangerously hasty veer into the left lane.

"Hey pal, there's just no way to get over that quick from here," the driver said matter-of-factly.

Two fifty-dollar bills flew over the seat and landed in the driver's lap.

"Just do it!"

There was a harsh squeal of tires as the cab skimmed past a Jaguar. The radials spun in the sludge that covered the centerline. The driver crossed himself quickly as he jerked the wheel one way then another, but his words weren't nearly as Catholic as his gestures.

The headlights from the taxi pointed the way along the expressway. Joel stared out the window at a car in the next lane. He had missed his flight home, though he'd had no real plans to be on it anyway. Above them, in the night sky, a jetliner was blasting its way west. Maybe it was his USAir flight.

The Ford's suspension was shot. It stunk of gasoline fumes. Joel clawed the cheap upholstery. Passing lights swept over him as they cut in and out of traffic. It occurred to him then that he had no clue where this little jaunt might take him.

The Ford shot through an impossibly narrow gap. Joel could hear the engine begging for a rest. They hugged the right lane.

Joel's neck and back were as stiff and tight as newly milled lumber. He lowered his head for only a few seconds, propping his elbows on his knees, and worked his fingertips down the back of his neck, drumming out the knots that had collected there over the past few minutes. When he raised back up, her taxi was nowhere in sight.

"Where'd it go?" Joel's arms were up over the seat.

"I don't know, I don't know—sit back! It was right up there just a second ago. A bus changed lanes and cut me off. And by the time it got out of my face, it was gone!" The driver's photo ID had the name *Jimmy* beneath a face only a mother could love.

"Listen, Jimmy," Joel said, digging out his wallet. He held up a wad of cash pinched between his index and middle fingers and said, "You find that cab, and this'll be your tip. Understand?"

Jimmy mashed his ancient Reebok to the pedal.

They exited Grand Central Parkway and Jimmy's eyes went wide and his neck craned, his head turning this way and that, hoping for even the faintest glimpse. He knew he was looking for cab number 1881. He'd seen the ID number printed in bold black lettering. But as they crossed the Triborough Bridge, 1881 was nowhere to be seen.

"I don't know what to tell you, pal," Jimmy offered with a shrug. "I'm not a miracle worker."

"Just drive!"

Everywhere he looked were dozens of yellow cabs that were carbon copies of the one they were hunting. And they multiplied by the second. His field of view was a chaotic mess. Joel pressed the side of his face against the cool glass, and scolded himself.

Stupid . . . stupid . . . stupid! The cab was gone. She was gone. *Gone.* She'd been nearly within his grasp. Yet as suddenly as she had appeared to him from among the passing throng outside JFK, she had now disappeared back into the cityscape.

Hers was a face he hadn't seen in ten years, and one that he'd become certain he would never see again. But he had—here in this city, tonight.

Joel clutched his hands to his face in disbelief, uncertain whether to weep tears of anguish or those of intense relief. A moment he'd longed for had arrived with the abruptness of a brick to the head, then passed, and was now gone. Ten years of hope and loss rushed back at him in a torrent.

He had seen the face of an angel, *his* angel—his daughter.

8

IT WAS FULLY DARK OUT NOW, AND WITH THE arrival of night came a new wave of sleet and snow. The cab had dropped Joel across the street from a coffee shop. He stood in the cold and the elements, his toes and fingers growing increasingly numb. He waited for a break in traffic, clutched his luggage and darted across the street to the warm sanctum of the coffee shop.

Once inside, Joel found a table. A waiter took his order. His thoughts were a jumble. It was early evening, but he'd already put in a long day of business, and suddenly he found himself stranded in an unfamiliar city, without a room, without a way home, without a plan. It was just days before Christmas, making the prospect of finding an open seat on any flight in or out of the city anytime in the near future so remote it seemed ludicrous to even consider the odds.

This was not like him. Not at all. He was a man of strict habit, of routine. He'd had a schedule to keep. But recent developments had altered circumstances dramatically. Seeing Megan brought all other thoughts, all other plans, all other considerations, to a bone-jarring halt. Seeing Megan changed everything.

Last month had seen an infamous milestone for forty-seven-year-old Joel Benjamin. It had marked the tenth anniversary of the disappearance of his family.

In an earlier lifetime, as a freshman at USC, Joel Benjamin had fallen in love with a high school cheerleader named Ariel Matthews. They married a week prior to his graduation. Ariel dropped out of school, well shy of completing her degree. Her parents frowned upon this, but she and Joel had to follow wherever his career path led.

He took a sales rep job in San Diego, which allowed them to take out a mortgage. They found a decent neighborhood, a three-bedroom house, with a tree in front and two in back, dishwasher, disposal, stone fireplace, chain-link fence, and a mailbox with a dent in one side the shape of an aluminum bat. The mortgage was for thirty years.

The company manufactured adhesives. Tape. Glue. Caulking. Paste. Industrial-strength gunk designed to adhere and harden and fasten one thing to another for nearly eternity.

Joel's territory included Southern California and much of Nevada and Arizona.

Rental cars, flights in coach, fast food. Gray suits, blue suits, red ties, striped ties. Wing tips, deck shoes. A firm shake. Fake smile. Forms in triplicate. Sign here. Initial there. How about those Dodgers?

Days at a time slipped away on each of his trips. A week or more on the road was commonplace. The life of a salesman.

Ariel was twenty-one when their daughter was born. She took to motherhood with ease. Joel stayed home for the first two weeks after Megan's birth. He could see the fresh spark in his wife's eyes. Two made a couple; three made a family. They were in debt up to their armpits, but they somehow managed to keep their heads above water, and though this new arrival added extra weight to an already teetering load, they bore it the only way an up-and-coming couple can— with love and determination.

He approached life on the road with renewed vigor. His accounts blossomed, and the little annoyances of the day-to-day business world bothered him much less than they had previous to his baby Megan entering the world. The proud papa stood tall, his chest puffed out. Joel vowed to give her the world on a string.

Megan was her mother incarnate. Her nose. Her mouth. Those ears. Those eyes. And that hair, as dark as the deepest night. She was a gorgeous child, sublimely blessed with her mother's flawless genes. Her tiny smile produced enough raw wattage to power entire cities.

But in time, the child brought discord. Joel's extended absences left Ariel feeling terribly lonely, and often alienated. Megan was a handful, and Ariel resented being stuck at home 95 percent of the time, cut off from real, adult company and conversation. She threatened to leave him, to take their daughter and go. They sought counseling, and for a short time the tension eased up. But his accounts multiplied, thus expanding his route. Exasperated, Ariel moved in with her parents. She was tired and frustrated and sick of being a married single parent.

During this period, Megan blossomed into a radiant little girl. By her tenth birthday, Joel had taken a desk job, mercifully granting him the luxury of being home every night. But the damage was done. The days of possible reconciliation were over. The divorce was final a week before her eleventh birthday. Ariel was awarded full custody.

Joel stood by helplessly for months and watched as Ariel repeatedly denied him his visitation rights. He pleaded with his attorney, who in turn pleaded with the judge, who in turn scolded Ariel, ordering her to cooperate or risk losing custody.

And for six months the cogs of their dysfunctional arrangement turned without incident. Joel again had a relationship with his daughter. For her twelfth birthday, he took Megan and a cluster of her giggly little friends out for pizza and a movie. It was his best and last memory of her.

Two Fridays later, Joel pulled up to Ariel's house and found her car was gone. The closets were emptied. Ariel and Megan were gone. The neighbors didn't know a thing. Her parents pled ignorance. Joel nearly went mad.

When they first disappeared, he later learned, they hid in Oregon. For a week, Ariel laid low in a rented cabin a half mile outside a national forest. She sold her Volvo for twelve thousand dollars cash, and flew with her daughter to Miami. And it was there that Ariel and Megan Benjamin, mother and daughter, disappeared. Once and for all.

Miami was where the trail went cold. Joel paid a California PI to track them down. The man returned from Florida with nothing more to offer than a shrug and a bill for expenses. And that was it.

Joel was thirty-seven.

His depression hit like a tsunami. It consumed him without warning and hammered his psyche for ten years. He battled the pain with prescription antidepressants and booze, using one to control the other. *How do you forget the past? How can you simply walk away from one life to begin another?* Megan's sweet face haunted his dreams. Sometimes the all-consuming void opened up great and wide, hungrily tugging at him.

He dodged suicide twice: the first attempt was thwarted by an observant secretary who phoned 911 when he locked himself in his office and stuffed into his mouth an entire bottle of over-the-counter sleeping pills. The second occasion had come to pass barely an hour ago; Joel had purchased a small-caliber handgun from a pawnshop, fully intending to lock himself in a rest room stall in JFK and shove the muzzle down his throat. Then he had glanced up for a fraction of a second and seen the one face that could make him hold on for just a little longer.

9

As the boat continued toward Nantucket, his old nemesis, paranoia, began to tap on his shoulder. It was a nuisance, but such things kept you alive. Especially in his business.

St. John slept fitfully. He tossed and turned, battling the wool blanket. The bed was six inches shorter than his body, so he spent much of the night fantasizing about stretching his toes. The mattress was abused and lifeless, and air wheezed from it every time he moved or adjusted. It beat sleeping on the floor, just not by much.

His dreams were the spaces where the paranoia liked to creep in first. Such ugly visions. This was another reason to sleep in narrow shifts. An hour here, a half hour there. Fifteen-minute naps when he could afford it. The visions were never as bad between jobs, when he'd pulled it off and managed to merge back into the anonymity of the masses. It was the act of fleeing, that awful slinking into the shadows, that wrecked his sleep.

This morning he brewed thick, black coffee. St. John set an opened package of graham crackers on the corner of the table behind the navigation equipment and munched in the darkness. The moon was faint. Green and red lights from the navigational instruments blinked and formed patterns.

The boat rocked with the sea. The old diesel sounded strong. He was making good time. There was another two hours before sunup.

Midmorning, the radar chimed. St. John was below deck, tending to the oil and motor fluids. He shot up the ladder and approached the console with a shop rag in his hands. The sweep of the green readout clearly identified an oncoming vessel 5.63 kilometers due south, and closing in at close to eleven knots.

St. John snatched the Leupold field glasses from a hook above his bunk and went up on deck. The sky looked gray and threatening but the weather was not altogether unpleasant. His middle finger toggled the viewfinder into focus. He leaned his midsection against the railing at the very nose of the boat. Nothing but open sea.

Whatever it was, it was coming straight at him.

With nothing yet on the horizon, he slipped below to the cabin to ready himself. The mattress lifted up and out, revealing a stowage compartment. He pressed one clip into the grip of the 9mm, and slipped a second into the back of his waistband. The loaded Glock waited patiently on the wooden lip of the instrument console. He popped the protective caps from his scope, and opened the bolt action to arm the rifle with six shells.

St. John eased the rifle onto the nylon bench-seat at the table and took up the Glock to have another look-see.

On the far horizon, a mast appeared. In no time, he could see the fishing nets, and the crew aboard her moving about, working the hooks and baiting lines. She was a fishing vessel. St. John took in a deep breath and stuffed the 9mm down his waistband. He watched with suspicious curiosity as the oncoming vessel grew larger and more defined. He wheeled his own vessel off course just slightly, and the two boats passed within five hundred yards of each other. The crew was busy at work, and if they noticed him they ignored him. This set well with his frazzled nerves.

A quick retooling of the instruments, and he was back on course. He stowed the rifle back inside the hold beneath his bunk, but left the Glock atop the navigation console. If there were more visitors, anytime soon, he'd be prepared.

He washed his face at the sink and fixed something of substance for his shifting stomach. St. John took his lunch and his field glasses on deck.

The paranoia twisted its talons into his back and shoulders as he sat cross-legged and watched the horizon.

It wasn't an enormous charge of plastic explosives, just enough to do the trick. St. John had rigged them himself, and now he knelt on deck, making a final inspection of the timer and the detonator.

He wasn't a novice at these games, but handling enough plastic explosives to instantly incinerate his upper body never failed to elevate his anxiety level by a marked degree. It was a simple rigging—nothing fancy—designed for a straightforward task. He fingered the device gently, examining all the connections, making sure this wire went here, that wire went there. The soldering was clean and holding firm. The battery pack had plenty of juice.

It was early evening on his last full day at sea. The bow of the boat rose and fell at the prompting of the sea. The sun hung low in the sky, brilliant and massive, gradually nearing the unbroken line of the horizon.

Here, the sea was a deep blue. The water was choppy and rolling. He glanced at his watch, anxious to get his chores under way, yet still holding to the peace of this moment at sea. These next few hours represented the end of a way of life, which had been the only one he'd known for more than half of his lifetime. And like this boat, he hoped that the burden of his past would settle to the ocean floor to be forgotten by time.

When the light of the moon replaced the light of the sun, St. John struck the tip of a wooden match and lit the lantern hanging above the table in the cabin. The gear he'd need was stowed in a pack on the bench-seat. He put on his wet suit.

He headed on deck with his diver's mask and snorkel, finding his way by flashlight. He played the light across the explosive held in his hand just to make certain he'd not forgotten anything, then adjusted the mask over his face, took in a long breath and held it, and dropped over the side rail with a mild splash.

Beneath the boat, the water was smoky black. The beam of the flashlight followed the contour of the underside as he finned his way along the hull. He came to a good spot and treaded water as he pressed the plastic explosive against the rotting wood. The boat was at least twenty years old, and plenty in need of repair, a fact chief among the reasons why he'd selected it in the first place. The boards were rotted and flaking, eaten away by more than two decades in saltwater. All of this would make his task much easier to accomplish.

He attached the device to the hull of the boat. St. John held the flashlight against one cheek as he set the timer. With his free hand he tapped a setting into the touch pad. 30:00. Then, with a final keystroke, the device was activated.

29:59 . . . 29:53 . . . 29:37 . . .

Satisfied, he ascended to the surface and hauled himself up the rope ladder. He stood on deck in his wet suit, catching his breath, a puddle spreading out around his feet. The night was breezy and cool. He strapped his pack over his shoulders, and eased into the raft, which he'd trailed behind the boat these past days. It started without a hitch.

The charge went off, blowing fire out both sides of the hull. St. John watched from a quarter mile away. The salt-soaked wood caught fire and burned quickly. As the hull filled with water, first the forward deck slowly submerged, raising the prop high over the surface of the water. Then the vessel sunk rapidly, taking on water with greater speed by the minute. In twenty minutes, all that was left was a foam of white bubbles, then nothing at all.

St. John turned away and motored at a steady clip in the opposite direction. The raft slapped against the choppy water, surging forward against a stout headwind. By his map and his compass and the last reading he'd taken from the radar on the boat, he estimated he was four hours from shore. A *long* four hours.

He'd be there by midnight.

10

ACTUALLY, IT WAS A FEW MINUTES BEFORE
midnight St John unfastened the clamps that secured
the ten-horse motor to the raft and let it drop into the
black water. He fitted the oars into the oarlocks and
manually powered the inflatable craft the final two
hundred yards to shore.

The island of Nantucket was draped in gloom.
Drizzle and a low fog blew in off the sea. It was a
rough night to be outdoors, particularly on the water,
without refuge. St. John was wearing a military-surplus
slicker from his pack. It did reasonably well at keeping
out the wet but had little or no success against the
cold. The slicker fluttered as a gust howled across the
bow of the dinghy. He made smooth, strong strokes
with the oars, surging forward in the choppy water.

He brushed back the hood, glanced up at the
drizzle and the cloud cover and frowned. The question was how long the sour weather might cling to
the island. The weather was one of the few things he
couldn't control or at least manipulate. If it stuck
around, his flight, scheduled to lift off late tomorrow
afternoon, might not be allowed to leave the ground.

Periodically, lightning would flash in the distance, flickering behind massive columns of cloud, but his instincts told him it wouldn't be a long-term hindrance. It was crucial that he be on that plane, and nasty weather was the primary threat to keeping him grounded.

He beached the rubber dinghy among the rocks where the island sloped gradually into the sea, and eased over the side, knee-deep in the shallows. Though the moon remained well hidden, he had no trouble seeing well enough to drag the raft up on the beach. He yanked a diver's knife with a serrated blade from his ankle sheath, and plunged it into the rubbery meat of the bow. Air wheezed out through the gash, and the raft rapidly deflated. He heaved it into the trees, concealing it with whatever was available nearby. Next, he slipped out of the wet suit, tied it into a bundle, and tucked it out of sight.

He shouldered his pack and checked the batteries in his rubber-armored flashlight. He came to a paved road and followed it. This was his second trip to Nantucket. A month earlier he'd come to scout the area.

As he walked, an occasional car whizzed past on the narrow strip of two-lane asphalt. At the crest of a hill, he could see lights from town. His reservations had been made on his prior visit, paid in full in advance. The bed-and-breakfast was quiet when he hurried up the walk and stepped inside. Most of the lights were out, but St. John had made arrangements to accommodate a late arrival.

When he got to his room he locked the door and collapsed onto the bed. Every muscle in his body ached. Nothing would have pleased him more than to sleep for thirteen hours. But he'd be lucky to snag six. There was still a schedule to keep. And he was ready to get on to the next step. A better life awaited him once he was off this island. A fresh beginning.

He'd sleep hard, clean up, and try to feel human again. There was no TV in the room. That was just as well. He stretched out on his back on the bed and stared at the cracks in the ceiling until his eyes grew heavy. By the time he fell asleep, it was 1:20 A.M.

There was hardly any traffic on Pennsylvania Avenue when the small caravan of four black Lincoln Town Cars motored through a few hours before dawn and turned into the entrance to the White House.

They idled at the security checkpoint while word of their arrival went to the Oval Office, where the president had adjourned one meeting only moments before in anticipation of the one to come.

In the second Lincoln, Anthony Philbrick rode in silence, as he had for most of the trip up from Florida. What was happening around him, even in his wildest dreams would have seemed perfectly absurd. Less than twelve hours ago he'd sat in the sand with his grandchildren, pink from the sun. Now here he was, a few feet and a few minutes away from being tagged as second-in-command.

They drove down a ramp and into a heavily fortified passage that turned hard left, iron barriers slamming shut behind them. Armed soldiers saluted from their posts, automatic weapons on straps over their shoulders. Sodium-arch lamps lit the subterranean world of cement. They stopped, and a well-armed sergeant, who saluted as he stepped aside, opened his door.

Philbrick was nearly eighty, and he considered himself relatively fit for his age, but suddenly he felt overcome by the gravity of the moment. He did not smile as he was escorted through a maze of corridors and high-security clearance zones.

Now they stepped into an elevator. The doors slid shut without so much as a sigh, and he could feel the slightest hint of movement as the box headed up the shaft.

The speaker was certainly no stranger to the White House. He'd been a guest on countless occasions, but this level of welcome was, to say the least, new to him. He'd always come by the normal channels, above ground, with far less urgency. The realization suddenly struck him that he'd entered an entirely new stratosphere of existence. His days from here on in would be spent with little sleep, being shepherded to the far ends of the globe to act as mouthpiece for the president wherever he himself could not be. This, of course, was the unspoken dream of every speaker. But as reality slammed him in the face, all those years of longing seemed illusory and misguided. He took a deep breath as the elevator settled to a halt. The doors parted.

A hand came up to meet Philbrick's.

"Ah, Tony!" Russ Vetris led him through another stretch of corridors. "The president is anxious to get the ball rolling. He's been expecting you. There's no time to waste," the chief of staff said.

"I understand," Philbrick said, nodding, his long legs matching Vetris's spastic pace stride for stride.

He had a billion questions but held his tongue. He'd be told what they wanted him to know. Ettinger was dead. How? When? These things would be answered in time. And no sooner. What he did know was that within the hour he'd be sworn in as vice president of the United States of America.

Vetris passed his ID card over a digital scanner. Three seconds elapsed before a door receded and they were through and beyond. The chief of staff briefed him with the basics. It had happened at Ettinger's vacation home in Maine. Details, even now, were sketchy. He'd been declared dead almost immediately. Miriam? The kids? All fine, all safe.

Another door, then they were inside the Oval Office.

Yates stood at his desk in shirtsleeves. The tie was loose around the collar. He looked beat. He smiled at Philbrick and took the speaker's hand in both of his.

"Tony."

"Mr. President."

There were others in the room. Philbrick turned and saw all familiar faces. Among them, the chief justice, who would perform the brief ceremony that would officially change the nameplate on the VP's desk. They all shook hands. Said their grim hellos. And business got under way.

11

SHORTLY AFTER DAWN, ST. JOHN WAS AWAKE and out of bed. His beard was beginning to chafe, and he couldn't wait to have it off his face. He leaned over the pedestal sink in the small bathroom and went about the annoying process of snipping at it first with a pair of travel-kit scissors.

Next, he lathered up his face. A cheap Gillette razor made quick work of cleaning off the remaining stubble. St. John showered and dressed. He had a satisfying breakfast downstairs—infinitely superior to the wet oats he'd conjured up aboard the fishing vessel—and then excused himself when a conversation-hungry guest latched on to him.

The clean-shaven face and full stomach replenished his strength as well as his morale. His was a nasty industry, and many who made their living at it were soulless creatures. To survive, you had to respect assassination as a business. Whether you killed for a living or traded bonds, you had to conduct yourself with dignity and professionalism. To do otherwise was to risk slipping into a sort of lifestyle that quickly narrowed the psychological gap that divides human and beast. If he did manage to pull out now, he might still have a life ahead of him. There was plenty left to salvage.

Just the thought of the promise of things to come put a snap in his stride and brightened every sight and every sound. All he had to do was get on that plane today. Just get on that plane and get off this island. There was money awaiting him. More money than a reasonable adult could ever spend. And he already had a load of money. He'd been wealthy for years, though not a penny of it could be traced back to him, directly or indirectly. He had millions scattered in banks all over the world. He could have given up the business five or six years ago, and lived in luxury.

And why hadn't he? That was the question he'd pondered increasingly in recent years. Why not buy a goat farm in the Netherlands and slip into peaceful anonymity? But a satisfactory answer evaded him. Recent months had changed everything, though. The past six months had seen a . . . *palpable* shift inside him. A new man was growing inside his old skin. And what he'd finally discovered was that the answer to his question was simple: he had never had anything worth giving himself wholly to, as he had his work. Money meant little. Money represented the power to choose. He'd simply never felt drawn to anything other than to the art of hunting people. Until now.

During his previous visit to the island, St. John had rented a postal box. As per his usual routine, he had telephoned a number and given the box address. The box would be used only once. The number he'd dialed was to a suite of offices in New Zealand, which encrypted the call and rerouted it to a second suite of offices in Tulsa, Oklahoma, where the call was further encrypted and redirected to a mainframe computer in Gdansk, Poland.

All of his business, for the better part of the past decade, was routed through the office in Poland. It was a system he trusted and one that had served him remarkably well, considering the very nature of his trade. But the next forty-eight hours would put an end to it, for good. In two days he would have his money and his new life, and he would sever his ties to the office in Poland.

Midmorning, a taxi delivered St. John outside the post office. Dressed in chinos, leather boating shoes, and a sports coat, he removed the single item from the box and promptly returned to the taxi. The item was a pink envelope, the size of a small thank-you card. He tucked the envelope in an inside jacket pocket and gave the driver new directions. Save for a few specifics, which of course changed with each job, he didn't need to open the envelope to know its contents. It had to do with his payment of $5.9 million.

The taxi stopped at a red light, and St. John made a concerted effort to breathe in the moment. Here he was, stepping out of old shoes and into new ones. How many people had an opportunity like this? He had pulled the trigger for the last time, taken his last life for profit. No longer would he be the angel of death. So many of his thirty-two years had been spent squinting through a scope, concentration creeping icily through his veins. Those were the moments he'd lived for. Nothing had compared. The addiction to taking aim at a mark and easing down on the trigger had been complete and absolute. He was the hunter. Could he live without it? Yes. Without question.

He had discovered a force much more addictive than the kill: love.

12

NELSON ETTINGER LEARNED OF HIS BROTHER'S
death as he stood staring at the half-eaten carcass of a
bison calf. Wolves had gotten to the young bison, sep-
arating it from the herd. This was southern Montana,
where the yearly snowfall made the daily search for
food a vicious contest of kill-or-be-killed. The pack
was dining on the dead youngster when Nelson came
over the ridge in his Dodge extended-cab 4x4.

He had taken his Wetherby rifle from the window
rack and fired a pair of rounds at the sky. A half dozen
of the predators had spooked, pounding off through
the tree line. A stubborn male stood his ground, dipping his snout into the open chasm of the bison's rib
cage. Ettinger dropped the animal with a single round.

The cell phone in his truck rang. He tromped
through the snow and grabbed the phone through
the open window of the driver's-side door, answering
the call as he made his way back to the corpses of the
bison and the wolf. The voice of a young man asked
if he were Nelson Ettinger. "You got it," he answered,
kicking at the wolf's hindquarters.

"Thank you, please hold," the voice told him.

Nelson looked up, scanning the tree line slowly for any sign of the rest of the pack. He'd have liked to kill them all. Nothing against the animals themselves, but they were systematically wiping out his stock of bison. He had accumulated nearly two hundred head, in addition to his cattle, and had no intention of letting those four-legged savages pick his herd off one by one.

There was a series of digital tones over the phone line, and then a familiar voice said, "Nelson?"

"In the flesh."

"Nelson, this is Miriam." Miriam Ettinger's voice sounded tired and spent.

Nelson was surprised to hear from her. His brother had never been big on maintaining contact, but Miriam had *never* phoned him herself. Not that they didn't get along. It was a simple matter of a clash of cultures. Nelson preferred wide-open spaces and fresh air, without cars, and as few people as possible. Miriam *needed* people, masses of people, and the only mountains she felt comfortable among were man-made structures of iron and glass and cement.

"Well, I'll be," he said, grinning.

"I hope I didn't interrupt anything."

Staring down at the carnage, he said, "No, ma'am, not a thing."

"Good. Good."

"How's my little brother?"

"Nelson, that's why I'm calling. Something terrible has happened." Her throat tightened. She had made a concerted effort to stay strong. It was hard to tell if he could sense her struggle to control the rush of emotions. If he did, he didn't let on.

"Oh?"

"Nelson . . . James is dead."

He glanced up from the blood and gore, his gaze tracking up across the snowy landscape. This was his land, all fifty thousand acres. Miles and miles of it, as far as the eye could see in any direction. It was bordered on three sides by national forest. It was populated with his livestock. He had twenty-five full-time hands who worked to keep the ranch immaculate and profitable. He'd paid a pittance for it. It was now worth millions. His pride in his land was immeasurable. Thirty years earlier this massive piece of real estate was nothing but wilderness. Careful planning and a delicate touch had maintained its natural beauty. All that stood before him now was a result of the grand vision and boundless energy he'd had as a much younger man. Now he was seventy, with neither the energy nor the willpower for such a brutal undertaking. Any fool could see that there was much to take great pride in. But suddenly it was all forgotten.

"Come again?" he said, furrowing his brow, nudging his hat with a knuckle. Perhaps he hadn't heard quite right.

"James was shot. He's . . . he's dead, Nelson. James is dead."

"You're telling me Jimmy's *dead*?"

"Yes, Nelson. Two days ago."

"Two *days*?"

"Yes, I . . . I'm sorry, Nelson. I wanted to call you straightaway, but the president has asked that I keep this as quiet as possible until the FBI can get their bearings and are able to get their investigation moving in the right direction. Believe me, you're one of the first to know. I . . . I just . . ." She trailed off, shakier than ever.

There was a glare off the snow from the sun. Nelson Ettinger used his arm as a visor. He stared off into the distance, groping for words, his thoughts in a jumble. His baby brother was gone, dead. When was the last time he'd seen Jimmy? Two years? Three? What did it matter, they'd chosen different paths their entire lives. He was Jimmy's senior by fifteen years. What had they had in common, besides a mother and a father and a last name? In the end, they were just different people, living in separate worlds. But none of that mattered—brothers were brothers. Period.

"I don't know what to say, Miriam," he said. An honest declaration.

"So far, this hasn't leaked to the media. We've been lucky for that. We are hoping . . ." Miriam paused, her throat tightening again. She was still trying to be a good politician's wife. She went on, tremulously, "They keep telling me that every person who knows about this is an additional security risk."

"I understand." And he did.

"The press will be on this day and night for weeks and months and on and on, once this breaks."

"For years," he said, knowing full well the feast this would make for the news-gathering business.

"Yes, for years." There was thunder in her voice.

"Miriam, what do you need for me to do?"

"It would mean a tremendous amount to me if you could just be here. James would have wanted it."

"Of course. I'll be there by late tonight."

"Thank you."

"What else can I do?"

"I . . . don't know. Everything has been chaos. I can't eat. I can't sleep. I'm exhausted, Nelson. I can't believe he's . . ."

"Please, Miriam. Hold together till I get there."

She was nodding. "Okay. I'll make certain there's a car waiting for you at the airport. The kids will be glad to see you and—"

"Miriam, don't worry about me. This old cowboy has seen a lot, and there's not much that scares me off. Don't let those government crows spook you."

"Thank you, Nelson."

"I'll be there in a jiff."

He hadn't been to the office in three days, and hated having to put off some business responsibilities that had probably piled up. Nelson did not fit the mold of the traditional businessman. He was casual, even rustic, in his lifestyle, but he took finances seriously and was certainly not one to slack off when it came to getting the proper paperwork taken care of to get the job done and keep his customers happy.

The snow and the wolves kept him doubly busy during the winter months. For every hour of daylight, it seemed he needed three more just to stay on par with everything that piled on his to-do list. When he'd moved out west more than three decades earlier, his intention hadn't been to become a corporate goon. And really, he *wasn't*. But he was seventy years old, and the prospect of keeping his nose to the grindstone till he slumped over into the grave appealed to him about as much as life on an island of lepers. On the other hand, turning over the reins so that someone else could run the business made him more than a little nervous.

Thus he found himself in the regrettable position of having to somehow go on with business even as he began to grieve the loss of his sibling. He dialed on his cell phone and told his wife to book the first flight she could get him on. His office was in town, twenty minutes from the ranch. He asked her to phone him there once the arrangements were made.

The telephone on his desk was ringing when he unlocked the office door. Nelson threw his denim jacket on the coatrack and grabbed the phone. His flight left in ninety minutes. She would have a carry-on bag packed and waiting for him at the house. He'd have just enough time to tie up a few loose ends at the office, swing by the house for a quick shower and his bag, and make a dash for the airport. Opal even promised to have a tuna fish sandwich waiting for him on his way out.

He shook the snow from the brim of his hat and dropped into the leather captain's chair behind his desk. There were a half dozen messages on the answering machine, which he absently listened to as he shuffled through files and bills and receipts on the desk. He logged onto his desktop Mac and opened his email program. There were at least a dozen messages, but at the moment he had no time for them. He'd just print them and thumb through the stack on the flight out east.

Nelson printed off the emails, folded them, and tucked them away. He was suddenly weary, overcome by the gravity of it all. It would've been nice to take a few minutes and sit back in the leather captain's chair behind his desk. But he did not want to risk missing his flight. He'd be back in a couple of days, and right now he had to go bury his baby brother.

The first official public absence came on the third day after Ettinger's death. It was at a tiny, insignificant event. It was a pancake breakfast at a Methodist church in Portland, Maine, to raise money to upgrade the county's 911 system. The vice president was to make an appearance of no more than forty-five minutes, but an appearance nonetheless. Just his presence alone would raise the number of charitable donations exponentially.

The morning of the event, a call was placed to an official in charge, apologizing for the VP. It seemed he had come down with a nasty viral infection and was under doctor's orders to stay in bed.

If the absence raised any suspicions that anything might be out of the ordinary, none were voiced.

The president met with his advisors in the afternoon, their second gathering of the day. He was getting anxious. Philbrick was being kept under wraps for the moment. Even Mrs. Philbrick had been left in the dark up to this point, at the president's request.

The director of the FBI, Curtis Martindale, presented what little data his people had managed to compile in the past six hours, none of which seemed very promising. Martindale assured the president that every available agent was being activated.

The director of the CIA, Guy Palmer, for his part, read from a printed list of possible suspects. Most of them were members of various militant extremist groups scattered throughout central Europe and Asia. There was a Palestinian group that Palmer expressed particular interest in. But there was nothing tangible yet, nothing to link any of the parties in question to the crime at hand.

The president had his reading glasses perched on the tip of his nose. He'd slept three hours in the past forty-eight and was quickly tiring of these two birds pointing fingers at each other. There was enough blame to go around, he figured. How this clown had been allowed near enough to Ettinger's property to get a clean shot *through his bedroom window* was beyond him. More than that, it scared the living crap out of him. If some goon could get to Ettinger, it was just as likely there was a blind spot for getting to him, as well. And he had no plans to die in office.

Both the FBI and the CIA laid out their tentative game plans for the next twenty-four to forty-eight hours. Russ Vetris probed them for anything they might know and might be choosing not to share at the present time. These boys were masters at telling you only what they wanted you to know. Harboring secrets was their stock-in-trade.

Every international flight, whether inbound or outbound from U.S. soil, was being monitored. Analysts at Langley were reviewing security tapes of passengers boarding international flights at seven major airports in the United States, going back three days.

The president had the fourth draft of a speech on his desk. It was the speech he would give when the time came to address the nation to officially announce the untimely death of their vice president.

He was marking it up with a red felt-tip. He would be sitting right there behind his desk in the Oval Office when he read it directly into the television camera. Briefly he considered which suit he'd wear to convey the proper mixture of sadness and strength. He dismissed the thought—after all, that's what his advisors were for.

They scheduled a third meeting for 9 P.M., and the congregation queued up and marched out of the Oval Office. The president looked at his editing job, and frowned. How long should they wait to make the announcement? It was the biggest story in four decades. If they held out too long, the story would break through less proper channels. And that would be no good. This was news that the American people should hear directly from their leader.

13

A SMALL ARMY OF FLIGHT ATTENDANTS CON-
verged near the front of the jet to assist with a kid in
a wheelchair. The kid's head was shaved, and he
looked to have had a pretty sad run of things over
the course of his short life. His arms were lined with
needles that fed tubing, which in turn trailed off to
hanging bags. A battery-operated ventilator kept his
lungs pumping. The attendants and his harried-
looking parents and a nurse maneuvered his wheelchair down the aisle toward the exit. The rest of the
passengers waited semipatiently as the small caravan
shuffled along.

St. John remained seated for a few minutes,
watching people brush past him. In front of him, the
sweaty real-estate agent from Nebraska tussled with
his carry-on, having wedged it against its will into the
overhead compartment. The guy's wife nagged for
him to step it up a notch or they'd never catch a cab.

The crowd thinned slightly. St. John fetched his
hanging bag from the overhead compartment and
waded into the aisle and off the plane. The air was
static with the spirit of the holiday and the sighs of

weary travelers. St. John moved along in the queue of heads and bodies heading down toward the terminal.

As the ramp opened wide, the masses dispersed in all directions. He had an inch or two over most of the crowd, and his sharp blue eyes made a broad, patient sweep of the immediate area. It was surprisingly warm here. There were enough bodies in this room to heat a rural community. A Korean and three small children bumped past him like ballistic missiles. They shot down the thin carpeting to where a cluster of smiling relatives engulfed them with hugs and kisses.

St. John stood straight and tall. His gaze had made it halfway back across on the survey when he saw her. His breath caught for just a moment, and he smiled. She saw him too. She'd been watching him, he could tell in an instant. She'd seen him step a foot or two out of the traffic and pan the crowd for any sign of her.

St. John took a breath, then a big step forward. In that instant, he forgot the swarming heat, the half a billion winter-clad travelers milling around him, and the chaos of La Guardia Airport and New York City.

She waited, standing next to a support column. The deplorable overhead lighting did nothing to diminish her beauty. Her dark hair framed her face like an angel. And her smile produced a current far more substantial than electricity. She wore a long coat over a short skirt, and held dainty leather gloves in her hands.

St. John approached and stopped less than a foot away. He looked down at her, then took her hands in his. Two weeks, had it been, or an eternity? It was a question that each asked as they stared into each other's eyes. When he could stand it no longer, he let go of her hands, touched his fingers to the smooth slopes of her neck and leaned in to kiss her.

He kissed her deeply, and Megan received him in the way that he'd grown to crave. She groped her way beneath his coat and felt the tone of the muscles along his sides and back, and all the luscious memories of their time together came back to her in a flood. They had yet to speak a word.

Chills fingered down her spine as he kissed her neck and chin.

She managed to say, "How was your flight?"

"Lonely, without you."

She couldn't help but grin. His lips were warm against her flesh. Why had she ever let him leave her? Never again, she swore.

"I have a cab waiting."

"Good. And you'd better have a *room* waiting," he purred, working up toward the lobe of one ear.

She nearly melted. Megan nodded. "A big one. With a big bed, and room service."

"We don't need a big bed, just a stout one."

"Let's find the rest of your clothes." Megan motioned in the general direction of the baggage carousel.

"I don't plan on needing them." He attacked her other lobe with his tongue.

"We'll at least have to *eat* sometime."

"You said we have room service."

"New York is a city where a woman needs to be wined and dined," she teased, pulling away with a laugh.

"Very well. One meal. Then it's back to bed for the two of us!"

Megan Durant took Olin St. John by the hand. He collected his bags and they hurried to the cab. Even before the taxi had left the curb, he was kissing her again.

Hardly nine months had passed since they'd first met. A mutual acquaintance had introduced them. It was at an exhibit opening at a large art gallery in London. The acquaintance was a major figure in certain circles in Europe and was ushered away to join another conversation mere seconds after Olin St. John and Megan Durant had said hello. Their eyes met, and in that instant, fate let its intentions be known: they were meant for each other.

Though they'd met in England, they were both American by birth. Megan was hesitant to speak at any length about her parents. Her parents had divorced, she explained, and there wasn't much more to add. She cared to remember little or nothing of life before the age of ten and was clearly determined not to dwell in the past.

Olin lied. His family, he said, had been missionaries to Scandinavia for years. When they returned to the States he stayed behind, eventually building a career that had made him quite wealthy. In truth, his grandfather had fought in the Second World War and married a German woman and had a son. His father had worked as a watchmaker for thirty-five years until a thief put a knife in his back. Olin was raised on the streets, where he learned to make a living with a gun.

She scribbled her number on the back of his program. He phoned within the week, longing to hear her voice. Soon he was visiting regularly. They fell in love hard and fast.

Olin had traveled the world, and he enchanted her with stories of Moscow and Hong Kong and the Middle East. She let him make love to her in palatial rooms overlooking the Thames. It seemed clear that they were soul mates.

Olin found himself increasingly distracted from his work, his heart longing for Megan more with each passing hour that they were apart. She thought of little else than Olin St. John, her body craving his touch.

They'd known each other for such a short time when, only two weeks ago, Olin phoned out of the blue and proposed marriage. He was away on business. This, he declared, was his final account. He was retiring so that he could be her husband. He told her that he had accumulated enough wealth for them to populate the earth with their children and for neither of them to lift a finger for the rest of their lives.

"Meet me in New York in two weeks," he'd said as she listened breathlessly. "Then we'll do something hokey—fly to Las Vegas or something, and be wed on the spot. No friends, no family, just the two of us, starting our life together on our own terms. Then we'll make love till we go blind."

Through tears and laughter she accepted.

Several more calls followed in the days to come, as they whizzed through the arrangements. Never again would they be apart, they promised with each conversation. With an ocean standing between them, they declared that their love would burn forever.

A pair of stark-looking figures in dark suits and dark sunglasses were waiting when Nelson Ettinger appeared in the terminal at Ronald Reagan National Airport. They had been provided with photos of the vice president's brother and were briefed on how to handle transporting him to the Ettinger estate in Washington, D.C.

Nelson had barely stepped out of the narrow jetway into the terminal when the two gentlemen presented themselves and quickly ushered him into a waiting car. There was no conversation. Nelson had expected none.

He was still perplexed by something he'd read during the flight. Among the emails he'd printed at his office was a message from his brother. The message was both intimate and cryptic, and Nelson had no idea what to make of it. Nelson ached at the thought that he'd not had a chance to say good-bye to James. But in some small way it helped to have these final words printed out on office paper. It was as if James had reached out to him one last time, and that meant the world to him. He intended to show it to Miriam. Maybe she could shed some light on what James had written.

The estate in D.C. was massive. The mansion sat on a ten-acre, partially wooded spread. It was gated and, at the moment, guarded like the Pentagon. The Lincoln eased through security. One of the men in dark glasses carried Nelson's bag for him. Nelson noticed the man run a detection device over and beneath the bag.

Miriam's sister, Elaine, was in the kitchen, giving instructions to the staff. It hadn't occurred to him that Elaine would be there, though it made sense. He tipped his hat to her and she offered him a hug. Her kids were in Connecticut with her husband, she said. Bradey and Jude were in the family room watching TV.

"How's she holding up?" he asked, removing his hat and running a hand through what scraps of hair he had left.

"She's coping."

He frowned.

"Have you eaten?"

He shrugged. "Don't fuss on my account."

Elaine led him down a series of hallways, finally heading up a flight of plushly carpeted stairs. Along the way, she introduced him to various clusters of serious faces, presenting him as the vice president's brother. Everyone offered condolences.

The ceiling was high and vaulted. The place was much too fancy for his taste.

"Miriam has been understandably withdrawn, the past day or so." Elaine gestured as they walked. "She absolutely dreads the media blitz. Those scavengers are never going to leave her alone."

Nelson nodded, following a half-step behind. "When does Yates plan to make a statement?"

She took an exasperated breath. "I honestly couldn't tell you. I mean, the FBI wants more time, but Miriam needs *closure*. There is a funeral to plan. She has to bury him, and it's just not right to drag this out any longer."

"I couldn't agree more."

"But they're not concerned about her, they have their politics to worry about."

"Like what?"

"What little I've heard, Yates has tapped Anthony Philbrick to fill the VP's vacancy."

"As in *Speaker of the House* Philbrick?"

They came to the closed double doors of the master bedroom. "Just a second," she said, and knocked lightly. There was no answer. Elaine turned the door-knob and eased open the exquisitely detailed raised-panel mahogany door. Once inside, she left the door open only a crack.

Nelson Ettinger stood with his Stetson held at his side. He turned away from the door. Back down the hall, the way they'd just come, a Secret Service agent paused and flashed him a suspicious look. He had short auburn hair and a strong jawline. The old cowboy spotted the tiny receiver in the man's ear. He offered the young man a courteous nod. The gesture was not returned.

"Nelson." She motioned for him.

He followed Elaine beyond the door. They stopped beside the huge bed. Nelson observed his surroundings. The master bedroom was the length and breadth of a modest home. *I wonder how much hay I could fit in here?* A quarter of the opposing wall was composed of floor-to-ceiling windows. Beyond the glass, a balcony protruded from the mansion.

"She's out there," Elaine said, crossing her arms over her chest. "I'll leave you two to talk, and I'll make sure your dinner is ready when you are." With that, she was out the door.

He spotted his sister-in-law seated in a deck chair on the balcony, a blanket across her lap. He could only guess how long she'd been there. Perhaps the harsh winter chill helped her to deal with the shock and the pain.

He tapped on the glass before stepping out.

"Don't get up," he said. He bent down to hug her. She kissed him on the cheek.

"I don't imagine you expected to fly all the way from that ranch of yours to stand out here in this nasty weather?" Her complexion was pale and her eyes were noticeably streaked.

"The cold isn't a problem," he said, a big warm grin revealing startlingly white teeth. "Enduring the traffic in this city, though . . ."

"Still just an old cowboy?"

"Yes, ma'am."

"Thank you for coming on such short notice, Nelson."

"The security around here is nuts."

"Yes it is. Perhaps James would still be alive if they had exercised such rigid precaution on a regular basis. He was shot in our *bedroom*, Nelson. How could they have allowed that? There is no excuse!"

"No one can be kept safe one hundred percent of the time."

She met this comment with silence.

"If there's anything you need from me, Miriam, don't even hesitate. Jimmy and I weren't the best at keeping in touch, but I know full well that he'd have been there for Opal in a flash if the tables were turned. The sad truth is that he was the second most visible and powerful man on the planet. Not the safest job you could choose. There are some awfully vile folks out there with a lot of hate. And they've got to direct that hate toward somebody." Nelson looked out over the lawn beneath the balcony. Arc lights cast elongated pools of light across the largely undisturbed snow. He could see Secret Service agents moving about along the perimeter of the grounds.

He could tell she was freezing but wagered that the discomfort of the biting cold was a small price to pay to keep away from all the activity inside the house. He could spout all sorts of encouraging, uplifting drivel, but her life had been washed away in one fatal blow. The heart heals in its own time.

The corners of her blanket fluttered in the crisp breeze. Nelson could feel his own nose going numb, and his ears were beginning to sting, as well.

"My visit will be as long or short as you request," he continued, aware that his presence would serve very little purpose other than moral support. "I'm here for you and the kids. If you need help with funeral arrangements, just say the word."

She turned to him, tears glistening, the weight of the world reflected in her eyes. "You're a good brother."

"Ah, don't get carried away, young lady." He gave her a wink. "I loved my brother. And I love his family."

Miriam reached out a hand for his, giving it a squeeze.

"That sister of yours promised me a hot meal. You reckon there's any truth to that?"

"Absolutely," she said with a forced smile. "The food around here might even impress an old dog like you."

His grin faded as he unbuttoned an inside pocket of his sport coat. "Listen, Miriam, real quick. I was curious, was something peculiar going on with Jimmy?"

"I'm afraid I don't follow."

Unfolding the email printout, he handed it to her. "Well, I didn't understand it myself. It's the strangest thing. I didn't know what to make of this. But perhaps it might be of some interest to you."

14

OLIN SURPRISED HER WITH TICKETS TO *THE Producers*. Sitting at a small round metal table at lunch, Megan was dreamily lost in his eyes. The restaurant had a generous view of Central Park. He slid the matching pair of tickets to her, banded with a Christmas bow.

They'd frequented shows in London. He kept a brownstone in the theater district. It was a place to unwind, with a fireplace in the den and a tree out front, nothing fancy. Megan hadn't been much on theater until they'd met, but now she was addicted.

"These are for the eight o'clock show. Are you pleased?" He didn't need to ask. She was beaming. She took his hand and leaned to kiss him.

"Very much so. Thank you."

They dined on pasta and white wine. The small table was very intimate. They talked, keeping their faces close together, and flirted like teenagers, hands groping, kissing, eyes sending plenty of uncoded signals. The flirting flowed with an energy of its own. These past few weeks had seemed unending. All they wanted was to be near each other, to touch and hold, and to know that the wait was over.

Even with the cold and the wind and the ice-crusted sidewalks, it was a pleasure to stroll together along the streets of New York. Megan nestled herself against Olin. He bundled her in his arms.

They shopped, leisurely browsing. She tried on this and that, modeling for him, and turning in front of the tall mirrors. Olin carried her bags.

Midafternoon, they stopped for cappuccinos, sipping and chatting as flakes of snow specked the windows.

"I want a whole house full of children," she said, a bit of foam from her hot drink clinging to her upper lip.

"That's what you've said."

"What do you think?"

"I think we need to get in lots of practice first."

"A girl first, though; a sweet little thing, with a huge red bow in her hair, and lots of frilly white lace on her dress. Then a few boys, as handsome as their father. Then, whatever happens to come along after that."

"I'm glad you've put in your order early." *A father?* The thought was like shrapnel tearing through his consciousness. It sounded absurd. Sure, he was setting sail into a new life, a new existence, but hurtling headlong in paternity—how could it be? He'd spent more than half of his life killing for profit. How could he expect to be an example to another human being? Not that his nurturing side didn't exist. But how can you discipline your child for picking a fight or not cleaning her room, when you've opened up a man's chest with a foot-long serrated blade as he begged for mercy that you never for a second considered granting? These were the questions that would haunt him in the future, he knew. For now he'd pursue only what was directly in front of him, here in this moment.

An icy finger of cold, absolute terror trailed up President Clifton Yates's spine. He read the words again, and again he choked hard on his panic. This had to be a joke. But there it was in black and white. His stomach lurched. He felt like he would be violently ill, right there on the steps of the monument. But to his credit, he held it in. For the moment, no matter how nauseating the sight of the message made him feel, he had to remain cool.

> *Nelson,*
> *If and when you hear my taped statement,*
> *please forgive me. I've turned out to be*
> *neither a good brother nor a good citizen.*
>
> *I'll call you in a few days.*
> *James*

Taped statement? What on earth could that mean? His imagination was spinning out all sorts of feverish scenarios. But Yates had to focus . . . focus and breathe.

"This is as baffling to me as it is to you, Miriam. I assure you," Yates said.

Miriam Ettinger stood only a few feet away, her countenance the very definition of sober. She was bundled in an elegant fur coat and a scarf. It was after two in the morning, Wednesday. She had phoned him personally, shortly before 1 A.M., and was adamant that they meet right away, alone, to talk. How could he say no?

His driver delivered him, per her request, to the Lincoln Memorial. The temperature was scraping zero. They stood at the base of the magnificent edifice of the Great Emancipator, his likeness bearing down on them.

The president had adjourned the last meeting of the night at eleven-thirty, and had settled in for some ESPN. When her call came, he had muted the game he was watching, and spoke to her as if he'd just been thinking of calling. But the voice on the other end had been, as it was now, all-business. She was slightly enigmatic on the phone, stating only that it was urgent that she see him immediately. And he'd honestly seen no harm in humoring his running mate's grief-stricken widow.

But now, more than anything on God's green earth, Clifton Yates wished he could rewind to that moment and simply pacify her with some benign words of sympathy, just to get her off the phone. Instead, he was holding a copy of an email written by James Ettinger mere hours before his assassination. An email containing two infinitely volatile words. Words, that in a city like Washington, had the potential to bring down administrations.

Taped statement.

"Was it something he was *planning* to do, or something he had already done?" Miriam Ettinger asked him, as if he should know.

Most of the color had left the president's face. The extreme cold was a blessing, otherwise she might have noticed the terror-induced whitewashing of his features. "Miriam, I . . . couldn't even begin to explain this message. Clearly, he had something on his mind, but I think it would be unwise to jump to any conclusions on this. James and I talked almost daily, and he was in perfect spirits the day before his death. Perhaps this was just something between brothers."

Miriam shook her head violently. "No, Clifton. Nelson has no idea what James was trying to tell him. He brought it to my attention because of his own bewilderment. Besides, if it were between brothers, why would he call himself a bad citizen? What would he mean by that?"

"I wish I knew," Yates said. Indeed, he did wish he knew yet feared that maybe he *did* know. Most paralyzing at this moment was the amount of room there was for speculation. He knew very well what James Ettinger might have meant by those words. But it seemed unlikely.

Ettinger had been faithful to the party for so long. Faithful to the machinations required for success. Faithful to the administration. Nobody *liked* living with what they'd done. Yet nothing worth doing ever got done without discomfort or sacrifice. And they had managed to slip under the radar, to accomplish something that was all too necessary for the country they loved to remain strong and great, for the nation to remain the most powerful force on earth. They had lived under the weight of paranoia for nearly eight years now, but they'd finally made it out of the danger zone.

Taped statement.

The focused heat of speculation was boring a hole through his chest. This woman wanted an answer. He would not be able to provide her with one. Not today. Not tomorrow. Not ever.

"Was he planning to speak before Congress? Could that be it?" There was rising desperation in her voice.

"Miriam, I can look into this—and I assure you that I will immediately—but for me to speculate at this time would be unproductive and foolish. I'm in no better position than you are. I need time, Miriam. You've sprung this on me out of the blue. And you've got to leave room for the possibility that this means nothing at all, as painful as that might be to accept. After all, it says right here that James had planned to call Nelson in a few days to explain. It's probably nothing." Glancing at the massive likeness of Lincoln and thinking of how many tremendous sacrifices Abe had made in the name of the greater good, he wondered whether he himself—if the truth were ever made known—would be held in such high regard.

Miriam Ettinger wanted none of it. Her first reaction was to cast off his argument. But the voice of cool reason finally offered its counsel, stripping her rebuttal of its momentum. Maybe the message was benign. Could it be that her urgency to find meaning in James's message to Nelson was fueled merely by the desperation of a woman grieving the loss of her husband? Possibly, she thought.

A stiff breeze brought leaves skittering across the top steps leading up to the memorial. She took a step toward the president. "Clifton, I apologize. You're probably right. Please forgive this inconvenience. I've kept you out on such a miserable night. You were a good friend to James." She motioned to the printout in his hand. "Feel free to throw that in the garbage. You've always known what's best."

"James was my friend, Miriam. You have become like a sister to me. You could never inconvenience me. And I mean that. I will not rest until his killer is brought to justice. You have my word." The president put his big hand on her shoulder, offering her the same look of unquestionable sincerity that had won him back-to-back elections.

Miriam thanked him. She turned and descended the steps to her waiting Jaguar. The car whisked her into the night.

President Clifton Yates looked down and read James Ettinger's words again. He would not let that man destroy him from the grave. He crumpled the paper in his fist but did not discard it. It did not belong in the garbage. In time, it would be burned, and the ashes scattered. But not yet. Before that could happen, other eyes would have to see it.

A frantic call was made at 3 A.M. The call originated from the car carrying the president between the Lincoln Memorial and the White House, and was answered by a sleep-soaked voice at a behemoth stone mansion in Silver Spring, Maryland. The person on the receiving end of the call was H. Glen Shelby, the president's attorney. The conversation was short and enigmatic.

A short time later, Shelby parked his Lexus next to a playground at a local junior high school and waited with the engine idling. In no time the president's car appeared at the street corner and then stopped at the rear of the attorney's car. Glen Shelby climbed inside, and the president offered him coffee in a tall paper cup.

The car turned out onto the street, the deep, cold night passing over its black-tinted windows. The excursion, which took them on a meandering route through D.C., lasted three-quarters of an hour. The point of the drive was to have a private conversation. The topic of conversation was decidedly not fit for the Oval Office—or any other space within the walls of the White House, for that matter—where unseen electronic eyes and ears were far too prone to eavesdrop.

A few minutes after 4 A.M., the black limousine dropped Shelby back at his car. He started his Lexus, feeling rattled. He sat in the cold, staring straight ahead, thinking, both hands on the wheel. He put the car in gear and started to pull away from the playground, but then eased the gearshift into neutral, taking a moment to catch his breath. He lifted his phone but suddenly realized he wasn't sure who to call first with the news he'd just been given by the most powerful man in the world.

15

AFTER SIX DAYS IN AN NBC NEWS EDITING
booth, blurry-eyed from piecing together a story that
had been in the works for nine months, with her
brain reduced to mush from absolute zero daylight
for the past eighteen hours, a very scary thing happened to Brooke Weaver: she found herself suddenly
attracted to Barry, the cameraman who'd made
dozens of passes at her in the past two or three
months. The thought of it made her skin crawl. But
her rods and cones were so warped and distorted
from staring at archival footage that nothing made
sense anymore; up was down and down was . . .

Get a hold of yourself! Brooke shook her head,
trying to clear up whatever had short-circuited in
there. She found her Diet Coke can sitting behind a
computer keyboard, and shook it. Empty.

Barry Hickman was on the other side of the massive glass partition, working on something with Darla
Donovan, her boss. Darla had been a producer for
NBC News for nearly twenty years and had estab-
lished enough clout in the industry to pretty much
write her own ticket. For her age—for *any* age—she

looked stunning. Brooke could not imagine why a woman with Darla Donovan's beauty and brains hadn't wanted to work *in front* of the camera. Actually, Brooke *knew* the answer to that question. The truth was that the real fun of TV news was behind the scenes. The talking heads on camera got the big bucks and all the special perks, but the *real* journalists were off camera, doing the legwork, putting the stories together.

That's why Brooke had begged, pleaded, and come just short of committing a felony for the chance to work with Donovan. And by some miracle, she'd gotten it straight out of graduate school.

And now here she was, worn down to the point of actually thinking Barry Hickman looked *pretty good!* Ouch. It was sad and ultradepressing to even acknowledge. But after four years at Harvard, two more years for her masters in journalism, and three years of the brutal work schedule of Her Majesty, Darla Donovan, she was exhausted and had no social life to speak of.

At twenty-seven, she was Donovan's personal assistant and had been granted more responsibility than she could have ever dreamed possible. This was *precisely* where she'd dreamed she'd be at this age. But she was ready for some sleep, some spicy Chinese takeout, and, more than anything else, she needed . . . *a man!*

Barry peered over the cubicle where he and Darla were talking and he caught Brooke staring at him. A big, beaming smile stretched from ear to ear. Then he winked at her.

Brooke suddenly felt three inches tall. She could

feel her face flushing red. More than anything in the world, she wanted to crawl under the desk where she was working and die. If she thought Barry had been a parasite before, there was not a shadow of a doubt that he would never, *never*, let her live this down. Out of frustration with herself, she snatched the empty Diet Coke can from the desk, crushed it, and then hurled it across the room, missing the wastebasket by an embarrassing distance.

She flipped a page in the script she'd been working with to edit the raw camera footage and stared blankly at the typescript, the words suddenly incoherent to her. *Thank heaven for Christmas*, she thought, rubbing her eyes and yawning. All she had to do was to get to Darla's designated stopping point, and then she could call it a day. Then she'd run across town and barricade herself inside her apartment. Tomorrow evening was the party at Darla's. She'd sleep late, apply badly needed makeup, and spend the evening at Darla's condominium with the rest of their production team at their annual Christmas party. And the morning after that, she'd be off to the country to celebrate Christmas with her family.

Her brother, Wyatt, was dying of leukemia. He was living back at home so that their parents could take care of him. Most likely, this would be their last Christmas together. The thought of losing him filled her with . . . well, it was simply too much to contemplate.

First, though, there was work to be done. Brooke shook off her musings in an attempt to focus. Just a few more hours and she'd be free. The minutes simply couldn't tick by soon enough.

An hour later, Brooke made the mistake of passing Darla's open door. Brooke barely got three steps beyond when she was summoned inside. She cringed, debated hurrying on, then reluctantly entered her boss's domain.

"Have you called Richmond?" Darla said without looking up from her desk.

"Not yet."

"We needed that nailed down a *month* ago!"

Cringe. Clearly, Darla was in one of her pissy moods today. They came and went like the tides. Maybe it had to do with the holidays.

"If you need a baby-sitter to hold your hand, Brooke, to help you get this done, I guess—"

"I'll make the call, Darla." Brooke blew a tuft of blond hair out of her face. Her lean figure, shoulder-length blond hair, average height, stylish skirt and top, and tortoiseshell horn-rimmed glasses made her the absolute picture of a corporate go-getter. Brooke was accustomed to her boss's fury. The woman's angelic face and movie-star smile could turn vicious in a millisecond. "You have my word."

"Fine, fine!" Darla wheeled around in her executive-style swivel chair, turning her attention elsewhere. In an instant she was on the phone and quickly had a new victim. "Jonesy, where is that documentation? No, no—you said Wednesday. Jonesy, you're late, *again!*"

Brooke took advantage of the window of opportunity, and backpedaled out of Donovan's den of terror. Deadlines generally put Darla on the warpath. She could be your best friend, your pal, your amigo, but when the screws began to tighten, as a story came due for broadcast, well . . . frankly, she transformed into a shrew. Although, in comparison to the remaining 99 percent of the women in the industry, she was a saint.

Brooke nearly escaped. She had her arms stacked to overflowing with file folders, videocassettes, and script binders as she navigated the foot traffic toward the relative solace of her own tiny work space. Darla sprang out the door, still holding the phone to her ear.

"Brooke! Brooke, hold on!"

Brooke Weaver froze, midstep.

"Brooke!"

Brooke pivoted on her heels.

Darla motioned her back to her office. *Cringe.* That could mean anything. Being called to Darla's office was a nerve-shredding grab bag of the unknown. Whether good or bad, the result was invariably *more work.* She shuffled toward her boss's door.

Brooke poked her head in, and Darla set the phone down. "Sorry," Darla said, as apologetically as her nature allowed. "Favor to ask. I'm swamped. Haven't been home since, like, July. So I haven't made it down to check the V.I.P. box for at least three or four days." Darla sighed, sweeping an open palm above her desk, acknowledging the immense clutter.

Brooke caught the hint. "Say no more, Chief. I'll hit it on my way home."

"You're a champ."

"So they say."

"You *are* coming to the party tomorrow night, right?" Darla flashed her *the look.*

"I'll be there with bells on."

"Great! If you would, swing by the post office on your way home today, and bring any mail from the box to my place tomorrow evening. Six o'clock sharp. You're a doll—oh, here's the key." Darla dropped the key on the videocassette case atop Brooke's load.

"I'll be here all night. Think about me when you're lounging about, eating chocolate and watching cable."

Brooke smirked. "You know very well that you are *all* I think about." Then she turned back into the corridor, NBC employees rushing past her. Over her shoulder she called, "See ya, Chief!"

The V.I.P. box was Donovan's special secret. She'd developed enough faith in Brooke, over an exhaustive period of time, to trust her to periodically messenger its contents to her whenever the need arose. It was nothing more than a garden-variety post office box. Darla had maintained it for years. It was her way of keeping "sensitive material" away from prying eyes in the mailroom at NBC. She had dozens of trusted informants scattered throughout the various realms of industry, politics, and power, and the vast majority of these "anonymous sources" were understandably paranoid. So, there was the "V.I.P." box. It had served her well. Darla was violently possessive over the box's content and had laid down two nonnegotiable rules regarding Brooke's occasional assistance: first, she was to tell no one of the box's existence; and second, under no circumstances was she to open *anything*—period!

The walk from Rockefeller Plaza to the post office seemed twice as long because of the bitter cold and the biting wind. A tall gentleman with close-cropped hair and a long wool coat held the door for her, and nothing had ever felt so good and right and lovely as stepping into the great heated expanse of the United States Postal Service.

Brooke snatched off her gloves with her teeth and waded through a sea of fellow New Yorkers to the opposite end of the building. 1124, 1123 . . . 1122. She turned the key in box 1122 and removed two business-size envelopes and a parcel wrapped in brown paper. She felt her hand around deep inside the box, just to be sure.

She found some breathing room and set her Eddie Bauer backpack on a table by a window. The table was littered with change-of-address forms. She brushed them aside. Her pack was filled with a change of clothes, a water bottle, the script she'd worked on for the last nine months of her life, and an entire compilation of other odds and ends from her daily existence.

Neither the letters nor the parcel possessed a return address. Nothing from the box ever did. If anything, there'd be a symbol or a code word written in the upper left-hand corner. The first envelope had nothing more than the box number and the proper postage. The second envelope had a small, hand-drawn sunflower, in red ink. She could only guess what shadowy figure had doodled that bit of hokey artwork.

Brooke unzipped the outer compartment of her pack and managed to wedge both envelopes alongside a Pottery Barn catalog she spent most of her free-time lusting over. The parcel, she estimated off-hand, was the size of a hardcover book or a small gift box. The word **BEACON** was written in block lettering in the upper corner. The outer compartment of her pack was stuffed, so she pulled back the flap, yanked out a fleece pullover, and stuffed the parcel deep inside.

She glanced up and saw fresh flakes sticking to the outside of the window. She dreaded going back out in the cold. Just then, a cab pulled alongside the curb and let out a passenger. Without hesitation, Brooke swiped up her pack by its straps and made a mad dash for the door.

16

Early afternoon

PRECISELY TEN MILES (AS THE CROW FLIES)
from the post office where Brooke had just hailed a
cab in Manhattan, Joel paid his driver and stood on
the street corner in a working-class neighborhood in
Queens.

He had exchanged his usual attire of mindless-
gray business suits for newly purchased khaki pants, a
turtleneck sweater, and a casual-looking midthigh-
length hooded coat. From a pocket of his coat he
unfolded five sheets of blue paper from a legal pad.
The contents of these pages represented close to
forty-eight hours of nonstop legwork and desperation. The subject of interest was an address jotted
near the bottom of the fifth page. The name that
accompanied the address was that of Louis Vena. The
road to Louis Vena had been a long and winding one.

He had begun at the only point he could, with
what little he had. New York was an enormous place
to find something or someone, even if you had a
name or a destination to work with. But with Megan,

he'd had neither. She would be twenty-two now, and given her and her mother's flight a decade earlier, they likely had taken on a new last name, at the very least. Perhaps entirely new identities. But all of that was pure speculation. The sum of what he had was a face and a description of a young woman and a taxi number.

He had begun with those small clues on Monday evening. Now, just forty-eight hours after his mind-blowing sighting at JFK, Joel was inching closer, taking hold of one small piece of the puzzle at a time.

Monday night he had hardly slept at all. His adrenaline had been pumping. More than once he had questioned his own sanity. Was there even the remotest chance he had actually seen his daughter? The question seared through his brain. Megan had been twelve years old when they disappeared, yet he'd seen a full-grown woman at the airport. So, how could he even begin to convince himself that it was truly her? Was this merely self-deception on a grand scale? Perhaps.

Genuine doubt, though, had never really entered his mind. His conviction lay in the fact that when he'd first seen the woman's face, he'd have sworn she was Ariel. Standing there, luggage in hand, his mind on other matters, he had believed wholeheartedly that he was staring at his ex-wife. There had been no doubt. It was the face he'd married. The face he'd loved.

Yet in a fraction of a second he had realized that the woman was much too young. Ariel would be in her forties. And in that instant, the synapses of his mind aligned, producing the answer to the riddle:

Megan had grown up in the mirror image of her mother. It happened every day, in millions of homes across the globe. Mothers and daughter. Fathers and sons. Simple biology. Something deep in his gut told him there was no doubt about it.

Monday night, in the earliest stages of the hunt, her face and description were of no use to him. Neither was her name. His only lead was the taxi number, 1881.

He rented a room in Manhattan and opened the phone book to the Yellow Pages. There were dozens and dozens of listings for taxi and livery companies in the greater New York area. Across the street from the hotel was an all-night grocery, where he purchased a legal pad, a pack of four ballpoint pens, and a New York street map.

With the map spread across the small reading table in his room, he pinpointed JFK and, using the mileage scale in the corner of the map, drew a measured circle around JFK. The circle indicated a twenty-mile radius. He repeated the process with a second circle, this one half the distance, establishing a ten-mile radius.

Then came the lengthy process of pinpointing, on the map, the street address of each cab company in the Yellow Pages. If an address fell beyond the twenty-mile radius, it was crossed out. Anything between ten and twenty miles was underlined, and any company inside the ten-mile radius was circled. This assumed that any taxi company outside the twenty-mile radius was less likely to service JFK on a regular basis.

Abiding by this strategy, he was able to instantaneously shrink the search parameter to fewer than twenty miles. On his legal pad, he compiled a list of companies falling within the ten-mile radius. This was his A-list. Next, he compiled a B-list, those companies falling between the ten- and twenty-mile marks.

Calls made to the companies on both lists produced fourteen cars with 1881 as their identifying numerals. By this time, it was early Tuesday, and only a third of these companies operated around-the-clock. Joel was connected to the dispatch offices of the available five and, under the guise of being a detective with the NYPD, requested information regarding any fares picked up at JFK between five and seven, Monday evening. Of these five, there'd been no fares from JFK.

That left nine.

He'd have to wait until morning.

As painful and frustrating as it was, Joel had resigned himself to the cold reality that he might very well have run aground. This might be the end of the road. He had nine more shots. Nine more arrows in his quiver. Nine smooth, flat stones to fling into the abyss. But it would have to wait until daylight.

He fell asleep on the floor, his head on the map. By the time he awoke, sunlight poured through the drapes. He had struggled to his feet, bleary-eyed and half-alert. His head had felt strange, dense. It was Tuesday, 11:20 A.M. He had overslept.

Joel had run across the street for coffee and then jumped on the telephone. A stupid mistake had cost him a lot of daylight. Nobody was very forthcoming with information. His first call was on the money, or at least began that way; car number 1881 had picked up a fare at 6:30 P.M. at JFK and delivered the fare to an upscale apartment building in Manhattan. The dispatcher informed him that no log was kept regarding passenger description. "We don't care what they look like, Detective, so long as they pay their fare." He was hesitant to divulge the driver's name and home phone number.

The next six companies produced only negative results. In each case, 1881 hadn't gone anywhere near JFK. But the last companies on the list were pay dirt. Each had had fares from JFK around the time frame in question. Joel spoke with one of the drivers right on the spot. Sure he'd picked up a fare a few minutes before five—an older fellow with his wife.

Dead end.

The remaining driver was already on duty. At the request of *Detective* Benjamin, the dispatcher radioed the driver and patched him through to Joel. Yes, he'd picked up a fare at JFK, but it had actually been well after 7 P.M., and he'd not followed the route into Manhattan that Joel described. Joel thanked him.

By now it was late Tuesday evening.

The sole remaining lead was through Cross-City Taxi & Livery. The cabdriver's name was Louis Vena of Queens, New York. Repeated attempts to reach Mr. Vena by phone on Wednesday had failed. No one answered, and either the Vena family did not have a machine or had failed to turn it on upon leaving for the day. The dispatcher had stated that Wednesday was Vena's day off.

All of this had led Joel to the street corner in Queens on a cold, overcast winter's day. The written address led him to a small brick house with one window overlooking the street. Joel ascended the front steps and pressed the doorbell button. A minute's wait, and no answer. A mailbox hung from the brick facade to one side of the door. Joel cast a glance over each shoulder, and lifted the flap to peek inside. He pulled out a gas bill. It was addressed to Mr. and Mrs. L. Vena.

Joel waited in the cold with no assurance that his man would show. He waited across the street. He didn't have to wait long. He watched as a short, stocky man wandered down the sidewalk, stopped at the door, unlocked it, and disappeared inside. Joel took a breath and headed back across the street.

Thirty minutes later, Joel added a crisp fifty-dollar bill to the two he'd already handed Louis Vena. Vena folded the bills into a shirt pocket and showed the stranger to the door. Joel thanked him again, and again found himself alone on the street in working-class Queens.

He buttoned his coat, chilled by the sudden cold, yet pumped by sudden exhilaration. Every sound, every visual stimuli, every evidence of life in the city was lost to him. He was blind to all things save for the realization that he'd taken an enormous leap forward, a monumental step closer to Megan.

During the hours in question, Vena had picked up several fares. He vaguely remembered a young brunette wearing a maroon beret but failed to offer specifics. Where he'd dropped the brunette, he couldn't state with any amount of confidence. What he *could* offer, though, were the three stops he had made in Manhattan somewhere within the desired hours. Who he had dropped where was simply beyond recall. Three separate fares at three separate stops. And he was pretty confident that one of the fares had been the brunette.

The sum of his new knowledge did not point him directly to Megan. It only narrowed his area of focus. Thirty minutes of conversation and $150 had wrenched every available drop of recollection from the memory of a cabdriver from Queens.

Joel departed with three street addresses. How his investment in Louis Vena would pan out, only time would tell. Was Vena trustworthy? Perhaps. There was presently no room for debating the issue. If there was any substance to the information at all, one of the most populated cities in the world had just shrunk dramatically.

17

SET AGAINST CRUSHED VELVET, UNDER ARTFULLY arranged lighting, the five-carat diamond glowed and shimmered, seeming to produce a life and light of its own.

Each point of light danced in the eyes of Megan Durant. The spell had been cast. No other hypnotic in the universe can match that of a diamond over a woman. Her lips parted ever so slightly. She leaned against the glass display case. For the longest time she didn't blink. She didn't breathe. If her heart continued to beat, she didn't notice. Every molecule of her existence froze in the perfection of the moment.

Olin was poised at her side, arms crossed over his chest. It gave him great pleasure to gaze on her profile. He made no attempt to hide it. A smile lit his face. The deep blue of his Armani suit amplified the blue of his eyes, which never left Megan.

The gold band glided down the length of her slender third finger. Megan held out her hand, raising it slightly, turning the diamond at different angles to the overhead light.

"Well?" Olin said, knowing she was completely enamored.

"It's fabulous." Her voice came out as a dreamy sigh.

"Yes, absolutely," the saleswoman agreed, seeing that she had them hooked. Now it was time to play the fish, to work the line, to reel her in. "Stunning, really."

"You make it look beautiful," Olin said, not caring about the ring except that it brought such joy to Megan's eyes.

Megan took a step back from the counter. She ran the tip of a finger against the stone, feeling the perfection of the cut. It seemed to be nearly the size of a dime and gave off the light of an entire galaxy.

"I really don't know what to say," she said, clearly out of breath.

"Say you love it."

"Oh, I do. I do. It's just so overwhelming."

"It's one of our finest. One of the finest we've ever had in stock, really."

This morning they had made the rounds. A dozen different jewelers. Countless rings. A mine of diamonds. Megan had been like a child in a candy store. She found herself filled with a giddiness that made her feel slightly embarrassed. But what could she do? Every girl's fantasy was to spend a day as she had today. Olin simply let her wander the display cases, offering encouraging words. The prices were outlandish. But he seemed only to care that she find precisely the one jewel that she could not do without.

At Tiffany's she tried on dozens, oohing and aahing and enjoying herself immensely, though never arriving at the stone that truly met her expectations.

Manhattan, as a whole, was a shopper's paradise. And Megan wallowed in it.

Around noon they broke for lunch, dining on crab salad and a delicious white wine. Megan merely picked at her meal, her thoughts still floating across acres of crushed velvet. The wine helped her nerves. She sipped it and clung to Olin's arm.

Money was never a topic of discussion. Olin wouldn't hear of it. If she questioned him about a steep price, he'd simply touch a finger to her lips and convince her that the only issue of concern was her complete satisfaction, not price.

So now she stood at the counter, bathed in milky light, transfixed. She set the ring at the edge of the crushed velvet display pad and made a disciplined effort to peruse the rest of the selection. But Olin could almost read her thoughts. She'd found the one, he knew.

A clear anxiety filled her as she drummed her fingers along the top of the glass counter.

"They're all so gorgeous."

"Absolutely," the saleswoman echoed.

Olin waited, watching. Another couple shopped a few feet away. As if drawn by some unseen force, Megan steered back to her place at Olin's side, nearly floating on air.

"You were born to wear that piece," the saleswoman continued, sensing the sale but doing everything in her power not to appear too anxious.

"What do you think?" Olin knew the answer.

Megan had the ring on her finger, once again adjusting the angle in the light. She turned and looked at him with tears in her eyes. "This is the one."

In many ways, their relationship was, however intense and passionate, still in its infancy. There had been no time for the newness to wear off. They had known each other barely nine months, and had been separated for weeks at a time, communicating either by phone or by email. And when they managed to find time to be together, it was usually spent in bed, not in extended conversation.

By nature, Olin St. John was self-contained, disciplined, remote, introverted. He was cool and in control at all times, whereas Megan's energy was on display. She was not hyper but *alive*. That appealed to him. He was warmed by her glow.

Megan had left the States at the age of twelve, under circumstances she'd been too young to understand. She'd known only that her mother and father had stopped loving each other and that her mother had decided it might be best for Megan and herself to begin a new life in Europe. Her mother married a man from Italy named Durant, and now lived with him in Rome. Megan had been relinquished to a Catholic school in London, where she spent much of the next six years under the tutelage of a host of nuns at the Church of the Holy Trinity, including Sister Catina. It was a lonely way to grow up. Sister Catina had taken her under her wing, helping her with her studies and encouraging her in her art. Now the old nun was near death's door, a fact that without Olin's presence in her life would have been a devastating reality to face alone. Her mother had little to do with her, ignoring her periodic letters and calls. Her new husband was a success of some sort. Megan remembered little or nothing of life before Europe.

Her father was gone so much of the time when she was small that not having him around somehow felt normal. And given that he apparently hadn't made an attempt to contact them during their years in Europe, she had never felt the need to take steps to fill that vacancy. Clearly, he'd not come after her, so why bother?

She had her art studies to fulfill her and she had Olin to love. She had a glorious diamond ring on her finger, and the promise of a fairy-tale life awaiting her across the Atlantic. She asked nothing of the past, except that it stay behind her. Her vision of the life ahead was idyllic, blissful.

Olin did not have the luxury of dismissing his past so offhandedly. His past had fangs and wings, and thrived on fear—his fear. A childhood in the streets had taught him to survive by way of the gun and the blade. Both his parents were long dead. Megan's innocence was another thing that he relished. To her, everything was a delight. She possessed a freshness, an optimism as yet unscathed by a crass and odious world. And perhaps his money and his love and worldly ways could protect her from it. It would be his mission to build a wall around her innocence. Long ago he'd lost count of how many men he had killed, but he would kill a thousand more in her honor if she demanded it. She was his one solitary hope of surviving a world that had made him what he was. Megan was a beacon on a hill, a point of reference on a rolling, thrashing sea. He could not, would not, under any conceivable circumstance, give her up.

As they moved casually along, Olin put his face in

her hair, breathing in the sweet perfume. She turned her face to him, kissing him full on the mouth. How had he lived without her? How had she lived without him? He hooked an arm around her, bringing her in close against him as they walked. With the afternoon came an increase in the snowfall. The wind picked up, but neither of them noticed or paid the weather any heed. They sauntered through a splendid museum, and later stopped in at a quaint bistro for coffee. In the bistro, they stole to a corner table and made out like a couple of teenagers, flirting and giggling, sipping expensive coffee and ignoring the world around them. Later, over an early dinner, they whispered conspiratorially in a darkened booth, lost in each other's eyes.

The day was a dizzying contest to catch up on lost time.

18

LESS THAN AN HOUR EARLIER THE CITY HAD seemed to shrink simply on the basis of Louis Vena's testimony. Their conversation had sounded so profitable. Vena was so matter-of-fact. But now, standing at the first of three destinations Vena claimed to have stopped at on Monday evening, Joel slowly came to the realization that the real work, the real hunt, had only just begun. Suddenly, Vena's recollections appeared brutally detail deficient.

Panic began to flower in his chest. He'd burned two full days already, with no assurance that Megan was even still in New York. His window of opportunity, however broad it might have been to begin with, was creeping shut with every passing moment. The stress was claustrophobic, like cold damp hands around his throat.

Joel came out of a deli a half a block from the intersection of East Fifty-seventh Street and Lexington Avenue, taking a big bite from a meatball sandwich wrapped in wax paper. He paused on the cement steps as the door eased shut behind him. He'd considered taking the time to find a table inside and take a load off his feet while he ate his sandwich, but thought better of the idea in light of the ticking clock. Rush hour had arrived. The congested streets and sidewalks of Manhattan would surely not help. From a pocket of his coat he removed a Discover Card envelope, folded in thirds. He unfolded it and saw the crude map Vena had sketched in red ink. Vena had come down Lexington and then turned left onto East Fifty-seventh Street. His recollection had been fuzzy, too fuzzy for Joel's comfort, but he swore he'd made a drop in front of a large apartment building, an apartment of either limestone or gray cinder, he was almost certain.

Joel followed Vena's directions, dodging foot traffic as he looked from the envelope to street signs to the walls on either side of him. Suddenly, he found himself in front of what must be the right building. It was a nine-story cinder block L. He stood staring up at it. This had to be it, he thought. Looking up from across the street, at the building, Joel started to count the windows, but stopped himself. There had to be a couple hundred on this side alone.

"How many hundreds of people live there?" he wondered aloud, shaking his head in disgust and disbelief. From the outside the apartment didn't appear run-down. On the contrary, it looked like a nice middle-income residence, which meant he'd likely either have to be buzzed in by a resident or get by a doorman in order to get inside. And even if he got in, what then?

If the apartment were her home, if there was some means by which he could nail that down as fact, time wouldn't be a crucial factor. Otherwise, the clock was the enemy. If Vena could have definitively stated that Megan was a fare that night, and that he'd delivered her to this apartment building, Joel could have had some room to play with his strategy. But as it was, this was just the first of three stops, and the more time he wasted at one, the more likely it was he'd miss her somewhere else. The point of pain was radiating outward, pounding through his head in rhythm with his pulse. He patted his pockets, hoping to find a small bottle of Excedrin, remembering then that he'd left it in his briefcase in his room.

He was having to think on his feet—always a bad way to lay out a plan of action. There were no good answers, no good options. If he managed to gain entry into the building, a door-to-door canvassing would likely get him quickly booted to the curb. And loitering outside, simply waiting for her to make an appearance, would burn precious time.

He stood on the curb across the street from the building, his eyes moving from window to window. Lights were on in many, though not all, of the apartments. She could be in any one of them, he thought. Or none at all. She might be somewhere on the other end of the city, or in New Jersey, or Connecticut . . . or just about anywhere on earth. He'd seen her forty-eight hours ago. In fewer than forty-eight hours, a person could easily get from New York to Moscow.

I might as well be looking in another country.

Standing there staring at the nine-story structure was useless. He needed to move on. Glancing both ways repeatedly, he dashed across the lanes of traffic. Again he found himself being brushed on all sides by fellow pedestrians, most of whom were probably heading home after a long day at work. He side-stepped his way among moving bodies until he found himself pressed against the hedge that separated the apartment building from the sidewalk. Up close, the place seemed even more immense. Surely he'd never find her in there. It was time to move on.

Joel turned to go, then paused. He took a step closer to the building, reaching a hand through the hedge, hesitantly pressing the flat of his hand to the brick facade. For a long moment the cold and the wind and the frustration eased away. In that instant his only desire was to reach out to his daughter. As desperate a gesture as it was, desperation was all he had.

He was a generic-looking government worker with a blond comb-over, and glasses nearly thick enough to be bulletproof. He did his best to make eye contact with absolutely no one in the world. His office was located among innumerable others within the walls of a massive government complex that was itself a part of the web of office structures in and around the D.C. area.

His official title was lame and interchangeable with any other in the building. It was stamped onto a name-plate that stood at the edge of his cheap desk. Apart from his everyday responsibilities, this man was also the liaison for a very "unofficial" government agency.

Today he forged an erratic route through the city in his gray sedan. If anyone had been following him, they were by now pissed off and thoroughly lost.

Finally, at a supermarket, he parked near a chain-link fence, locked his door, and crossed the parking lot on foot. By taxi he traveled four miles, walked another three blocks, periodically throwing a cautious eye over his shoulder, then flagged a second cab. The cab dropped him at a corner where he waited less than five minutes and caught a city bus. At the third stop, he spotted his contact out the window. His contact wore a Red Sox ball cap, as specified. Comb-over and Red Sox climbed in the emerald green Mercury Marquis, without a word between them.

The Mercury Marquis stopped at a private airfield where the man with the comb-over boarded a Bell 430 helicopter. Thirty-seven minutes later, the Bell 430 touched down on a helipad inside a guarded 500-acre estate. The estate was surrounded by dense timber on all sides. The helipad faced a huge mansion built of white stone that had been imported from a quarry in Afghanistan. The rotors from the Bell whipped up the snow on and around the pad. He could see faces waiting for him from a stone terrace. Opening the door of the chopper, he raised an arm across his face to block the wind coming from the rotors.

Hurrying toward the warmth of the mansion, he glanced up at the terrace at the men awaiting him.

H. Glen Shelby was the first to shake the liaison's hand.

"Mr. Susnick," Shelby said.

Susnick was not his real name. No one here cared what his real name was. They didn't need to know about him, only what he was here to tell them.

None of those present here, except for Susnick himself, were government employees. Shelby was retained by the president on a private basis. Susnick recognized his face from television. The remaining two men he'd never seen before, but he had some idea who they might be.

The old man frowning from his wheelchair owned the property on which they stood. It was his mansion, and it was his Bell 430 that had brought Susnick here. His name was Albertwood. The other man was Eamon Desmond, here as representative for another party that held a very strong interest in the information Susnick had come to deliver.

Susnick's coat was taken by a stunning Puerto Rican maid, and he was ushered down a wide hall with a marble floor and a massive, vaulted ceiling. Susnick wiped the lenses of his glasses on his shirt, squinting to see where he was walking. Everyone seemed very interested in his metal briefcase. And well they should be, he thought.

They went to a room that was furnished with a beautiful, long conference table. Susnick was offered a seat, which he declined. After the winding journey he'd taken to get there, he was plenty happy to stand. He set the briefcase on the table and opened it, rifling through its contents.

Shelby was not familiar with Susnick but had little doubt that the man had been exposed to all levels of classified information over the course of his career. He was one of the faceless subordinates who served as messengers for those who could have no "official" contact with the people paying for the information being delivered. Shelby didn't know from where in the D.C. area Susnick had crawled out of; only that whatever he had to offer had come from deep inside the Pentagon.

Susnick eyed each of the three men who flanked

him. He was beginning to bear the look of a man who knew too much and was not important enough to actively protect. He knew his days were numbered. Someone would find him in an alley one day, or in a runoff ditch in some rural county, gutted and bled out. It was difficult to retire from the intelligence racket.

Shelby was there on behalf of the president, because the chief executive couldn't have firsthand knowledge of these matters but had to make sure nonetheless that they were handled promptly and efficiently. Desmond was there on like terms. Albertwood had brought all the parties together. There was as much pressure on him in these matters as on anyone else.

Clifton Yates had informed Shelby of the email message to Ettinger's brother only this morning. Yet now, barely fifteen hours later, Shelby was here, hoping that a possible solution had been discovered. The predawn excursion with the president had left him at the edge of his nerves. Yates was rattled, understandably. If Ettinger had pulled something, they had to know exactly what it was and stop it. That's why Susnick was there.

The old man in the wheelchair, Julius Albertwood, glared up with wide eyes and a gnarled grin, his only expression. His entire right side was paralyzed. Albertwood was ninety. His body had essentially given out on him, but the old man's mind was still as sharp as a knife and twice as deadly. Over the years, the skin of his face had constricted, pulling his lips back from his teeth. This left him with a nasty, perpetual grin. It was startling, to say the least. He used his good hand—the left one—to work the steering wand on the arm of the wheelchair. He backed away from where he'd wheeled up to the table, and parked himself at the corner of the table, as close to Susnick and his briefcase as he could manage.

Shelby did not bother with introductions. Susnick did not wait for permission to speak. From his briefcase he removed three glossy eight-by-ten photographs, each in black and white. He spread them on the table in front of his small audience.

"Those are still-frame photographs taken from a security camera in the vice president's residence in Maine," Susnick said without looking up.

"Beagle Run," Shelby added.

"Yes. The camera is mounted in a short hallway leading to the kitchen area of the lodge. The Ettingers have a slew of such devices mounted throughout their homes, both here and abroad. These cameras are monitored by satellite at an off-site location. They have a long-running contract with a security outfit in Maryland. This outfit also does contract work for the Pentagon." Susnick glanced over the top of his glasses, his hands still busy in the briefcase, and added, "Convenient, I know. This permits us special . . . *access.*"

The photos were black and white, and rather grainy, and no one had any question who the subject captured on film was. The photos were captured images of the vice president taken from digital video footage. These three shots showed a progression of movement, and the time-and-date stamp and the bottom of the photos indicated the time lapse between the three shots to be fifteen seconds.

Susnick noted, "The cameras relay an image to

the satellite every five seconds, twenty-four hours a day."

"Why five seconds instead of a continuous feed?" Desmond asked.

"Storage considerations."

Desmond folded his arms over his chest, a frown on his face.

"These images," Susnick continued, "show James Ettinger at six A.M. on the seventeenth of December."

Shelby pondered the time-and-date stamps—6 A.M., December 17. Ettinger died in the evening, and the email was sent in the middle of the afternoon.

"As you can see, the last frame shows Ettinger opening a door in the hallway. This was curious to our people because the floor plans to the lodge in Maine show this door to lead down a narrow flight of stairs to a basement. Not much was thought of this in the beginning, but it was the one movement of Ettinger's we couldn't readily account for. Understand, there are no security cameras mounted in the basement. So the archives from the entire week prior to the seventeenth were thoroughly checked. And sure enough, two days prior, we found these . . ." Susnick lifted another stack of photos and flopped them on the table.

Julius Albertwood clawed at the glossies with his one good hand, hungrily groping for a look.

The photos documented a full half a minute of five-second intervals taken from the camera mounted above the hall that led to the kitchen at Beagle Run. In them, Ettinger approached the same door, only this time he was carrying something in his arms. Something fairly cumbersome. The image wasn't terribly clear, making it difficult to identify exactly what it was.

"We managed to blow up the clearest frame and touch it up a bit," Susnick said. "This is what we got." He slid a ten-by-twelve exposure onto the conference table. Only Albertwood was unable to control his reaction.

"Gggghh!" Albertwood gasped, grasping at the arm of his wheelchair with his good arm.

Shelby looked over at Susnick, who kept his attention on his briefcase. Susnick, he'd observed, avoided eye contact at all costs. Shelby then glanced at Desmond. Desmond didn't say a word. Shelby knew they were thinking the same thing he was thinking. Again, the video-capture was grainy, and having been magnified had lost much of its detail. But the magnification had succeeded in enhancing the view of what Ettinger was carrying. It was a video camera attached to a tripod.

"Tell me that's not what I think it is," Desmond said to Susnick.

"It is a Sony home video camera," Susnick informed them.

Bingo, Shelby thought. Good news and bad news. This was what they'd needed to know but hadn't wanted to hear. Ettinger had indeed made a tape. He'd somehow slipped beneath their radar just long enough to pull one over on them. He stood with his hands behind his back, already contemplating what he'd tell the president. Yates was nearing the very edge of sanity. Miriam Ettinger had sprung this little grenade on them out of the blue, knocking them for a loop. If they'd been able to see this coming, maybe they'd have made certain preparations. And perhaps they had, Shelby thought, casting his eyes across the table to Desmond. James Ettinger was dead, after all.

"Okay," Desmond spoke up. He was a broad man, thick through the chest, with a mat of red hair and a neatly trimmed red beard. "Where's the tape? Ettinger said something on tape. Where is it?" he demanded.

"That was a little stickier to come by," Susnick declared, again busy with the contents of his briefcase. "You must realize, we've had less than fifteen hours—total—to piece this thing together. And considering that fact, it is actually quite astonishing to be as far along as we are." Susnick peered over the heavy frames of his glasses, conveying his point. "Precisely *where* the tape is, we can't say for certain," he continued. "But we have a very solid prospect."

Susnick withdrew yet another photo from the briefcase. "In the basement of Ettinger's lodge at Beagle Run, there was indeed a video camera set up, facing a chair. The cassette had been removed, just as we assumed it would be. There was also evidence in the basement that Ettinger had packaged something to be mailed." Susnick paused, then withdrew a printed page and placed it before them. "Most of the clutter had been deposited into a waste receptacle in the basement. Among the garbage, this was recovered . . ."

A cab took Joel Benjamin down Park Avenue, past the Waldorf-Astoria, the second possibility Vena had mentioned. It was clearly in the running. But, again, without a photo of his daughter to show around, all he'd be able to do is wait for her to make an appearance. And under the circumstances, waiting idly seemed like a terrible waste of time.

Next, they swung by a Cuban restaurant at the corner of West Fifty-first and Ninth Avenue. The third and final destination given by Louis Vena. Joel asked the driver to hold tight for a few minutes, and stood looking around. The eatery was a compact joint, situated on a corner, with a dry cleaner on one side and a pool hall on the other. A trio of Latino punks huddled outside the door to the pool hall, eyeing him. What business Megan might have at a place like this, he couldn't imagine.

He opened the door to the Cuban dive and ducked inside. The lighting was subdued, and the place smelled of something he couldn't readily identify. A waiter appeared before him with a menu, speaking rapidly to him in Spanish. Joel took a long look around. Surely this couldn't be the place. He backpedaled his way to the door.

His gut was telling him to cross this place off the list. If there was anything of value in Vena's information, it would revolve around either the apartment building on East Fifty-seventh or the Waldorf on Park Avenue. End of discussion.

"Take me back to the Waldorf," he told the driver after he was back inside the cab.

The driver nodded.

Joel stared out the window, his forehead against the glass. Of all the places in the world to try and hunt down someone you hadn't seen in a decade, nothing could have been worse than New York. He was from the West, and now lived in the Midwest. This was not his turf. If he were on track at all, it would be a miracle. Megan had been in the city Monday night. He'd seen her. Where she'd gone from there was anybody's guess. But she'd been here. For the past two days he'd strained to listen to his inner voice, his voice of reason and logic. It was a voice he trusted. He'd listened for that voice to speak its mind, to pop him on the back of the head and tell him this was idiotic, that the girl was just some girl, nobody to him. He listened hard and long, struggling to be objective, but ultimately he heard nothing that warned him to end his search. He received no answers he could fully trust.

Joel was an unmarried man, with no one waiting for him at home. He had a little time. As sad a fact as it might be, if there was anyone in the world whose absence could go unnoticed for the better part of a week, it was Joel's. Except for a handful of curious neighbors and colleagues from work, there was no one to really raise an eyebrow. Normally such a thought might cause a ping of melancholy, but given the current status of things, it granted him a bit of space within to work, to think, to plan. It was his one chance to find Megan. She was in New York. He could almost bet the farm on that. He'd seen her. And his gut was telling him she hadn't gone far.

He paid the driver, and the cab disappeared into traffic. Evening had settled in, and with it had come a biting wind. Joel needed to find someplace warm, and he needed some food and some sleep. But all of that would keep him from doing the very thing he was there to do: watch for Megan. He wondered how long he could loiter in the lobby of the Waldorf before they'd politely ask him to leave. Probably quite awhile. Then it occurred to him. Why not get a room in the Waldorf himself? It would give him a base to work from. He could roam the halls more freely. The odds of bumping into her there were remote but better than on the street.

Joel hurried inside and smiled at the young woman behind the counter. He needed a room for three nights, he said, presenting her with a credit card. She smiled. Indeed, there were rooms available.

The knot in Joel's stomach relaxed, and he pocketed his credit card. Tomorrow he'd have to retrieve his belongings from the other hotel. Tonight he'd sleep in a warm bed with a full stomach. And if his search up to that point hadn't been completely in vain, it was quite possible that he was spending the night beneath the same roof as his only child.

19

THERE WAS A BOTTLE OF WINE IN THE CABInet, three-quarters full, just as Brooke hoped and thought there would be. Maybe she would have a glass later. Throughout the late afternoon and into evening, the temperature had progressively dropped, and the snow came in fits and starts. It was now coming down pretty steadily. Brooke lay on the couch in front of the TV, watching fat flakes stick to the front window. The TV was off.

Terri, her roommate, was out. She worked at an advertising agency and oftentimes kept odd hours. The two of them saw each other primarily on weekends, which worked out nicely, since half the rent was paid yet one or the other had the apartment to themselves most of the week. At times, though, this arrangement could get lonely. Brooke would have liked to have another face around to keep her company, and the Queen Bee—Darla—made sure that she had no love life.

It was better, for the moment, that Brooke had the place to herself. She'd come home to find a message from her mother on the machine. Brooke called her back on the spot. Wyatt was getting worse. The past few days he'd seemed to be fading fast. Her parents had taken him to the doctor yesterday, and the news wasn't good. Could she come sooner? Of course.

Of course.

Her body was in a fetal position on the couch. A blanket was spread over her legs. The temperature in her drafty apartment was probably sixty-five degrees. If she lay real quiet and still, with her eyes shut, and listened really hard, she could hear the flakes *ticking* against the panes of glass. The silence only served to make the room colder. She wriggled about on the couch, adjusting herself and tugging at ends of the blanket. She hadn't phoned Darla yet. She'd need to call and let her know that she'd not be making it to the party, which would not please her boss at all. Darla was fully aware of her brother's terminal condition and had in fact been gracious enough to let Brooke take the occasional three- or four-day leave of absence when necessary. But Darla also possessed the rather phenomenal perspective that the universe, and everything in it, was there for her personal satisfaction and benefit. Thus, she dealt very poorly with alterations in her carefully crafted schedule. Dealing with Darla Donovan was always a volatile and unpredictable job.

She peeled off the blanket and headed to the kitchen to find something for dinner. She saw a casserole dish on a low shelf, wrapped loosely in foil. She worked the foil off one corner and peeked inside, leaning in close to take a cautious sniff. Her upper lip curled. She put the casserole dish back on the shelf. There was a package of cheese slices. A tub of cottage cheese. A bag of celery sticks (Terri had a thing for celery). In the back of the fridge, behind a half-gallon of milk and a bottle of tomato juice, was another dish covered in foil. She dipped her head for a closer look. It was a dinner plate with a dozen or so fudge brownies. Terri, it seemed, had kept herself busy baking. Brooke took a brownie, making sure to refold the foil around the edge of the plate. The brownie was a little dry, but the sugar hit her system like a bolt of lightning. She hadn't realized how starved she was.

She peeked in the freezer but found only empty ice cube trays and a carton of low-fat yogurt. Desperate times called for desperate measures. She dialed the phone and ordered Chinese takeout. A place around the corner had free delivery and the best egg rolls on the planet. She pledged to stock up on groceries when she got back from her parents' house. She ate so much crap at work, she figured her arteries would slam shut by the time she turned thirty-five.

Her thoughts drifted to Wyatt. He would turn thirty on Christmas Eve. He didn't look thirty. He still had a baby face, but the cancer had aged him far beyond his years. He was so thin now, and the chemo had taken his hair.

She was glad he was home. Their mother had kept his old room pretty much as he'd left it when he got out of high school and headed out into the world. There was still the *Star Trek Enterprise* model hanging from the ceiling by fishing line. His collection of rock-and-roll albums and his turntable, his baseball trophies, and the concert poster signed by Jon Bon Jovi. He even still had an ancient Atari game system, with all the old favorites like Pac-Man and Centipede.

There would be a certain comfort in taking his final breaths in the bed that he grew up in. Adulthood had offered him only misery. He'd see thirty, God willing. But there'd be no fortieth birthday. He'd never marry or have kids. He'd had the last few years to dwell on, and come to terms with, these certainties. Brooke couldn't fathom shouldering such realities in her own life. And it was surreal to see her brother handling it with such grace and dignity.

When they were kids, Brooke idolized Wyatt. He was her big brother. He was her protector. Her passage from adolescence through the awkward teenage years to the world of young adulthood had been immeasurably smoother because of his presence and his protective hand. Even now, a small but distinct fear rose inside her at the thought of not having him in her life. Wyatt was her reassurance. With him gone. . . . That was a thought too horrific to ponder.

They looked a lot alike, she and Wyatt. Both had blond hair and were very nearly the same height. They shared the same eyes and the same bright, beaming smile. She was slimmer, with delicate, feminine features. Wyatt's body, especially when he was younger and really into sports, had some density to it. In high school he'd played on all the varsity teams. Because of his short height, he spent most of the basketball season on the bench. But football and wrestling and track, those were the arenas in which he excelled. He'd been such a strong kid. He had broad shoulders, and when he got into weight lifting, his physique pumped up rather impressively. Back in the old days, most of Brooke's friends had wild crushes on her brother.

The doorbell rang. Brooke rummaged through her purse, grabbing a handful of ones. The lanky Asian at the door swapped her a stained paper bag for the cash, and she set the bag on the table and grabbed a Diet Pepsi from the fridge. The smell of the food reawakened her empty stomach. She popped the tab on the diet soda and took a sip on her way to the couch with the paper bag.

She found the TV remote between the cushions of the couch. Working in television had slightly jaded her toward the medium; like peeking behind the curtain at a puppet show, the magic and mystery were gone. But still, when you were alone, it made a faithful companion. She stirred the rice with her chopsticks, letting a bite cool for a moment before devouring it.

On the Discovery Channel, they were explaining mummification. She passed on that one. The six o'clock news was over. Just as well. Again, her *life* was the news. She'd had enough of it for one day. The sweet and sour pork melted on her tongue. She'd chosen wisely.

It was hard not to think about the day to come. Her mother's voice over the phone had given away a lot. Brooke knew that Wyatt's death would cripple her mother. It would cripple them all, but Grace Weaver above all others. Her father would deal with it the way he dealt with every crisis or new wave of stress; he'd slip out to his work shed to saw and nail and measure and sand. Brooke imagined that he'd likely already logged untold hundreds of hours this winter out back in that ten-by-twelve A-frame building of his.

The leukemia had sucked the joy out of their relatively tight-knit clan. Wyatt was dying before their eyes. There was simply no justice in taking someone so good so young, especially in such an excruciating manner. At her last visit, Wyatt had weighed barely 110 pounds. She figured he'd dropped significantly since then. The bones of his face were more prominent now. Mom had mentioned that tonight.

"I didn't think he could get much thinner," Mom had said. "But his face . . . I don't know, it's just so drawn up and bony. He's just a skeleton."

"Fatten him up, Mom," Brooke said. "Make him a big crock pot full of your famous pork chops, put on a roast. Fill the oven with baked potatoes and slap on the sour cream and butter."

"You think?"

"If anyone can put some meat on that boy, Mom, it's you. You know?"

Her mother had agreed. But the big meals would not be prepared. There was no reason to waste food that wouldn't be eaten. Unless they got rid of the leukemia, Wyatt was not going to pack on the weight. Brooke knew this. She merely wanted to give her mother hope and a feeling she was useful.

When the eleven o'clock news came on the TV, she thought of the script she'd lugged home from work. Ordinarily, she'd have trudged into her bedroom, snatched the script from the backpack, and sat down with it at her laptop computer. There was still a ton of work to be done on it, and the segment was scheduled to air the second week of January. A morbid thought occurred to her: by the time the segment airs, Wyatt might be gone. She squeezed her eyes shut to fight the tears.

Beyond the grief and foreboding, Wyatt's imminent demise had a secondary effect on her. It forced her to confront her own life. Not her mortality, per se, but the direction she'd chosen. Sure, she was living her dream, at least to some extent. She'd gone to school to become a journalist, and she was first mate to one of the most respected and most successful names in her chosen field. The work was exciting and challenging, and even in her short stint at NBC News, she'd been exposed to things most people could never imagine. But it was a profession fueled by sacrifice. Free time was scarce. What few friends she had she rarely saw. She hadn't been on a date in four or five months. And really, she'd only gotten a taste of the business. Darla Donovan had logged twenty years in the news business, and look at her. Divorced, and not looking. She lived at the office. Brooke wondered how many nights a week the woman actually made it home to sleep in her own bed.

As much as she loved it all, she was tired. Sure, she'd put in some ungodly hours lately, putting this piece together, but still, she was only twenty-seven. There was still time to bolt and run if she had doubts. She was still young enough to go into anything in the world she desired. And she was bright enough to *do* anything she desired. She was not racing the clock, by any means. Her great fear was that for now she was simply living off adrenaline. But what would her life be in ten, fifteen years? When she turned forty, would she look back and smile, a gleam of satisfaction and fulfillment in her heart? Would Wyatt be smiling down on her? Or would she be a Darla Donovan clone, a slave to success?

Nuzzling her face against a pillow on the couch, she closed her eyes, breathing deeply. A scene blinked onto the blank canvas of her mind. It was Wyatt—the *old* Wyatt—from years ago. He was standing in the backyard of the house, his jeans muddy up to the knees, the collar of his letter jacket flipped up. His blond hair was tousled. A football was clutched under one arm. She was standing at the patio door, and he was smiling at her. Java, their chocolate Labrador, was bounding up and down, ready for more fun.

He didn't wave, didn't move a muscle. She didn't wave. They didn't need to. Everything they had to say to each other was implied, understood, and reciprocated. Wyatt just smiled at her, and she smiled back at her brother. And for that moment, the world seemed like a good place to be.

Shelby had been up for nearly twenty-four hours now and would be lucky to get shut-eye anytime soon. Initially, there had been hope that the Ettinger email would add up to nothing, that is was just a brother-to-brother sort of thing, that it was meaningless, benign, and ultimately nonthreatening. But that had not been the case.

In the beginning, he would have never dreamed that Ettinger might be a loose cannon. Stott and Albertwood had expressed their concern for some time, but Shelby had shrugged off their paranoia, at least early on. But in recent months Ettinger had become uncooperative, a bit reluctant to be a team player. It became apparent to all that the vice president was unreliable. And yes, actions had been taken to silence the threat. But it had all been done in the name of security.

He'd had to shelter the president from any knowledge from the beginning. That was the nature of the beast. What the president didn't know, the president wouldn't have to cover up. Regardless of whatever Yates might have suspected, he had no direct knowledge or involvement. Except the email, of course.

It was unfortunate that Ettinger's widow had come straight to Yates with the email. That was something that Shelby would have preferred to protect him from, if at all possible. Now she expected an answer, and from his mouth to her ear. That required Yates to lie. But lie he would.

The president was standing in snow up to his shins. It was late and he was exhausted, having spent another day licking his wounds and rallying the troops, bracing for the inevitable. His Irish setter was playing in the snow, pouncing at his own shadow. They were on the lawn outside the Oval Office, and the flowers and landscaping were out of sight beneath the blanket of white crust. Shelby stood beside him.

Shelby had his hands deep in his coat pockets, his breath escaping in silvery plumes. He'd come with bad news. Very bad news. His job now was to brief the president on where they stood and give him the prognosis.

"Were our friends there?" Yates said. They had

stepped outside the Oval Office, where they could speak a little more freely.

"Yes, of course," Shelby said.

"Is it bad?"

"Yes."

The president looked off beyond the lawn, toward the lights of D.C. The day had started off all wrong, and he had no doubt that what his attorney was about to tell him would not end it on a positive note. "Have they been busy?"

"Yes."

"And?"

"There was a home video camera set up in the basement at Beagle Run," Shelby began. "We don't know what he said on tape, but the tape is gone. It's nowhere in the lodge. Our boys turned the place inside out," Shelby said. He kept his voice low, periodically throwing a glance over his shoulder toward the lights in the windows. He was paranoid about mikes and cameras. He eyed the setter, wondering if there was a tiny mike hidden on the dog's collar. "But we think we have some idea of where it went."

Shelby was vaguely aware that the president had turned to face him. Shelby cut an eye his way.

"Our man on the FBI tech crew found something in the trash near the video camera setup. It was the thin plastic backing from an adhesive shipping label. It had been crumpled and tossed into a wicker wastebasket near a worktable. The tech guy apparently didn't think much of it at first, but then he held it to a light, and clearly whatever was written on the address label left an impression on the backing. You know? Like pressing down with a pen or pencil. It leaves a very slight impression. So they scanned it onto a computer and enhanced the image."

"And?" Yates said.

"We got an address."

"Who is it?"

"It was addressed to a postal box in New York."

"Who is it?"

"It would be in your best interest if you limited your knowledge of these things. You know that, Mr. President."

"How bad is it?"

"Very bad."

"Can we do anything about it?" The president was staring off into nothingness again. The setter had made his way over and was sniffing at his shoes. Yates ignored the dog.

"We're working on that."

"Don't pull that crap with me, Glen. Just tell me whether or not the matter can be handled."

"With the proper resources, nothing is beyond our reach."

"Is that a yes or no?"

"It is a yes."

"Glen, you know I can't tell you to do what I need you to do."

"Of course."

"You have an address?"

"Yes."

"You have a name?"

"We have the name that the postal box is addressed to, yes."

"Has the tape arrived yet?"

"That, I don't know. We're working on that. If it

has arrived and by some miracle the tape is still in the box when we get to it, everybody can stand down. Crisis averted. The tape, after all, is what we're after. If it's been picked up . . ."

"Just . . . get it taken care of, Glen. Whatever that entails. I don't know *what's* on that tape, if anything. But if it's even remotely close to what we assume, our little kingdom will topple like nothing this country has ever seen."

"I understand."

Yates was clearly growing agitated. "Tell me this much, Glen. This name you have, on a scale of one to ten, how dangerous is it?"

"In all honesty, Mr. President," Shelby said, shaking his head and turning to leave, "if the name that box is registered under turns out to be legitimate, you might as well throw away the scale."

Hearing this, Clifton Yates pivoted slightly in the snow and said to his lawyer's back, "It's really that bad?"

Shelby did not turn around to face the president. He simply said, "Worse."

Terri Bryant worked her key into the lock and opened the door quietly. She spotted Brooke asleep on the couch and eased the door shut. She peeled off her coat and draped it over the back of an upholstered chair.

Terri didn't wear watches; didn't believe in them. She glanced up at the digital clock on the microwave as she passed through to the refrigerator. Her eyes rolled back in her head in ecstasy as she bit into a brownie and chewed it slowly. She snatched a paper towel from a roll atop the fridge and stacked three more brownies on it. If Brooke had burgled her stash, she couldn't tell. Before exiting the kitchen with her snack, Terri wrapped her hand around the bottle of wine from the cabinet, then tiptoed in and flopped down about eighteen inches from the TV screen.

She uncorked the wine and took a big swig. Terri was the polar opposite of Brooke Weaver in most every area of life, not the least of which was the simple biological fact that she was black and Brooke was white. In addition, Terri had grown up the daughter of a very successful federal judge, had never had to do without, and viewed life as a leisurely pursuit. They meshed well because of their differences.

Brooke twisted beneath her blanket, then woke with a start.

Terri, who was sitting Indian-style with the brownies and wine between herself and the TV, leaned back on an elbow and smiled at her roommate.

Brooke rubbed her eyes, coming out of a haze. "What . . . time is it?"

"After midnight."

"Ugh."

"I'm surprised Darla let you come home tonight," Terri said, biting a brownie in half and talking with her mouth full.

"She's about to run me into the ground." Brooke yawned, working her way into a sitting position, bunching the blanket in her lap. "I wasn't going to be any good to her if I didn't get some R&R." Terri's mention of Darla pulled her from the groggy haze of sleep. She'd meant to call her boss, either at home or the office, and give her the heads-up that she wouldn't make the party.

She grabbed the cordless off the wall and dialed

the office at Rockefeller Plaza. It rang several times, then Darla's voice mail recording kicked in. Brooke disconnected. She considered her options. She would have liked to tell Darla in person, but she couldn't keep calling until Darla got back from wherever she'd gone. And if, by chance, Darla had headed home, she'd be in bed by now. Her boss only went home to sleep. She didn't cook. She did carryout, or ordered in. And Brooke knew better than to wake her. It was a quick decision. She'd try the office again, and if Darla didn't pick up, she'd just leave a message on her voice mail, apologizing and wishing her a merry Christmas. She dialed, waited for the snappy voice of the recording, and succeeded at sounding adequately contrite.

Fortunately, she already had her bag packed for the trip home, so she would not have to mess with that tonight or in the morning. Considering Wyatt's rapid deterioration, and not knowing how long she might actually end up having to stay at her parents' place in case things went downhill fast, she figured it might be a good idea to take her backpack and her laptop so she wouldn't fall quite so far behind at work. That way she could email back and forth with Darla.

She headed to the front room for more brownies and to watch late-night television with Terri.

The mail from the V.I.P. box never entered her mind.

20

Thursday morning

OLIN WAS GONE WHEN SHE AWOKE. MEGAN could smell him on the sheets and the pillows and on her own body. She nestled herself down in the fluff of the bed, craving his embrace. The sun was high and bright in the window.

She had no idea what time it was, and didn't care. They had not left their room since yesterday afternoon. Long sessions of lovemaking bridged the hours and exhausted them. Their time apart had carried the weight of an eternity. Having him with her again, kissing her, touching her, was like slipping into a warm soothing bath and melting into the soapy bubbles. She closed her eyes and a dreamy look washed over her face. Olin would be back soon enough, she knew. He'd gone on his morning run. So in the meantime she'd just have to dream about him.

For the first mile and a half, Olin always took it easy. It was a time to limber up, get the old bones loosened and flexible. Then he'd kick into gear and push pretty hard for the next three. The last mile was the cooldown.

This morning, nature and New York were conspiring to upset his routine. He was used to the chill and slop of Europe, but this was just a mess. By the time he hit the four-mile mark, his ears burned, his lungs were on fire, and his nose was lit up like an emergency flare. Out of breath, he backed against a wall, hands on hips.

Going against his precise and disciplined nature, he cut the run short by a good half a mile and walked briskly to a corner near the Waldorf. He plucked a copy of the *Times* from a tall stack at a newsstand and folded it under his arm, heading quickly for the warmth of the hotel.

Once outside their room, he twisted the doorknob and eased the door open, silently, careful not to wake her. He took cautious steps on the deep carpeting.

She was not asleep. Even with his stealthy approach, she had heard him enter. And she was waiting for him.

He froze when the bed came into view. His fiancée was on display. And what a sight she was. The covers were in a mound at the foot of the bed. Except for the pillows and her glorious body, the bed was bare. Megan had posed herself seductively. Smiling, he walked over to her and they kissed deeply. She pulled him down against her. When he pulled away, she pouted playfully.

"Just for a little while," Megan said, her voice throaty with desire and need. "Please."

Olin grinned. Who wouldn't? "Before I can survive another round with you, I need fuel, replenishment." He jabbed a thumb toward the phone on the nightstand.

Room service delivered a cart filled with breakfast goodies.

Megan draped herself with a tissue-thin gown and curled up in a chair at the table to eat. Olin sliced strawberries on his waffles and sipped coffee from a heavy ceramic mug decorated with the Waldorf's logo. His copy of the *Times* was spread out to one side of his plate.

His chosen profession had taught him many lessons. But first and foremost, to leave a job behind once it was finished. By doing this, you mentally separated yourself from the details, training your mind to delete the fact that your involvement ever existed. He blanked the episode from memory. It never happened. This protected him from his own reaction if ever questioned or confronted. In essence he remained an outside observer. And so, on this cold but lovely morning spent with his beautiful fiancée over fruit and croissants and waffles and coffee, Olin St. John read with great interest the breaking story that covered the entire front page of the *Times*. It concerned the assassination of the vice president of the United States of America.

Russ Vetris was breathing fire. He screamed at junior staffers and a cluster of secretaries, the secretaries tripping over one another, scurrying to take cover at their desks. The chief of staff had a copy of the *New York Times* rolled up in his fist. He ordered everyone out of the Oval Office, and then slammed the door.

Yates was pacing around the room, proofreading the statement he'd be making in half an hour. Thanks to the banner headline on the front page of the

Times, the old speech had already taken a fatal trip through the shredder. The people wouldn't be hearing the news firsthand from their leader, as he'd planned. Word was already out. The call had woken Yates before dawn, informing him that word of Ettinger's death had leaked.

He had on pinstriped slacks and a bathrobe. No shirt, no socks. The makeup girl would be in any minute. The president's red pen was bleeding all over the latest draft, which had been delivered to his desk merely seconds earlier. He'd spent the last ten minutes pacing, shaking his head, cursing at the wall, kicking at the large hand-loomed Egyptian rug in the middle of the room.

"I told you we were going to wait too long!" Vetris hissed, whacking the back of a couch with his copy of the *Times*.

The piece in the *Times* quoted an unnamed source, listing a string of facts, including such things as the vice president's time of death to the caliber of bullet that had exploded his skull. The piece was dead-on, and it had surfaced at the worst of all possible times. Now it would be all about damage control. Now was the time to lie. And you had to lie with sincerity burning in your eyes. Later on, if facts surfaced beyond your control, the lies could and would be doctored. In politics, nothing was absolute and nothing was final.

"Someone's gonna burn on the cross for this!" Vetris went on, flopping down behind the president's desk.

"Have you spoken with Martindale today?"

Vetris shook his head. "This thing has set the

Hoover Building on fire. Martindale is ducking for cover. That's what the FBI is good for—nothing."

"The American people are going to want to hear our list of suspects. I go on camera and confirm that Jim Ettinger got a new part in his hair courtesy of some schmuck with a sniper's rifle, and tell them we sat on our haunches for half a week, and now we've got nothing to show—no suspects, no leads. That'll fly, Russ. That'll fly real well!" The president kicked at the rug again. He stopped in his tracks and stared down at the copy of his speech. As he reread it for the two-dozenth time, he clenched his teeth and shook his head. Every word of the thing was drivel.

"How long till showtime?" Yates asked. He owned a dozen Rolex and Omega watches yet had nothing on his wrists.

"You're going live at nine," Vetris said, badly wanting to scream at someone over the phone. *Anyone.*

"What time is it now?"

Vetris tugged on his sleeve and glanced at his arm. "Nineteen minutes till."

"Get Fortner in here," the president said with a snarl.

The phone rang.

Russ Vetris jerked it to his face. "Vetris. Yeah. Okay. No . . . no, I want it within the hour or they'll be finding pieces of you scattered all over the Bible Belt!" He slammed the phone, then slammed his fist against the desk.

The president just stood there in his bathrobe, with no shoes or socks, his gut peeking over his slacks, waiting for his chief of staff to say who'd been on the phone.

"That was Heins, with the Secret Service. They think they've found the leak. They're not too anxious to hand out a name until they've dug a littler deeper." Vetris put his face in his hands, and then raised his eyes, locking glares with Yates. "When we find this cretin, I want to be locked in a room with him for ten minutes. Just ten minutes. I'll have him squealing . . . *begging* for an expedient death. Anyway, I expect to receive word by the time you get done dancing for the TV camera."

"Get Fortner on the phone. I want him in here, pronto."

Two minutes later, Vetris was out the door, and President Yates was at his desk. The hair and makeup women entered the Oval Office and went to work on the shipwreck the week had turned him into. Robert Fortner, his head speechwriter, found a seat on a couch with his laptop balanced on his knees.

Eleven minutes and counting. The camera crew had already set up, and they now assumed their positions with the speed and efficiency of a well-lubed machine. The hair and makeup people departed, and Fortner printed up a new draft, complete with all the president's changes. He handed the page to Yates, who scanned it and grunted. He gave the speechwriter a sour look. Fortner bolted for the door and was gone.

The lights were hot and bright in his face. He cleared his throat, sweating profusely under his suit and tie. The final draft of the speech came up on the TelePrompTer. A man wearing a headset counted down from three, then gave the thumbs-up. The president faced the camera and confirmed what the world already knew.

— —

Brooke had managed to find a seat to herself on the train, and now she struggled to catch a nap. She'd snuck out the door this morning without waking Terri. Terri had her parents' number and her cell phone number if she needed to get ahold of her for any reason.

She put her head against the window, feeling the cool glass against her forehead.

In a way, she was glad she'd found a way out of Darla's party tonight. After all, these were people she saw day in and day out, and she had no desire to see them every moment of her downtime. Besides Darla, there was Barry, Joyce, Lipton, Connor, Jill, and Lesley. They were her team, and she loved them to death, but please . . . enough was enough. She shifted in her seat, searching for a comfortable position that simply did not exist.

It was just now 9 A.M., though it seemed like they'd been traveling forever.

The train was packed, with the exception of maybe three or four empty seats. Brooke said a silent prayer of thanks that no one had asked to slide in beside her for the long trip north. Her guilt for bailing on Darla faded with every passing mile. Every mile the train put between them and New York City was another mile closer to Wyatt and her folks.

21

IN A RESTAURANT AT THE WALDORF-ASTORIA,
Joel ate a big breakfast.

He hadn't realized how hungry he'd been. It seemed now that he'd been running primarily on nerves and adrenaline. He'd slept like the dead in his plush room. He woke recharged and ready to roll. He sipped from his coffee, and spooned eggs and hash browns into his mouth as fast as he could chew.

He had stared at the ceiling late into the night, debating what his next move should be. Whether he lost her now, or not, he had to bring it down a notch and exercise some good judgment.

A certain level of peace had settled over him last night as he lay in bed, listening to the sounds of the city. Either he'd find her or he wouldn't. The rest was out of his hands. He could sweat blood day and night, and not draw any nearer to her. If she was still in New York, if she was or had been at the Waldorf, he'd reach her step by step.

With the peace had come a plan. Nothing elaborate, but a place to start. Last night, for the first time, he'd entertained the idea of hiring a private detective. New York was a huge city, and in the few days in which he'd stumbled about in the streets, he'd felt terribly overwhelmed. Maybe a PI would get quicker results. Today he planned to give that option some serious thought.

He'd get to it after breakfast. He buttered a biscuit while a waitress topped off his coffee mug. She smiled at him, and he blushed slightly. She was cute. He didn't see a ring on her finger. He'd leave her a generous tip.

The thoughts she aroused in him reminded him of how long his life had been on hold. But just maybe things were beginning to change for him. In seventy-two hours his universe had been tipped on its head. Simply *pondering* what the next seventy-two might have in store for him scared him to death.

Shelby sipped his coffee and kept his face down. The table was in a corner in the rear of the little coffee shop, where it was darker and where there was less foot traffic. Even with the British driving cap and the pair of tinted Oakley glasses on his face he still felt terribly visible. The coffee shop was in Little Italy, not an area of New York where his face would exactly stand out. But he was still the president's attorney and might be recognized.

He pulled the bill of his cap down and stared straight down the aisle. The piece in the *Times* had him on the ropes. They'd expected the news to break, but they'd also hoped to control the *flow* of news a little better. This development simply meant they had to mobilize and get matters resolved before they escalated out of control.

They had to find the videotape. If they were right in their assumptions, the contents of the tape would put them all away for the rest of their lives. Shelby dabbed his brow with a paper napkin, beginning to perspire simply thinking about it. The address they'd found at Beagle Run led to a postal box at a post office in Manhattan. The box was registered to Inez Mulkey. Some quick legwork last night had uncovered the fact that Inez Mulkey was deceased. She'd been dead for eleven years and had lived in Utah for the five years previous to her death. Why the postal box had never been taken out of her name had stumped them for a while, but not long.

It turned out that Mulkey was the name of her *second* husband. Her first marriage ended with the death of her spouse, Frank Donovan, from a heart attack. That marriage produced one child, a daughter named Darla. It hadn't taken long to piece the puzzle together and determine who Darla Donovan was. This revelation caused much activity in Shelby's chest cavity.

James Ettinger had mailed the videocassette to a producer at NBC News. It was a beautiful setup for her, really. Who knew how long she'd maintained that box, but hats off to her for the ingenuity. Shelby massaged his temples. He glanced at his watch. Desmond was late.

He wondered how long Ettinger had had this little trick up his sleeve. Months? Weeks? Days? Had it been a long-term plan, or had it merely occurred to him in a moment of sudden remorse? Either way, they'd screwed up big-time. They hadn't thought to check his mail on a daily basis; in hindsight, it seemed obvious. Shelby wadded a paper napkin in his fist and squeezed down on it, his knuckles going white under the strain. They let their guard down, and now they might pay for their apathy. Sure, they'd suspected for a couple of months that Ettinger was getting weak and might crack, and that's why they'd taken the initiative to have the threat eliminated. And there was *some* satisfaction in knowing they'd read the signs correctly, that Ettinger had grown weak and dangerous. But they made their move twenty-four hours too late.

Desmond parked his yellow Ferrari Modena a block and a half from the coffee shop and continued on foot. He wore Ray Bans and a leather bomber jacket. He jerked the glass door open and walked to the rear of the coffee shop, sliding in across from Glen Shelby.

"You're late," Shelby said, staring down at his coffee.

"Traffic."

"Where's the tape?"

"Good question," Desmond said, flipping open a laminated menu. He was not really reading it. It just gave him something to do with his hands. "It wasn't in the postal box by the time we got there. I've had my people watching it round the clock since late last night. The box was empty when we found it, and it's still empty. Given that it's coming up on Christmas, the postal service is running a tad slower than usual, so there's every chance it simply hasn't arrived yet."

Shelby drummed his fingernails along the rim of his coffee mug. He raised his face slightly, glaring at Desmond from behind his glasses.

"If Ettinger dropped the tape in the mail Monday morning, after he recorded his statement and packaged it up, it most likely went out Monday afternoon," Shelby said. "Today's Thursday."

Desmond nodded.

"Monday to Thursday. Maine to New York. No, it should be here by now. I say it's been in that box already, and Donovan has picked it up." Shelby paused to consider his own line of thought, then continued. "Yes, she has it. She may not have viewed it yet, and in that case she doesn't know what she has in her possession. She likely receives a lot of mail at that box. I imagine she checks it five or six times a week, maybe daily."

A waitress stopped at the table and topped off Shelby's coffee. Desmond ordered a cranberry juice and bagel with cream cheese.

Desmond said, "You may be right. But it hasn't hit the news yet, and you know very well that if she has the tape and has viewed it—if it's even what we *think* it is—it would be everywhere by now. We wouldn't be sitting here, and Yates wouldn't—"

"*Shut up!*" Shelby hissed. "Don't mention his name. Not *here.*" He glanced around the coffee shop. If anyone was paying attention to their conversation, it certainly wasn't obvious. The coffee shop was only about half full, and no one seemed aware in the least of their presence at the table in the rear.

Desmond shrugged.

Shelby adjusted the bill of his cap, shaking his head, clearly on edge.

"Anyway," Desmond continued, "if the tape comes in at any time now, we'll be all over it."

"We've got to be proactive," Shelby said, stabbing his index finger at the table between them. "You can have your people watch the box from now till eternity, but you'd better start sniffing around Donovan. My money says she already has the tape."

"What if she has it at her office?"

"I don't know. We'll look there, as well."

Desmond took a bite of his bagel, and said, "If she's got it, we will find it."

"You'd better have it by noon today, or the walls may begin to crumble," Shelby said.

Desmond assured him, "If I don't have that tape in my hand by twelve noon, I'll be very close, I guarantee it."

The past ten years, Joel had lived alone. He was a bachelor by both choice and circumstance. For the past seven years he'd made his home in a decent neighborhood in St. Louis. He paid nearly eight hundred dollars a month for two bedrooms, a small kitchen, a single bath, a large front room, and a garage with a tiny utility area.

His neighbor was a retired draftsman named Howard Tate. They got along well. Mr. Tate was a widower with lots of time on his hands. He was bored with life and invited Joel over for dinner every two days. Mr. Tate collected Joel's mail for him, and kept his newspapers from piling up in the driveway.

Tate didn't answer his phone at 8:30 A.M., when Joel first dialed him from the Waldorf. He was likely out on one of his half a dozen daily walks around the neighborhood. He had a pug named Cedar, and he and his dog had logged more miles than Delta Airlines. Joel tried again in ten minutes, and again in twenty. Still no answer.

Joel took a cab across town to the hotel where he had stayed previously. He gathered his things from his room, settled up with the clerk at the front desk, and dialed Mr. Tate's number at a pay phone in the lobby. Maybe Cedar had escaped his leash and was making a mad dash for the Great Wide Open. Joel grinned at the mental image, then stepped out into the cold and waited for a cab to return him to the Waldorf.

Joel was betting that Megan had either gone to the Waldorf on Park Avenue or the apartment building on East Fifty-seventh, and now the fear was building that he'd spent too much time watching one and not the other. That might spell disaster, which was why he so desperately needed to get ahold of Mr. Tate.

An accident up ahead had traffic bottlenecked. Joel sat in the back of the cab, fidgeting with nervous energy.

"I'll just walk from here," he said, looking over the seat.

"Suit yourself, bub," the driver said.

He threw the cash over the seat and crossed a lane of traffic to the sidewalk. He walked quickly, his hands stuffed in his pockets. The wind cut him in half. He noticed a copy shop up ahead. He went in the door and had to wait in line for a few minutes before being helped.

"How much do you charge to receive faxes?" Joel asked the woman behind the counter. She was haggard-looking and didn't smile at him.

"Three bucks first page," she said. "Two bucks every page after that."

Steep! he thought, shrugging it off. "What's the fax number?"

She handed him a business card from a stack on the counter. "Here," she said. "It's on there."

"You take cash, right?"

Miss Congeniality shot him a look, which reflected her assessment of this man standing before her. She said, "Uh, yeah."

He thanked her and hurried out the door.

He found a pay phone a half a block down, and dialed Mr. Tate.

Surprise, Mr. Tate answered on the second ring.

"Hey, hey . . . Joel!"

"Hi, Howard. Everything good with you?"

"You betcha! Me and Cedar, we been out on the town. How about you?" Mr. Tate said.

"I'm good, real good, Howard."

"Great. I figured you'd be back home by now, Joel."

"Yeah, me too." Joel hoped to cut the small talk short, something scientifically impossible to do when dealing with the old and bored. "I'm stuck out on business."

"Oh, yeah boy. I been there, yessir. I been there."

Cut to the chase. "Listen, Howard. I have a small favor to ask of you."

"Anything, my boy!"

"Great. Thanks, Howard, you're a lifesaver. You know where my key is?"

"Sure, under the air-conditioning unit out back on the cement slab."

Joel wondered for a moment how many hours Howard Tate had spent roaming through his house. "Good. Okay, in the spare bedroom, in the closet, are several unpacked boxes. In the one on top, should be a picture frame with a photo of a young woman. She has on jeans and a T-shirt. You follow?"

"Got it, boss."

"Great. Remove the photo from the frame, then run into town to the supermarket and fax it to me."

"The picture?"

"Yes, Howard, the picture."

"Won't it bend it up a little bit going through that machine?"

"That's okay, Howard. I just need it in a hurry."

"Whatever you say, boss. I'll have it to you in a jiffy."

"I owe you one, Howard."

Joel read off the fax number for the copy shop, and they hung up. He offered up a short prayer that Howard would find the right photo and wouldn't somehow botch this one simple errand. The photo was of Ariel, taken a year or so before Megan was born. It was one of the few mementos he had left from their life together, and it might just be the one tool he needed to get his daughter back.

22

DESMOND PARKED THE FERRARI A BLOCK FROM the van. He spoke into a handheld radio, cueing his people into action. Two men and a female exited the van and crossed the street to the high-rise apartment building. Desmond walked past the van at a steady clip. He glanced up at the high-rise. It was fifty floors of glass and steel.

He entered an office building that rose from the street corner a few hundred feet from the apartment building. He rode an elevator to the eighteenth floor and followed a hall around to the right, stopping at a locked door. He looked around, saw no one, and took a thin length of metal from his coat pocket, working it in the lock. In less than seven seconds he was inside the office with the door locked behind him. He pocketed the length of metal and strode to the window. The view overlooked the street, and from where he stood he could see the glass and steel high-rise that Darla Donovan called home. They'd had no luck at her office finding what they were after, so it was on to the next step.

Forty-five minutes earlier, Desmond had scouted

the area around Donovan's building. There was a bank branch located directly across from her apartment. That was useless to him. Next to the bank was a catering business. There was space available to rent or lease on either side of the apartment, but he needed to face the building, he had to be able to watch it. He settled on this skyscraper, determined which floor would allow him the best view, and within minutes was on the phone with the property's real estate agent. She gave him the lowdown on which office units were vacant and available, as well as the lease prices. Desmond thanked her and hung up the phone. All he needed was an empty space where he could set up his equipment and wait.

Desmond removed a handheld radio from his coat pocket and keyed the transmission button.

"Echo-Two, do you read me?" Desmond stood close to the window, watching the reflections in the enormous glass building that his team had infiltrated.

"Affirmative, Echo-One."

"What is your position?"

"We are in and moving into position," the man's voice stated.

"Good. Proceed." Desmond unzipped the bag he'd carried with him and removed a pair of rubber-armor field glasses. Donovan's apartment was on the eighteenth floor, just as he was now. Her apartment number was 1840. He knew that her apartment overlooked this street. He would have to wait a few minutes before he found out precisely which one was hers.

The woman who entered the target's apartment building wore large sunglasses and a brown wig over her blond hair. The earpiece was tucked neatly inside the auditory canal of her left ear. A tiny mike was clipped to the underside of the lapel of her long coat. There would be cameras in the elevators, she knew. She used the stairs. Her name was Carmichael.

Carmichael's partner, Lewis, found a metal access door that led to a basement-level room. He left the lights off and removed a bulky flashlight from the sleeve of his coat. He thumbed the spring-activated button and the flashlight splashed a broad spot of light onto the wall. The walls were lined with electrical breaker boxes, which supplied power to all the tenants in the building. Also he found where the telephone cables fed in from an outside source. The telephone lines were housed in metal boxes mounted on the walls. Strips of masking tape that had been written on with laundry markers labeled both the breaker boxes and telephone boxes. Each apartment unit had a corresponding set of breakers and phone lines.

He spoke into his lapel mike. "Echo-Four. Thumbs-up on the phone."

Working quickly, Lewis played the beam of light across the boxes and their strips of tape until he happened across the masking tape labeled 1840. He then took a small wad of putty from his pocket and affixed it to the door of the metal box, marking it for later. He moved to the other side of the room and quickly found the phone lines belonging to apartment 1840. Here too he affixed a wad of putty to the metal door.

"Echo-Four, moving out," he said, following the beam of his light back to the metal access door.

The second man, Porter, had taken a separate flight of stairs. He wore wraparound sunglasses and a San Diego Chargers ball cap. He and Carmichael met at the door to apartment 1840, and he rang the doorbell. If anyone answered, they would simply apologize for having the wrong apartment number and continue on, regrouping per Desmond's orders. But no one came to the door. They waited for nearly a full minute before the man worked his wizardry on the bolt lock, and in a flash they were inside.

"Echo-Two and Echo-Three are in position," Porter said.

"Acknowledged," Desmond responded.

Porter stepped cautiously through the big main room of the apartment, and then hurried to the picture window that overlooked the street below. He removed a bulky flashlight from the sleeve of his coat. He thumbed the switch, activating the light, then pressed the glass of the flashlight's lens to the glass of the window, and clicked the switch off and on, repeatedly.

From his post, catty-corner down the street, Desmond spotted the flicker of light through his powerful field glasses. "Roger that, Echo-Two. I have visual."

Over the course of the next twenty minutes, the two of them scoured Donovan's apartment in search of the VHS videocassette. At this stage in the ball game, it was important not to tear the place apart. It was important to leave everything the way they'd found it. If they caused even the slightest suspicion, she might really tighten the screws on them.

Desmond made periodic radio contact, watching

anxiously through his field glasses. Each time he was met with a negative report. There was no sign of the tape.

In less than half an hour, the two intruders had done an admirably thorough room-by-room search of the premises. Still no tape.

Desmond cursed under his breath. His reflection in the window frowned at him. He cursed at his reflection. Time was becoming the enemy. If he failed to find that tape, and find it soon, Mr. Stott would have his head served on a platter.

A final sweep of the apartment produced no further results. Careful to cover their tracks, the pair made sure that nothing had been disturbed, then eased out of the door, locking it behind them. They hurried down the stairwell and crossed the street to the van. When the van's sliding door slammed shut, Lewis put the van in gear and accelerated into traffic. It was time to move on. But they'd likely be back very shortly.

Desmond set down his field glasses.

Static crackled from his radio. Then a voice said, "Echo-Two and Echo-Three are clear, over."

It was nearly 10 A.M. They needed results, and they needed them fast.

Desmond held the radio at his side, still staring out the window at the glass-and-steel facade across the street. He thought of Mr. Stott, Yates, Shelby, and of Julius Albertwood. He wasn't sure whom he hated more. He hated them all. But only Mr. Stott truly frightened him. If he didn't get results very soon, Mr. Stott would certainly not be pleased.

Desmond had killed men in rain forests and

deserts and at sea with his bare hands. He could live
in the wilderness, surviving off nothing but roots and
dirt. He could disappear from the face of the earth at
the snap of a finger. But he could never hide from
Mr. Stott. No one could. "Roger that, Echo-Two. On
my way." He put the field glasses in his bag and
headed for the door. He eased open the door, and
ducked his head into the hall. When the door clicked
shut behind him, he inserted a business card between
the door and the doorjamb about three inches above
the carpet. He'd plucked the card from his windshield wiper that morning after his meeting with
Shelby. It was a solicitation from a weight loss company. If anyone opened the door before he returned,
the card would provide the evidence.

As per the usual routine, the drop could be made at
any time over a three-day period. Olin St. John
entered the bank at a quarter to ten, Thursday morning. They had used this particular bank a number of
times over the past few years, so St. John was familiar
with the layout and atmosphere of the place.

The arrangement was simple: once a job was
completed, there was a four-day safe zone, an interim
allowing him to slink away and lay low. Following
this period, he was to be notified within the next
three days as to where his payment would be wired
and when. The notification was deposited in a safe-
deposit box at the agreed-upon bank. Then he simply
had to go where the money was to be wired.

St. John carried a leather attaché case. He strode
across the expansive atrium. This part of the job
always made him uncomfortable. He was conscious

of the cameras staring down from all over. He knew exactly where to go and was prompt at finding the person who could help him. A woman wearing a business suit led him down a flight of stairs to the sublevel, where many of the safe-deposit boxes were located. She asked him to wait in a room furnished with long, narrow tables. St. John set the attaché case on a table as the bank employee disappeared through a vault door.

This was the part he hated. Considering who he was and what he did for a living, it was nerve-racking having to voluntarily step inside such a fortified environment. The only disguise he now wore was a pair of nonprescription eyeglasses. The process of collecting his money made him feel maddeningly vulnerable.

An old man was sitting in a chair at the far end of one of the other tables. St. John watched him closely, but the man appeared harmless. He had a box on the table before him, but St. John could not tell what had been stored inside.

The bank employee returned carrying a metal deposit box. She gave him instructions for when he was finished. He thanked her and she left him alone.

Olin St. John took a seat at the table and removed from his attaché case the small pink envelope he'd received in Nantucket. He slit open the envelope with his pinky finger and dumped its contents out onto the table. A small brass key toppled out, making a metallic chime as it skittered across the surface of the table. He scooped up the key, unlocked the box, and opened it.

The box was empty.

St. John exhaled. They hadn't come yet.

This frustrated him somewhat, only because he'd hoped to be done with it. He was walking away from the life he'd known, and the sooner he could be rid of it the better. But this was only the first day. The notification would be ready for him, Saturday at the latest, but hopefully Friday. He and Megan had plans, and he was itching to get their life together under way. And sure, he'd already collected enough money over the past ten years to retire in opulence. He could walk away now, and no great harm would be done. But he'd agreed to this last job for a reason. The $5.9 million was the great brass ring. It would ensure them a life without worry. It would ensure that he'd never have to work again. Two more days and the money would be his. All he had to do was be patient.

He notified a bank employee that he was finished with the box and ascended the flight of stairs to the main business floor of the bank. He looked around as he crossed the broad expanse toward the exit. Hopefully he'd be making only one more trip inside these walls. Two at the most. But two was one too many for his taste.

Be patient, he told himself. *Just be patient.*

The old man exited the bank a safe distance behind St. John. He ducked out of sight behind a massive support column, peeled the facial prosthetics from his nose and jowls and chin, and removed the too-thick reading glasses. He was in his midtwenties, and his name was R'mel. He knew that the man he'd followed from the bank was an assassin, and he knew the assassin's name was Belfast.

R'mel dumped the pieces of his disguise into a receptacle as he descended the steps from the bank. He straddled his Ducati motorcycle, keeping his man Belfast in view. The Ducati roared to life. R'mel put on his helmet, and spoke into the built-in mike.

"This is R'mel," he said in his native French. "Belfast has left the bank, and I am pursuing." He received instructions through the earpiece in his helmet.

St. John hailed a cab, heading back across Manhattan.

The Ducati followed at a reasonable distance.

The news of the vice president's death was screaming through the airwaves. Satellites far above the earth worked overtime, bouncing signals from dish to dish. The media tasted blood. The face of President Clifton Yates was broadcast nonstop from the moment he began his announcement.

Darla already had a tape of the president's statement in her office, and her production staff had gathered around her desk, gawking at the television screen, still unable to grasp the full reality of the earthquake that had hit. She knew that Brooke would be sick that she'd missed it.

Darla had befriended James Ettinger early on in President Yates's first campaign. She'd treated him fairly, and he'd rewarded her with interviews at times when nobody else could get a word out of him. But she was still a member of the media, and therefore not high on a politician's list of favorite faces. She and Ettinger weren't friends, not by any means. But over the course of the Yates administration, she'd managed to earn a certain level of trust. For that, she'd been grateful. And because of that, she'd miss him.

Now Darla was on the phone, pounding away at the usual places for more info from the White House than they were offering in the official press releases. She'd be on the phone all day. She was exhausted, and it was only just beginning.

23

THE PI'S NAME WAS CROUDER. HE WAS DIRECT and to the point. He asked specific questions that Joel did his best to answer informatively. Crouder charged $125 an hour, which was the best price of the dozen agencies Joel had found in the Yellow Pages. Crouder wanted a picture of Megan, and luckily Howard Tate had come through for him. Howard had done a good job getting the photograph of Ariel faxed. Crouder wasn't pleased with the quality of the facsimile. It looked almost as if it had been snipped from a newspaper.

The meeting lasted barely twenty minutes. Crouder said he'd need three days. He said he thought he could find her but wouldn't make promises. He gave Joel a card with his office and cell numbers on it, but he told Joel not to call during those first three days.

Joel left Crouder's office feeling some sense of relief at having another set of eyes on the lookout for Megan. He told himself to give it a rest while Crouder went about his work. Just take a break, get some rest, have a nice meal, take a load off. Crouder was the professional, and Joel was simply wasting time chasing shadows around the city. Let the man do his job, he told himself firmly.

At noon, the main lobby of the Waldorf-Astoria Hotel was busy with the rush and flow of travelers and guests, businesspeople and hotel staff. Joel sat in a wing chair, an unread paperback in his lap.

Reading wasn't possible. His mind simply couldn't stay still long enough to care about anything but finding Megan. He eyed the people in the main lobby, studying the faces of the hotel staff. He rubbed his eyes, feeling useless. Surely he could do *something*.

The page that Howard had faxed to him was folded in half and tucked between pages in the book. Four days had passed since Joel had spotted Megan outside La Guardia. In that time his mental snapshot of her had altered and faded into sort of an ambiguous image. Staring now at the photo of Ariel, taken nearly twenty-three years ago, he found himself startled anew at just how eerily similar Megan was to her mother. Whatever doubt had arisen in his mind between Monday night and this moment as to whether the young woman he'd caught only a fleeting glimpse of was his daughter was gone. The face in the photo brought the face from La Guardia into clear focus. The image in his mind's eye sharpened into a distinct still-frame. He knew it was Megan.

An elderly couple was checking in at a reception desk, and a tall blond kid in a Waldorf uniform loaded their bags onto a wheeled cart and headed for the elevator. The elderly couple remained at the desk, taking care of business. Joel arrived at the elevator ahead of the kid, holding the door for him until the luggage cart was safely inside.

"Thanks," the kid said.

"My pleasure," Joel said, nodding. The kid looked to be no older than nineteen or twenty. He was tall and clean-cut. They rode in silence.

The bell chimed, and the doors opened onto the tenth floor. The kid rolled the cart forward, and then headed down the corridor. Joel came out and turned in the opposite direction, walking slowly away toward his own room but glancing over his shoulder to see where the kid was headed. When at last the kid stopped the cart and unlocked the door to the room where the luggage belonged, Joel paused and turned around, watching. He watched the kid lift the bags and tote them inside. He suddenly felt inspired.

The bellboy crossed the big suite carrying the first two of six pieces of luggage, then turned and hurried back for the next load of luggage.

The man standing in the doorway startled him. He stopped suddenly. For a moment he thought perhaps he recognized the man but couldn't put his finger on just how.

"Excuse me," Joel said, smiling, doing his best to come across as friendly and nonthreatening. "I'm sorry if I spooked you," he said, noting the kid's name badge said TODD.

"No, sir." Todd shrugged. "I simply didn't notice you there. Can I help you, sir?" It was then that Todd recognized the man as the fellow in the elevator. He relaxed a little.

"Well, yes, actually . . . you can. I *hope*, anyway." Joel took a step inside the room, easing the door closed a hair, so that he and the bellboy were out of sight of anyone who might happen by in the corridor. He pulled a folded bill from a pocket and offered it to the kid.

Todd unfolded the fifty.

"I'd like to ask a favor of you," Joel said.

"Yes, sir."

Joel smiled. He unfolded the photocopy of Ariel's picture and handed it to the young man. "I was wondering if by chance you had seen this woman here?"

The kid frowned at the picture and said, "Not that I remember, sir. No." He looked up and then handed the photocopy back to Joel. "But I'm not supposed to discuss our clientele, sir. It's hotel policy." Now he was frowning at Joel, suddenly suspicious and uncomfortable.

"Oh, I understand, I understand," Joel said on the defensive.

Todd reached out to return the fifty.

"No, no," Joel said. "You keep that." And he pulled out another fifty-dollar bill and held it out. But this time, the kid only looked at him. "I'm not asking you to tell me anything about anyone, except if you've happened to see this young lady around the hotel at any point in the past couple of days. There's no harm in that, is there?"

The kid studied him for a few seconds, staring him dead in the eye.

A bead of sweat trickled down from Joel's armpit.

Finally, the kid said, "I suppose not." And he snatched the fifty from Joel's grasp. He took another, longer look at the face on the photocopy. "No. I don't remember seeing her. Doesn't mean she wasn't here though, sir. So many people come and go every day. And I only see the folks who come through during my shift."

"Of course." Joel nodded.

"Why do you need to find her?"

Joel had prepared for this. "Well, to be honest with you, Todd, she's my daughter."

Todd looked at the photo, then looked skeptically at Joel. "Looks a little old to be your daughter."

"It's a long story."

Todd considered this. He examined the picture more closely. Then he asked, "Why not show this to the front desk? They see everyone who comes through. They could help you more than I could."

"You're right, and I probably will. But I saw you, and just thought I'd ask."

Clearly uncomfortable, Todd said, "I wish I could help, sir, but—"

"Tell you what," Joel said. "You keep that photo. And you keep the cash—you've earned it. Just keep your eyes peeled over the next couple of days, maybe show it around to some of the other staff. You can find me in room ten-eighteen. Or ask her to call me there. Okay? It'd be a big help, Todd."

Todd looked very uncomfortable, but a hundred bucks was a hundred bucks, and all he had to do was throw the photocopy in the garbage and forget he ever saw this guy. And that's what he fully intended to do. He shrugged. "I'll keep an eye out."

"Great, great. Listen, Todd. I appreciate it."

Todd watched the man open the door and step out into the corridor.

Joel had half a dozen copies of the photo in his

room. The conversation with the bellboy had been spur-of-the-moment. It couldn't hurt. Perhaps he could have one set of eyes working for him at the Waldorf and one set at the apartment building on East Fifty-seventh. That way he didn't have to be at both places at all times. If somebody spotted her, they could contact him in his room or leave a simple message for him at the front desk. For a moment he seriously considered approaching a manager or the front desk with the same request but quickly shrugged off the notion. It was probably best just to leave the footwork to Crouder.

He wasn't sure how much he trusted this Todd character to do any more than rip off his hundred bucks. But the money was the last thing on his mind, and anything the kid might see or hear could very well make the difference between finding Megan or losing her forever.

Megan had retained very few memories of the United States from her childhood. She hadn't been back to America since she was twelve and had spent nearly all of those years in California. This was her first visit to New York City.

She inserted her quarter and looked through the viewer that was mounted to the railing at the top of the Empire State Building. She couldn't help but smile. Olin St. John stood behind her, his hands in the pockets of his coat. He'd been to New York many times on business. And though he had some business to take care of while he was here, he had designated this trip primarily for leisure and for celebration.

Megan was acting like a child with a new toy. She

pivoted the viewer, taking in the cityscape. Olin took a step forward and put his arms around her. She giggled, pointing to this and that in the distance. He kissed her on the neck. A biting wind coursed through the viewing area, and she grabbed him by the wrist, urging him to hurry back to the warmth of the elevator.

They found a cozy little bar a few blocks from the Empire State Building. She found a table while Olin waded through a crowd to the bar and ordered drinks. Megan took a long sip of her Chivas, plenty happy to finally have her insides kick-started by a little alcohol. Olin ignored his Heineken and stared at her.

Olin had explained to her that they only had to stay in New York until he had finished up a little business. Then they could jet off to Las Vegas and have a quick wedding. Neither of them had any desire for a big, family-style wedding. She hadn't heard from her mother in ages and no longer knew if her father was alive. The only members of Olin's family who had mattered to him were long dead. There were some relatives somewhere out there among the world's vast population, but none that he cared to see. Besides, his past required him to stay low. There were countries with bounties on his head, and the fanfare that accompanied a big public wedding is not the best way to keep your face among the shadows.

Part of what worked for them as a couple was the fact that they were bound only by each other. He had no ties to friends or family, and her few acquaintances were chums she'd met at art school. It was a perfect fit. Certainly, her lack of familial ties had attracted him to her. Families tended to be protective and were often leery of outsiders. Olin St. John could not afford to be analyzed this way. Megan would believe the lies he'd told her concerning his past; parents and grandparents, aunts and uncles, and siblings very well might not. She had come with no baggage, and this made all that he saw in her that much more worth possessing.

So they would be together for another day or two in New York, and then fly out to the desert. Maybe he'd even do some gambling. With $5.9 million as good as in his pocket, he had money to burn. They could spend without thinking.

Megan finished her drink and was ready to go. Olin had barely touched the Heineken. They planned to catch a movie matinee before having a nice dinner back at the hotel. All they had was time and each other.

Getting up from his seat at the end of the bar, R'mel paid for his tonic water and followed the couple outside. While they waited for a cab, he fetched the motorcycle parked nearby. He was aware enough of Belfast's reputation not to get careless and follow too closely, but the two were clearly so enamoured of each other that they seemed oblivious to everything.

The girl was an interesting development. He now knew where Belfast was staying, and whom he was with. R'mel was certain that his employer would be pleased.

The movie started at three, and they'd have to rush to catch the coming attractions. The theater was sparsely filled. They settled into their seats and Olin wrapped an arm around her shoulders. He stared at the screen, but his mind was far away.

He worried about the money. Until it was safe and sound, transferred to his holding account, it would be difficult to rest or relax. There were simply too many things that could still go wrong. In his experience, there'd rarely been any sort of complication when it came time to collect his fee, but no one let loose of this amount of money too enthusiastically.

As important as the money was, the chance at a future and having peace of mind were more important. That was the driving force behind his retirement. He was still young and healthy, with a chance to grow old with the woman he loved. He wanted to walk the streets with his wife, shopping and talking and laughing. Maybe he would grow a garden. Or build a boat. He had the money to buy a yacht, but within him was the desire to have calluses on his hands, to sweat in the heat of the day, and to take pride in accomplishing something.

And he was certainly free to do any or all of these things. But if he had to worry that someone from his old life might be hiding in the shadows ready to pounce, if he had to glance over his shoulder wherever he went or wake from sleep at the slightest sound—he'd never be a whole man.

Even though it might take another decade of his life to outrun the ghosts of his past, there was enough time ahead of him to slowly become a new being. He thought that perhaps if he stayed out of the game long enough to forget about them, they would forget about him.

That would likely be many years away, but he could make it. He was sure of it. In the meantime, he would sleep with his gun within easy reach.

24

A CATCH IN HER BREATHING WOKE BROOKE. She unwound herself from the precarious and terribly uncomfortable position her body had twisted itself into during sleep. Her head was on her backpack. She sat up, feeling a crick in her back and neck. A patch of warm, bright sunlight was full in her face. She squinted into the light and looked ahead at the rows of seats and into the distance. She had no idea where they were. It had to be afternoon by now.

Raising her arm to check the time, she realized her watch was in her backpack. She lifted the pack onto her lap, twisting it around, unzipping the small outer compartment where she thought she remembered stashing her cheap Timex. The digital readout confirmed that it was 2:00 P.M. She fastened it on her wrist.

As she fussed with the zipper on the outer compartment of her pack, a bubble of realization caused her to dig her hand into the compartment and pull out the two envelopes she'd retrieved for Darla from the V.I.P. box.

"Great," she muttered to herself. She put her head back against the seat and closed her eyes. Darla was gonna kill her. She didn't plan on heading back to the city for at least a week. So if there was anything inside the envelopes that might be of immediate interest to Darla, there was little doubt that her boss would be screaming bloody murder very shortly. She opened her eyes and stared at the back of the seat in front of her.

"Smooth move, Brookster," she said, sighing. She fanned herself with the envelopes, shaking her head in disgust. "Sometimes I amaze myself with my stupidity."

A middle-aged man in the seat ahead of her stuck his head between the seats and gave her a concerned look. She glared at him. He faced forward again.

Then she remembered the package she'd crammed into the bottom of her pack. She tucked the two envelopes between her thighs, peeled back the flap on her backpack, and unzipped the main compartment. Her pullover was stuffed on top, and below that, just as she remembered, was the parcel wrapped in heavy brown paper. Everything was now accounted for. And each second that she sat there with them in her lap, staring at them like a dumb ape, she was creeping farther away from her boss.

Brooke chewed her lower lip, restraining the impulse to curse aloud. It was very likely that all that would happen was that she'd phone Darla, explain her lapse, and Darla would either have her hold on to the items until she returned from her parents' place, or she'd have her FedEx the stuff overnight. If the latter were the case, Brooke would offer to cover the shipping charges out of her own pocket. In either case, Darla would hold the incident over her head indefinitely. That was her way.

She looked at her watch again. It seemed impolite and unprofessional not to give Darla a heads-up. Surely she was still at the office. She quickly dialed the number. Voice mail. She hung up and tried again. Voice mail. She hated voice mail. She needed to talk to her boss directly. Either Darla wasn't in the office or she wasn't answering the phone.

She dialed a third time in the hope that Darla might get sick of the incessant ringing and answer the blasted thing. Again, the voice mail picked up. Brooke took a breath and waited for the curt recorded message to finish. Then she spoke into the phone. "Hi, Darla, it's me, Brooke. Listen, I need to talk to you. I'm still on the road, call me when you get this. I guess I'll try to get ahold of you this evening. Okay? Bye."

She pressed the End button, and set the phone on her knee. This had accomplished nothing. Her message had told Darla absolutely nothing. But she didn't feel comfortable discussing the V.I.P. box on voice mail. Perhaps Darla had taken off for home already. Of course. She'd called it a day and run home to get things ready for the party tonight. And even if she hadn't made it home just yet, Brooke could leave a more specific message on the machine at Darla's apartment.

She paused for a moment, tapping the phone against her chin, straining to recall Darla's home phone number. Then she dialed. It rang three times, then the machine picked up. Brooke winced, gritting her teeth in frustration.

The recorded message was followed by a beep. Brooke thought for a second, then said, "Hey, Darla. It's Brooke. I'm still on the road. I, uh . . . I picked up your mail from the box yesterday . . . and completely forgot about getting it to you before I took off this morning. I *really* apologize. I feel pretty stupid about it. Anyway"—she glanced at the small pile of mail on top of her backpack—"you've got three different items here. Two envelopes. Neither with a return address. One of them has a cheesy little sunflower design in the corner. And there's a parcel wrapped in brown paper—looks and feels like a book or something." She squinted at the word written in the upper left-hand corner. She said, "And it's got the word *Beacon* jotted on it." She shrugged, not really knowing what else to tell her boss about the items. "If that stuff rings a bell, leave a message at the number I left with you. They'll be happy to talk your ears off, believe me. Either way, I'll give you a call as soon as I arrive. You can give me eighty lashes when I get back. I'll talk to you later. Bye." She pressed End, vaguely satisfied, though still plagued by guilt.

Darla Donovan had that effect on you. No matter how out of your way you went to please her, you always felt as if you'd missed the mark.

It was a harmless accident. She'll get over it, she thought. *No big deal. Whenever I talk to her next, tonight or tomorrow or the next day, we'll laugh about it.*

More than anything, there was a great sense of relief that all the secrecy was over. Miriam Ettinger was finally free to grieve. She had watched the president's short statement on the major networks just like everyone else in the nation. She could now act like the widow she was.

The president himself called less than ten minutes after he'd finished his televised statement. It had not been scheduled, but she'd expected the call. Again, it all had to do with protocol.

"I'm sorry we had to wait so long, Miriam," Yates said.

"Me too."

"I have asked Anthony Philbrick to assume the office of vice president."

"Yes. I heard your speech."

"Ah, of course you did," Yates said, sweating bullets.

"I have no ill will toward you or anyone else with involvement in the investigation, Mr. President. There is a job to be done. An important job. James would have understood that, therefore I must as well. Under the circumstances, there would have been no pleasant way to handle it. There is only one person to blame here, and I want you to find him, Clifton. I want you to give me your word that you'll exhaust every available resource to find the man who murdered my husband." Miriam Ettinger spoke with very little emotion. At this point, four days after the assassination, she was simply numb. She hadn't slept, and she'd lost weight.

"I vow to you that the responsible party will be hunted down and brought to justice. I will make it my personal mission, by whatever means necessary, Miriam," the president lied with absolute sincerity. "James contributed more to my administration than I could ever hope to repay. And for that, I will be eternally grateful. He was a leader, a public servant, and a true man of the people. No one in this city or this country will soon forget him."

She had heard him speak these words already

today, on television, and she wondered if he was even aware of the repetition.

"Thank you," she said, only vaguely aware that she'd spoken at all.

"I'm always available if you want to talk, Miriam. My door is always open."

"Thank you."

"Please, Miriam, I mean it. Let me know if you need anything, or if there is anything I can do."

"Yes. Of course." She was hearing him but not hearing him.

"And give Bradey and Jude my condolences."

"I will."

"Good-bye, Miriam."

"Oh, Clifton?"

Startled, he replied, ". . . Yes?"

"Has anything come of that email James sent his brother?" she asked. "You said you would look right into it."

His mouth went dry. His tongue turned to putty.

"Clifton?"

He managed to work up enough saliva to speak. Nothing has come of it, Miriam. We did our best. Everyone's perplexed by it, I'm afraid."

"Hmm. I thought perhaps James had tried to tell us something. Perhaps we'll never know. Or perhaps we will," Miriam said.

Yates attempted to speak, but nothing came out. He sat frozen in place, afraid to make the least little sound, lest he betray himself.

Miriam hung up the phone.

They knew what Donovan looked like. They knew where she worked and where her office was inside the NBC studios at Rockefeller Plaza. The woman with the blond wig, Carmichael, had loitered for hours on a bench just outside the entrance to the NBC studios, watching and waiting. She spoke into the mike on her coat lapel when Donovan walked out the door well after dark.

"Here she comes," Carmichael said.

Lewis and Porter were waiting inside the van, parked several blocks away. Carmichael followed Donovan on foot. She spoke into her mike, updating their movements. The van appeared at a corner where Donovan was headed. Just short of the corner, she turned into a liquor store. In a matter of minutes, she exited the liquor store with a paper bag in her arms. She stepped to the curb and flagged down a cab. Carmichael jumped in the van, and the van fell into pursuit, several car lengths behind the cab.

Lewis spoke into his radio. "She's in a cab, and looks to be heading in your direction."

"Roger that," Desmond said, seated behind the wheel of his Ferrari. He snatched his bag from the passenger's seat and locked the doors, heading to the office building on the corner. It was after dark, and many of the offices had been abandoned for the remainder of the evening. The business card was still wedged in the doorjamb, precisely as he'd left it. He jiggled the metal instrument into the lock, making quick work of it. Inside, he left the lights off. He opened his bag, removed the field glasses, and set them on the window ledge. Next, he removed and assembled a standing tripod. He mounted a telescoping microphone to the bracket at the top of the tripod. He picked up the field glasses, adjusting the focus until the window to Donovan's apartment came into clear view.

Darla rode with her head back against the seat, nearly asleep. She was exhausted. The day had turned into much more than anyone could have expected. Her repeated calls to her most dependable sources had gotten her nowhere. Tomorrow would be a new day, and perhaps with a decent night's sleep and some food and champagne in her system, she'd be better prepared for the endless hours of work ahead of her.

She had stopped at a favorite liquor store for several bottles of champagne for the get-together tonight. Given the day's developments, tonight wouldn't have quite the festive holiday spirit that they'd all counted on. There would be a constant buzz about the news—what it could mean, who might be responsible for Ettinger's death, and how or *if* they, as a production team, would go about putting together a big piece on the story.

She'd spent most of the day in meetings. The higher-ups were going nuts. The network's stars—the so-called *talent*—were fighting tooth and nail for the big interviews. They wanted Miriam Ettinger, the widow. They wanted Clifton Yates. They wanted to dissect the FBI's investigation. They wanted shots of the Ettinger children, looking weepy and distraught. And of course, there would be a trillion profiles of Anthony Philbrick to assemble; he was now number two, and the world would demand to know every last detail of his life.

The day had left her in disarray. Her desk was now piled high. The other story her production team had worked on for months would now suffer.

There were dozens of Post-it notes across the surface of her desk, messages requiring her immediate attention. She had not checked her voice mail since early morning. Her email, she didn't even want to think about.

Riding silently in the back of the taxi, Darla wondered if she'd even stay awake till the guests arrived. She opened her eyes, her head canted against her shoulder. The taxi was at a dead stop in traffic. She didn't know what time it was and didn't care. There was a throbbing behind her eyes. The rest of the gang would be over momentarily. She'd be lucky to have ten or fifteen minutes of peace before they arrived.

Desmond's people managed to stay close. The taxi was in the next lane over, two cars ahead. The view of Donovan's head was slightly obstructed by part of the cab. But they knew she was in there. Lewis sat in the driver's seat in the van. Carmichael leaned forward between the seats. Traffic inched forward, ten or twelve feet, then halted. Donovan had come out carrying a handbag. They were very interested in the contents of that bag. They radioed this detail to Desmond up in his crow's nest.

Desmond thought about this. If Donovan had, in fact, picked up mail from the postal box at some point prior to the beginning of their surveillance late last night, she apparently hadn't found the time to take a look at it. If this were the case, they were in a good position to snuff this fire out free and clear. The president's announcement had sent the media into a frenzy. The talking heads on CNN and elsewhere had prattled on endlessly since that morning, and Donovan was part of that same universe. In fact, he was somewhat surprised she'd even left work tonight.

Desmond tested his equipment. He placed a headset over his ears and aimed the telescoping microphone at the window of one of Donovan's neighbors. He tuned the sensitivity level until he could hear even the slightest nuance of any conversation. There were sounds of dinner being prepared, of ice being dropped into glasses, of channels changing on a television.

The liquid crystal displays on his equipment glowed red and green in the darkness of the office. When he was satisfied, he pivoted the tripod mount, aiming the long, cone-shaped microphone directly at the window of Donovan's apartment. He'd be able to hear everything. He raised the field glasses to his eyes.

The streets were clogged. The taxi puttered forward a few feet at a time. A block from Donovan's apartment building, the van pulled down a side street and then into an alley behind a frozen yogurt shop.

The van's side door rattled open, sliding on its tracks, and Carmichael barreled out, looking both directions down the alley. A stray cat watched them from atop a Dumpster. Porter stepped from the passenger's door, saying something into the mike on his lapel, and then nodded. Standing in the slush and muck of the alley, he faced the van, double-checking that his weapon was loaded and ready to go.

Carmichael checked her weapon, also. They nodded at one another, then walked as a group, hurrying through the alley.

25

CONNOR KINGSTON, THE NEW INTERN, AND JILL Palmgrass, who'd been on her research staff the past eight years, were sitting in the hallway with their backs against the wall when Darla stepped from the elevator.

"Well, hey," Darla said, surprised but not startled by their presence.

"Hiya, boss," Connor said, getting to his feet. "We thought maybe you could use a hand getting ready, before the rest of the gang shows up."

Darla was tired and half-asleep from the cab ride from Rockefeller Plaza, and had fully intended to have time to sit down and enjoy a moment's silence before the festivities began. But maybe this was better, she thought. Jill and Connor could get things cranking in the kitchen, while she stole away to the bathroom and ran some warm water over her feet in the tub.

"Sounds fine to me." Darla fumbled through her purse for her keys.

"Joyce called me from her car," Jill said. "She and Lesley are on their way up. They had to park a couple of blocks away."

Darla nodded, fitting the key and pushing the door open with a knee.

"Here ya go, let me take care of that," Connor said, taking the paper bag from Darla. "Mmm, champagne! You know the way to a man's heart!"

Darla set her purse on a tall, narrow table just inside the door and pitched her keys into a pewter dish on the table. The keys settled in the dish with a clatter.

Desmond's people moved along the outside wall of a brick building a few hundred feet from their destination. They moved quickly and with purpose. Carmichael kept a hand on the Walther automatic in her coat pocket. It was fitted with a silencer, as was her associate's weapon of choice.

From where they now stood, their view of the apartment building was obstructed by another highrise. They turned to the left, stepping into an adjoining alleyway, which would lead them out to the sidewalk that ran along the street. A small import car was parked there. They stepped around the car, hurrying toward the light from the street.

Porter adjusted his cap.

Lewis did not have a wig or a cap, but a trim mustache was attached to his face by spirit gum. When this business was over, he would discard it in a trash bin or just out the window of the van. He glanced at his watch, noting the exact time, and thought they should be done and out in less than ten minutes.

The same voice crackled into all three earpieces. "Hold tight," Desmond instructed.

Lewis put his arm out, halting his associates just short of the sidewalk. "What gives?"

"She's home, but she's not alone."

They eyed one another, momentarily bewildered, and then crept back into the shadows of the alley.

"Okay, what's your call?" Porter said.

"Hold up," Desmond ordered. "Wait for my signal."

Porter adjusted the Chargers cap, shrugged at the others, and said, "Roger that."

There was a platter of sandwiches in the neighbor's refrigerator. A deli had delivered it in the afternoon, and Darla had requested that Miss Landers please keep it in the refrigerator until she got home. Barry Hickman had arrived by now, so he and Connor took a stroll next door, where they received a snooty once-over from Miss Landers.

The platter smelled heavily of green onions and mayonnaise.

When they returned to Darla's apartment, Lipton Stephenson was seated in an overstuffed armchair in the front room. The armchair was against a big window that overlooked the street. He had a coffee table book on his lap. He flipped pages slowly, scanning the pages through rimless glasses. Lipton was the oldest and least social of the bunch. He was from the old school of print journalism, and carried an air of superiority, which goaded his colleagues.

The sounds of activity in the kitchen carried into the front room. Lipton looked up from his book for just an instant, then returned his attention to the page. He did not offer to help.

There was an indoor grill already set up on the counter in the kitchen. Darla had directed them to the buffalo wings in her refrigerator. The chicken was divided between two crystal plates on the bottom shelf. Joyce pulled them out and peeled off the Saran Wrap. The grill heated up in a matter of seconds, and Joyce found a set of stainless steel tongs in a drawer and set about spacing the chicken pieces above the burner. She then basted the meat with a prepared sauce that Darla had worked up. The meat began to sizzle.

Barry and Connor stood around one of the islands in the kitchen, shooting the breeze. Barry lit a cigarette. Connor grabbed a wine cooler from the refrigerator. Lesley worked on a salad. Around this time, everyone echoed the same sentiment: too bad we have to work tomorrow.

Desmond listened to every word, every sound, every breath.

He crouched in the darkness. The only light was that of the moon coming through the office window. He listened through the headset, closely monitoring the sensitivity level of the telescoping microphone. So far there was nothing of value. But he would give them a little time to say what he wanted to hear.

Then he would be forced to get physical.

The flashlight snapped on in the basement, pitching an oblong spot of light across the wall. Lewis played the beam of light across the rows of electrical boxes, then turned and spotted the metal boxes that housed the telephone lines. He ran his tongue along his lower lip.

The lump of putty was still in place. Lewis picked it off and tossed it over his shoulder into the darkness, then opened the hinged metal door. He scanned down the rows of masking tape until he found the strip of tape that had been labeled with Donovan's apartment number. Disconnecting the phone line was an elementary task. He simply reached up and twisted the connector, detaching it from its post.

Lewis spoke into his mike. "Phone is down," he said.

Across the street, a spot of moonlight on his face, Desmond dialed his cell phone. The line rang fifteen times without being answered. He had dialed Donovan's apartment. He keyed his radio and said, "Let's do it."

Lewis nodded to himself. He left the hinged door open, and then turned and moved across the small, cinder block room, approaching the metal boxes that housed the breaker units. Again, he found the lump of putty on the proper box. He found the appropriate unit and swung the metal door open on its hinges. Each room in the apartment had a separate breaker switch, and at the top of the unit was a main breaker, which would cut all power to the apartment.

He held the flashlight against his collarbone, making sure that everything was in order. Then he spoke into his mike. "Ready and waiting."

Porter and Carmichael were in the stairwell. They came through the door and into a hallway on the eighteenth floor. The hallway was empty. They moved with precision, staying shoulder to shoulder. They stopped at the door to Donovan's apartment, checking to make certain no one had entered the hallway on either side of them. There was light visible beneath the door. They removed their weapons and readied them. They prepared to pull the night-vision goggles down over their eyes.

Porter spoke into his mike. "Let's do it."

Lewis nodded, reaching up and putting his thumb on the main breaker switch. "Say good night." His thumb flipped the main breaker into the off position.

The light beneath the door was suddenly gone. Porter shoved a thin metal tool into the lock, and turned the knob.

Everyone but Lipton was in the kitchen. Lipton looked up from his book in the dark. He furrowed his brow, a bit put off by the sudden loss of light.

The instant the lights went out, there was a brief hush in conversation, then a mix of humorous chatter and subtle dismay broke out. The guys loved it. The women, though, had reservations about how long they were willing to spend in the dark with them.

No one heard the gunshot that killed Lipton. By now he had crumbled into a heap at the foot of the overstuffed chair. The coffee table book was spattered with blood.

Darla felt her way to the end of the counter, where a phone was mounted on the wall. The numbers on the phone glowed a sickly yellow in the dark.

"Must be the snow," Lesley said. "It builds up on the power lines."

Everyone nodded in the dark.

Darla dialed the super's office downstairs and

put the phone to her ear. No dial tone. She frowned. "The telephone is down, too."

"You have matches around here anywhere?" someone asked.

There was a coughing sound and a flash of light in the archway that led to the kitchen, followed by a clatter as someone fell to the tile floor.

"What was *that!*" someone yelled in the darkness of the kitchen.

Another quick flash of light and a coughing sound. Someone standing beside Darla, maybe Barry, slumped to his knees, then fell forward lifelessly. There were screams, followed by flashes of gunfire.

Suddenly there was scrambling in the unlit space. Then another flash of light, and another body crashed into a service cart that was parked along a wall. In the chaos, those who remained found themselves tripping over bodies, no one too sure of which way to run. They collided with one another, slipping and fumbling as the tile floor became increasingly slick with blood.

Darla found herself frozen where she stood. She heard a rapid succession of coughing sounds; bullets ringing off of pots and pans. Someone screamed, but that scream was quickly silenced as a body hit the floor. Someone was lying against her leg. She dashed forward, her hands groping blindly in the dark. She felt a hard edge topped with Formica. The island. The flashes of light seemed to be coming from the entrance to the kitchen. She squatted behind the island, with her knees tucked against her chin.

Bullets chipped away at the wooden cabinets.

Suddenly it was quiet. The firing stopped.

There was no more scrambling. No more flashes of light.

Darla could smell the acrid odor of what she suspected was burnt gunpowder. She shook uncontrollably. She was going to die. She knew she was going to be shot but did not know why or by whom.

There were no screams or moans, and she feared she might be the only one of her staff left alive. She began to weep. For what had already happened, and for what she knew was still to come. Now there were footsteps. They drew nearer to her. The footsteps stopped inches from where Darla huddled at the base of the island.

A voice from the darkness said, "Darla Donovan?"

Tears streamed down Darla's face. She was afraid to look up, afraid to open her eyes. Death was imminent, but her instincts had her convinced that as long as she kept her eyes closed, she could prolong the inevitable.

"Are you Darla Donovan?" The voice was stronger this time, more insistent.

She felt a cylinder of warm metal pressed to her forehead.

The tears burned her eyes, and she began to blubber. But she managed to say, "Y . . . yes."

"Where is the videotape?"

She turned her face up, daring to confront the voice in the darkness. There was not enough light to make out a face or a definite shape, only a vague outline of someone standing before her. She was shaking so badly she could hardly enunciate. "What?"

The warm cylinder pressed harder against her head. She knew it was the barrel of a gun.

"Where . . . is . . . the . . . TAPE?"

"I . . . don't understand! What tape?"

The barrel pulled away from her head and an instant later there was a coughing sound and a flash. A bolt of indescribable pain shot up from her thigh. She'd been shot in the leg.

Darla rolled onto her side, clamping her hands around her thigh. Sticky gore seeped between her fingers. She wanted to scream but feared the repercussions.

She felt the metal cylinder press between her eyes again.

"Let's try this one more time," the male voice said. And she had no doubt that his patience was quickly expiring.

Videotape? What was he talking about? Why would she have a videotape worth killing over? None of it made sense. But that did not matter, she decided. All that mattered was that this man, whoever he might be, was dead set on obtaining something she did not have.

"What videotape?" she said, beyond desperation.

"The one you found in your secret little box."

Pure insanity! "I don't know what you're talking about!" Her sobs overpowered her ability to think clearly. "Please . . . *please!* I *swear* . . ."

Speaking to someone else, the voice said, "She's useless." In a moment, he said, "Roger that."

The heat of the cylinder was burning the flesh between her eyes.

"You have two seconds to tell me where it is. One . . ."

Breathlessly, "I *swear*—"

Her brains sprayed throughout the kitchen, speck-ing the cabinetry and the tile floor. Porter kicked her legs out of his way so that he could get by. They were careful to collect each of the spent shell casings. Carmichael had gone back to the front room. She came back now, her gun in one hand and something else in the other.

"What is that?" he asked her.

"Donovan's answering machine," she said.

He nodded. He stepped over a corpse and paused in the front of the oven range. From a fanny pack on his waist, he removed a small device the size and shape of a track-and-field stopwatch. On the back of the device was a small mound of incendiary putty. The front of the device had a digital readout. The readout had been preset. It read: 03:45:00. He opened the oven door, firmly attaching the explosive inside the appliance.

Standing, he reached over the range and turned the gas knob, cranking it clockwise until it would turn no farther. He squatted, leaning in, listening, making certain he could hear the hiss of the gas line. He gave her the thumbs-up. She waved him out.

The explosive he'd planted in the oven would cover their tracks. It would only create a limited det-onation, and the digital device would melt to the size of a guitar pick. An investigation would find that the resident had failed to turn off the gas for the oven after cooking dinner.

They exited the apartment, descending the stairs, the way they'd come. On cue, Lewis reinstated power and telephone communication to the home of Ms. Darla Donovan. He came out an access door and awaited his confederates outside the building.

Desmond had seen only the initial muzzle flash, the shot that had killed Lipton. Less than two minutes later, he'd given the okay to off Donovan. She had had nothing to offer them, and they could not let her live. One of his agents had reported finding something of interest, not the videocassette, but something she said might be of use to them.

For now, he needed to get out of the office building. There'd be quite a pyrotechnics display very shortly. And he didn't want to stick around for it. He radioed them from the Ferrari. They were already at the van. The tape was still at large, so that put them still very much in the thick of a crisis. Another day was coming to an end without results. Tonight he'd have to answer to Mr. Stott, Albertwood, and Shelby—a truly bleak consideration. The only possible upshot would be if the item from Donovan's apartment happened to put him within arm's reach of the videotape. He felt pessimistic, but he uttered a quick chant to the twin gods: Luck and Chance.

26

DEAN AND GRACE WEAVER HAD OWNED THEIR home in Syracuse for the better part of three decades. It was a 2,700-square-foot timber-frame structure, with three bedrooms, a large family room, a well-furnished kitchen, and a large stone fireplace. It had been a great home to raise kids in, and would make a fine place to live when they reached retirement.

The back door was open, and the wind was slapping the storm door against the doorframe. It was late in the evening, Thursday. Dean Weaver shuffled across the patio, his arms heaped with split firewood. He kicked at the storm door, nudging it open with his house shoe enough so that he could catch it against his hip.

The storm door clacked shut behind him. A narrow hallway led from the back door, through the kitchen, dissected another hallway, and ended at the family room. His wife moved the metal screen from in front of the fireplace, and Mr. Weaver carefully added the pieces of split wood to the fire. The flames rose, warming his face. Satisfied, he then headed back the way he'd come, to lock up and turn off the patio light. He was pleased to have both his children home.

Wyatt's hospital bed was set up in his old bedroom. The bed was raised so that he was sitting up. His mother had added a second pillow behind his head. IV stands stood to the side of the bed; tubes ran to his nose and arms. The smile on his face was weak but genuine.

Grace Weaver had brought in a dining room chair for Brooke. Brooke sat right up against the hospital bed, her hand wrapped around Wyatt's fingers.

"I'm glad you came," Wyatt said. His voice was tired, and the act of speaking drained him of whatever tiny reserve of energy he possessed. He would close his eyes for long stretches, even during conversation.

"It's Christmas," Brooke said. "I wasn't going to miss out on the presents, Mr. Wiseguy." She smiled at him. Indeed, he had lost another ten or fifteen pounds since her last visit.

"How is the big city?"

"Big and noisy," she said.

"Are you a star yet?" he said with wink.

"I was *born* a star."

"Amen."

"I'd like you to come stay with me for a few weeks when you get better. You'd love my roommate. In fact there are a lot of girls who'd fall in love with you."

"Women," he said, coughing. "Life's too short. Especially mine. Hey, let's go sit by the fire."

"Are you sure you feel strong enough?"

He nodded.

Brooke called her father in, and they helped Wyatt into the wheelchair.

"Maybe we could go jogging tomorrow," Wyatt said into her ear as she steered him down the hall toward the family room. "I do four miles a day now," he said, perfectly deadpan.

"I bet you do. I could chain this chair behind Dad's car, and get you going about sixty-five."

Wyatt laughed out loud and then coughed until he was gasping for air. Brooke suddenly felt horrible for making him laugh, but knew he needed as much laughter as he could get. Laughter wasn't what ailed him.

She parked Wyatt catty-corner to the fire, where it would be warm, but not too warm. Then she sat cross-legged on the floor beside him. Within a minute or two, he was asleep, his chin against his chest. She walked over and sat beside her mother on the couch. They caught up on news of friends and relatives and neighbors, and Brooke talked about work and how Darla was driving her crazy.

"She sounds nice enough," Mom said.

Brooke nodded. "She is. She's just driven."

Brooke had remembered to phone Darla about an hour after arriving in Syracuse. She phoned the office first, but did not leave a message on the voice mail. She then phoned Darla's apartment, got the machine, and again decided against leaving a message. She was done leaving messages.

Her father was asleep in front of the TV, and her mother was mesmerized by the work in her lap. Brooke stood, and walked to the kitchen. She took the cordless from the wall mount and dialed Darla's home number.

There was no answer, but the machine did not pick up.

Odd, she thought. Darla must have come home and turned off the machine, and had then either gone out again or just wasn't answering. Perhaps she had turned the ringer off. She looked at the clock on the kitchen wall. The party should still be going on.

She dialed the number again. But again, no answer and no machine.

Enough of this, she thought, returning the cordless to the wall mount. *I'll try her in the morning.*

She leaned against the countertop, enjoying the dark and quiet of the kitchen. It smelled of her childhood. Above the sink, through the glass pane of the cabinet door, she spotted her favorite Christmas cocoa mug. Half of the painted-on snowman on the front had rubbed off, and the handle was chipped in two places, but she'd sworn to her mother that if she even *thought* of throwing it out, she would commit her to an old folks' home the first chance she had. One of those really bad ones, she'd promised, where they steal your money and won't change your bedsheets.

Wyatt woke himself up, coughing.

Brooke checked his IV drip and offered him something to drink.

The wind had really picked up outside. It wasn't snowing much, but it was ten degrees colder than in the city. She had arrived late in the afternoon, but in winter the sun went down around 4:30 P.M., so she hadn't gotten to see much of her hometown in daylight. Tomorrow maybe they'd get out and do a little shopping. But getting Wyatt in and out of the car was an ordeal. And if he got really sick while they were out, they'd have to rush back and put him to bed.

It was getting late, and she was tired. She asked Mom if Dad would need help getting Wyatt back into bed.

"You go on," Mom said. "We'll take care of that."

Brooke gave her mom a hug.

"It's good to have you home."

"It's good to be here."

00:00:32 . . . 00:00:31 . . . 00:00:30 . . .

For the past half an hour or more, Miss Landers had been absolutely positive she smelled gas. At first she ignored it, blaming her overactive imagination. Then her curiosity got the best of her, and she began sniffing around her apartment. She went straight to the kitchen, sticking her head in the oven and taking a big long whiff. She roamed from room to room. Curiously, the farther she moved from the front door, the weaker the smell got.

Miss Landers turned down the volume on the television, as if her sniffer might function better once immersed in silence. She raised her nose high in the air, a look of determination in her eyes. As she passed through her front room, the odor drew her toward her front door. She worked her way down into a kneeling position, putting her face as close as she could to the gap beneath the door. Here the odor was strongest. She frowned and went to find her shoes.

Outside her door, she stood in the hallway, catching the scent. Out here it was particularly strong. She walked a dozen paces to the right, and though the odor was still present and strong, the farther she walked the more it faded. She moved back toward her door, and the smell of fumes increased. It seemed to be heaviest just at the door to Darla Donovan's apartment.

Miss Landers frowned. She started to knock on Darla's door but hesitated. Was it her business to deal with a neighbor? Perhaps not. She went back inside her own apartment and shut the door. She picked up the phone and started dialing the super's number. Again, she hesitated. Why get a third party involved? It was a simple matter of broaching the subject to her neighbor, and asking the woman if everything was in order. And if something needed to be fixed, Darla could then contact the super herself.

00:00:12 . . .

Miss Landers approached her neighbor's door. She and Darla were not cozy with each other, but were on good speaking terms, and often aided each other in various capacities when the need arose.

By now she'd grown quite dizzy from the fumes. She raised her thumb to the doorbell button, and for the fleetest of moments reconsidered phoning the super.

00:00:03 . . .

Miss Landers frowned, nearly sick to her stomach because of fumes coming from beneath her neighbor's door. She gathered her resolve, stood her ground, straight and tall, and jabbed the orange-glowing doorbell button with her thumb.

00:00:01 . . . 00:00:00 . . .

The explosion rocked the city for a radius of

about a half a mile. Ada Landers was flash-fried in the span of a nanosecond. Several apartments on either side, as well as above and below the epicenter of the explosion, were decimated. Glass and mortar and brick and steel showered down into the streets below. Cars and pedestrians were crushed by falling debris.

The shock waves set off hundreds of car alarms in the surrounding neighborhoods. Flying debris crashed through the windows of the bank directly across the street, setting off its alarm system. Fires burned big and bright in the enormous gash left in the side of the apartment building.

It would burn for most of the night.

The total number of dead would not be tallied for at least a day, maybe two.

The explosion happened too late for the evening news, but just in time to make the next day's early editions. Photos of massive flames shooting up out of the gutted carcass of the apartment building would be splashed across the front page, and thirty-second snippets would run endlessly on CNN.

It would take weeks or months of investigation to decide upon the point of origin of the explosion, and only after another lengthy investigation would the gas line from a kitchen oven be blamed.

The seven victims of gunshot wounds had been incinerated in the blast.

They listened to it again.

> *"Hey, Darla. It's Brooke. I'm still on the road. I, uh . . . I picked up your mail from the box yesterday . . . and completely forgot about get-*

ting it to you before I took off this morning. I really *apologize*. I feel pretty stupid about it. Anyway, you've got three different items here. Two envelopes. Neither with a return address. One of them has a cheesy little sunflower design in the corner. And there's a parcel wrapped in brown paper—looks and feels like a book or something. And it's got the word Beacon jotted on it. If that stuff rings a bell, leave a message at the number I left with you. They'll be happy to talk your ears off, believe me. Either way, I'll give you a call as soon as I arrive. You can give me eighty lashes when I get back. I'll talk to you later. Bye."

Albertwood hunkered down in his wheelchair, snarling at the digital answering machine on the table. It was the one from Donovan's apartment. He growled at Desmond, "Play it again—just the middle part."

Desmond, who had been standing a few inches from the big round table, with his arms crossed over his chest, reached out a hand, briefly pressed the Rewind button, and then released it.

. . . *two envelopes. Neither with a return address. One of them has a cheesy little sunflower design in the corner. And there's a parcel wrapped in brown paper—looks and feels like a book or something. And it's got the word* Beacon *jotted on it* . . .

"Again?" Desmond asked after he had pressed Pause.

Albertwood shook his head. "No."

They were in Albertwood's penthouse in Trump Tower. Albertwood had flown into New York on his Bell 430 helicopter, where he was met by Desmond. After the discovery of the phone message, Desmond had anxiously phoned Mr. Stott, to relay the news. Mr. Stott instructed him to contact Albertwood.

The two of them were alone in the room. Shelby was on the speakerphone.

"We've found it, gentlemen," Shelby said from his office in Washington, D.C.

"It's not good enough just to *find* it," Albertwood grunted. "We have to *possess* it. It must be in our hands. Nothing less will do."

Desmond said, "The girl with the tape works for Donovan. That should make remedial work of finding her. We track her down, get the tape, kill her, and the crisis is resolved."

"I agree," Shelby said.

Albertwood nodded. He sat with his clawed hands groping the armrests of his wheelchair.

Clearly, they had made light-years of progress in the last hour. They knew who possessed the tape. Now all they had to do was get it in their hands.

"We know she has a package," Desmond said. "But can we be absolutely certain it's from Ettinger?"

"Yes," Shelby said over the speaker mounted in the phone console. "In the message, she mentions the word *Beacon*. That was the code name the Secret Service gave James Ettinger. I'm actually astonished that he used something so obvious."

"The problem is that her message says she is out of town," Shelby said. "So where is she? And for how long?"

"We know the girl's name is Brooke, and that she works in the news division at NBC," Desmond said. "I should have a New York address for her within the hour. But finding where she is at the moment is a different challenge."

"She has to disappear, *forever*," Albertwood said. "This all still has to do with Ettinger and his death. I want Belfast to finish the job he started."

Over the phone line, Shelby said, "You said yourself that Belfast was going into retirement. You'll never find him."

Albertwood coughed hoarsely, then said, "I already have."

"Oh?"

"He is here in New York, waiting to be paid. I've had him followed. He's with a girl."

"What if he refuses the job?"

"Then he doesn't get paid," Albertwood said.

"And if he doesn't care about the money?"

"Then . . ." Albertwood began, "we are forced to conduct business on a more personal level."

"Ah," Shelby said. "We use the girl."

"That is correct, Mr. Shelby," Albertwood said. "If Belfast is difficult and refuses to cooperate, we use the girl."

The president excused himself from a meeting to take the call. He could barely contain a smile.

"Have we got it?" the president asked.

"We're close," Shelby said. "We are doing all we can as fast as we can."

President Yates lit a cigar, exhaled in relief, blowing smoke at the ceiling fan. He thought he'd held up pretty well after six-plus years in office, but the last seventy-two hours had cut him down to size. He had confronted one crisis after another during his administration. He could handle the Russians and their nuclear warheads. The oil-mongers over in Sand Land were a walk in the park. Even the Communists in the East hadn't caused him nearly as much stress.

"What kind of timeline are we talking here, Glen?"

Glen Shelby hated that the president used his name over the phone. If things ever broke down somewhere along the line and worse came to worst, he could deny a lot of crap, but if any of this found its way onto tape, it would be a tough bullet to dodge. His skills as a lawyer could only carry him through so much, then he'd have to face the music with everybody else. But, with any luck, it would never come to that.

"I really couldn't say, Mr. President."

"Glen . . ."

"Twenty-four to thirty-six hours." Shelby sighed, suddenly sweating out of every pore on his body.

"Less than two days?"

"Best-case scenario."

"Call me the instant you hear *anything*," the president said.

Shelby hung up the phone and sat for a long moment, just holding his breath. They were close. So close it was scary. If they managed to pull this off and cover their tracks, it would be a miracle. He thought about the assassin called Belfast. If anyone on the planet could find the girl with the tape and ensure its safe return, Belfast was the man.

He found his secret stash of Camels and lit one, hoping his wife was fast asleep and wouldn't smell the smoke. The only light in the room came from an ornate lamp on his desk. He kicked his feet up on his desk and crossed them at the ankles. It was after midnight.

He thought of how far they'd been and how far they had yet to go. He thought about Yates and Albertwood and Desmond and Stott. But most of all his thoughts were of Belfast.

27

MORNING CREPT INTO THE WEAVER HOUSE. As a family, they were generally early risers. But the cold made it hard to venture out from beneath the warm blankets. Dean Weaver headed straight for the woodpile at the back of the house. Gas prices were up again, so lately he had kept the fire blazing in an effort to ward off higher utility bills.

Brooke lay in bed awake for half an hour before she bundled herself in heavy socks and a robe, and went across the hall to the bathroom. She stared at herself in the mirror, rubbing her bleary eyes. She washed her face at the sink and patted herself dry with a hand towel hanging from a plastic ring on the wall.

Coffee was brewing in the kitchen. Brooke could smell it from the far end of the house. She returned to her old bedroom and slipped into a pair of sweat bottoms and one of Wyatt's old baggy New York Islanders sweatshirts. She ducked her head inside Wyatt's bedroom. He was fast asleep, facing away from the door.

Brooke stood with her back to the fireplace, soaking up the warmth of the fire and the aroma of brewing coffee.

"Ah, how are you feeling this morning, honey?" her mother said, rounding the corner from the kitchen.

"Like a spring chicken," Brooke said.

Her mother pecked her on the cheek.

"Did Wyatt get through the night okay?" Brooke asked. She was a light sleeper but hadn't heard much hacking or coughing coming from across the hall. Per her routine, Grace had made numerous checkups throughout the night, making sure that there were no complications.

"I think he slept just fine. Nights are always hardest for him, you know. He dreads them. But he needs the rest. I think the dark is what bothers him the most. It's depressing. The sunshine keeps his spirits up a little better. He's been so excited to know that you were coming up. He has missed his little sister a lot."

"I know. I miss him, too." Brooke rubbed her hands together behind her back. The back of her sweatshirt was now pretty warm to the touch. She scooched forward a few inches in her stocking feet. "It's killed me not to be up here more, especially since he's gotten worse."

"Don't let that bother you, honey. He knows you've got an important job and that you're busy. He's so proud of you. I'd say he brags on you even more than your father and I." Grace put an arm around her daughter's shoulders. "And believe me, that's saying something."

"I'm proud of him too, Mom."

There was a sound outside the front door. Through the window blinds, Brooke could see her father in his gum rubber boots, trudging up the sidewalk through the snow. He had retrieved the morning paper. She could see it in his left hand, bound in a clear-blue plastic bag and rubber bands. He stepped onto the front porch and stomped his boots on the doormat. The front door opened and he marched in, bending to unlace the boots on the tiled half-moon of the entryway. He looked up at her and smiled. His cheeks and nose were pink.

"Ahoy there!" he beamed.

"Ahoy, sailor!" Brooke laughed.

Her dad held the paper up proudly. "Come rain or shine, blizzard or drought," he said, "I gots to have my paper."

The few seconds he'd held the front door open had let in a cool draft. Brooke backed closer to the fire.

Grace poked her head around the corner. "French toast in five minutes."

"You do still eat breakfast, right, city girl?" her father said, unfurling the morning paper.

Brooke shrugged. "Usually I only manage to choke down a half a raisin bagel with a tall cup of coffee."

"Well, your mother won't be satisfied unless you gain six or seven pounds during the holidays," he said.

"I guess I'll have to do calisthenics in front of the fireplace."

She noticed movement down the hall and saw the door to Wyatt's bedroom slowly swinging open. The chrome of his wheelchair gleamed in the morning light. "Ladies and gentlemen, Elvis has left the bedroom. *Thankyouverymuch*," he said as he patiently maneuvered down the hallway.

"Morning, Sunshine! I hope you're hungry," Brooke said, wheeling him toward the kitchen.

"Mom's frying up one of her famous artery-clogging breakfasts."

"Only kind I'll eat," Wyatt said.

Brooke's father brought his newspaper with him to the table. He settled into his chair at the head of the table, and shuffled through to the sports section. "The Nicks ate it again last night," he said to no one in particular.

Brooke parked her brother at the table and then flopped in a chair next to him. There were cartons of milk and orange juice on the table. She poured herself a small glass of juice.

Grace worked in front of the oven range, occasionally wiping her hands on her apron. She carried two serving dishes to the dining area, setting them on braided hot pads on the table.

"Everything smells *great*," Brooke said.

"Well, eat up, because there's plenty," Grace said, turning back to the kitchen.

Wyatt insisted on pouring his own milk. His thin arm strained to hold the carton of milk steady as the white stream gurgled in the bottom of his glass. There were splotches on the tablecloth where he'd missed his target. Brooke watched her brother, wanting to help him, but knowing that it was important that he feel that he was still capable of performing certain basic tasks for himself.

Curls of steam rose from the griddle. Dean worked his fork like a surgeon's tool. Without tearing his eyes from the sports page, he reached blindly toward the center of the table and grabbed the squeeze-bottle of ketchup. He squirted a whole blob on the side of his plate.

Wyatt went through the laborious process of transferring a fried egg to his plate. The result was a broken yoke. It oozed in streams, forming a yellow perimeter around his French toast. He glared at the mess for a moment, then cut a glance at his sister.

"I like to mix my food," he said with a shrug and a grin.

"It all winds up in the same place, anyway," Brooke said, then sipped her juice.

"Hey," Wyatt said, "how about some of that world-famous coffee of yours?"

"Coming right up, mister," Grace said, backing her chair away from the table.

"Keep your seat, Mom. I've got it." Brooke jumped to her feet and grabbed a coffee mug from the cabinet. "I can't tell you how nice it is to be away from the city for a while. It took me quite some time to decompress during the train ride up here. But the ride forced me to mellow out and catch up on a little sleep. And it's so peaceful up here. You don't know how badly I've missed *trees*, of all things."

Grace said, "I'm relieved you got here safely. I kept expecting to see your train overturned on one of those news reports."

"Yeah, we saw a lot of folks who'd slid off the road."

"Serves 'em right for getting out in this weather," Dean said, never looking up from the page before him. His mouth was full. "People can't stay home for ten minutes. Run,run,run . . . that's all it is."

Brooke's mother rolled her eyes.

"Yeah," Wyatt piped in. "Shoot, it's looking like I'll have to invest in snow chains for my wheelchair.

Otherwise I'll have to quit my job as a welder down at the docks."

"Welder? Uh, *yeah*." Brooke fiddled with her utensils.

"I for one will sleep better at night when you move somewhere less hostile," Grace said, peppering her eggs.

"New York is fine, Mom," Brooke said.

"Brooky here is bulletproof, Mom," Wyatt said.

"It's a mother's job to worry, you two," Grace responded. "Otherwise, I'd have nothing to do. Every time I see something on the news about someone being shot or getting into an accident, I'm always glad to know that the two of you are safe. Like those poor people in that apartment building last night. One minute everything was fine, and they were going on about their lives. The next minute— *Whooooosh!!!*—the whole place explodes in a ball of flames."

"We don't live in Libya, Mom," Wyatt said.

"It wasn't Libya. It was right there in New York City."

"What?" Brooke raised her head. "An apartment building in New York?"

"Mmmhmm."

"That's terrible. Where?"

"I'm not exactly sure. It's been on CNN all morning. They don't know if it was an accident or what. Pretty scary stuff," Grace said, shaking her head woefully.

"Probably a terrorist," Dean added from behind his paper.

Brooke's news instincts took over. She just couldn't

miss out on a good story. She headed for the front room. She turned on the TV and flipped through channels until she landed on *Headline News*. They were making the half-hour financial report. That meant she'd missed the top stories and would have to wait for it to come around in the rotation. She returned to the kitchen and took her plate from the table, taking it with her to the front room.

"Don't get anything on the carpet," Grace said behind her.

Brooke sat cross-legged on the floor in front of the TV, her plate on her lap. She picked at her French toast as she flipped slowly through the cable channels. The fire felt good on the side of her face.

It took ten minutes to hit on anything about the explosion.

"Oh, my gosh," she said, watching the footage of flames shooting from the rubble. She set her plate down on the carpet beside her. She studied the network footage, drawn to something eerily familiar, which she couldn't immediately put her finger on.

Wyatt steered his wheelchair into the front room. "What gives?" he said.

"Shhh."

They watched the television screen together in silence.

Finally, Brooke said, "I'm waiting for them to give an address. Something . . ." She shook her head. "There's something familiar about that building."

"You know that building?"

"Maybe, yeah, I think . . ."

The footage showed firefighters dousing the blaze with long hoses. Smoke rose high above the destruction. On the screen, reporters interviewed witnesses in the street, asking them what had happened. There were shots of the dead and injured being spirited away on stretchers and then loaded into ambulances. Text appeared at the bottom of the screen, identifying the location of the explosion.

Brooke's jaw dropped. "Please, God, no!"

"What? What?" Wyatt sat up straight in his wheelchair.

Brooke had jumped to her feet. She backed away from the television set. "No,no,no!!!" Her voice had risen in her distress, bringing her parents into the room.

"What is it, dear? What's wrong?" her mother asked, wiping her mouth with a corner of her apron.

"What's the problem?" Dean Weaver insisted, his newspaper trailing from his fist at his side.

Brooke Weaver stood ashen-faced. Her eyes looked as big around as soup cans, unblinking. "Darla!" she said. "That's Darla's apartment building!"

"No way," Wyatt said.

Brooke turned and dashed for the kitchen. She jerked the cordless phone from the wall and in her panic misdialed Darla's home number several times. She finally got all the digits punched in their proper order and listened to the line ring. She could barely contain herself.

"Comeoncomeoncomeon!" she muttered, staring at the countertop. "Darla, come on, pick it up. Answer the phone!" She could hear Wyatt and her parents talking in the front room, all of them clearly baffled by the situation.

There was no answer.

She dialed again.

Still no answer.

She hung up, then dialed Darla's office number. The voice mail picked up. She left a frantic message, "Darla, this is Brooke. Are you all right? I just saw the fire on the news. Please call me the minute you get in. I'm worried sick."

She hung up.

She dialed Darla's cell phone. No answer.

She tried again, praying that she'd misdialed the first time.

Again, no answer.

Then it occurred to her to try someone else in their production team to find out what was going on. She dialed Joyce's desk. There was no answer. She took a deep breath and dialed Lesley. No answer. Lipton Stephenson. His voice mail picked up.

She had failed to get ahold of a single member of their team. She hung up, brushing her fingers through her hair. Perhaps they'd gone to lunch together. But she glanced at the clock on the wall. It was still early morning. They should be at work by now, but the day had just begun. Everyone should be busy. A meeting, perhaps?

Then a terrible, terrible thought bubbled up in her mind. A thought so horrendous it frightened her to even consider it. She pulled over a kitchen chair and sat down. *Oh no, please no,* she thought, closing her eyes and taking a deep breath.

The Christmas party.

They would have all been at the party.

Brooke suddenly felt a sick lump in her stomach. *Okay,* she told herself, *remain calm, just remain calm. Take a deep breath and relax. There is a perfectly good explanation for what is going on.* But she knew there was not a perfectly good explanation. They had all been at the party—Darla, Barry, Joyce, Lipton, Connor, Jill, Lesley—and they had all been in the explosion.

Time seemed to stop. For a long moment, she forgot where she was.

Her hands began to tremble. She felt quite sure she would vomit.

She dialed the phone. A female voice picked up. "NBC News, this is Mandy."

"Mandy, this is Brooke Weaver."

There was a pause.

"Brooke? Oh, thank *goodness!* We all thought for sure . . . I mean, you didn't show up this morning and nobody answered the phone at your apartment, so we thought you'd been with the—"

"Mandy, where's Darla, and the others on the team?" Brooke said, her head growing dizzy with each passing second.

"You mean . . . you don't . . . you haven't heard?"

Brooke hung up the phone.

Her stomach began to lurch. The spasm grew stronger. It was all coming up. She rose from the chair and stumbled toward the bathroom, passing through the edge of the front room, heading down the hall.

"Brooke? Sweetheart?" her mother called after her.

"What's going on?" she thought she heard her father say.

She made it through the bathroom door, but she

hit the linoleum hard on her knees, barely managing to brace herself with her outstretched hands. She was breathless, her heart hammering in her chest. Her knees were like rubber, too shaky for her to stand. She was vaguely aware of the sounds of her family coming down the hall after her.

As she balanced there on the bathroom floor on her hands and knees, a mental picture flashed into her mind's eye: it was her seven friends, talking and laughing in the final seconds before the apartment building went up in smoke and flames.

Another call had been answered at the NBC studios at Rockefeller Plaza at a different desk, a few minutes earlier.

A female voice asked, "I'd like to speak to Darla Donovan."

"I'm sorry, Ms. Donovan is not in this morning," a woman at the reception desk said. "Would you like to leave a message?"

"No. No. How about Brooke? Could I speak to her?"

"Brooke *Weaver?*"

"Excuse me?"

The receptionist clarified herself, exactly as the caller had assumed she would. "Brooke Weaver is one of Ms. Donovan's assistants."

"Ah, of course. Yes, could I speak with Brooke Weaver?"

"I'm sorry, Ms. Weaver is not in the office this morning, either. I would be happy to—"

The line was disconnected.

The call had come from a pay phone a block

away. Carmichael, still wearing the brown wig, hung up the phone and turned to Lewis, who was standing beside her.

"Bingo," she said.

"Let's go," he said.

They hurried to the van and climbed in.

Carmichael dialed a cell phone from the passenger's seat.

"What?" Desmond said, answering the phone in Julius Albertwood's penthouse at Trump Tower.

"Her name is Brooke Weaver," Carmichael said.

Porter sat at a table near Desmond, with a laptop computer before him. Desmond nodded at him, and said, "Brooke Weaver."

Porter rattled the computer keys. In four minutes they had a phone number and an address.

Twenty minutes later, Lewis and Carmichael exited the apartment. Terri Bryant had told them everything they needed to know to find Brooke Weaver. They had found her in bed, sleeping off a bit of a hangover. They slit her throat and left her in the bathtub with the shower curtain drawn. Afterward, they stole the cash and credit cards from her purse and tossed the apartment. The police would think it was a robbery gone bad. Carmichael grabbed a framed photo of an all-white family; Brooke Weaver and her family, she assumed.

Now they knew where Brooke Weaver had been headed when she left the message on Darla Donovan's answering machine. She'd gone home to Mommy and Daddy. And they had a picture of her. Everything now seemed pretty clear-cut. Belfast should have no problem finding her in Syracuse.

28

THE PHOTO OF ARIEL HAD GOTTEN HIM nowhere. Joel had spent a long, cold night outside the apartment building on East Fifty-seventh. He'd gone almost entirely without food, and entirely without sleep. And now he was violently ill.

A hacking cough was ripping his chest out through his throat. He had a fever, he was sure of it. His head was pounding. What a stupid, stupid decision, he thought.

The night before, desperate for a lead, he had stood outside the front doors to the apartment building, approaching residents of the apartment as they came and went, showing them the black-and-white photocopy, asking if they recognized the face. Most folks ignored him, hurrying on through the door or out to catch a cab. Canvassing the apartment had turned into an abysmal dead end. Every ten minutes he fought the urge to call Crouder for an update.

He found a grimy little dive down the street and huddled over a steaming cup of coffee at a table against the wall. He sat coughing until his face was purple and his voice went hoarse. He could now barely talk. *Stupid, stupid, stupid!!!!* Maybe this was how it should end, he thought. Maybe this was a sign, a sign that he was meant to fail.

Megan was out there somewhere, but in his condition he could not go on searching for her. He felt like he was going to die. He needed a doctor. He was freezing, yet his flesh was hot to the touch. How his growing momentum from twenty-four hours ago had slammed to such a complete and absolute halt, he couldn't understand. He was growing increasingly depressed.

Leaving the coffee shop, he found a small, corner grocery and purchased a bottle of cold and flu formula. It was increasingly hard to focus, let alone navigate the busy city streets.

After all he'd been through in the last four days, after the peaks of emotion and flood tide of adrenaline, after entertaining the prospects of reuniting with his daughter, his only present desire was to simply make it back to his hotel room and pass out in bed until sometime tomorrow.

The Ducati motorcycle was parked at the curb between a Chevy Cavalier and a Fiat. The face shield on the rider's helmet was flipped up. He saw Belfast and the girl come out of the Waldorf-Astoria and hail a cab. It was 10 A.M.

As the taxi merged with traffic, R'mel flipped down his face shield, and the Ducati pulled away from the curb, fishtailing slightly as the rear tire fought for traction on a patch of ice. R'mel gunned the throttle, accelerating through traffic, making sure to keep the cab in view. At Fifth Avenue, the girl got out of the cab. She blew a kiss at the rear window, then spun on her heels and pranced off for a morning of shopping. Behind the face shield, R'mel smiled.

St. John was anxious. It was Friday morning, and he was just flat-out ready to put this whole circus behind him. Once the money was in place, he could shake off this anxiety.

He was glad that Megan was going to spend the rest of the morning shopping. He'd outfitted her with a string of credit cards—cards with no limits. He'd told her to go crazy, but he knew she was not like that. For her, life wasn't about the money. She loved him and would always love him. The money, if anything, was about security. It would allow them to focus on each other rather than worrying about how to pay the mortgage or where their next meal would come from. Sure, she'd grow accustomed to the finer things, but he was convinced that she'd not even flinch if he announced that he wanted to give the money away.

From the very beginning, he had called himself Belfast. A killer for hire could not feasibly use his given name when doing business. The only way to function, to carry on a normal existence outside of his chosen occupation, was to maintain an alias. When he was little, his family had had an Irish setter named Belfast. St. John had loved the dog.

He had managed to rigorously protect his birth name. It would have been devastating for his true identity to ever be made known to those with whom he came into contact in his profession. But now, after more than a decade of bearing the enigmatic label of

Belfast, the time had come to rid himself of the name forever.

The payment of $5.9 million U.S. was to be wired to an offshore account in the name of one Charles Masnad. St. John would then have the money transferred to a web of accounts throughout the Caribbean and Europe. Eventually, the money would wind up in six banks in Europe—five with one million dollars each, and one with nine hundred thousand dollars. There the money would remain until needed. By that time, "Belfast" would be no more. There was a knot in the pit of his stomach. *Just let this morning be the end of it*, he thought. There should be a small yellow envelope in the bank box. The envelope would contain the account number in the Caribbean where his fortune awaited him. St. John called the driver's attention to the bank ahead of them. "That's it," he said.

The driver honked at a Volkswagen sedan, then swerved into the right lane. He put the transmission in park and said something over the seat at St. John. St. John peeled off several bills, and folded them into the man's hands.

R'mel spoke into the mike in his helmet. He was instructed to hold his position outside the bank and wait for further instructions. He steered the bike up alongside the curb, within sight of the bank, and used the heel of his boot to knock down the kickstand.

They saw the girl. She was walking leisurely, with a look of contentment on her face, her mind a thousand miles away—everything pie-in-the-sky. They only needed a few seconds. Before she understood what was happening, it would be too late. Game over.

He patiently went through the routine. The bank employee smiled at St. John as he set the box on the table.

"Just let me know when you're done," the man said.

St. John nodded in return.

When he was alone in the room, he pulled out a chair and sat at the table. The box sat before him. There was no reason to delay any further.

He inserted his key and turned it. He lifted the lip and peered inside.

A ribbon of warmth and gladness lifted in his stomach. There inside the box was a yellow envelope. He reached in and pulled it out. Just the act of holding it in his hand was like taking the first, broad step away from his old life. He let out the long, deep breath that he had held ever since the bank employee had gone to retrieve the deposit box for him.

Could it really be over? It was hard not to break into a full smile, right there at the table. He wished Megan were sitting there beside him so that he could wrap his arms around her and kiss her on the mouth. This envelope would tell him how to find his money. Then Belfast would be a part of the past, and Olin St. John could step into the future and live the way a man was meant to live.

He pushed the metal box away and flipped the envelope around so that he could run his finger beneath the flap. The paper tore as he worked his finger along the edge. He took a breath, and smiled, then removed the folded card. He opened the card, read what was written, and the smile evaporated.

R'mel spoke into the mike in his helmet. He thumbed the ignition switch, and the Ducati eased away from the curb. It was time to move again.

Belfast had emerged, clearly in a huff. R'mel knew to hang back. Belfast's reputation preceded him. Belfast could kill him with a pencil through the ear in the time it would take to blink.

He watched him stop at a pay phone half a block dead ahead.

St. John was infuriated. The folded card was in his hand. He dug a fist into a pocket, looking for change. He snatched up the pay phone and looked at the phone number written on the card. The number had a Manhattan prefix, and the suffix began with 9, which told him he was calling a pay phone.

This was bad. Very bad, indeed.

The arrangement had always been simple: he did the job, the wiring information was left in the bank box, and then he transferred the money wherever he desired. This development, though, was highly out of the ordinary. And that made the hairs on the back of his neck stand up straight and tall. He struggled to remain cool. He wanted his money, that was all.

A bitterly cold wind rushed down through the street, but he did not notice. He looked up ahead on the sidewalk, at the faces going in any and every direction. Then he pivoted and looked down the way he'd come. A city bus had stopped a few hundred feet behind him, and passengers were boarding. Several car lengths behind the bus, a man with a helmet sat on an idling motorcycle.

He had to get control of himself. He hadn't survived the past decade by sweating every unexpected development. But something wasn't right. In fact, every molecule of instinct was telling him that something was very wrong.

He inserted the correct change into the pay phone and punched in the number, slowly, one digit at a time. He pressed his hand against the side of the phone booth and closed his eyes.

The call was answered on the first ring.

29

THE SUBWAY TRAIN CAME TO A GRINDING HALT and the doors slid open. A few passengers wandered in and out. St. John stood and exited. The voice on the phone had told him where to go. The instructions had been brief but precise. He found the rest room exactly where he'd been told it would be. A nervous flutter ran through his belly.

He stole up behind a trash receptacle and eased his Glock from a coat pocket, checking that the clip was fully loaded—he had come for his money but had no plans to die for it.

There was a derelict asleep on the ground on the other side of the trash receptacle. St. John stepped around with caution. He eased along the wall and stopped at the mouth of the rest room. There was grime and graffiti on the walls. Banks of fluorescent bulbs spewed puke yellow light on the tiled floor. He eased inside, his senses and instincts on full alert. He glanced over his shoulder to make sure the derelict hadn't moved.

A cinder block partition divided the bathroom entrance from the remainder of the rest room. He kept one hand in the coat pocket with the Glock. He stopped. The old paranoia was back. His palms were suddenly sweaty. His hand tensed around the gun.

It had been thirty minutes since he'd found the yellow envelope in the bank box. In that time, he'd had to think through his options. Something was afoot. Were they reneging on the payment? Was it their plan to get him alone and put a bullet through his brain? He'd made it very clear to those who needed to know, that the James Ettinger job was his last. His decision had not been questioned. There was no fuss.

True, this was the largest payment he'd demanded in his career, but they'd seemed willing enough to pay. There had been no quibbling; his client apparently had very deep pockets. Taking out the vice president of the United States was no small order, so his price had been steep. And if they had made a fuss, he would have politely declined the assignment. But they hadn't. The 5.9 had been acceptable to all parties involved.

What then? The voice on the phone had been vague. He was to meet someone named Albertwood.

The ground rumbled underfoot as a subway train roared past outside the rest room. It created a breeze that cooled the sweat on his face. The rest room had the stink of neglect. He was mindful of any hint of movement, any alteration of heat or light.

He stood with his shoulder against the partition, facing a corner where the wall opposite him led into the open expanse of the rest room. He parted his lips to speak, running his tongue along his lower lip. He breathed in and out, his eyes fixed on the opposite wall; if there was a shift in light from within, that was where it would show up. Finally, he called out, somewhat tentatively, "Albertwood?"

His voice boomed off the walls and the tile floor, and carried outside the rest room, where it finally died out over the tracks. The sound of his own voice startled him. It reminded him of how alone he was down here.

"In here," a voice said.

St. John tightened his grip on the gun. It was not the voice from the phone; the voice from the phone had been more muscular.

"Please, come forward."

St. John eased into the light.

There was a row of urinals opposite a long countertop fitted with rows of metal sinks. The mirrors above the countertop had all been broken out. There was a small, round drain in the center of the room, to which the floor on all sides sloped. Beyond the row of urinals were six or seven toilet stalls. St. John would have liked to check the stalls. If he'd had earlier notification of this little rendezvous, he'd have staked it out, to know the terrain. But, of course, that was the reason it had been sprung on him. They wanted him shaken. They wanted him off guard.

In the center of the expanse sat an old man in a wheelchair. His lips were drawn back in a sickening grin. He looked ancient. One hand lay across his lap. The other gripped the steering wand on the wheelchair. His long gray hair was fastened in a ponytail that looped around over his shoulder. He was a grotesque sight.

"Albertwood?"

"Of course. Thank you for coming on such short notice."

St. John had his finger on the trigger. He stood tall, facing the old man and wondering where this all might lead.

"I apologize for the inconvenience and for the change of plans. If you plan on using the gun in your pocket, I'd have to discourage it on the basis of the three automatic weapons aimed at you at this moment," Julius Albertwood said. He was pleased. He could have had Desmond handle this matter, even Shelby. He could have simply shown up and watched. But to have a legendary assassin on the ropes was more than he could bear to pass up. Very few had ever seen Belfast. He hadn't been photographed since his teens. Many did not believe he existed. As with Carlos the Jackal, no one knew for certain whether the man behind the name was a myth. Actually, he appeared younger than Albertwood had imagined. No one knew his birth date or age. Hiring him was no easy matter, either.

A ghost in the flesh, Albertwood thought. All the stories he'd heard were chilling. He was all too familiar with Belfast's work. He was a fan, in fact. It was heartening to find the legendary Belfast so human after all. He was really just a kid. He'd seen and done a lot, traveled many miles, but in the end he was just a kid with weaknesses. Weaknesses that could be exploited.

Looming retirement had blinded Belfast, mused Albertwood. He'd gotten sloppy in these last days. He'd allowed himself to be spotted and to be tailed. He'd fallen in love—amateur mistake. Love deadens the survival instincts. And perhaps he thought he was being cautious, even with the girl. But her mere presence had divided his attention. Every second spent with his eyes on the girl was a gap in his defense. Of course, even as he congratulated himself, Albertwood never let Belfast's potency slip far from his mind. There was at that moment enough lead pointed at the assassin to ground a zeppelin.

St. John did not move his head. His eyes found the toilet stalls, and he had to assume that at least one gunman had followed him into the hellhole, but he did not turn to find out. He'd gone against his better judgment, coming here, and now he felt like a fool. But if they'd simply wanted to kill him, it would have been easy enough to take care of the job on the street. He removed his hand from the coat pocket.

Albertwood signaled his approval with a slight nod.

"I've come for my money," St. John said.

The wheelchair surged forward twelve or eighteen inches, Albertwood's upper body jerking from the sudden thrust. He controlled the machine with three fingers curled around the shaft of the steering wand. "Payment will be forthcoming, I can assure you. It will be wired to your account, as prescribed. In addition, a second payment of three million dollars will be wired. Both payments will be available when completion of your new assignment is confirmed."

New assignment? A plume of fury rose in St. John's chest. He could feel the sudden heat spreading across his face. "I have retired," he said.

Albertwood ignored him. "Because of an unforeseen development, your further services are required."

"I'm not interested."

"When you've completed this task, you will be paid in full. Until that time, you will receive nothing."

"I want only what is owed me."

"That is not an option, Mr. Belfast," Albertwood said.

St. John touched his right hand to the lump in his coat pocket. He could kill Albertwood with a single blow to the larynx. The old man saw the movement but ignored it; he was ninety and paralyzed, and had been within spitting distance of the grave too long to fear it.

"Like I said, my services are no longer for sale—at any price."

"It's a lot of money, Mr. Belfast."

"Keep your money."

The old man stirred where he sat. He released his grip on the steering wand and raised his good hand, fishing something from a pouch strapped to his armrest. "Syracuse, New York. There you are to find a woman named Brooke Weaver. She has gone there to visit her parents for Christmas. She has in her possession a VHS videocassette. You are to return the videocassette to me. Payment will be made upon delivery."

Olin St. John, enraged, turned to go.

"Before you go . . . ," Albertwood called out.

He ignored the old man.

"I've enjoyed the company of your fiancée."

A cold spike shivered down his spine. He turned slowly.

The old man's posture hadn't changed. He was still a stooped, crippled, grinning . . . freak.

"What?"

Albertwood held a small manila envelope in his good hand. He set it on the corroded corner of a metal sink. "Megan is safe. She will remain in excellent health until midnight, tomorrow. If you are mathematically impaired, that's thirty-six hours from now. If I have the videocassette by then, you will have Megan and eight-point-nine million dollars— not bad for a day's work. I don't think it's necessary to discuss the alternative, do you?"

He staggered back a step, then braced, and took a long stride forward. He had made a catastrophic error. There had been absolutely no need—*none*—to take this job. He was among the wealthiest one percent of the population on earth. All he'd had to do was walk away. Marry the woman he loved, and walk away. Simple as that.

His ears were buzzing. The room spun. All his instincts had crashed and burned around him. He could have passed on the offer to kill Ettinger, and some other hired gun would have gotten a shot at him. Nobody was as good as he, but he was no magician. He'd simply mastered his craft. Now this was no longer just about him, this had become completely about Megan. They had her. And she could be dead by midnight tomorrow.

"How did you—"

"What's important is that you have only thirty-six hours, and the clock is ticking," Albertwood said.

"Where is she?"

"Where she will be at twelve A.M. Sunday morning is the only relevant question, Mr. Belfast."

St. John had a sudden impulse to jam a key

through the old man's throat. He could saw the man in half with three swift strokes. In the past, he'd done more with less. If indeed they had Megan, most likely they'd kill her anyway. This was his one shot at vengeance. If not, they might kill him in addition to Megan.

Could the old man be bluffing? The question hovered over the shifting waters of his mind. If so, where did he get her name? Then it hit him: the bank, he'd been followed from the bank yesterday. The realization was like vinegar in his mouth. In his newfound bliss, he'd disregarded the rules that had kept him alive all these years. The rules had been his lifeblood. And now he was bleeding.

"Where do I bring the videocassette?"

Albertwood made a sweeping gesture with his good hand. "Call the same number you received from the bank box. It is a pay phone, but I assure you the call will reach me."

A thumb between the ribs, St. John mused, that's what the old man needed.

"Now, if you'll excuse me," Albertwood said, manipulating the steering wand on the armrest. The wheelchair motor whirred to life and the wheels squeaked on the tile.

St. John watched him go.

His gut told him that the envelope on the corner of the sink contained a photograph. His chest was tight, his breathing forced. He took a hesitant step forward. Then another.

The photograph was facedown in the envelope. He snatched it out with two fingers, holding it down at his side for a long moment. He then strode across to the entrance to the scummy rest room. The subway tracks stood before him, running into infinity in either direction. He looked both ways and saw no trace of Albertwood or his henchmen.

Then he raised the photograph, and saw Megan's face, a gag of duct tape twined around her head and a Colt .45 automatic shoved in her ear.

30

WHEN SHE CALMED DOWN, SHE PLACED ANOTHER call to NBC. Yes, it was Darla's apartment that had exploded, but neither Darla nor the other six NBC employees had been accounted for. Rescue crews were still sifting through the rubble, searching for survivors. Everyone seemed relieved to hear that Brooke had not been in the building. Next, she phoned her apartment. There was no answer, which didn't astonish her. Terri came and went like the tides, only not nearly as predictably. She lay on her bed, staring at the ceiling. She should have been dead. The talking heads on the news were saying that a possible gas leak was suspected. Someone had likely lit a candle or a cigarette and the place ignited. It would be, they said, weeks or months before anything more specific was known.

She was supposed to be at that party. And she would have been, had her mother not phoned her with word of Wyatt's decline. She stared at the ceiling, raising her hands above her face, studying her fingers, moving them in a wavy motion. She was alive. Her eyes filled with tears. As she slept last night, Darla's apartment was ablaze.

The tears streamed down the sides of her face. She closed her eyes and stared into the dark void. She pressed her hands to her face, weeping violently.

There was a knock at the door. Grace Weaver poked her head in the door. "Sweetie, you all right?"

Brooke wiped the streaked tears from her cheeks with the backs of her hands. "Yeah," she sniffed. "Yeah, Mom. I'm okay."

"You want some soup or something?"

"No. Thanks. I'd just like to be alone."

Her mother nodded, offered a sympathetic smile, and withdrew, shutting the door behind her. Her face ached. She would have to see about catching a flight back to the city in the next day or so. If Darla and the others were in fact dead, there would be a ton of details to be taken care of. She would be needed in the office. She would have to—

Something needled her. Something from the back of her mind.

She rose from the bed and opened the door, marching down the hall to the kitchen.

Her mother was working on the breakfast dishes, rinsing them and stacking them in neat rows in the dishwasher.

"Mom?"

Her mother looked up from her chore, and smiled.

"Where'd Dad put today's paper?"

"It's in the magazine rack beside his chair in the family room."

Brooke ran in and grabbed the local paper, staring dumbfounded at the front-page headline: **VP ETTINGER ASSASSINATED.**

"Mom!" She felt breathless.

"What? What?" Grace Weaver headed toward her daughter's frantic tone.

"This! What is this?" Brooke held the paper out.

Grace, shaken and confused at exactly what her daughter wanted, drew a blank. "What?"

"The vice president is *dead*?" Brooke's words came out in a gasp.

"It's been all over the *news*," Grace said. "The president made an announcement yesterday morning. You didn't hear?"

"No! No! . . . I . . . I guess it was while I was on the train." Brooke fell into the big recliner, every inch of her psyche flooded beyond overload. "James Ettinger . . . *killed*?"

"Yes. Not much has been released, yet. I thought—"

Brooke shot out of the chair. "I've got to get back to New York! Now! Today!"

"But—"

Brooke was already moving past her, wide-eyed and frenzied. "This is phenomenal! I can't . . ." She threw her closet door open, stumbling over yesterday's clothes heaped at the foot of her bed. "I can't believe it!"

"Brooke! Please," her mother was saying, doing her best to calm her daughter.

"I've got to call the airport . . . get a flight out in the next couple of—"

"Brooke . . . I—"

"How can this be . . . I mean, the explosion and the vice president killed, all in the same—" Brooke suddenly froze.

"Honey?" Grace said, touching a hand to her hair. "Are you okay?"

Brooke was silent. She stared at the closet door. "Mom, can you give me a minute?" she said as she swung her bedroom door toward her mother. Grace backed away as the door snapped shut.

Brooke sat on the edge of her bed. The gears of her mind were churning, and her heart was racing. A thought had occurred to her. An absurd consideration. It was ludicrous, preposterous—but there it was all the same. Her mouth went dry, and a hammering pain started in her head.

Her backpack was on the dresser. She stared at it for the longest time from her perch on the edge of the bed, paralyzed by a foreboding notion. The springs of her bed groaned as she slowly stood. She opened the zipper of the main compartment of her pack. She took a deep breath, releasing it slowly through pursed lips. The window above her dresser looked out over a small patch of lawn bordered by chain-link. The snow outside the window was undisturbed.

She removed the parcel from her pack and set it on a cleared space on the dresser. She fetched a pair of scissors from the desk in the corner and made a long gash in the brown paper. She peeled back the brown paper, revealing the cover of a book. She flipped the book over, then back, studying it. It was just a book.

Great Expectations.

But she knew there had to be more to this than met the eye. So, following this instinct, she touched a hand to the book's cover, and opened it.

The book was hollow. And inside was a videotape.

A creeping sensation raised the tiny hairs on her arms. The tape was not labeled.

The word *Beacon* had struck her as oddly familiar when she'd first seen it at the post office, but nothing specific about it had come to mind. It had simply seemed curious. But now a cold chill creeped through her as she remembered the Secret Service's designation for James Ettinger.

Directly opposite the foot of her bed was a thigh-high unfinished wooden table with drawers. Atop the table was her VCR and nineteen-inch television. She sat cross-legged on the floor in front of the TV and fed the videocassette into the VCR. The remote was in the drawer. She thumped the Play button.

The machine whirred, and the screen went from fuzzy to black. She leaned back against the bed. When the face of Vice President James Ettinger appeared, she gasped reflexively. He was dressed in a bathrobe, and his hair was slightly disheveled. He stared awkwardly at the camera for a moment or two, as if unsure whether it was yet recording. He took a sip from a glass of water, and cleared his throat to speak. Brooke sat transfixed. The man on the screen took a breath, and then spoke directly at the camera:

> *"Hello. My name is James Highfield Ettinger, vice president of the United States. Today is the seventeenth of December. By the time anyone views this tape, I will have resigned from office . . ."*

—▪ ▬

A few minutes before noon, St. John entered the Waldorf-Astoria and rode an elevator up to his room. His self-loathing had peaked. All his greatest fears had come to pass. To allow himself to stop thinking and acting like a professional, even for a minute, was so amateurish it was vile. And now he was paying for his lapse.

He had taken a cab to the bar and grill where he and Megan had agreed to meet for lunch. He'd gone there in the off chance Albertwood was bluffing. But the photo was all the truth he'd needed. The photo didn't lie. Megan had not been at the bar and grill. If they harmed her in any way, the remainder of his existence would be a campaign of retribution devoted to making sure that each of those involved died a heinous death at his hands. He was trained to find anyone, anywhere. And he was trained in methods to make the pain last just as long as he desired. He almost wished they'd provoke him. They had found him. He could most certainly find them. It would be an utter joy to pick them off one at a time. Maybe skin them alive.

The room was just as they'd left it that morning. The bed was in disarray, the sheets twisted into vines and sagging to the floor. Clothes were strewn about. What to leave and what to take?

The clock was ticking.

The girl's name and her address in Syracuse were written on the back of the photograph that the old freak had provided him. If he booked a flight now, he could be there this afternoon. But if all flights were booked for the day, he'd have to drive. That would eat up valuable time he simply couldn't afford. A private aircraft would cut down on travel time and let him focus on the girl and the tape. He decided the latter would be best. He'd also keep the room and come back to it when this whole mess was over. His time would be better spent in the air, not folding shirts.

Twenty-four hours ago he and Megan had been two lovers beginning a new life together. Now she was a hostage of his trade. Even if he managed to pluck her out alive, their relationship would change forever. She would probably know who he really was and what he'd done for a living. Whether that would matter to her or not, he couldn't say. He'd lied to her. He'd deceived her. She was engaged to a professional killer. And now she knew it. Or soon would.

If the planets aligned in his favor, he could even be back in the city late tonight. It was simply a matter of putting a bullet through the girl and getting the tape to Albertwood. But something in his gut told him this wasn't going to be that clear-cut.

It was tempting to consider shucking the whole business. What if he spent the day and a half tracking down Albertwood, freeing Megan, and leaving a trail of carnage in his wake? The obvious problem with this strategy was that it put their future in jeopardy. Albertwood clearly had powerful connections. Albertwood's people had no trouble picking him out of the multitudes of New York City. And he had no qualms about sticking a gun in a young woman's ear.

No, he'd be going to Syracuse.

He'd take no luggage. Just the Glock and the info on the girl.

He sat in a chair at a table by the window and

opened a phone book, flipping through entire chunks of pages until he found the Yellow Pages. He overshot the *A*s and had to backtrack. There was a slew of private charter services in the *Aviation* listings. He only needed one. Money was no factor.

Near the bottom of the page was an advertisement for Atlantic General Aviation. AGA's fleet included both Learjets and prop-driven aircraft. It was a place to start. They were located at a private airfield in Long Island. St. John dialed the phone. They were booked for the day.

He had better luck with his second choice, Eastern Charter, which, based on their small ad, appeared to be a smaller outfit. Their hangar was located in the general aviation section at JFK. He got them on the line. A woman with a husky smoker's voice quoted him a price for a one-way flight to Syracuse, New York.

By the time they fueled up the Cessna and went through the whole maintenance routine, he'd be lucky to be off the ground by 3 P.M., more like 3:30. He made the reservation under the name Allan Price. He tore the page of the phone book, folded it, and tucked it in a coat pocket.

There was bottled water in the minibar. He screwed off the cap and took a long sip. His thoughts went to Megan. He hated himself for putting her in danger. His chosen profession was vicious and cutthroat, and he had to treat the threat against her life as impending. At the same time, though, he could not afford to dwell on her safety and treatment. There was a job to do, and there was a deadline. He simply had to perform, do it right, and be swift about it. No hesitation, no second-guessing.

All he had was the photo of the girl, Brooke Weaver, and her parents' address in Syracuse. That should have been enough. He'd make it work. He folded the info into a pocket.

He looked at his watch. 12:30 P.M.

He needed to be at the airport in two hours.

There was a full clip in the Glock. He tucked it away. Thankfully, since he was flying out of the general aviation section of JFK, he wouldn't have to pass through any metal detectors. He could carry the gun on him every inch of the way.

He made a quick pass through the hotel suite, making certain that everything was in order. When he was satisfied, he stepped into the hallway and pulled the door shut. It locked automatically. He headed to the elevator.

The elevator doors opened onto the main lobby, and St. John strode purposefully past the service counter, heading for the Park Avenue entrance. A dozen paces from the doors, a hand touched him on the shoulder. Startled, St. John jerked away quickly, turning to look.

A young man dressed in a Waldorf-Astoria uniform smiled sheepishly, and said, "I'm sorry if I startled you, sir."

St. John had been lost in his own thoughts. Lost in the day and evening ahead. "No . . . not at all." He noticed the boy's name badge said *Todd*. "Not at all, Todd."

Todd glanced around him anxiously. "I hate to bother you, sir. But I think there's something you might want to know."

"What is it?" he said to the boy impatiently.

Todd cleared his throat nervously and said, "Sir, perhaps it would be better if we spoke in private."

St. John hesitated for a beat, then nodded. "Very well."

Todd motioned for him to follow through a side door, which was posted with a metal plate that read STAFF ONLY. They descended a short flight of stairs. Todd led him into a small utilities area and pulled the double doors closed.

Todd reached behind his back and removed something from a pants pocket. It was a folded sheet of paper. "Sir, yesterday morning a man approached me and handed me this, asking if I'd seen the woman in this photo. At the time, I hadn't. He said he was trying to find her. Said he was related to her or she was his kid or something, but was pretty vague. This morning as I was working, I believe I saw the woman in the photo leaving the hotel. And she was with you." Todd unfurled the sheet of copier paper, handing it over.

Ever cautious, St. John took the page in his hand, his eyes still on the bellboy. Then he let his gaze fall to the black-and-white photograph. What he saw stunned him. On the page was a photo of Megan, or someone who looked astoundingly like Megan.

Todd continued, "I was a little suspicious of the guy. He paid me a hundred bucks to keep my eyes out. I shrugged him off. To be honest, I'd forgotten about it. Then I saw her with you this morning, and thought you'd want to be made aware."

"What else did he say?" St. John said. He took the boy by the sleeve of his shirt and ushered him farther back into a corner, away from the door. "What did he look like? Did he give his name or say how to contact him?"

The kid nodded. "That's his room number there on the page." He stabbed a finger at the photocopy. "He jotted it there himself."

Suddenly swept up in an all-new wave of nervous energy, St. John struggled to take it all in. *It had to have been Albertwood's people*, he thought. *That's how they found us! They must have seen—*

What? What had the kid said?

"Room number? Room number *where?*" St. John asked.

Todd's eyebrows went up, as if the answer was obvious. He said, "Well, here in the hotel."

"The hotel? You mean, *here?*"

"Right. The number's right there on the page. Room ten-eighteen."

Someone had been looking for Megan, had come to their hotel showing around a crude photo of her, and had even taken a room there. Could he still be there? Clearly, Albertwood had had the hotel staked out. There had probably been copies of the photo passed out all over the city in hopes of finding them. But how had they known what she looked like? Or that she would be with him? Or even that they were together? It had been years—that he knew of—since he'd last been photographed. So how would they know anything about him, let alone whom he was dating?

And why would they have needed to keep tabs on him? Had that been the plan the whole time? None of it made sense. Why hadn't they told him about the girl in Syracuse in advance? Then he would have been able to better prepare.

"Did he speak with anyone else in the hotel, that you know of?" he said to the kid.

"I really don't know."

St. John took out his wallet and tipped the kid handsomely. "Listen," he said. "You did the right thing coming to me. If you see this guy again, leave a message for me at the front desk. I'm in room eight-oh-seven. Got that?"

Todd nodded. "Like I said before, I'd forgotten about him altogether until I spotted you and your wife. Then I got to thinking it was kind of creepy that this guy would be trying to hunt down somebody's wife or whatever, you know."

St. John nodded, a thousand nerve endings curling beneath the skin of his back. "Keep this to yourself," he said.

He returned to the main lobby. He noticed then that he'd begun to perspire. His armpits were damp. The old fears were rising. His throat was tight. He needed to mellow, to fall into the zone, to let his instincts take over. Someone had hunted Megan down within the Waldorf-Astoria. And whoever it was might very well still be there, or come back very shortly. But now St. John had the man's room number. Charge a mistake to their team, he mused. Finally he'd gotten a break.

If he could surprise the guy in 1018, he might just be able to turn the tables on Albertwood. Surely the man in 1018 would know where Albertwood was keeping Megan. If they were expecting him to be in Syracuse tonight, he could catch them off guard and snatch her out from under them. Besides, he had no guarantee that Albertwood would honor the business deal. He had already reneged once. What was to stop him from pulling the same stunt twice? He now had an hour and a half to get to JFK. He couldn't miss that flight. But the man in 1018 might just make the flight to Syracuse unnecessary. Either way, he had to make a move.

He double-checked that his Glock 9mm was handy, then left the rest room, crossing the lobby to the elevators. It was time to deal with the man in room 1018.

31

JOEL LAY FACEDOWN IN BED, SLEEPING LIKE A rock. Two and a half hours earlier he'd staggered to his hotel room and fussed with the buttons on his shirt, finally peeling the thing off his arms and slinging it to the floor. He'd fallen into bed, then kicked off his shoes. His pants were still on.

The shades were drawn and all the lights were out. The only illumination in the room was the slight glow of daylight coming through the heavy drapery over the window. There was just enough visibility to vaguely make out the shapes of the furniture.

The cold and flu formula had gone straight into action. It hadn't occurred to him to check the box to see whether or not it was a nondrowsy formula. No matter. It had knocked him out like a board to the side of his head, but he needed the sleep. His head had no more than hit the pillow before he was unconscious and he was floating along through kaleidoscope-patterned galaxies.

\- - →

St. John had trained himself to work with little or nothing. In this case, his only available choice was a butter knife from a room service cart back down the hallway. The cutting blade was rigid and smooth, and just flat enough for him to slip it between the doorjamb and the door facing. He sidled up to the door to room 1018, throwing a glance over his shoulder to check that no one was coming. There was no light coming from beneath the door—either the guy was gone, or he was sacked out. He was confident he could enter the room undetected, even if the guy was a light sleeper.

He worked the blade of the knife down the narrow groove until he hit something solid, then angled it as best he could, held it firmly in place with the one hand, and gave the butt of the knife handle a good thump with the ball of his free hand. The knife sank in about a half an inch—just right. He double-checked over his shoulder, then, using the doorjamb as a fulcrum, pressured the knife handle to the left. He turned the doorknob and eased into the darkened space.

Having stepped from the well-lighted hallway, he was momentarily blinded by the darkness of the room. He eased the door shut gently. He then squatted in the corner where the wall and the door met, making time for his eyes to adjust a bit. He remained frozen and silent.

St. John took a careful step forward, easing the sole of his shoe down onto the carpeted floor. His eyes were still adjusting. The entry opened into a sitting area, and in the dark he could make out an open doorway to his immediate right that he presumed led to the bedroom. He eased the Glock from his coat and squirreled the silencer onto the end of the muzzle. The bedroom, like the sitting room, was dark and silent and still.

A figure was lying sprawled facedown on the bed, covered from the waist down by blankets. St. John wondered what kind of thug Albertwood had employed who would be asleep in the middle of the afternoon? Then he noticed the cold and flu formula box on the bedside table, and put two and two together. *That should make my work easier,* he thought.

He readied the Glock in his right hand as he approached one side of the bed. He wanted to make as little mess in the room as possible. Also, he wasn't too keen on leaving a body in the room. If the man's body was discovered in the hotel, there would be an investigation, and eventually the bellboy, Todd, would come around with his story, and suddenly the authorities would have a very good description of the man responsible for the murder.

No, he needed to find out what the guy had to say, what he knew about Albertwood and Megan. Then he needed to get him out of the hotel where he could deal with him on a more primitive level.

The guy didn't look like anything special. Thinning brown hair, maybe a little extra padding around the middle. He looked more like an accountant from Toledo than a gun-toting thug. None of that mattered. He had clearly been asking around about Megan, and that was enough to make him dangerous. St. John pursed his lips, planning his assault. The guy was just dreaming away, not a clue in the world that his life was coming to an abrupt end.

The dream—whatever it had been, wherever he'd been floating—snapped shut. Joel's head was jerked backward by his hair. At first he didn't make a sound. For the first few seconds, his mind was still asleep. His eyes bulged from their sockets, his mouth hung open, and he sucked air. The force from whatever had ahold of him was pulling too hard, tugging his head back too far. His neck wasn't designed to bend backward like that. The extreme angle cut off his air supply.

St. John was on the bed, on his knees, straddling Joel's waist. He put the silencer under Joel's chin, jamming it into the soft flesh. Joel winced in pain.

"You are going to keep your mouth shut, or you will die right here right now—understand?" St. John said, leaning down, speaking with his lips barely a half inch from Joel's ear.

Desperate for breath, Joel nodded.

"I've got a nine-millimeter under your chin. I'd love to use it, and I will. Do you understand?"

Again, Joel nodded.

"Good."

St. John relieved the pressure on Joel's neck slightly. Joel gasped, desperate to fill his lungs. He coughed and gagged. St. John adjusted his position, lifting his right leg, driving his knee into the small of Joel's back. This forced him to hold the gun against the back of Joel's neck instead of under the chin.

Joel's mind was shaking itself awake. The sensation of someone mounting from behind, seizing him by the hair of his head, and taking him at gunpoint, had at first seemed to be only a dream. But now the pain and the bewilderment were all too real. He was in bed, in the dark of his hotel room, barely able to see at all, and only able to face the pillow under his head and the headboard and wall six inches directly ahead. The weight pressing down at a single point in the small of his back was like being pinned down by the leg of a grand piano. A four-inch circle of scalp felt as though it were being uprooted. A billion points of pain prickled from the back of his head on down his backside.

Finally, his mind steadied enough for a clear, cognitive thought to crystallize: *What is going on? What . . . who's . . . what's happening?*

"Are you gonna behave?" St. John said, barely above a whisper.

Joel nodded as best he could.

"Are you listening?"

"Yes."

"Good. I am going to make this as simple as possible so that we can get this over with. Understand?"

Joel felt a tickle rise in his throat. He coughed hoarsely, then forced out, "Yes."

"I'm going to ask you a question," St. John said. "And as soon as you've given me a satisfactory answer to *that* question, I will ask another question. When you've answered that, I'll ask another—and so on. Understand?"

"Yes."

"And if you fail to answer any of the questions satisfactorily, I'm going to use the contents of your head to repaint this room."

Joel might have laughed if he could have gotten any air. Six days ago, he'd been on the road, just another businessman from Missouri following the same basic routine he'd known for most of his adult life. Five days ago, he'd been almost home. New York had been nothing more than a layover on the way to somewhere else. Then he'd glanced up and seen a face. He could have ignored it. But he hadn't.

Now here he was on his belly in a ritzy hotel room with the lights off, with a stranger on his back, whose face he could not see, with a gun jammed into the back of his neck.

There was a few hundred dollars left in Joel's wallet on the table by the window, the last of an ATM withdrawal he'd made with a Visa. Also in the wallet was a meager assortment of credit cards, but little else of value. There was an extra suit in the hanging bag in the closet. The briefcase on the table held only paperwork. That would not be a windfall for a thief, but he'd gladly offer it up if the man would just take it and go.

What confounded him was the fact that all these things had been readily available to the thief without need of waking him. Joel had been in a deep sleep and would not be of any further value to the man if awake. The guy could have simply strolled around the suite, gathered the goods, then eased back out into the hallway. Joel would have woken stripped of his things, with no further harm done. But now he was a witness to the crime. The man couldn't leave a witness, and the gun pressed to his neck told him he had no intention of doing so.

Now he deeply regretted leaving the other hotel. He'd been safe and sound. Not only had he failed to find Megan, but now he was being robbed at gunpoint.

He needed to swallow, but his windpipe was still awkwardly contorted. His lips were pulled back from his teeth, and his tongue stood in the gap, as if not knowing where to lay.

"Tuh . . . take what you want," Joel Benjamin said, coughing.

Olin St. John tightened his grip on the fistful of disheveled brown hair and twisted. "Shut up!" he hissed.

Pain sparkled around Joel's scalp. For a thief, he thought, the guy sure is sadistic.

"Where did they take her?"

"What?"

The fist twisted the knot of hair. "Where is the girl?"

Joel's eyes flashed open. *Huh?* What the crap was this? Who was this nut job? The tickle ran up his throat again, and he coughed in terrible heaving spasms. "I don't . . ."

St. John leaned down, putting his mouth right against Joel's ear. "Have you forgotten our little agreement?"

Joel's eyes went wide and frantic.

"Tell me where the girl is? How did you get the picture of her?"

"What picture . . . what . . ."

St. John found the photocopy the bellboy had given him. He pulled the folded page from a pocket and slung it open with several snaps of his left wrist. Then he propped it on the pillow, inches from Joel's nose. St. John leaned over and switched on a lamp on the bedside table.

Joel's breath left him in a gasp. He was staring at

his photocopied picture of Ariel. The realization bloomed with stunning, awful suddenness: the man on his back was no thief.

"Look familiar?"

"Where'd you get—"

"Yeah, I thought that might jog your memory," St. John said, interrupting. "Now, where is she?" He rubbed the barrel of the silencer against Joel's cheek.

St. John was warming to the process of interrogation. "Okay, so you show the photo around and you camp out waiting for someone to call up saying they've found her. Then you find her, and some of your people haul her away while I've got my back turned for a minute. I get everything so far. What still has me puzzled, though, is why you're still here. I mean, you've got the girl. And yeah, she was in the hotel, but . . ." St. John pondered his own train of thought. Had this guy been waiting for *him*? That didn't make sense. They'd sent him on a mission. And he had to get out of the city to complete the mission. Clearly this guy hadn't been on his toes. He looked like death warmed over. The only realistic possibility was that the guy's work was done, but he'd taken ill and just collapsed in bed. He nodded slightly. Yeah, had to be. *Too bad for him*, St. John mused.

The guy had found Megan, and they'd waited until he and Megan went their separate ways for the morning before they moved in on her. But the guy had had the dumb fortune to return here for a little afternoon nap, unaware that their mutual friend, Todd, had double-backed on him and given up the goods.

"Who . . ." Joel tried cranking his head around to

catch even a glimpse of his assailant. "Who are you?" That was a mistake. St. John leaned in with his knee, driving it against bone and muscle. Joel wheezed, his cheeks fluttering. The pain was so intense that his thoughts blurred.

"Who I am," St. John began, "is the last person in the world you wanted to screw with." He wasn't going to accept this guy mouthing off. "Where'd you get the photo?" He craned his wrist so that the muzzle of the silencer pressed against Joel's closed eyelid. He wanted him to always remember the reality of the gun's presence.

"Can't breathe . . . *please.*" Nausea was quickly rising from his nether regions. It was beginning to take real concentration not to vomit. Joel repeated, "Can't . . . *breathe.*"

St. John maintained his hold on the mass of hair but eased the head forward slightly, clearing the guy's windpipe enough for him to speak coherently. "Make it good or I'll snap your neck in half." Again, he said, "Where'd you get the photo?"

"It's mine."

"What?"

"I had it faxed from home."

Sweat had formed along St. John's brow. The room was warm, and he'd suddenly become aware that he was perspiring. The man's response struck him as odd. He adjusted his posture, now sitting nearly erect. His brow furrowed as he considered the absurdity of the man's words. *Home?* A feeling of subtle but intensifying trepidation crept over him. What he was hearing was far from what he'd anticipated.

"Don't *screw* with me!"

"I swear."

Reaching for the photocopy, snatching it up, St. John said, "Who's this, in the picture?"

In the last few minutes, based on the chaos that had erupted around him, Joel had submitted various data to himself for debate. First and foremost, he had no earthly idea who this guy was or what business he had with Megan. He was wielding a gun. What involvement would Megan have with such a character, and why? He didn't have any answers.

"Who do you think she is?" Joel said, fishing.

The time for games was over. St. John put the muzzle of the silencer to Joel's head, just behind his ear, and pressed it brutally hard. "Two seconds," he said. "That's how much life you have left. In two seconds your brains will be displaced and—"

"My wife! My wife!" Joel blurted in a panic. "The photo's of my wife!"

There was a knock at the door.

St. John froze.

St. John said, "We're gonna wait right here until whoever it is goes away. You're not going to make a sound. Understand?"

Joel nodded.

Another knock at the door.

They waited on the bed in utter silence. He kept the gun pressed firmly to Joel's head.

A voice called from the hallway, "Mr. Benjamin? Hello?"

St. John's heart rate quickened, and the perspiration on his face thickened. Sweat was getting in his eyes, and with one hand in the guy's hair and the other holding the gun, wiping his face was a bit awkward. He lifted the gun away for just a second and dragged his right forearm across his eyes and forehead, then put the muzzle back against the guy's scalp.

"Mr. Benjamin?" the voice called again. "It's important that I speak with you."

Then St. John made a decision. The guy at the door would have to be dealt with. They'd have to get rid of him and get back to business. But the situation had evolved, and there was no longer a clear definition of what was to be accomplished. There was no evidence that the guy beneath him was a hired thug. No guns lying about. But he'd been looking for Megan. And what about the photo?

First, though, they'd deal with the clown at the door.

"Okay, get up—*slowly*," St. John said, easing off Joel's back but maintaining the grip on his head and keeping the gun in place. Joel eased up, pushing off with his hands pressed flat against the mattress.

"*Easy.*" St. John steered him to the side of the bed, and Joel got to his feet. "Now, you're gonna keep your mouth shut, right?"

"Yuh."

"We're gonna ease over to the door and find out who it is and what they want."

"Okay."

Moving through the doorway that led from the bedroom to the sitting area, St. John kept the gun aimed at his temple.

"Mr. Benjamin? Please, sir. Are you in there?"

St. John put his eye to the peephole mounted in

the front door. Through the distorted glass lens, he saw a man dressed prissily in a nice suit, with a name badge pinned to his left breast. A hotel employee. He considered this for a moment, running through his options. Finally, he whispered softly to Joel, "Answer him."

Joel faced the wall, and loud enough for the guy on the other side of the door to hear him, he said, "Yes." St. John watched the man's reaction through the peephole.

"Ah, Mr. Benjamin. My name is Jonathan Thayber, the hotel's concierge." St. John could see that Thayber had a printed form in his hand. He nudged Joel's temple with the cold steel of the muzzle.

"What can I do for you, Mr. Thayber?"

"Sorry if I woke you, sir. I tried to call first, but you weren't answering your phone."

"Is there a problem?"

Thayber cleared his throat, taking a step closer to the door. "Actually, Mr. Benjamin, this is a matter, perhaps better handled in private. If I could step inside, please."

Joel glanced at St. John, who shook his head no.

"Not a good time, actually. I'm not decent."

Thayber stiffened, with his arms straight at his sides. "Mr. Benjamin, this concerns your payment status—your credit card, to be more specific—and I'd rather not have to discuss it through the door. I'm sure you'd understand."

St. John made sure the brass security chain was fastened from the wall to the bracket on the door. He let go of Joel's hair, dropping the Glock to the middle of Joel's back. Again, he whispered, *"Easy."*

Joel worked the lock, then opened the door until the chain caught. His face appeared in the narrow gap between the door and the doorframe. He offered an awkward smile.

Mr. Thayber inched closer, extending the form in his hand. "Sir, we've been notified that your second night's stay here has taken you beyond the credit limit on your credit card, and has thus been denied."

"Oh?" Joel was much less concerned with his credit card than he was with the 9mm jabbing him in the spine.

"Perhaps you could use another card to cover the rest of your stay with us," Thayber offered.

"Right. Could you give me a moment?"

Thayber nodded, "Of course."

The door shut and the lock engaged. St. John backed away and motioned with the gun for him to head for the bedroom.

"You have another card?" St. John asked in a whisper.

Joel pursed his lips. He gave a slight nod, "Yeah." *Ping.* A lovely and unexpected thought struck him. This whole wave of madness, from Monday evening at JFK till now, had followed immediately on the heels of a stopover in some other section of Manhattan. The layover in New York had been four hours. At some point on Monday afternoon, he'd reached the end of his rope. He'd sat and stared at nothing until he'd run out of excuses to keep on as he had for so many years. The depression he'd battled for so long had gotten ahold of him again, and this time with a maddeningly tight grip. He took a cab into the city, heading nowhere in particular. The cab waited while he made a purchase in a pawnshop, which he then stashed in his briefcase, an item intended to end the pain, to end the misery, to snuff out the depression.

But he'd never gotten the chance to carry through. Megan had changed everything.

"Get the card," St. John demanded.

Joel nodded, suddenly awake with new hope and new possibilities. His credit cards were in his wallet, and his wallet was in a coat pocket. But Joel had no interest in the cards or his wallet or the coat. "Right. I think it's over here," he said, motioning with his head toward the table and his briefcase.

"Get it. Let's go."

Joel switched on a lamp so he could see better. The brass fasteners on the briefcase flipped up in crisp synchronization. He quickly opened it and immediately began shuffling through paperwork and fishing his fingers into pockets, putting on quite a show. He glanced at St. John, swallowing hard at the sight of the gun. "I know they're in here somewhere." He needed to go unobserved for three or four seconds. Mr. Thayber helped him out.

Three brisk knocks on the door, and, "Is everything all right, Mr. Benjamin?"

St. John took several steps toward the sitting area and peeked his head around at the front door. He didn't want the concierge wandering in on them.

In that instant, Joel slipped his hand beneath a leather-bound portfolio inside the briefcase and found the .22 pistol he'd purchased Monday afternoon, and then he stuffed it in his waistband.

St. John motioned with the Glock.

Joel shrugged. "I thought it was in here."

"Get rid of him."

The door opened, drawing the chain taut.

Mr. Thayber stood with his hands behind his back, his mouth creased in an impatient but reasonable frown. He flashed his best PR smile and raised his chin attentively when Joel's face appeared at the door. He put out a hand, expectantly.

Working hard to mask the tremor in his voice, Joel said, "I'm a little under the weather at the moment, Mr., uh . . . Thay . . ."

"Thayber."

"Right. Anyway, I've got a card around here *somewhere*. How about if I scrounge one up, jump in the shower and run it down to you in, let's say, about an hour?"

Jonathan Thayber stiffened, the frown deepening. "I see."

The Glock was drilling a hole in his back. Joel stood there in his slacks, with bare chest and bare feet, his face in the narrow gap of the door.

"Very well," Thayber said. "In that case, Mr. Benjamin, I most certainly hope to see you at the front desk"—he made a flourish with his wrist, making a big show of checking his watch—"one hour from now."

"Great, thanks for your patience." The door shut and the lock engaged. Joel took a deep breath, and St. John rushed to the door to see if the concierge had in fact gone. He pressed an eye to the peep—his left-hand palm flat to the door, the Glock momentarily at his side. His one mistake. A second later, St. John felt a cool ring of steel, the size of a dime, pressed to his right temple. It was a familiar and unmistakable shape. A sinking, terrible lump filled his gut. In that breath of time, the assassin understood the score.

"Drop the gun," Joel ordered, his voice shaky but insistent. St. John nodded, and the Glock hit the floor between them with a soft *thud*.

32

TWO HUNDRED AND FIFTY MILES NORTHWEST OF
New York City, the videocassette finished rewinding,
and static fuzz filled the TV screen. Brooke was dizzy
with mental overload. She had sat on the floor in
front of her bed, barely breathing. Vice President
James Ettinger had spun an incredible tale.

The reality of Ettinger's words had yet to fully
sink in, yet she understood perfectly the implications
of what he had described. And those implications
involved the total collapse of the current White
House administration, not to mention more federal
indictments of high-level government officials, and
others, than she could even begin to conceive. In
comparison, Watergate seemed like a puff piece on
the local news.

Her legs had fallen asleep, a fact that didn't make
itself apparent until she tried to unfold them to
stand. They wobbled beneath her, and she made a
mad grab for the footboard of her bed. The clock
radio on her bedside table told her it was now after
1:30 in the afternoon. She stood, her knees aching.
She pulled the videocassette from the VCR and

tossed it onto the bed. Right now, she thought, she needed to shower and get dressed. She'd think this through in the shower. As she walked down the hall toward the bathroom, her mother popped into sight from the family room and asked if everything was all right.

"Fine, Mom. Just going to grab a shower."

Grace nodded hesitantly, but then shook her head and stood her ground. "Brooke, you're scaring me! I want to know what is going on and I want to know it *NOW*, young lady!"

Brooke closed the bathroom door, tugged the shower curtain aside, and sat on the edge of the tub until the water temperature felt about right.

Her mother stood outside the bathroom door asking, "Brooke, did you hear me? I'm worried about you."

Brooke ignored the clammer outside. She yanked up on the little knob on the faucet, and the shower-head sprang to life. She disrobed and stepped into the plume of steam.

Darla Donovan was dead. James Ettinger was dead. Barry. Joyce. Lipton. Connor. Jill. Lesley. But most of all, Darla and the vice president. Dead within a week of each other. Ettinger by an assassin's bullet. Darla in an explosion—its cause still in question. And now, a taped confession by the vice president, hours before his death, had been mailed directly to Darla's postal box, and the fact that it had been labeled with only Ettinger's Secret Service designation. It would take a mighty persuasive explanation to convince her that the two incidents weren't related.

Brooke was aware that Darla had a positive working relationship with Ettinger. But that Ettinger would send his mind-blowing confession only to Darla Donovan would have never even entered her realm of consideration. It was a journalist's dream.

The most explosive piece of political documentation in the history of the nation was on ninety minutes' worth of VHS on the quilted bedspread in the bedroom where she grew up. Vice President James Ettinger had played a part in a crime that would level Washington, D.C. Clearly someone knew what he'd had to say, and had killed him for it. They somehow also knew that he'd sent the confession tape to Darla Donovan, and Brooke would bet every penny she'd ever make in her lifetime that whoever *they* were, also had been responsible for the explosion at Darla's apartment building. And if that were the case it wouldn't stop there. The information on that tape was too volatile. If and when it hit the news it would—

Brooke's eyes flashed open in the spray from the showerhead. Something had fallen through the trip wire in her subconscious. She stood stone-faced in the rising steam, and she put a hand to the wall to keep her balance.

The phone call from the train. The message she'd left on Darla's machine from the train.

They knew. They knew she had the tape.

I have to get out of here, she thought, her chest tightening.

I have to take the tape and run. I don't know where to go, but I have to run!

But then she paused and thought for a second,

and realized that in fact she *did* know where to go. She knew *exactly* where she had to go.

Using his right foot, Joel kicked away the Glock, sending it coasting lightly across the hotel carpet. His heart was pounding madly, and his upper body glistened with sweat. He backed away slowly, the snub-nosed .22 aimed dead-level with the guy's ear.

"Keep your hands where I can see 'em."

St. John slowly raised his hands. His palms faced out at shoulder height. He was sick with himself.

Joel knelt to retrieve the Glock, then stood and aimed the 9mm at St. John. He took a deep breath, the fire in his throat still roaring. He coughed. "Turn around," he said. St. John pivoted slowly where he stood in front of the door. Joel motioned with the gun. "In there," he said, indicating the bedroom.

They moved together, St. John six or seven paces ahead of Joel.

"Sit."

St. John eased into a wing chair against the wall. How that gun had materialized, seemingly from nowhere, had him baffled. He cursed himself for the lapse of judgment. Now for the second time in a matter of hours he'd allowed someone to get a drop on him.

Taking a shirt from the hanging bag in the closet, careful never to turn his back to the guy in the chair, Joel put on the shirt, shifting the gun from hand to hand as he put his arms through the sleeves.

"What do you want with me?" Joel said, awkwardly buttoning the shirt using only one hand.

"The woman in the picture."

Joel unzipped his fly and tucked in the shirttail "Why?"

"I am engaged to marry her."

Engaged? Joel hesitated, puzzled. "Why'd you assume *I* have her?"

St. John pointed at the crumpled photocopy on the bed with one of his upraised fingers. "You were looking for her, no?"

"Okay . . ."

"And now she's been taken from me, and I was led to believe you might know where she is."

"What is her name?"

St. John considered, then went ahead, "Her name is Megan Durant."

The chills began at the toes, sizzled up his legs, and branched out in gooseflesh throughout his upper body, reaching the tips of his fingers, and crackling up the back of his neck. Had he really said *Megan?* Joel wondered. Had the past week not been in vain after all? *Megan . . . Megan . . . Megan.* His mind had not betrayed him after all. His eyes had seen what they thought they'd seen. That face in the crowd had indeed been a face from his past. His only child. His daughter. His angel.

His knees suddenly felt like rubber. He didn't know whether to smile or cry, but he resisted the temptation to do either. *Durant.* Ariel had changed their last name; he'd figured as much. But Megan was still Megan. He had indeed found her. Never could he have imagined that it would come about in such a fashion, standing in a hotel in New York City, holding a stranger at gunpoint, a stranger who'd held *him* at gunpoint only moments earlier.

"You said *Megan?*"

St. John nodded. "That's right."

From a hanger in the closet, Joel put on his coat. What, where, how? These were the questions he had no answers for. What to do with this guy? And where? And how?

"What do you want with her?" St. John said.

Pulled from his thoughts, standing on the far side of the bed, Joel looked up, brushed his hair back with his free hand, and said, "She's my daughter."

The blood drained from St. John's face. It had to be a lie. It simply *couldn't* be the truth. It was too impossible. It was inconceivable. Megan had spoken so little of her family that there was limited resources for him to draw from. He worked to play back their many conversations, desperate to run across even the smallest scrap of related data. Hadn't her parents divorced? Megan avoided the subject at all costs, and Olin hadn't pressed her. She *was* American born, and this guy was clearly from the States. But that alone was not enough to even begin to prove such an absurdity to be the truth.

St. John lowered his arms a hair, his eyes unblinking and locked on the guy across the room. When he spoke, he spoke slowly, clearly, choosing his words. "My friend, whoever you are, I can assure you that Megan Durant is not your daughter."

"Where is she?"

"She is being held against her will."

"By whom?"

St. John lowered his hands nearly to his lap.

"Heyhey! Up with the hands!" Joel took a step forward, the gun in front of him, aimed at St. John's chest.

St. John raised them level with his chin.

"By *whom?*" Joel repeated.

"Actually, I'm not altogether sure."

"Where?"

"Good question."

"Why are they holding her? What do these people want?"

"They want me to do something for them."

"What?"

St. John shrugged. "That's between me and them."

"It just became my business. What do they want you to do?"

"Someone has something they want, and I have to get it for them."

"Where?"

"Syracuse."

"Syracuse?"

"New York. Syracuse, New York."

"And if you don't, if you don't bring them what they want, what then?"

"They will kill Megan." He watched the shock register in Joel's eyes. St. John watched the Glock, watched it dip slightly in the man's hands. If he got the slightest opening, he'd rush in, take his chances.

Joel looked away, his stunned gaze sweeping the floor. It had become unspeakably difficult to differentiate between reality and fiction. But this man sitting in the wing chair before him was the one and only link he had to Megan. And he refused to let the trail end here.

"You're lying!"

St. John shrugged. "Am I?"

Propelled by a sudden rush of burning rage and confusion, Joel stormed across the expanse between them, and thrust the muzzle of the Glock in the man's face, his face wretched and hard and shaking with determination. *"LIES!"* he screamed.

St. John faced straight ahead, expressionless. If this were to be his moment of death, he would accept it without flinching. So much had gone wrong so quickly. But behind the cool demeanor was a tempest of cognitive activity. There was a way out of this. And eventually he'd find it.

Joel held the silencer's muzzle at St. John's nose. And he wondered if he truly had the resolve required to jerk the trigger and put a bullet through the man's head. His right index finger quivered against the curved steel of the trigger. His fist was wrapped tight around the pistol grip. But the awful truth was that he needed this guy. If a word of what he'd said was even half true, he'd need him. Frustration sparkled up his spine.

St. John released a long-held breath through his nose. "I have till midnight tomorrow, then they kill her. Believe what you like, but you're just wasting my time and putting Megan in further danger. We both want to find her, and we can't do that sitting here threatening each other."

Joel backed up three paces and motioned with the Glock. "Up," he ordered.

St. John stood.

Syracuse, Joel thought. We've got to go to Syracuse, New York. How?

"How far is Syracuse from here?" he said.

Hands still in the air, St. John shrugged.

"You have a car?"

St. John shook his head no.

Joel rubbed his chin, in need of a decision he'd rather not have to make. "What was your plan?"

There was no reason to hold back. "I've chartered a plane."

"Where's the plane?"

"JFK."

Joel considered this, then shook his head. "Won't work." He waved the gun. "I don't think they'd appreciate our . . . *situation*." He waved him ahead with the Glock. "We're going to walk out of the hotel now. We'll take the fire exit. I want you three steps ahead of me."

St. John led the way, hands in the air.

Joel rounded up his few pieces of luggage, shoving the hand with the Glock in a deep coat pocket. He realized then that the silencer made the gun too long for the pocket. He set the bags down and detached the silencer tube from the muzzle of the gun, then tested how it fit in the pocket. Good.

He folded the hanging bag over his left forearm, taking up his briefcase with that hand. Now there was a small bulge where the Glock pressed against the inside of the coat pocket. St. John eased out ahead of him.

"When we get in the hall," Joel said, "put your hands at your sides, but don't get stupid on me. Just take it easy."

St. John moved ahead in silence.

Joel followed him into the hall. An elderly couple hobbled by. St. John offered them a nervous smile and a polite nod. Joel swallowed hard. He had no real idea where this was going. He was playing this by ear. St. John almost made his move right then and there, and he should have; Joel was facing away at an angle, pulling the door shut.

"Move," Joel ordered, keeping his tone low.

St. John progressed forward. "Do you really think you're helping Megan, doing this?" he said.

"Shut up and walk."

It was a good question. Was this really being productive? Would this bring him any closer to Megan? It was something he'd asked himself dozens of times over the past five days. And his answer now was the same as it had been every other time. *Dear God, I hope so.*

33

THE GARAGE WAS A BARN-SHAPED BUILDING separate from the house. Both of the family's cars were parked inside, behind double doors. The only way in without a clicker for the door opener was to go through the side door, which led down a short cement walk to the front door of the house. Dean had shrugged on his heavy coat and hurried out to the garage to start his wife's Subaru wagon.

His glasses slid down his nose as he sorted through the jangling mess on his key ring. The doorframe on the side door shifted in winter, the wood puckering in the cold. He had to put a shoulder to it, and it popped with a jarring vibration. He brushed a light switch with the back of his hand, and a bulb flickered on somewhere in the open rafters.

The Subaru was cold, having sat idle for five or six days. In bad weather like this, he and Grace tended to run their errands together, taking his four-wheel-drive Ford Expedition, which was parked on the far side of the Subaru. He found the Subaru key and turned it in the ignition. The battery struggled, then the ignition rolled over a half-dozen times before the engine finally sparked to life. Dean punched the clicker button clipped to the sun visor over his head, and a chain-drive contraption slowly raised the garage door. The gas gauge registered at three-quarters of a tank. He didn't know how long Brooke would need the car, or how far she had to go, but he understood from her frantic state that it was urgent that she get going, and get going *now*. The wagon got nearly forty miles to the gallon, so three-quarters of a tank could send her scooting a good piece down the road.

Exhaust coughed from the tailpipe and swirled at the rear of the car. Dean climbed out and shut the door, having popped the hood to check the oil. He knew good and well that the oil was fine, but it was habit, and it gave him something to do with his nervous energy.

Back inside the house, Grace was wound tight. Her daughter had locked herself inside her bedroom for over an hour and a half, then hurried to the bathroom for a shower. Now suddenly she was babbling about having to get out of the house, that she had urgent business to take care of. She needed to borrow a car.

"I don't understand," Grace was saying as Brooke finished dressing, her face pallid and sober. "Where are you going?"

"Mom . . . Mom . . . please." Brooke shouldered her bag, marching out her bedroom door and past her mother. "It would really be better if you didn't know. Just *trust* me on this one, okay?"

Grace frowned, her hands on her hips.

Wyatt sat in his wheelchair at the end of the hall.

Whatever was up with his sister, he sensed quite accurately that it was not something they should waste time discussing. He reversed in his chair a bit as the two women flew past in a storm of words.

"At least let me pack you something to eat," Grace said, desperate to have a hand in the situation.

"Mom . . . *please.*"

"I don't understand what's come over you all of a sudden," Grace called after her daughter. "You're rushing around here like the world's coming to an end!"

Brooke spun on her heels and gave her mother a big hug. "I love you, Mom, but I've just got something I have to do. I'll call you as *soon* as I can and let you know that everything's all right. Something has come up, and it just can't wait. Okay?"

Dean barged in the front door, kicking snow off his boots, flurries whipping around his head. "Brooke, you be careful on these roads. It's a mess out there."

"Will do," Brooke said. She looked at Wyatt, parked at the edge of the kitchen, watching her. Nothing cut deeper than the thought of leaving him. How much time he had left was anybody's guess, and she hated herself for rushing away when he needed her most.

"Mom . . . Dad . . . ," Brooke said.

Dean crossed from the front room, disregarding the trail of slush and slop he was leaving. He stood next to his wife, and Brooke put a hand on a shoulder of each of her parents. Her face was suddenly stern.

"Listen, you two . . ." She craned her neck around to catch her brother's eye. "This goes for you, too, buddy boy. No one is to know that I was here. If someone asks about me, I'm still in New York. You haven't talked to me on the phone for a week or so, and you have no idea when you'll see me next. I never came home for Christmas. I was never here."

"But I—" Grace tried to pipe in.

"No, you've got to promise me. I know it's hard, but please trust me . . . I know what I'm doing. And it's a *good* thing I'm doing. I'll explain later," Brooke said, flashing them a hurried, loving grin, then dropping her hands from their shoulders.

Dean put an arm around his wife's shoulder. "You raised her to be tough," he said, winking at Brooke. "She can take care of herself."

Grace shrugged, then nodded, but didn't like it a bit.

"Like I said," Brooke added, "zip your lips."

The three of them—Grace, Dean, Wyatt—made zipping gestures across their mouths.

Brooke smiled. "Good." She grabbed her bag and said, "I've gotta go."

Her father hurried out ahead of her to back the car from the garage. Grace followed her daughter out the front door, and they headed along the cement walk toward the driveway.

Halfway down the walk, Brooke paused, then turned back toward the house. Wyatt was parked at the threshold of the front door, watching her from his wheelchair. She flew back up the front steps and knelt in front of him.

"I'll be back in a flash," she said, holding his hands in hers.

"By Christmas?" he said, making an effort to smile.

"I hope. More than anything in the world."

Wyatt nodded. He looked so frail.

She kissed him on the forehead, and turned to go.

Wyatt waited in the cold, watching as her car backed the length of the driveway to the street and accelerated past the mailbox, zooming beyond the fencerow and out of sight.

34

JOEL WAS IN CONTROL, BUT NOT BY MUCH. THEY had descended by the stairs, and on their way to an emergency exit, he had spotted some men at the end of a corridor carrying boxes of crated vegetables through a service entrance. This would be better, he thought. And it was.

They came out in an alley, where a Volvo flatbed delivery truck was parked and piled high with crates. Joel pushed St. John forward. The cold hit them the moment they were out the door. It felt like the temperature had dropped.

A shiver ran up Joel's arms. He felt truly out of alignment with the universe. He was holding a man at gunpoint. It was absurd. Just the thought of it was absurd. He was scared to death. Scared and at wits end. This man, whoever he was, claimed to have a relationship with Megan. That, too, seemed absurd. But what if it were true? Where would that leave things? This man had ambushed him in bed, spiking a knee into his back and threatening him with the very gun Joel now held on him. If it was as he said, and Megan was being held against her will until a delivery was made, what kind of business was this guy in, and how had his sweet little baby girl become involved with him? All of it surged through his brain, creating a pressure that made his head want to explode.

"What's your name?" Joel asked over the howl of the easterly wind.

St. John glanced over his shoulder, and had his mouth half open, when he hesitated, deciding which of his aliases he might choose for the occasion. He remembered the name he'd given to charter the flight out of JFK. Allan Price. It seemed as good as any.

"Price," he said into the wind.

"What?"

"Price. My name is Price."

Joel doubted it, but he had to call him something. If they were going to Syracuse, they'd need transportation. Holding a man at gunpoint made renting a car a difficult issue. It would be next to impossible to maintain the current state of things in crowded areas. Price had to be thinking that Joel would be hesitant to fire if there were witnesses around.

A taxi was out of the question as well. He'd never he able to hold the gun on Price with a driver watching. They'd simply have to make do. They had a long drive ahead of them, and from the sound of it they were on a deadline.

Joel was only a step behind him now.

They were coming to the mouth of the alley, where it gave onto the sidewalk and the street. "Steady, man," Joel said.

"You know you can't shoot me."

Joel ignored him, his face burning in the wind.

"Without me you can't find Megan. And without me, Megan will die."

Joel said through gritted teeth, "I've done a lot of things these past few days that I never dreamed I'd have the guts to do. Killing you might be the best thing I could do for her."

Joel jabbed the Glock into his back. St. John winced, the collar of his coat shuddering in an icy gust.

They turned onto a sidewalk, both men thinking hard about the other. Joel said, "Can you wire a car?"

"No," he lied.

"A man with your skills? Please."

St. John nodded. All things being equal, that was fine with him. It was simply too cold to walk much farther. And besides, killing this guy would be simpler in a confined space.

The military cargo jet carrying the remains of James Ettinger received clearance from the tower at Andrews Air Force Base, then circled around and dipped into its final approach. The flight and its cargo were not public information, but word had leaked and members of the media had arrived, complete with camera equipment and microphones.

Yates and Philbrick waited in the president's limousine, along with a handful of advisors. Philbrick was all eyes and ears. This was to be his first official appearance as vice president.

The president had canceled much of his schedule for the next three or four days. His announcement yesterday morning put him in the awkward position of having to deal with matters on his home turf rather than the scheduled engagements on foreign soil. The world would have to wait.

Someone spoke up, then pointed at the sky, and most of the heads in the car turned to look. The day was cloudy and gray, and snow flurries whipped and swirled in brisk white waves. At first it was hard to spot, but as the cargo plane descended, it passed through the cloud cover and grew larger against the bleak background. The president didn't look. He could have cared less. There'd been no word from Shelby. The president had slept little last night, then got up and had scotch for breakfast. Lunch had been with a visiting dignitary, an oil sheik, a hassle he couldn't avoid. Oil prices would have to go up again. Big deal. In a week he might very well be in prison. If not, it would be business as usual for the leader of the free world. What a job.

The cargo plane taxied onto an apron, rolling to a stop a few hundred feet from the massive hangar where government officials and the media had gathered. The nose of the plane opened and a group of uniformed soldiers marched out carrying Ettinger's casket. At the front of the gathered crowd, the president and his new vice president looked on with somber faces. Cameramen recorded the event, flashes popping. A hearse was parked and waiting not far from where the cargo plane had come to rest. Its rear doors were open. Two men in dark suits spoke instructions and pointed as the soldiers approached with the casket. When the casket was loaded, the doors were shut, and the hearse headed off the apron and around one side of the hangar. The gathering disbanded, and within minutes the hangar was barren.

The president's limo headed back to Interstate 495.

35

THE SOUND OF BREAKING GLASS WAS MOSTLY muffled by the wind and by the din of the traffic. The window hadn't shattered, which was good. Joel had managed to make a hole using the Glock's pistol grip. An alarm screamed at them. Careful not to shred his hand, he reached in and unlocked the back door. St. John was a step ahead of him, leaning against the driver-side door.

Joel slipped inside and reached up to unlock both of the front doors. "Get in," he said, keeping a cautious eye on his man.

St. John lifted up on the handle and slid in behind the wheel of the Saab. He ducked his head beneath the dash, and in a matter of seconds the alarm was silenced. His hands working above his face, he sorted through a tangle of wiring.

Joel rounded the front of the car, moving quickly but with discretion. He opened the passenger-side door and eased into the front seat, quickly shutting the door. He was finally free to pull the Glock from his coat pocket. He squirreled the silencer back onto the muzzle of the gun and touched it to St. John's head. "Let's go!"

St. John's breath came out in gray vaporous puffs. "One minute," he said.

Joel spotted a cop on the other side of the street, nearly parallel to them. "Come on!" He slouched down in the seat, his heart drumming in his chest.

The wiring was a jumbled mess. He connected two wires, and the ignition fired. The engine began to purr. St. John sat up in the seat.

Joel said, "Pull into traffic."

The Saab couldn't have been more than a year old, and the engine hummed like a sweet strum on a Stratocaster. They were parallel parked along the curb, with a car in front and a small pickup behind. St. John shoved in the clutch and guided the stick into reverse. The car revved as he gave it a little gas. Joel kept his eye on the cop, who seemed to have nothing to do but have a good long look around. Joel could feel every muscle in his chest crunching into knots.

R'mel hadn't spotted them right off. The stranger's face meant nothing to him, and he'd only caught sight of Belfast by chance as the two of them emerged from the alley and turned south on Park. He'd been working on a chocolate bar wrapped in foil and was crossing at a traffic light when he happened to glance toward the alley at a lucky moment, spotting Belfast being ushered onto the sidewalk by a man he couldn't place. He'd followed Belfast from the subway station to the Waldorf and had been waiting for him to come out the main entrance.

There was a split second of indecision as R'mel debated whether to pursue on foot or retrieve his bike. His fear was that if he headed around the corner he might lose them in the bedlam of traffic. There was no time for debate. He chose the bike.

St. John cut the wheel, inching forward, then backing the same distance. Finally there was space enough to pull into the lane. He glanced at Joel, who held the gun steady. St. John figured he could have taken the guy at anytime, but he couldn't afford a miscalculation. All he wanted was to get this guy out of the picture and get Megan to safety as quickly as possible. He certainly didn't trust Albertwood to keep his word, but he couldn't concern himself with that at the moment.

They followed the southbound traffic down Park Avenue.

"You know where you're going?" Joel said.

St. John nodded. Yes, he knew the way. But he had no intention of taking this schmuck with him. Sooner or later there'd be an opening, and the tables would turn. When the time came and he found an opportunity, he'd have to act with precision. He just had to hope the fool didn't do something stupid between now and then, something they'd both regret.

Joel had bitten off a bigger bite than he could chew. They were caught in a clog of midday traffic. The gun made him nervous beyond measure. The car sat low enough to the road that passing motorists could easily see in. If anyone reported him, that would be the end of it. Thinking this, he covered the Glock with the tail of his coat. The muzzle of the silencer protruded out from the fabric of the coat about three inches. If anyone could see that, he thought, they had too much time on their hands and much better eyes than he.

St. John steered into a center lane, the turn signal arrow flashing among the dashboard gauges.

Joel swelled with anxiety. Price was clearly a professional, and could regain control of the situation in the blink of an eye. And the more time he gave Price to think about it, the more likely it became that he'd get the better of him. But Joel had the gun. He simply had to focus and remain composed. Much of his concern now shifted to the drive ahead of them. Once the sun went down, it would be difficult to watch the man's hands in the dark.

They turned onto Park Avenue and St. John accelerated into a gap between cars, braking, then downshifting, cutting the wheel, then pounding into the next gear. Joel found himself switching hands with the gun, bracing himself against the dash with his right hand.

St. John noticed this and smiled to himself. The gun was now in the weaker hand. If he caught the man off guard, he'd be slower to react, and his aim would be less accurate. He might even be able to reach him with a blow to the throat right now, but again, that was a big risk.

They crossed an intersection, running a yellow light.

"Watch it," Joel said. "If you run a light, it won't benefit either of us."

St. John downshifted, braked, and took a hard left, accelerating briskly.

Suddenly agitated by their speed, as well as by his unfamiliarity with New York streets, Joel whipped his head back and forth in an attempt to get his bearings. "You're sure you know the way?"

St. John ignored him.

Joel tried to relax, but the knots in his neck were tightening into rope. His fingernails bit into the dash. He turned his head and faced the rear window, on the lookout for police.

It was while Joel's attention was off of the road ahead of them that St. John was struck with inspiration. Up ahead, maybe thirty feet, a Mayflower moving van was stopped in traffic in the right-hand lane. The Saab was now going nearly forty miles an hour, and at that rate St. John had barely two seconds to react. He braced himself and jerked the wheel hard to the right.

36

THE SAAB CLIPPED THE MAYFLOWER VAN, ITS right headlight catching under the van's rear bumper. The impact crushed that side of the car, blowing out Joel's window, spiderwebbing the shatterproof windshield, and activating both of the car's air bags.

Joel was pitched forward for a fraction of a second before the air bag inflated and sandwiched him against the seat. The Glock was gone. Simply gone. Perhaps it fell to the seat, perhaps to the floor. Perhaps it was sent flying out a window or into the rear of the car. Either way, for the first minute or so after impact, thought of the gun never entered Joel's mind.

The car spun out of control, freewheeling across lanes of traffic. St. John had prepared for impact but still had the breath knocked from his lungs by the wallop from the driver-side air bag. The car slid forward, its tail end careening around, slamming into a red Pontiac Sunbird, caving in the Pontiac's rear passenger door. The force of this second collision reversed the rotation of the Saab, jerking it back toward the far-right lane. The driver of a transit bus braked hard, seeing the projectile hurtling toward him, but it was too late. He flashed a look of panic, but the Saab merely nicked the bus, only smashing a reflector panel attached along one side. The small rectangular reflector disintegrated, blowing out in a puff of red plastic.

Joel was aware of the rush of cold air blowing in from behind him. The world spun around him— flashes of color and sound, carried on long blasts of arctic-cold wind. The grating racket of metal on metal rang in his ears. He felt sure he was either dead or soon would be. The blow and its immediate aftermath had come suddenly, unannounced, and seemingly out of nowhere.

With no hands on its wheel and no feet on its pedals, the car was at the mercy of inertia. It skidded forward at an angle, finally coming to a full and complete stop with most of its front end in one lane of traffic and the rear end in another.

St. John blinked his eyes open, shaking his head. The air bag felt like being kicked in the chest with a work boot. He'd read stories about young kids having their necks broken by air bags, and now he fully understood the concern. But his had worked like a charm. He fumbled at the door latch.

The sudden squeal of clashing metal startled the ordinarily composed R'mel, nearly causing him to lose control of the Ducati and tip it over. He steadied the bike then flipped up the visor on his helmet. Up ahead, he could see a cloud of smoke rising from the Saab. Then one of the doors opened and someone got out.

— • —

Joel was vaguely aware of activity from the seat, but when the dome light came on in the ceiling, he put two and two together and realized that the situation had begun to quickly unravel. *The gun*, he thought. *The gun!*

The door had pushed open with only the normal amount of resistance, and St. John rolled out and landed on his knees on the wet pavement. The accident had only lasted a few seconds, but it felt like the car had bounced around in traffic for an eternity. He hit the ground on all fours, sucking for air. Smoke was pouring from the rumpled hood of the Saab, and the horn was blaring. He lifted his face and saw that a few folks had gotten out of their cars, watching him and approaching cautiously.

"You okay?" a voice off to one side asked.

Something was wrong with Joel's right arm, the one that had taken the full direct force of the air bag. Maybe it was broken. Maybe his shoulder had dislocated. Regardless, he couldn't raise it beyond a forty-five-degree angle.

He saw that the driver's seat was empty and the door was open. Battling the fluffy bulge of the air bag, he hunted desperately for the Glock. The sound of the horn was deafening. Someone spoke through the window behind him.

"Do you need an ambulance?"

Joel ignored the voice. He couldn't find the Glock, and there wasn't time to dig around. The snub-nose .22 was in his coat pocket. It would have to do. His man was getting away.

A hand came down on St. John's shoulder. He looked up and saw a concerned face.

"I'm all right," he said.

St. John got to his feet and staggered between two vehicles stopped in traffic. He stumbled, his feet going willy-nilly on the slick roadway. He put a hand on the trunk of a car in front of him to keep from going down on his face. When he'd made it past the second row of cars, he stopped and looked back the way he'd come. The man was still in the car, struggling to get out of the wreckage. St. John had no way of knowing if the Glock had been flung free; he'd not seen it. But this was his window of opportunity. He was confident that even if the guy got out with the gun, he could lose him in the streets.

Voices shouted at him. He was leaving the scene of an accident, an accident he had caused. He ignored the shouts. He dug in, ignoring the sharp pain radiating from his left knee, which had struck the steering wheel when they'd collided with the truck, and he ran against the blast of wind coming down the avenue, wanting to put as much distance as he could between himself and the man who'd claimed to be Megan's father.

R'mel remained calm. They knew precisely where Belfast was headed. But this new face, the man who'd held Belfast at gunpoint and forced him to drive the Saab, was a problem. Who was he, and what business did he have with Belfast? These were not questions for R'mel to answer or to even bother with. No, his job was simply to follow the man and update his employer. And follow he did.

37

SHE DIDN'T REMEMBER MUCH. IT HAPPENED IN a flash, and most of it was a blur. Megan had no idea where she was or why. Wherever she was, it was cold. And she was blindfolded.

Periodically there were voices. Footsteps came and went, and she was pretty certain she could smell someone's constant presence. One of them—if there was indeed more than one—wore a very distinctive cologne. She smelled it now as she lay on her side with her hands tied behind her back. There was also a musty odor. That made her wonder if she was somewhere near water.

She'd been awake for what she guessed was close to half an hour. She had woken from a hazy sleep, most certainly drug-induced. Her mouth was gagged and made breathing a bit of an effort. She grunted through the gag. She wanted a drink. Her throat felt scratchy, dry.

Footsteps approached, and she grunted again.

"What?" a man's voice said. It was a deep voice, lungs full of tar.

"... ursty," came the plea through the fabric of the gag.

Hands worked at the back of her head, loosing the knot on the rolled strip of fabric.

"Water . . ." she managed to say in a thin, hoarse voice.

"Go back to sleep."

"No, *please* . . ."

There was a long moment of silence. She was lost in a world of darkness, and in that world her only source of vision was her imagination. She had a mental image of the hard surface on which she lay, and of the man standing before her, and of the room that they occupied. Every sound, every smell, every texture and taste produced a new snapshot against the canvas of her mind. And now she pictured this brute standing above her, deciding whether her thirst was a priority.

Apparently it wasn't.

"Later," he said. "I'll see what I can find."

The ball of fabric was crammed back into her mouth. Footfalls echoed across what could only be a broad, empty cement expanse and faded from the room.

The rag stuffed over her tongue and down her throat only served to make her even more thirsty. It dried up her saliva. And the drugs, whatever they'd injected her with, had left her dehydrated. Megan had never been so scared in her life.

She'd ridden in the taxi with Olin, intending to spend the morning shopping while he took care of his business errand. She walked half a block, rounded a corner—and the rest was a blur. The best she could dust off from the wreckage in her brain was a memory of being seized by the arms, and then a quick stinging sensation in her right arm. Within an instant, the world around her grew fuzzy, and then went black. Now, she lay in this cold damp room, thirsty, and with a raging pain in her skull.

As the glazing effect of the injection slowly dissipated, the numbness was replaced with absolute fear. Who had done this? And why? In this cloud of panic and horror, her own words floated back to her, the mild thoughts of trepidation she had silently voiced to herself on the flight to New York. It had all sounded so immature and paranoid on the plane. Why had she not insisted on accompanying Olin on his errand? The answer was comically simple: after spending three or four days with Olin, her insecurities had melted away.

Now all she could do was wait and listen, and prepare for the worst.

A flash of color dodging between cars about three hundred feet dead ahead, and Joel knew he had spotted his man. Pain twanged from the shoulder to the elbow of his right arm. Price cut to the left, disappearing for a moment, then reappearing on the other side of a silver Mustang. Joel made a similar move and found himself skating across a sidewalk.

Behind him, in the mash of the intersection, there was honking and shouts and general confusion because of the Saab they'd abandoned in the middle of the road. This Price character had pulled a rabbit out of his hat. Joel had to give him that much.

As he ran, plowing through foot traffic, heading southbound on the sidewalk, he patted his left hand down the front of his coat, trying to feel the hard lump. He felt it, suddenly, and skidded to a stop, pausing long enough to fish the .22 from his coat pocket.

Price had a good jump. And he looked to be widening the gap with every second that passed. Joel's heart felt like it might explode, and having run so hard in such freezing temperature had set his lungs on fire.

St. John raced around the corner and stole into the alcove of a storefront. Shoppers squeezed past him, entering the store. He bent at the waist, hands on his thighs, catching his breath. His breath came out in puffs of white vapor. He leaned out slightly, rolling forward on the balls of his feet, peeking back down the street. No sign of his friend.

He checked his watch. It was nearly 2 P.M. He had thirty minutes to be at JFK. Realistically, he figured he could show up an hour late and still be okay, but he wouldn't risk it. By the looks of things, he'd lost the guy. He waited another two minutes, then flipped up the collar of his coat over his ears and then hurried on.

Joel's eyes were watering from the cold, and the brisk run in cold air had reawakened the virus clinging to his insides. He doubled over, hacking. He braced himself with a hand to the wall of a building, and just stood there, bent at the waist, trying to keep from coughing up a lung. An intersection lay before him. He looked north and south down what he thought was Park Avenue. Looking to his left, he thought he saw his man hurrying east with a slight limp.

St. John flagged a taxi. Stepping from the curb, he

sank to his ankles in slush. The taxi angled toward him, slowing and then easing to a halt four or five feet from him. He jerked open the back door.

The driver turned his chin, a toothpick sticking out from the space between his teeth. "Where to?"

St. John had his hands cupped around his bad knee. Every beat of his heart sent gusts of pain through his leg. "JFK," he said.

"You got it."

He leaned over the seat, resting his weight on his elbow. He was out of breath; his jogging routine didn't generally include wearing a suit, coat, and leather-soled shoes. St. John glanced out the rear window, barely seeing over the backseat from his lowered position. If the guy was back there, he couldn't pick him out among the faces on the sidewalk. Had he lost him? Maybe. Probably.

It didn't matter now.

The taxi was mulling through traffic, putting masses of cars and people between him and the guy from room 1018. St. John pursed his lips, letting out a long breath slowly. This one had been too close for comfort. He'd wasted time and energy going back to the Waldorf. It was hard for him to accept the possibility that the guy wasn't one of Albertwood's people.

Regardless, the detour to room 1018 had been a waste of time.

With his lungs heaving, and webs of fire spreading throughout his legs, Joel had been near total collapse when he spotted Price jumping into the taxi. He shoved the .22 back inside a coat pocket. No matter how hard he panted, he simply couldn't suck down oxygen fast enough. He watched the taxi merge into the flow and bleed into anonymity. Price was gone.

In a rush of emotion, the events of the past week blazed through his mind in rewind, and suddenly he was back standing at JFK. The passage of time between then and now was dreamlike. He half expected to wake up in his bed at home any minute now, his body and bed and clothes drenched in a cold sweat from this otherworldly dream. Because certainly none of this could have really happened.

I am a no-name businessman from St. Louis!

If he'd developed a mantra for the week, that had to be it. It was the tune to which he danced.

Only a few days earlier Megan had climbed inside a taxi and vanished into the streets of Manhattan. And now the taxi carrying Joel's one concrete link to her had vanished into the crush of Manhattan as well.

He'd been so far behind Price that he wasn't close enough to catch the cab number. That was just as well. Price was on his way to Syracuse, and that was all Joel knew. Without a name or a street address, he would be just as lost in a city of less than two hundred thousand as he was in this city of millions.

Price had mentioned something about chartering a flight out of JFK. But Joel pondered what good that knowledge would do him. He could only guess that there would be dozens, if not hundreds, of charter companies stationed at JFK. The odds of finding the right one in time were astronomical, especially when he considered that Price was likely not the man's real name. He could easily be anybody or nobody. Price, whoever he really was, was gone. There would be no catching him. It seemed the end of the line had finally come.

38

IF SHE DROVE STRAIGHT THROUGH, STOPPING only for food and to use the toilet, the drive to Chicago would take twelve hours, maybe more in this weather. That was way too long. By that time she'd be dead. If she stayed on the road, they'd catch her eventually.

Brooke hunkered down behind the wheel of the Subaru, driving like an escaped convict. The wipers made *wick-wock* sounds on the windshield, brushing off the snow as it fell. She started out going north on US-11, then took a left onto NY-5. Even in such hazardous weather the traffic was amazingly heavy. She blamed it on the holiday.

It broke her heart to leave her family as she had, but she knew she was in immediate danger, and staying home would have served no other purpose than to put Mom, Dad, and Wyatt in danger as well. A mile down the road, she saw the sign for the N West St. ramp, and she slowed to make the turn. She expected any minute to see a dark sedan with tinted windows pull in behind her, guns blazing. It could happen in the blink of an eye.

She kept her eyes open for signs leading to Baldwinsville. A left turn took her up the ramp to I-690 West. Once she hit I-90, it would be nothing but a meandering line due west. Just set the cruise control and hang on tight. But she wasn't ready for I-90 just yet. A few miles before the exit, she pulled into a Shell station and parked back around on the side. A pay phone hung on the wall.

She hadn't dared use the phone at her parents' house. If the phones weren't bugged, any calls could still be traced, and then they could begin to unravel her strategy. It would be pay phones for her from here on out. She slipped inside the convenience store and purchased a thirty-dollar calling card. Outside, she dialed operator assistance and got the number for Syracuse-Hancock International Airport. All flights heading to Chicago were booked. She could land in Detroit or Toledo and rent a car, but that still meant too much time on the ground. Once she got in the air, she didn't want down until Chicago.

Another operator connected her to Niagara Falls International Airport in Buffalo. There was a seat on a United flight bound for O'Hare International leaving in two hours and twenty minutes. She made the reservation and read her credit card number over the phone. Less than two and a half hours to drive from Syracuse to Buffalo. The odds weren't good. But it was all she had.

The Subaru sailed out of the Shell station and hit the I-90 ramp screaming like a banshee. She turned on the radio, scanning channels for the news. The clock readout on the radio told her it was 2:40 P.M. As soon as the speedometer pegged at eight-five, she punched the cruise control and prayed for a little understanding from the highway patrol. She set the radio on scan, and stopped it at the tail end of a report that stated that the funeral for James Ettinger was scheduled for tomorrow morning. That got her blood pumping.

Time was the enemy. The longer she was on the ground, the more she was at risk. If they knew she had the tape, they'd be on their way. She needed to get in the air, but that was two and a half hours in the future. Her next concern was O'Hare International. If they'd done the math, there was every reason to believe they'd try to beat her there. And her greatest fear was of stepping off the plane and being greeted by a huddle of men in dark suits with dark glasses. If she was lucky, she'd be on the ground and in a rental car before these guys wised up to her plan. But she wasn't counting on being that lucky.

She found a station playing Jimmy Hendrix and cranked the volume until the windows shook. Then she gave the gas pedal a little nudge, and reset the cruise at ninety.

The snow and ice had wrought havoc on the electrical and phone lines of the neighborhood, and did so every year. So it didn't seem the least bit out of place when a white van with telephone company insignia on the side stopped at the edge of the trees around the block about 2:17 P.M. A fellow in a hard hat and equipment hanging from his belt climbed a pole. The van had a nice view of 87 Birchlawn Drive. Inside, two men in navy turtlenecks and coats listened through headsets and watched through field glasses.

Their orders were to not make a move unless absolutely necessary. They were to simply watch and listen, and report anything out of the ordinary. They sat there for half an hour, and there was no movement. Another van was parked near the entrance to the subdivision, ready to give chase if the girl made a break for it. But after an hour, it was clear that the family was settled in for the afternoon.

Inside 87 Birchlawn Drive, Dean, Grace, and Wyatt Weaver sat in front of the television, warmed by the fire. Grace fixed a late lunch. Periodically, Dean would go to the front window and peer through the drapes. As of yet, he hadn't seen anything unusual. He was certain that Brooke was just being paranoid. Whatever had spooked her was surely no big deal. Around 2:40 P.M. he peered out again, and shrugged. He backed away from the drapes, and strolled to the kitchen to pour himself some coffee. He shook his head, smiling with amusement at his own foolishness. He'd seen nothing unusual out there, nothing but the falling snow and a guy from the phone company working on their line.

39

"AFTERNOON, SIR. MY NAME'S YANCEY, AND I'LL be your pilot today."

The fellow was tall and slim, and a gee-shucks smile gleamed across his face. He shook St. John's hand and led him out across the asphalt apron to where the twin-engine Cessna sat waiting for them. St. John followed him, snow flitting in sheets across the asphalt.

"Not a great day to be in the air," Yancey called over his shoulder.

St. John nodded.

"Been like this 'bout every day for two weeks."

The Cessna looked like a small red and white bird sitting on the broad expanse of the apron. A small knot stiffened in St. John's stomach at the thought of putting along in the flimsy little aircraft in such nasty weather. But the plane looked well maintained, and Yancey, on first impression, seemed capable enough.

"Any bags, Mr. Price?" Yancey asked over the howl of the wind.

A shake of the head. "No."

"Okay, then. Let's saddle up and get this bird in the air." Yancey gave him a big thumbs-up. Yancey jerked up on a lever, and the door swung open. "Hop on up there, Mr. Price, and I'll get you buckled in here in a jiffy."

St. John nodded, climbed into the cockpit of the Cessna, and wormed his way into the front passenger's seat. He'd flown in Cessnas before—many times in the rain—but the thought of ice building up on the wings or the propellers gave him pause. True, he'd earned his living by dangerous means, but he'd always maintained a level of control in every matter on every occasion. And he wasn't big on letting the elements get the upper hand.

Yancey had on a Yankees cap. He handed St. John a radio headset, and put one on himself. The windshield was peppered with moist flakes.

"You fly often, Mr. Price?"

"Too often."

Another big thumbs-up.

The engines fired, and the props on each wing went into action. Yancey radioed the tower, and they sat in the wind and snow, waiting for clearance to taxi onto the runway. Fifteen minutes passed before they began to roll. The Cessna maneuvered onto the long gray strip, its propellers buzzing in the cold air. St. John could feel the vibration coming up through his seat. The tower gave them the all clear, and Yancey throttled up. The Cessna eased forward, then quickly picked up speed. St. John looked out the window and watched the gray asphalt sink away beneath them.

"Sit back and enjoy the ride, Mr. Price," Yancey's

cheery voice crackled through the headset. "It's smooth sailing from here."

"Just call me Allan," St. John said, congenially.

Yancey liked that. He grinned and gave his new pal a nod. "Will do." He scanned the instrument panel, and keyed the radio, saying farewell to the tower. "So, *Allan*, you have big plans for the holiday?"

The engines droned on as they pushed northwest toward Syracuse. There was a bit of turbulence, but actually not as bad as St. John had figured. He listened to the hum of the engines and watched the snow fling past outside the windows. Finally, without turning to face his pilot, he gave a slight shrug and said, "Nothing special."

He brought her water. Megan wrapped her lips around the plastic bottle, suckling at it, desperate for fluids. She sucked hard, then choked when a long, breathless gulp went down the wrong pipe. Her hands were still bound behind her back, the blindfold over her eyes, but the man who'd brought the bottle of water helped her sit up so she could drink. She choked again, coughing violently until her face flushed red.

Droplets of the distilled water beaded on her lips and chin, while she futilely moved her head about, struggling to become aware of her surroundings.

"Thank you," she finally managed. She received no reply but could hear the plastic cap being twisted onto the bottle. There were no departing footsteps; he remained in place in front of her. "How long have I been here?"

"Awhile," the male voice said.

"Where am I?"

No answer.

"Why am I here? Why are you doing this?"

No answer.

"When can I go?"

"It would be best if you'd just lay back down and sleep. The time'll pass faster," he said.

Megan's face tracked back and forth, her chin upturned, trying to pinpoint the source of the voice. "I just—"

There was the sound of leather soles pivoting on cement, and then footsteps retracting into the distance.

"No, no, please . . . *please* . . ." She remained as she was, sitting up, slightly hunched over, her wrists twisted and bound awkwardly behind her by what felt like thin plastic straps. Was this it? Did life boil down to a moment like this? Perhaps she was destined to be just another statistic, just another young female who disappears from the face of the earth to never be seen again, just *poof*—now you see her, now you don't. Every post office in the nation had hundreds of photocopied faces pinned to their walls. Thousands every year. And one day that face doesn't show up for school or for work, or hasn't made it home by dark, and someone, maybe a guardian or a boyfriend or a mate or a work associate, starts getting a little worried. Then the phone calls begin. *"Have you seen so-and-so, she should have been here by now and—"* And within a matter of hours there's panic, hysteria.

Cold shivers flanked out across and up and down her flesh. Her coat had been stripped off, and she was freezing. She could still smell him, cigarettes and pork on his breath, and that heavy cologne. The smell of her assailant. She worked her wrists against the cords, but there was no give. The outsides of her wrists were raw.

She thought of Vivian and Anna, Sister Catina and her mother. She thought of the apartment in London. But most of all she thought of Olin and the life together they'd never have. What a shame and what a waste it was to die at the age of twenty-two.

Was he already looking for her? They had agreed to meet at a little bar and grill in Manhattan for lunch. She didn't know what time it was, but surely he had arrived and would be getting anxious the later it got. Had she been here an hour? Two? Was it evening already? Could it be Sunday or Monday by now? With the effects of the drugs still fuzzy in her brain, it was impossible to know how long she'd slept.

Olin would go to the police. He'd file a report and there would be a citywide search. Olin would find her. Did he have a picture of her? She didn't think so. Olin wouldn't let her down, that much she was sure of. She had lasted this long, she would hang on until he found her.

Sixteen miles outside of Rochester, the Subaru got pinched among a gaggle of semis. The trucks behaved surprisingly out of character, easing cautiously through the growing blizzard. Soon they had geared down to a leisurely fifty-five miles per hour. Brooke jammed her fist to the horn, but the whiny falsetto did nothing but attract brake lights. She pressed back in her seat, her arms out straight, elbows locked.

"Come ON!" she screamed at the scummy mud-flaps of the eighteen-wheeler directly in front of her. "MOVE!"

There was no space on the shoulders of the inter-state. Even if she thought there might be room to squeeze by, in the back of her mind she knew if she edged the Subaru off the visible pavement, it might be the last mistake she made today. It would have been equally unwise to attempt to shoot through the gap between trucks. The Subaru was tiny compared to these monsters, but the way those big rigs tended to sway back and forth in the lanes, they'd crush her and not even feel it.

In total there were five trucks ahead of and around the Subaru. The snow was thickening on the road and on the windshield. The wipers were having to work double-time to keep up. There was progres-sively less visible blacktop beneath the layer of white on the road. At every exit they passed she cursed the trucks for not pulling off. It was midafternoon, yet the sky was fading to ever deepening shades of gray.

As they approached an exit, a semi flashed his turn signal and eventually swung onto the exit ramp. She gunned the Subaru, filling the newly vacant spot in line. Still no room to pass.

A sign read: BUFFALO 73.

Brooke slammed the heels of her hands against the wheel. Another hour and a half to Buffalo. Her flight out of Niagara Falls International departed in an hour and fifteen. As speed/time/distance calculations ripped through the lobes of her brain, the eighteen-wheeler cruising along beside her slowed a hair, open-ing a fissure between trucks about nine inches greater than the length of the Subaru. She held her breath, bit down on her lower lip, and punched the gas to the floor.

The Subaru wigwagged through a cloud of powder kicked up off the interstate by the huge rig in front of her. The wipers couldn't swish fast enough. For a full twenty seconds, she drove blind, keeping the pedal to the floor, hoping and praying not to see taillights through the smudged haze on the windshield. In her rearview mirror, the rig she'd cut in front of looked the size of a farmhouse. She couldn't have missed by more than the width of her head. He blasted his horn at her.

Brooke grinned to herself, pleased as punch to have nothing before her but open highway. She buried her nails into the foam of the wheel, squinting through the streaks made by the wipers. Buffalo was up there somewhere through all that endless white.

The vents in the dash blew nice hot air in her face. Brooke glanced at her backpack in the other seat. She put a hand on it. Twenty-four hours ago she'd been on the road, that same backpack at her side with that same videotape tucked inside. Now she was driving like a maniac, zipping through the storm, fighting to keep her mother's car between the lines. She had an hour to get to Buffalo.

40

THE TALE BEGAN IN SAN DIEGO, EIGHTEEN months before the election of Clifton Yates to the presidency and seven years before the death of James Ettinger. It began in the rest room at the rear of a greasy burger joint a quarter mile off the highway, with a paper bag stuffed with twelve thousand in cash being passed beneath the cheap wooden partition of a toilet stall.

The man's name was Macky Warren. He was a truck driver out of Houston, and was in San Diego hard up for cash and looking for work. He found it through the grapevine.

A friend of a friend set him up a meeting that ended with a promise for twelve grand in cash. Three days later, Macky Warren was in Mexico, smoking pot and flashing the money around. A month later he disappeared. A Mexican prostitute claimed to have found his body with three bullet holes in his forehead, but that was never confirmed and quickly forgotten. Macky Warren's diesel rig was dropped in a scrap yard and smashed into a cube the size a refrigerator.

At some point during those first three days, as Macky Warren sped south for the border, having earned his money, an emergency crew was pulling up the wreckage of a demolished Mercedes from the waves and rocks at the base of a cliff along a California highway. The car had smashed through the guardrail at a sharp curve, plunged to the rocks below, and exploded. The hunk of twisted metal the emergency crew hauled up the cliff had been reduced to shrapnel, blackened and burned out by the explosion. All that remained of the driver and passenger were two thoroughly charred corpses. They pulled the license plate and called it in. The Mercedes' registration matched the identities eventually produced from the dental records of the pair. The driver was Lyndon Peel, Democratic senator from Illinois. The passenger was his wife, Deborah.

They had been on vacation, touring the scenic coast. It was a trip they'd planned for months and had very much looked forward to. It was their last chance for privacy before all the fuss of the campaign was to begin in the coming months.

At the time of his death, Senator Peel was sixty-seven and in perfect health. He was a legend in the nation's capital. His thirty-five years in the Senate had thoroughly implanted him in the bedrock of Washington politics. He came from wealth and had built another fortune of his own. He came from a long line of outspoken liberals, and in his youth had been a favorite of Jack Kennedy's. He'd fiercely opposed the Vietnam conflict, supported the legalization of drugs, was more of a feminist than most women, and favored every sort of regulation of industrial pollution imaginable. In short, he was loved by the left and loathed by the right.

For the better part of three decades, his peers in the Democratic Party and many supporters of liberal causes had urged him to run for the presidency. But Peel was hesitant. He had a close-knit family, they were stinking rich, and the White House simply represented more anxiety and strain than the Peels felt obliged to weather. He remained astoundingly popular with the public.

The Republicans were more than happy to keep him in the Senate and out of the White House. It was hard enough working with the few bunglers the Democrats had gotten to the executive office, without having to deal with a monolithic figure like Peel. He was a magician with the public; they saw him as one of their own. For over three decades, he stayed put, and his liberal causes never came back to haunt him.

But times changed. Peel's kids grew up and left the house. The family oriented senator suddenly had time on his hands. There were whispers. Rumors circulated. The talk began.

In a secretly taped meeting with the chairman of the Democratic National Committee, Lyndon Peel acknowledged that he was indeed ready to take the plunge. Shivers of fear and dread coursed through the right wing. It was their worst nightmare realized. They were coming off a weak two-term Democratic president whose VP had no interest in filling his boss's shoes. During those eight years, no one on the right or left stood out as a bold-enough presence to overshadow Peel. If Peel ran, he'd be a shoo-in.

Enter Julius Albertwood. Born in South Africa to

British parents, he left home in his early teens and ended up in Hong Kong, where he thrived as a venture capitalist. His brand of commerce was the duck-and-weave art of coupling investors with high-yield opportunities. He made and lost many millions of dollars, for himself and for others.

On a Saturday evening in late June, he arranged a meeting with Clifton Yates, Republican governor of Mississippi. In Yates, Julius Albertwood saw a chance at the big score. They rented a beach house that overlooked the Gulf, grilled shrimp and lobster and drank imported beer, and watched fishing boats bob on the horizon while they talked. The meeting lasted several hours, and was attended by a handful of key players, among them, Clifton Yates's attorney, H. Glen Shelby.

Yates had developed a reputation among the Republican movers and shakers of the region as a man who was going somewhere in the party. This get-together was a sort of meet-and-greet. Albertwood was feeling him out. A couple of months later, there were a series of meetings, far more serious in nature. The intent was to tap Yates as the next Republican candidate for the office of president of the United States of America. Albertwood had a financial backer lined up—more soft money than a thousand campaigns could even hope to spend. It would ensure Yates the presidency in the upcoming election. All he had to do was agree to play ball once in office. Yates was all-ears.

The man with the money was Bertrum Stott. From an island compound off the coast of Belize, he ran an empire. Chief among his profitable operations was the manufacturing and selling of military hardware, primarily tanks and antiaircraft artillery. He had the money and the manpower to accomplish anything under the sun. No one outside his closely guarded circle had seen Stott in at least two decades. Many believed he was dead, and he liked that. His age and physical appearance were unknown. If he ever left that island of his, he did so secretly and rarely. Eamon Desmond spoke for Stott at the meeting on the Gulf. According to Desmond, what Stott wanted from his prospective U.S. president was a guarantee that several hundred billion dollars would be pumped into the defense budget.

Governor Clifton Yates came to the bargaining table drooling like a hungry dog. He could suddenly almost *smell* the presidency. He agreed to play ball. But no amount of money could sufficiently diminish the popularity of Lyndon Peel. He was a titan, and all he had to do to walk into office was stay awake at the wheel. Albertwood had the solution. And it would only cost their little consortium a few thousand dollars.

For their trip, the Peels had made reservations at several bed-and-breakfasts along their chosen route.

Macky Dean had followed them out of Del Mar. It was rainy, and that was good; it would be difficult to stop a skid on wet pavement. He rushed up on them on a straightaway that approached a hairpin curve. Senator Peel may have noticed the rig quickly filling his rearview mirror, but there was nowhere to go, and Macky Dean was flying. The impact lifted the rear tires of the Mercedes off the ground. He bulled them toward the guardrail for over a hundred feet. The Mercedes went tail up over the edge, rainwater spinning off the back tires. Macky Dean was around the curve and hammering down the hill when he heard the explosion. He smiled. But then, he was already dead, too, and didn't even know it.

The accident was front-page news. The Democratic Party went deep into mourning. Their savior was dead. The Republicans couldn't believe their luck.

The race for the presidency had suddenly taken a radical turn. Three weeks later, a relatively unknown governor from the state of Mississippi threw his hat into the ring, officially announcing his candidacy for president. Clifton Yates was suddenly a player. The country took notice in a hurry.

A Republican senator from California named James Ettinger had been approached early on by Albertwood's consortium. They offered him the VP slot in the Yates administration. Thanks to pressure from Albertwood, Ettinger made certain that the investigation of the deaths went away in a hurry. Soon, the tragedy on the California coast was reduced to nothing more than just another footnote in American history. And for seven years, Ettinger was a faithful puppet.

Yates was elected without any real contest, and under his regime the U.S. beefed up its military to unheard of proportions. Stott made billions off defense contracts, and Albertwood took a cut from every nut and bolt purchased by the government.

All the players were set to coast to the end of Yates's second term. The economy was strong, unemployment was low, and his approval rating was near 60 percent. Everyone was fat and happy. Everyone but Ettinger. The ghost of Lyndon Peel never left him.

41

THE WORDS PLAYED OVER AND OVER AGAIN IN Brooke's mind as she drove. James Ettinger had laid it out piece by piece on tape. She thought about Senator Peel and his wife, their faces locked in terror as the semi plowed them forward off the edge of the cliff, seeing the land giving way to the empty blue horizon, then the lapse of seconds before they hit the rocks that reached up out of the Pacific.

The look on Ettinger's face on the tape was so somber, so ridden with guilt. This thing—the knowledge of what they'd done for the sake of money, for the sake of power—had clearly eaten at him for years. Brooke ruminated on the last words of his confession . . .

> what we did, the death—murder! thought Brooke—of Senator Peel, Clifton Yates and I accepted as a worthy sacrifice. And even now, looking back, part of me still understands how we rationalized such a barbaric act. To us, money was just a means to accomplish what we sincerely believed to be

> *a necessity. To Yates and myself, Senator Peel*
> *became a threat, a threat to the safety of our*
> *nation. We believed that an expanded and*
> *well-funded military was vital for peace, and*
> *whatever means it took to ensure that peace*
> *was, in the end, for the greater good.*

Her stomach turned. Such concepts seemed impossible for her to accept. Brooke knew and accepted the fact that she was still young and a bit idealistic, and perhaps even still quite naive, but was it possible for her to be so blind to the machinations of governments? Yes. She knew the answer was yes. She wondered how many events in history had been shaped by such horrific acts of arrogance and ego.

The car surged against the wind. Visibility came and went. The windows fogged and made keeping the car on the road a challenge. Brooke reached for the instrument console and switched the heater to Defrost. Gradual oval patches cleared away on the inside of the windshield, turning bad visibility to poor visibility. Thinking about the content of the videotape made it difficult to keep her mind on the road.

She was a half hour from Buffalo. Every fresh wave of snow turned the knot in her stomach. It pained her to think about how many scheduled flights out of Niagara Falls International might have been canceled because of the weather. Every few minutes she craned her head over the steering wheel, her eyes scanning for blinking airplane lights in the patch of dreary sky above the interstate. Every flashing red light up there in the endless gray and white was an answered prayer. The needle on the speedometer hovered just below ninety. The engine was howling. She feared it might blow but snuffed out that fear with several even *greater* fears.

She envisioned the monsters pursuing her. Bertrum Stott. Julius Albertwood. Clifton Yates. H. Glen Shelby. Armies of men. Stockhouses of weapons and ammunition at their disposal. She only knew the faces of Yates and Shelby. The others were just names. But her imagination created villainous features for the others.

Chicago. Her plan was even more clever than she realized. And she'd done well, coming this far this fast. Based on the message she'd left on Darla's machine, they couldn't know for certain whether she knew what was on the tape. In fact, her message had only mentioned a "package." Perhaps they imagined they could catch her at her parents' house. But she had to figure that if they suspected she'd viewed the videotape, they would assume she'd make a mad dash back to New York and get the tape to NBC in a hurry.

At least that's what she hoped they'd think. And if so, by now they'd have eyes all over Rockefeller Plaza, not to mention JFK and La Guardia. They wouldn't let her within five hundred yards of the NBC studios. And they'd have her phone in New York bugged. Surely they had listened in on her call to the office this morning. So far though, her escapade down I-90 had gone undetected, and across the vast expanses of asphalt and snow and ice there had not been even the slightest hint of anyone keeping an eye on her.

Maybe she had actually slipped under their radar. Albertwood and his motley crew were expecting her to do the obvious. But the obvious would only get her killed. If they kept thinking inside the box, she just might pull this off. If she made it to Chicago, her likelihood of being out of harm's way would vastly increase. Because for the time being, she and she alone knew what was on the tape. Take her out of the picture and destroy the tape, and suddenly their troubles would be eliminated.

She didn't plan on letting that happen.

Joel sat on a barstool in a dank bar with music whining from unseen speakers in the walls. He stared at the bottle of beer in his hands. The music seemed far away. A chill slithered across his shoulders. He shivered and shrugged off the sensation.

Who was Price? Who was he *really*?

More than anything, Joel would have preferred to just dismiss Price as a liar. But his better judgment wouldn't allow that. Price had known too much, too many specifics. Regardless of the fiction Price had spun regarding Megan's current circumstances, he'd been in contact with her, and that put Joel in a more frustrating position than he'd been in before. Could Price really be Megan's fiancé? And was she being held somewhere against her will?

Either way, Joel had come to an impasse. At the end of these five days, one question and one question *only* had been answered: it had been Megan he'd seen at JFK. If only for the fleetest of moments, he'd seen her face. The snapshot of her was captured in his mind. Was that enough? After ten years of depression and misery, was it enough that he'd gotten to see her one more time? Perhaps at one time, he might have said yes. But it was no longer true. A part of him that had remained dormant had finally stirred.

It was astounding, really, how a single glimpse of a passing face in a crowd had turned his existence on its head. One glimpse. One moment. He'd found her. Whatever good that did him now was an altogether different subject. At the least, he could walk away with the knowledge that his Megan had grown into a woman. But was that all he wanted? Of course not. He wanted to be a part of his daughter's life. To know her. To talk to her. To try to salvage whatever he could from the years together they'd missed. He wanted to know about Ariel. What had become of her? And what was the meaning of Price's involvement in Megan's life? Was he lying or was she truly in danger?

Joel pushed the bottle away, planting his elbows on the bar, and putting his face in his hands. It haunted him that he hadn't pursued Price to JFK. True, he may not have caught him, but he could have tried. Instead, he'd simply let him get away.

A bolt of pain thundered through his arm. It probably needed a doctor's attention. He was certain he'd torn something in there. It would be a bear in the morning after the mush inside his arm had had a night to stiffen up. He climbed off the barstool and walked into the rest room.

As he faced the urinal, he decided to forget the beer and forget Price. There was nothing to profit from lingering on the mistakes he'd made. He figured he'd made more mistakes in life than he could count. What good would it do to beat himself over the head with them? None. No good at all.

He heard the rest room door open, and then the

door to one of the toilet stalls clattered shut. Joel jerked the lever and the urinal flushed. He turned and stood at the sink, running tepid water over his hands, lathering them with pink soap from a dispenser mounted to the wall. Then he rinsed. Then there was the barrel of a gun in his ear.

"Keep your hands in front of you, and keep your mouth *shut!*" a coarse voice said from behind. "One word and you're dead before you hit the floor."

R'mel grabbed Joel's left arm and twisted it behind his back, giving the wrist a good crank. He led him toward the door, which Joel noticed the man had locked on his way in. Quickly, they were in the narrow paneled passage that to the left led back into the bar, and to the right ended at a fire exit. R'mel pushed him through the door, which gave into a narrow alley.

"Where do you people keep coming from?" Joel said, and immediately regretted his words. R'mel wrenched the arm at the elbow, nearly driving Joel to his knees.

"Keep on your feet!" R'mel ushered him along the gray wall. Then Joel saw a fancy yellow and black motorcycle parked in front of a Dodge pickup with a windowless camper shell on the back. A stoutly built man stepped from the Dodge and approached. The barrel of the gun was drilling into Joel's ear.

Through gathering tears, he saw the man from the truck frown at him.

R'mel said, "This is him. This is the man I saw with Belfast."

Joel had no idea what he was talking about.

Then Desmond raised his gloved fist and knocked him out cold with a single powerful blow to the jaw.

42

FIFTY MILES OUTSIDE OF SYRACUSE, THE WEATHER let up. The wall of snow seemed to part to either side, opening an easily navigable avenue. This seemed to relax the pilot. St. John glanced over at Yancey, who up until a few minutes earlier had acted less than confident regarding the weather conditions. Visibility had been near zero. But now the sky had opened wide, and with fewer than fifty miles between their present position and a safe landing, they each let out a mild sigh of relief.

The Cessna touched down at Syracuse-Hancock International Airport without difficulty. The wind sock on the runway was flapping wildly, but Yancey guided the bird in for a smooth landing. St. John had paid in advance for the one-way flight. He'd paid for one-way only, mainly because he didn't want to be pressured on time. There were other reasons, as well, but none as up-front and critical as the time issue. He thanked Yancey for his services and then walked hurriedly into the terminal.

For much of the flight, he'd pondered how to best handle the girl with the tape. He'd foolishly given up his Glock to the man from room 1018. Perhaps he could take care of the job without a gun. The idea did not sit well with him. Even if he didn't use it, a gun was the most efficient way to cover his back, especially if a situation started going south in a hurry. Going in unarmed was akin to going in naked. But if he approached with caution, he should be able to take care of the girl by more primitive means, and without incident.

It would be dark in a couple of hours, and he would need that time to prepare. His target lived in a residential area, making it imperative to move only after the sun had gone down. St. John stopped at the Avis counter and paid for a Mazda hatchback. The young woman behind the counter handed him his key to the rental car, and pointed him in the direction of the parking lot. He thanked her and turned in the direction she'd instructed.

The car was cream-colored. He unlocked the door and slipped in behind the wheel. It smelled like a hundred-year-old ashtray. The smell gave him the sudden urge to brush his teeth. He wrinkled his upper lip in disgust as he inserted the key in the ignition and started the engine.

Hungry after his afternoon flight, St. John pulled through the drive-thru window at a fast-food joint in town. At a gas station, he bought a road map of the area and scanned it in the car while he dined on his Mexican feast. Birchlawn Drive was northwest of town. It looked easy enough to get to. He'd simply follow the main drag through the city, then turn north. Piece of cake. He put the car in drive and pulled out onto the highway, which dissected the city of Syracuse. In twenty minutes he'd jumped onto Interstate 81, heading north. As he drove, he noticed the sky rapidly darkening, and it began snowing harder. He switched on the wipers.

From the interstate he had a good view of the city. It took another ten minutes to find his exit. He referred to the map, his finger following the progression of street names until he found Birchlawn. *Birchlawn*, he said to himself so he wouldn't forget.

He found the turnoff that should lead to Birchlawn Drive, and then 87 Birchlawn Drive, and finally to Brooke Weaver. By the end of the night, there would be at least one body in that home, he thought to himself, and if anyone else was there and they complicated matters, they would die also.

Having been crippled for three decades, living life from a motorized wheelchair, Albertwood burned very little energy, and thus required very little fuel. He took one decent meal around midday, plus a small serving of fruit, both in the morning and an hour or so before bed. Today was broiled chicken and scalloped potatoes.

He ate at an oval table, watching the market recap on the massive television given him by the chairman of Sony. At the closing bell, the market was down for the day, no doubt a result of yesterday's revelation from the White House. The stock market wasn't a major concern to Albertwood. Such a response from the financial world was to be expected.

He'd spoken to Stott earlier in the day, updating him on the state of their affairs: Belfast was en route by plane to the girl's home. Megan Durant was safely in their keep, and the Weaver girl hadn't been spotted outside the house in Syracuse.

Conversations with Stott were always brief and directly to the point. He didn't spook Albertwood the way he once had, but Albertwood still bowed to the multibillionaire because, quite frankly, it didn't make good financial sense to piss off the golden goose. The conversations were abbreviated for a very practical purpose: very likely someone might be listening in. What was said was spoken in a sort of shorthand. On paper it would look like rubbish. The call was bounced through a million separate filters, and linked and relinked by a dozen satellites. Tracing one end of the call to the other through such a sophisticated communications web would take no less than the Pentagon's computer system, and Stott essentially *owned* the Pentagon.

At 5 P.M., with the sun going down and all systems fully operational, Albertwood was feeling quite optimistic. He didn't require a full night's sleep. He simply nodded off for ten or fifteen minutes at a time whenever he found there was a lull. A few minutes past five, his chin touched his chest, and he began to snore.

There was a sudden ping of activity from another room in the penthouse, and Albertwood raised his head, momentarily groggy. A cell phone had rung, and Porter answered. Albertwood could hear his voice but nothing of what was being said. The clack of boots on the polished floor announced Porter as he strode in, being careful not to block his boss's view of the television.

"That was Newbury," Porter said. "Nobody's come or gone. The house is pretty quiet."

"Have they seen the girl?"

Porter shook his head. "They are listening. There's some chatter going on in the house, but nothing of use. A man, they're assuming it's Dean Weaver, the father, periodically looks out the window. But that's the only face they've seen."

"Cars?"

"There's a garage, but they say it's too risky to approach in daylight. There are tracks in the street in front of the house, but cars have come and gone in the neighborhood since they arrived."

"Do we have an inventory of the Weaver vehicles?"

Porter nodded, referring to a scratch pad in one hand. "A teal-colored 1995 Subaru, and a blue 2001 Ford Expedition. Both of them registered under Mr. and Mrs. Dean Weaver."

Albertwood glazed his macabre grin with a single stroke of his tongue. "I want both vehicles accounted for!"

"Newbury said it should be dark enough within the next half hour."

"And I want confirmation that the girl's in the house!"

Footsteps approached from the adjoining room. Carmichael leaned her head in. She raised a printout in her hand.

"Mr. Albertwood, a United Airlines flight from Niagara Falls International Airport to O'Hare International was just charged to Brooke Weaver's Master-Card," Carmichael said.

"What!"

"That's . . . Buffalo to Chicago," Porter said.

Carmichael added, "Flight leaves at"—she glanced at her watch—"actually . . . it leaves in less than thirty minutes."

Albertwood pounded his gnarled fist into the armrest of his wheelchair. His sunken eyes glowered. "How did she . . ." His thought broke off, and he slammed his fist again. "Find Desmond!"

Porter was already dialing the cell phone.

"Chicago?" Albertwood was seething. It didn't make sense to him. Her friends and family and her connections at NBC were in New York, all in New York. Was she going into hiding? Was that it? Or was this matter innocuous, was this trip to Chicago simply part of her holiday travel plans? His mind conjured the face of Brooke Weaver from the photo taken from her apartment. Why would she be going to Chicago?

Then it clicked.

She was going to Chicago to find Lyndon Peel's son.

43

SOMEWHERE OFF IN THE BLACKNESS THERE WAS
a metallic clank, and then the shuddering sound of
roller wheels as a door rose. Megan became aware of
an idling motor just beyond the wall. Very soon she
could smell the noxious engine fumes. When the
door was fully raised, she heard the transmission
engage, and the vehicle eased into the space where
she was being held.

R'mel had raised the bay door. He watched the
girl in the far corner. She was lying on her side, with
her head raised from the elevated cement platform
where they had her bound and gagged. The pickup
with the camper shell backed slowly up the gentle
incline of the cement ramp. When the front of the
truck cleared the edge of the ramp, R'mel gave the
heavy nylon rope a tug, and the door came shuddering down its roller wheels. The sound of the door
slamming to a halt against the cement floor reverber-
ated through the cold, empty space.

Exhaust pumped from the tailpipe until the
engine was cut. The driver-side door opened and
Desmond hurried out. He snapped his fingers at

R'mel, motioning to the rear of the truck, and pitched a key to him.

R'mel nodded.

Megan reacted blindly to these intimidating sounds. She swung her legs around and sat up. Things were moving. Something was happening, and happening quickly. In the few seconds that the door was up, she'd felt an intruding chill from outside. Goose-flesh rippled down her bare arms.

Lewis had come out at the sound of the truck backing in. He was dressed in black fatigues and a heavy black turtleneck sweater, with a leather shoulder harness that carried a Colt .45 automatic. They hadn't contacted him prior to their arrival. He stood in the doorway between the small, paneled office and the storage area, his thick hands on his hips.

"Well?" Lewis said, chomping a stick of Juicy Fruit.

"We're moving the girl," Desmond said, hurrying to the platform where Megan lay.

"Oh?"

"Get her things, throw them in the back of the truck."

R'mel had the hinged door to the camper shell open and the tailgate down. He was leaning inside the back of the truck, the tailgate cutting into his thighs. He was shifting the cargo already in the bed of the truck.

Lewis ducked into the office and came out wearing his seaman's coat, his arms filled with Megan's coat and purse. He flipped the light switch and shut the office door behind him.

Heavy footsteps approached, then a hand caught Megan under one arm.

"On your feet," Desmond said.

Megan probed nervously for the floor with the toe of her right shoe. The platform was elevated some twenty-four inches off the floor. She slid cautiously on her rump, an inch or so at a time, and her toe stabbed at the rock-hard surface. Sensing that it was okay, she made a little surging forward motion, and hopped to the floor, balancing shakily. Eamon Desmond pulled her coat over her shoulders and fastened several of the buttons in front.

"Thank you," she said. "It's very cold in here."

Desmond glanced at R'mel, who had the upper third of his body angled over the bed of the truck. "Bring the blanket," Desmond ordered.

R'mel peeked his head out, nodded curtly, then ducked back inside. In a moment he pulled himself out, a rolled mover's blanket under one arm, and a roll of duct tape in his other hand.

She almost missed the exit. The Subaru took a bite of gravel and weeds, swaying off onto the shoulder, the little front-wheel-drive churning hard to make the cut onto exit 49. Brooke took a deep breath, her heart pounding, her knuckles hard and white around the wheel. She'd almost missed the turn, then almost bit it on the recovery. *If I keep this up*, she mused, *they won't have to kill me.*

The radials fought for purchase as she motored up to a stop sign. She signaled, giving glances in either direction. Then accelerating right onto RT-78 toward DEPEW/LOCKPORT before taking another right onto Aero Drive. The wind had picked up considerably, and what was falling was blowing horizontally passed her window. A mile or so ahead, she could see the lights of Niagara Falls International. The sight of it brought very little relief.

Snow flicked in her eyes when she forced open the door against the stout wind. The parking lot was half full. She locked the doors and wrapped her arms around her backpack like it might sprout munchkin legs and scurry away beneath the field of snow-shrouded automobiles. A jetliner screamed off the runway, appearing over the roofs of the terminal buildings, then disappearing amid the gloom. Brooke hurried inside.

She rushed to the United counter, breathless. She gave her name, and a gentleman behind the counter rattled his fingers on the computer keyboard. She felt like crying with relief. She squeezed her eyes shut tight, fighting back the tears. She had a long way to go still—it was too soon to waste energy celebrating or letting her guard down in any way, shape, or form.

The ticket agent handed back her ticket and a boarding pass. Brooke ran through the terminal, her backpack flailing at her side. Her hands were shaking, clamped around the boarding pass in a death grip. She found gate seventeen. An attendant stood at the entrance to the jetway. Brooke handed over the pass.

"Have a nice flight," the attendant said without a smile and without any eye contact.

Brooke's heart was still pounding. The flight was packed nearly to capacity. She saw only one empty seat besides her own and assumed she was one of the last to board. How lucky she had to have been to get a seat on the flight was too eerie and frightening to think about at the moment. She found her seat, in the rear, one row up from the toilet. She stowed the backpack under the seat in front of her, then settled in for the flight. Almost immediately, a flight attendant pulled the outside door closed and locked it. Brooke let out a long, slow breath. She'd made it by inches.

Within minutes, the plane rolled away from the gate. Brooke put her face to the window, snow skittering across the runway. They were out there somewhere. Whether her clever little plan had bought her a few extra hours, she could only guess. But sooner or later they'd figure it out. She was certain of that. And she was just as certain that it would most likely be sooner rather than later.

44

AT LEAST HE *THOUGHT* HE WAS AWAKE. BUT IN the darkness, Joel couldn't say one way or the other with any certainty. The pain in his head—his jaw, more specifically—had roused him to consciousness. There was a heavy stench of fuel. His mouth was taped shut, and his hands were bound awkwardly behind his back. He opened his eyes, but whatever they'd put over his face left him shrouded in blackness. There was no moving his arms, legs, or head. He felt as though he were encased within a cocoon.

They were moving, though. He could tell that much. It had to be the truck, he thought. He had to be in the truck. His jaw might be broken. For the moment it was difficult to tell. But the pain was not dimmed by his trappings or by the darkness. The pain was very real and quite present. He hadn't caught the face behind the gun, and the man who knocked him out was someone he'd never seen before in his life.

In the void of the all-consuming darkness, up was down and here was there. But the solid surface beneath him was a point of reference, and he knew he was lying on his back. Somewhere beneath him, the tires of the truck were rolling over fairly even terrain. Who had him, and *why*, were questions for debate. Where they were taking him, and what would happen when the truck finally rolled to a stop, was of more immediate concern and worthy of a greater level of speculation.

He swayed with every turn, his spine absorbing the brunt of each anomaly the road's surface had to offer. He was terrified but amazingly calm. Perhaps on some level, the past week had prepared him to endure such a bizarre scenario. Or perhaps some small part of him understood that he was here for a reason.

Boxxen Road ran north to Courtney Avenue. Courtney ran east to west. The Mazda turned onto Courtney Avenue, taking a westerly heading. It sped past Slatter Road, and St. John carefully watched the street signs flick by his window. The sun was edging toward the horizon, burning the overcast day a fiery orange-pink. Wind rattled the radio antenna sticking up from the hood.

He drove with one hand on the wheel, and one hand gripping the console between the seats. He figured there was a half an hour to forty-five minutes of daylight remaining. Enough time to make a cursory sweep, put together a rudimentary plan, drive the car several blocks away, and park it where it wouldn't draw unwanted attention. The gun still bothered him. Firearms made the work so much simpler. If the girl's family was home with her, and he had to assume they would be, the task of dealing with them by hand would add another dimension of stress and leave him open to too many variables. The issue would have to be addressed.

Birchlawn Drive came up on his left. He slowed the Mazda at the brick gate entrance to the street. There was an ironwork design inlaid against the brick. Ivy had grown in tangled vines, spreading across the gate. Snow lay in uneven dunes along the top edge. He stopped the car, glancing behind, gauging the flow of traffic. A single vehicle sped past the two-lane blacktop strip. Traffic shouldn't be an issue, he concluded.

Most of the homes had big lawns. It wasn't an overly developed plot of land, perhaps two dozen homes. Most were two-story dwellings, with asphalt shingles and long front porches and very few distinguishing architectural features. All in all, it was a bland finger of suburbia.

The house at 87 Birchlawn Drive had a single level with a separate garage. A cement walk led from the driveway to the front porch. Of the three windows overlooking the front lawn, lights were visible in two. The home was set against several acres of woodland, separated by a notched-post fence.

In his mind, St. John pictured the rear of the home. A cement patio. A sliding patio door that led into a dining area or the kitchen or a laundry area. After dark, this is where he would enter. He would find the fuse box, either in the garage or mounted to the wall along the patio. Cut the power, enter the home.

The videotape was the only thing that mattered. The rest was unfortunate collateral damage. The tape would get Megan back safe and sound. Nothing else was relevant.

The Mazda crept past the house and on down the lane. Birchlawn Drive merged into Birchlawn Elbow, a sweeping curve a half a mile in length. He pulled into a driveway in the middle of the elbow, and turned around.

On the return trip, he again slowed, studying number 87, its red vinyl siding glowing in the gloom of early evening. He then turned his head for an instant, making a cursory glance down Eberhard Street, which ran perpendicular to Birchlawn. He could see a handful of homes sprinkled among the gnarled oaks.

A van was parked two hundred meters down Eberhard. He slowed farther, rubbing the window with the sleeve of his coat. There was a man in coveralls stationed at the top of a telephone pole, tools dangling from his belt. He seemed busy with what he was doing.

Headlights turned into the road up ahead, and a Jeep Wagoneer eased past the Mazda in the narrow rut in the snow that acted as the other lane. By now he had crept past Eberhard. The light of day was fading fast. It was a quarter of six. He needed to get busy.

Back on Courtney, heading east, St. John was soon back at the edge of town. Businesses were closing shop for the day. He spotted several strip malls along the way. He stopped at a convenience store and purchased a sixteen-ounce bottle of water. He unscrewed the lid, took a long drink, then emptied the remaining contents onto the ground, tossing the empty plastic bottle into the passenger seat.

The Mazda motored through three lights, then pulled into the parking lot of a strip mall. One of the businesses listed on the tall sign by the road was what he needed. GIBBIN'S GUN AND PAWN. St. John parked and walked across the expanse of slush and ice. He kept his face downturned, his hands in the warmth of his coat pockets. The sign in the window said Gibbin's was open till six-thirty. It was now a hair after six. An electronic chime announced him as he entered.

A man as wide as an ATM machine sat on a stool behind a glass counter. He had a beard and a diamond-stud earring. His fingers were laced and resting on the shelf formed by his gut.

"Hep'ya, friend?" the fat man asked.

St. John half-smiled and nodded. In the glass case in front of the fat man were row after row of handguns. "I'd like to look at a few of those."

"What's your flavor? American? German? Russian?"

St. John moved his eyes over the selections. There were some decent guns in there. He saw a nice .38 Smith & Wesson revolver, but that was a heavy gun, and loud. No he wanted something light, and something more easily muffled. Then he spotted the one he wanted.

He tapped a knuckle on the glass. "Let me see that one."

"The SIG-Sauer?"

St. John nodded.

The man unclipped a tangle of keys from a belt loop on his enormous waist. He unlocked the sliding glass door, pushing it to one side, and reached inside the glass display case to retrieve the .40 SIG-Sauer automatic. He set it on the counter, the metal gently clacking against the glass.

St. John handled it, eyeing it for a moment, then aiming it at the wall. He liked it. He owned several, but this one wouldn't be added to his collection. It would be used then discarded.

"You sell ammo?"

The man licked at the curls of beard beneath his lower lip. "I got a box or two I could let go of, yeah."

"I'll take one box, plus the gun."

"I'll need to run your ID through the computer."

St. John produced a driver's license, one of a dozen bogus documents he carried at all times.

In the car, St. John loaded the clip and stashed the ammo box beneath the driver's seat.

It wasn't until he'd set the SIG-Sauer on the passenger's seat, under the map, and started the car, that he realized that the sun had set. It was dark now save for the lights of town. If all went smoothly, he hoped to be done with this mess and on his way back to the car by 7:30 P.M.

He easily retraced his route back down the highway, then onto Courtney Avenue. Birchlawn Drive passed on the right. The car's headlights washed over the brick and wrought-iron gate, and he continued on.

Three-quarters of a mile farther down, he turned left onto a well-graded dirt track. The road wasn't marked, but the headlights soon spotlighted a wooden sign affixed to posts in the ground that read Elmdale Reservoir. And fifty feet to the right, the road dipped into a marshy lagoon. He considered this for a moment, then backed the car under a natural arch formed by the vegetation. The tires of the front-wheel-drive spun in the previously untouched snow-pack.

He killed the lights, drowning his surroundings in cold obscurity. He gathered the .40 automatic and the empty water bottle, stuffing them in coat pockets. Then he put on his camel hair gloves and opened the door. His foot crunched down through six inches of crusty powder. He hoped there would be no problems getting the car out. The walk up the dirt track to Courtney Avenue would be the worst leg of the jaunt. There was no traffic on Courtney. He hurried across, hopping the ditch, slipping into the wooded acreage. It was time to find the videotape. Time for Brooke Weaver to die.

45

BERTRUM STOTT'S FACE WAS PITTED WITH ACNE scars. This was his one and only distinguishing physical feature. He was lean and muscular from daily laps in the exquisite Olympic-size marble swimming pool that overlooked the Caribbean Sea, but his well-toned body wasn't nearly as noticeable as his savagely pockmarked face.

He was standing in white cotton pants, a warm tropical wind fluttering his unbuttoned white silk shirt, leather sandals on his feet. He stood in silence and was nearly motionless. The flesh around the craters in his face had flushed to the color of ripe tomatoes. The tail of his shirt snapped in the breeze, matching the motion of the national flag of Belize hoisted high atop a pole that rose from the aggregate stone walkway along the perimeter of the terrace. He was a man whose personal fortune was more than he could hope to spend in a thousand lifetimes, but at the moment he burned with wild rage. He held a cordless phone at his side. He needed to quench the tide of emotion rising from his chest before he spoke again.

The swimming pool was built into the massive terrace facing out to sea from his island. A dozen teenage girls dotted the poolside, all of them very scantily clad. The girls did not live on the island. He imported them from neighboring countries, shipping them here for his pleasure until he bored of them and sent for a fresh batch. The girls were scared to death of him, but the money he paid for a week or a few days could last their impoverished families an entire year.

The sun was down, but the terrace was lit up like a Sunday afternoon. The moon hung like a jewel over the Caribbean. Just out of reach of the light were his armed guards. The guards were dressed in green fatigues and carried Uzi machine guns. All had formal military training. The guards were not permitted to touch the teenage girls, but they gathered in the bushes near the pool to catch a peek.

The phone call was from Julius Albertwood. Albertwood had bad news.

The deep gray orbs that were Stott's eyes were flooded with absolute fury. Somehow everything they had methodically plotted for so many years had begun to unravel. Ettinger's weakness should have been foreseen. Looking back on it now, that seemed obvious. And if not obvious, it should have at the very least been taken into consideration. In hindsight, the reality of what they'd overlooked in their selection of Ettinger as part of the consortium goaded him fiercely.

The consortium had thought long and hard over their choice for the vice president slot in the Yates administration. In the end it had come down to money. Ettinger had money. His father-in-law was a billionaire. Ettinger wanted to sit at the Big Boys' table in D.C. Coming to the table attached to Yates's hip would put him next in line for the presidency. What they *hadn't* considered, though, was that if he ever wearied of politics, they couldn't hold money over his head. No dollar amount would impress him.

Yates, on the other hand, had been the perfect choice. Yates was nothing but a fish. He swam in their toxic stew. He was their pet. Yates's payoff was yet to come.

Ettinger had been fully aware of the arms sales, and was fully supportive. But when he'd finally caught wind of the truth behind the Lyndon Peel scenario, the tide seemed to turn. Much of Stott's rage was for himself. That was the hardest thing to take. Albertwood had come to him some time ago with concerns about Ettinger. He was suspicious of the vice president and filled with anxiety over whether he could be trusted any longer. Albertwood's advice was to do away with Ettinger as quickly as possible. But Stott had hesitated. They'd given it several months, to watch and wait.

Then they struck.

They struck too late.

> . . . *If and when you hear my taped statement, please forgive me. I've turned out to be neither a good brother nor a good citizen* . . .

If the package from Beacon was indeed the taped statement referred to in the email to Nelson Ettinger, and if the videotape escaped their grasp, the floodgates would burst asunder. There would be nothing left to say. Yates would be useless, and he would be left to fend for himself.

Albertwood had called to say that Brooke Weaver was on a plane to Chicago. Smart girl, Stott thought. Chicago. Clever. Again, they should have suspected such a move. Ettinger had made the first chink in their armor. Now the girl was opening them up for the takedown shot. She was going to Senator Peel's boy. If she made it to Jefferson Peel, he would drive a sword through the heart of the consortium.

Belfast was on his way to Syracuse. A wasted trip. It would do no good to send him on to Chicago. Finding Weaver in Chicago would require more than one man. Belfast was of no further use to them now. He'd become nothing more than a liability. It was time for Belfast to check out. The girl in New York, Megan Durant, was of no value without Belfast. And this other man, Joel Benjamin, who R'mel identified as the man he'd seen with Belfast, seemed to be nobody at all. Why he'd taken Belfast at gunpoint was a mystery. But there was no time to waste on further investigation. The time had come to destroy them all.

Albertwood had a crew on a private jet heading for Chicago, as well as the small crew in Syracuse watching the house and waiting for Belfast to make his appearance. At this moment, as Stott bathed in the sweet smells of the island, Albertwood awaited the final word to give his people the go-ahead to put the entire matter to rest.

Stott went down the gently sloping steps to the edge of the pool. One of the girls sat with her legs dangling in the water. She reached out and caressed his legs with her small, soft hand. He stared down at her with a look of indifference. He bought and sold human life as easily as cheap farmland. He could have the current harem slaughtered, use their corpses to fertilize the island, and never be required to answer for his actions.

The fact that he'd so effortlessly manipulated the most powerful government on the planet was laughable. His money had not so much bought an American president as it had the American people. It was their money that funded his empire.

At that thought he nearly smiled. But another thought interrupted: the videotape.

He walked to the edge of the low wall that bordered the crest of a sheer hundred-foot cliff. Seawater foamed amid the rocks at the base of the cliff. Enough was enough.

Stott raised the phone to his ear, and said simply, "Do it."

46

AFTER THE ORDERS WERE GIVEN, NEWBURY closed the cell phone and set it on the console. They were sitting in the dark of the van, the varied-colored lights of the monitoring equipment twinkling like stars from a distant nebula. Newbury sat still in the swivel chair for a few seconds before turning to Adair.

"What?" Adair asked, the twinkling lights reflected in the whites of his eyes. "What is it?"

Newbury's throat was suddenly dry. He stared at the man beside him, then turned back to the console.

"They want us to kill Belfast," Newbury said.

A gust of wind shuddered over the van.

"Our orders are to kill Belfast and burn the body." Newbury blinked, a fearful vacant stare revealing his anxiety.

Adair keyed the radio. "Get in here," he said.

It took a couple of minutes for Watkins to unclip his harness and skim down the length of the telephone pole. He jerked open the van's sliding door. Flurries eddied around his shoulders. He started to speak, then caught his tongue as he looked in at his partners. They were dressed for combat. Watkins clambered inside and heaved the door shut. He snatched the hard hat off his head and clanked it against the rear door, then unzipped his coveralls.

"We are going to kill Belfast," Adair said flatly.

Watkins froze midzip and looked up at their faces.

Newbury nodded.

Adair and Newbury were zipped into their skintight jet-black neoprene bodysuits, each with a digitally calibrated night-vision monocular over one eye.

"You'll wait here," Adair said to Watkins. "If it looks bad, we'll call for you."

Watkins looked unsure.

They each were aware of the legendary assassin Belfast. Belfast had come to kill, and now they had been instructed to intercept and destroy him. This was not what any of them would have cared to hear. Finally, he swallowed, then offered a single, hesitant nod of acknowledgment.

All things considered, Watkins was beyond pleased to be the one staying behind.

Newbury twisted several latches then pulled up a rectangular panel from the center of the van's floor, revealing a small stowage compartment. From inside, he handed Adair an Uzi, and took one for himself. He handed Watkins a Walther and a pair of day/night field glasses.

Newbury said, "We'll stay put for ten more minutes, then work our way to the house."

"What if he doesn't show?" Adair said.

"He'll show." Newbury put the Uzi's strap around his neck. "And whatever you do, don't turn your back to him. It'll be the last mistake you make."

47

BY THE TIME ST. JOHN CAME WITHIN SIGHT OF the subdivision, he was in the killing mood. During the flight to Syracuse, he had fully intended to just take possession of the videotape, then get back to Megan. But now he was ready to shed blood. He'd leave no witnesses. This wasn't his usual style, but the current circumstances dictated a less delicate touch. His jobs were generally planned out weeks or months in advance. Today, though, he was forced to rush in and finish the job in a hurry, with whatever level of bloodshed that required.

Lying in the snow in the dark, he peered between two slats of the notched-post fence behind 87 Birchlawn Drive. There were several lights on in the house. Smoke was coming out the chimney. A dog was barking two houses down, and St. John considered whether the animal was yapping at him or just at its own dim shadow on the snow. The patio light was off, which was good. The patio was a cement slab, about ten feet deep and thirty feet long, with a woodpile that started just past the sliding glass door. From where he lay he couldn't make out a fuse box on the outside of the house. It might be inside, which would complicate his plan.

To the west of the house was a smaller building he suspected was the garage. It was possible the fuse box was in there. The fence ended on the far side of the garage. St. John eased through the shadows, staying low and not making a sound except for the soft crunch of his feet in the crusty snow. He wove between a series of contiguous trees. In the darkness, the house appeared alone in the universe. The neighborhood was sparse enough that there was only a lone streetlight, which stood a good fifty clips down the road from the front of the house. In the snow and haze, the streetlight added nothing to the visibility.

St. John crouched at the end of the fencerow, his breath clouding the air. There was a door on one side of the garage. He had to assume it was locked, so he thought ahead and prepared. The fence hit him chest-level. He tested the top slat against his weight. It seemed solid. He quickly slithered over the railing and crouched down in the snow on the inside corner. The wind picked up, biting at his face.

He stole up behind the garage. Working his way carefully around the corner, he watched for movement from the house, and saw none. The lights from inside bled out the windows onto the snow. But he was fully hidden by the dark of night.

The side door of the garage was locked as he'd expected. From his coat he removed a small pouch, the size and weight of a checkbook. He unzipped the pouch and chose a slender metal tool, which looked very much like a dental instrument. Also from the pouch he took a penlight. He twisted the penlight until a conservative spot of light shone on the door in front of him. Kneeling down on the door stoop, he played the spot of light onto the doorknob and inserted the fine end of the metal tool through the groove of the keyhole.

The tumblers gave, and he gently twisted the knob and eased into the calm air of the garage. He bumped the door shut and fortuitously spotted the fuse box on the wall to his immediate right. He swung open the access panel and shone the light on the breaker switches. In all likelihood, once he killed the power flow to the house, the girl's father would come out to check the box. St. John would kill him first. He'd leave the body in the garage. The family would be waiting in the dark. They would see a man's figure entering the house, expecting the father who'd gone outside. It would be impossible to make out any detail in the pitch-black of the house. Even if they'd managed to light a candle or two in the interim three minutes, there would still be enough distraction for him to march in and take down the lot of them in brisk fashion. He would save the girl for last. Get the tape, then end her. He wedged the penlight in his lips, freeing his hands. He found the SIG-Sauer automatic in a coat pocket, checking that a round was chambered. Then he fished the empty water bottle from another pocket, and fitted the muzzle of the gun inside the open end of the bottle, to form a makeshift noise suppressor.

The fuse box would be behind the door when the door was opened. The door had to be swung closed to get to the box. So he decided to simply stay put behind the door where he now stood. Mr.

Weaver would swing the door open, push it shut, turn, then *pop . . . pop!*—double-tap to the chest.

St. John twisted the penlight, and its thin beam of light blinked out. He stepped to the door and made sure it was locked. Then he repositioned himself in front of the fuse box. He opened the access panel, and took a breath. The flow of adrenaline had begun.

He put his thumb against the breaker switch labeled Main, then clicked it fully to the right, entirely cutting power to the house. He turned his back to the wall, raised the SIG-Sauer to his chest, and waited.

48

NEWBURY AND ADAIR WERE CROSSING THE FRONT yard from the east when the lights inside the house blinked out. They paused midstride and exchanged glances in the dark. They were both thinking the same thing: Belfast.

Adair squeezed down on his Uzi until his knuckles ached.

They crouched low to the ground.

There was a sudden flurry of activity in the house.

Both men scampered to the front of the house, concealing themselves in the hedge that bordered the house. Through the night-vision monoculars, the house and snow and sky were all static green. Their hearts beat madly. Belfast could be anywhere. Newbury tapped his partner on the shoulder, and with a flourish of hand motions, communicated their plan of attack.

When the lights went out, Dean was soaking in the bathtub, sudsy bathwater riding high up to the rim of the tub. Taking a hot bath in the evening was his ritual during the winter months. Steam rose from the water, and Dean had settled down low, his feet propped against the wall, his face the only part of his head not completely submerged. Then, the light fixture over the pedestal sink winked out, and suddenly he was alone in the dark, up to his chin in scalding water.

Grace and Wyatt were plopped in front of the TV. The screen was now black. The only light in the house was from the dancing flames of the fireplace.

"Oh, goodness," Grace said, sitting forward on the couch. Wyatt's wheelchair was parked between the couch and the fireplace. The flicker of firelight caressed his hairless scalp. He was half asleep.

Grace stood with a look of concern and worry on her face. "Dean?" she called down the hall.

"I'm in the tub."

"What happened?"

They could hear him splashing the bathwater, struggling to stand.

"Probably the ice and snow on the power lines. But I don't know. Do the phones work?"

Grace leaned across to the coffee table and grabbed up the phone. She heard the dial tone. "Yes," she called. "Phones are working."

She looked at Wyatt, who just shrugged.

"What do I do?" she called.

Dean was standing in the tub, as naked and slick as a newborn seal. He groped in the dark for a towel but was too disoriented to claw at the towel rack. He carefully stepped out of the water and just stood there dripping on the rug in front of the tub. He couldn't find a towel, let alone his clothes.

"Dean, what do I *do*? We need electricity."

Puddles were forming around his feet. "Just . . . just . . . I don't know. Have you checked the breaker box?" he said.

It took a few seconds for her to comprehend what he was saying. Then it dinged. "Out in the garage?"

"Yeah."

"Well, no."

"Maybe something threw a circuit. Other than that, I couldn't tell you."

She glanced at Wyatt. The walls of the front room were alive with licking firelight. She stood frozen, uncertain what to do.

"Want me to run out and check it, Mom?" Wyatt said.

At first the idea sounded appealing. But then a mental image of her cancer-ridden baby crossing the ice and snow to the garage popped up, and she quickly reconsidered.

"Don't be ridiculous, sweetie," she said. "I know where it is. You've got no business out in the cold." She set her reading glasses on the coffee table, eased through the darkened house to the kitchen, found Dean's coat on the garment tree by the back door, and snatched her keys from her purse.

She started to unlock the back door when Wyatt said, "Hey, Mom, you might wanna go out the front. The path is straighter. You're less likely to stumble over some piece of junk Dad left lying about."

She nodded and turned for the front door. Wyatt followed on her heels in the wheelchair. She unfastened the chain and turned the dead bolt. Out of habit she tried the porch light. Nothing.

"Careful out there, Mom," Wyatt said. She cracked the door, and a gust of arctic-cold air blew in around her. "Watch your step."

She found Dean's gum rubber boots sitting right outside the door, and stepped into them. They swallowed her tiny feet. They were stiff and cold. She crunched toward the porch steps, then hesitated and turned back to shut the door.

"I got the door, don't worry about it," Wyatt said. He sat in his wheelchair, one hand on the doorknob, the other on the armrest of his chair. Flurries circulated through the gap in the door and landed on his lap. In just those few seconds, his nose and cheeks began to turn pink against the cold. But he liked it. The cold at least made him feel alive. And these days he very seldom felt alive. He could have sat there for hours.

Grace took her time easing down the front steps. Snow had built up in drifts on the cement walk and had gotten crusty as the sun went down and the temperature dropped. She hobbled forward, unaware of the face looking up at her from behind the hedge barely three feet to her right.

Newbury held his breath, his back pressed against the front of the house. He was on his knees, bracing himself up with all his weight on his left forearm. The Uzi was raised in his right hand and resting against his cheek, ready to end her life if she turned around.

St. John could hear a slow progression of footsteps approaching just outside the door. Then they stopped. He tensed. He had his back flat against the wall, his eyes cut toward the door. The whites of his eyes glowed in the dark of the garage. Only a vague flush of illumination from the streetlight came through the narrow windows above the garage doors. Even in the immense cold, a single bead of sweat formed on his right temple and traced down his cheek.

The footsteps ended on the doorstop. And for a long moment there was no further movement, no further sounds. Only silence.

Grace was staring down at the set of tracks that led to the garage. They ran from somewhere over near the fence to the doorstop where she was now standing. She paused. They were large tracks. A man's tracks.

Had Dean made them earlier in the day?

The wind was nipping at her nose and her fingers.

What would he have been doing out at the fence?

It had been hours since any of them had gone outside. In fact, not since Brooke had left. And these tracks in the snow appeared fresh. At least they didn't appear to be filled in at all, and it had been snowing steadily the entire evening. The tracks led right up on the stoop, then disappeared at the door.

Her gaze slowly progressed up from the ground until she was staring dead-on at the door. The keys were cold inside her fist. She jangled through the mess, attempting to find the garage key in the gloomy darkness. She chose one, and leaning cautiously toward the door, slid the key into the lock.

It wouldn't turn.

She held the keys close to her face, squinting to see better. They all looked the same out here, she thought. Again, she leaned in, the teeth of the key skimming through the groove.

This time it fit.

Her mind would not let loose of those tracks. Their presence was simply . . . *curious*. She'd have to worry about them after the power was back on. She'd ask Dean to have a look. He would have a better idea about them than she.

She hoped she could find the fuse box in the dark. It was somewhere near the door, if she remembered correctly. The key turned easily, and she stepped inside.

49

THE DOOR SWUNG IN TOWARD ST. JOHN. HE leveled the gun and aimed about eighteen inches above the doorknob. He'd decided not to fire until he saw a face. The scuff of a boot came down on the cement slab floor. St. John steadied the gun.

Grace stepped aside enough to get around the door. She was momentarily disoriented in the sudden darkness. She looked to her left, but saw nothing on the immediate wall. She pulled the door against the surging wind from outside. She almost had it shut when she heard a click. . . .

The SIG-Sauer had jammed. St. John had taken quick aim, and when the figure at the door had turned, he pulled the trigger.

Grace's eyes widened. She saw a person's outline against the wall of the darkened garage. She momentarily froze, paralyzed in disbelief. Then, in a move of primal instinct, she grabbed for the doorknob and slung the door open as hard as she could.

St. John cleared out the shell, chambered a fresh round, and fired.

The .40-caliber slug blew through the end of the

suppressor/water bottle and punched a hole through the solid-core door, sending a spray of shredded wood dancing in the weak moonlight. The shot missed Grace's head by a fraction of an inch. The toe of one of her boots caught on the door's threshold, and she went down hard, falling forward, banging her knees on the cement stoop, then collapsing fully to the snow-covered ground, slamming first to her elbows and then planting her face in the snow. The force and surprise of the impact knocked the breath from her lungs. She lay there stunned. St. John's second round ripped a hole through the center of the door.

Adair leveled the Uzi and rattled off a half a dozen rounds at the garage. He had managed to take up position at the far edge of the patio. He'd not seen the woman crossing to the garage, but he'd witnessed her panicked retreat and hadn't hesitated to fire.

One of the six shots caught St. John in the right shoulder. It pushed him forward, and the SIG-Sauer fell from his hand and clattered off into the darkness. He stumbled, falling to one knee. A wave of tremendous pain roared from the opened meat of his shoulder.

He fell against the lone vehicle parked in the two-car garage and scooted around one side of it, seeking cover from the gunfire. *Where had those shots come from? Who fired them?*

His eyes scoured the floor immediately surrounding him for the gun. More shots ripped through the door, turning it into a funnel of blowing splinters. Several bullets chewed into the vehicle, ringing against the metal and shattering windows. He peeked around the fender, and through the outside door he could see fire spitting from the barrel of an automatic weapon. And it was quickly approaching him.

He certainly did not think that the Weaver family owned such high-powered weaponry. No, someone else was out there.

Dean was yelling at Wyatt to get on the floor. He had a towel around his waist. The gunfire rattled the windows of the house. Wyatt dropped from his wheelchair and lay facedown, firelight washing over his backside. He crossed his arms over the back of his head.

The Beretta .32 Tomcat that Dean occasionally took out to the firing range was in a desk drawer out in his cramped office in the back of the garage. He cursed himself for not keeping it in the house. He didn't know what good it might do against the guns he heard outside, but anything was better than nothing. His deer rifle, the Winchester bolt-action, was in the closet in the bedroom, but he didn't know if he had any shells. Because they'd spent the winter taking care of Wyatt, he hadn't so much as ventured into the woods this year. And he wasn't exactly the type to stockpile ammo in the off-season.

Dean scooted down the hall on his belly, holding the towel on with one hand. Another succession of gunfire crackled through the night. He couldn't help but wonder if this had anything to do with Brooke and why she'd left so abruptly.

He made it to the bedroom and squirmed to the

other side of the bed. It sounded like someone was firing just outside the bedroom window. His hand was shaking when he reached up and slid the closet door open. As always, it was immaculately organized, but in the chaos of the moment, his mind went blank and he couldn't find a thing.

Wyatt had worked his way to the kitchen on his elbows. He was determined to make it to the back door so he could see out to his mother, convinced that she was dead. Then he saw the telephone on the wall. He grabbed at it, fumbling it in his shaking hands, but finally managed to dial 911.

Grace was paralyzed by fear. She just kept her face planted in the snow and prayed to God that if she got hit by the flying ammo, death would come quickly. The shadowy figure in the garage had frightened her speechless, and even now she couldn't form words or even sounds in her throat. From the moment she'd slung the door back open till now, she'd scarcely breathed. Time moved in slow motion, every second lasting an eternity.

The shoulder was badly wounded. St. John pressed his left hand against it in an effort to slow the bleeding. His fingers came away sticky with blood. He had to find his gun.

The SIG-Sauer had skittered out of sight across the cement floor. He felt around beneath the Ford but came away with nothing. Then he had to ease down for a moment to give his shoulder a rest. He'd come unprepared to fend off this level of firepower. And now his shooting hand had been rendered useless. Even if he managed to recover the .40 automatic, his aim would be severely handicapped. He squirreled around on his butt, his back to the front-right tire of the Ford. He looked in either direction and up the wall, frantically seeking a route of escape. There was one window five feet up the wall. It was twenty-four-inches square, with wooden latticework on the outside. A tight fit at best, he figured. But it was what he had if the need arose.

Even if he managed to scuttle through the small window, without the SIG-Sauer he'd never get far in the snowbound world outside. St. John patted the front of his coat and fished out the penlight gracelessly with his left hand. A weak cone of yellow light fell on the floor beside his hip. He lay on his back, holding the light against the underside of his chin, playing the spot of light out away from him.

How had they responded so quickly and so effectively? St. John tried to piece it together as he searched for the handgun. He'd barely gotten off his two shots before they drowned the building with submachine gun fire. Had they expected him? How? How could they have—

. . . *Albertwood?*

The thought hit him with absolute clarity. It was impossible but undeniable.

Something was wrong. The plan had changed. For whatever reason, Albertwood wanted him gone. Wanted him dead. They'd waited for him, and he'd walked right into their sights. Either they had already gotten to the girl, or the girl had never existed. And now they no longer had any use for him. They were there to kill him. They'd likely already murdered Megan.

Albertwood.

He should have killed the old man when he had the chance. Albertwood had discovered his one weakness, and then exploited it beautifully. As a professional in the most dangerous game in the world, St. John felt out-and-out shame at being played for such a fool. The hatred and anger that seared through his soul was partially focused on Albertwood and partially on himself.

Just then, something glimmered at the farther outskirts of the penlight's reach.

Adair had the woman by the arm, dragging her free of the firing lane. She appeared to be unconscious, and her legs made long ruts in the snow as he pulled her to the rear of the smallish building.

The garage had been quiet from the time he sprayed his rounds through the door and wall. But he'd heard the cough of a silenced gun, and heard the double-tap to the wooden door, so he knew that Belfast was in there. Maybe the quiet meant that Belfast was hit. Surely it couldn't be that simple. Belfast was superhuman. He wouldn't die that easily.

He saw Newbury squatting at the far corner of the house. He signaled for him to make a dash for the front corner of the garage. Newbury nodded, then hunched low to the ground and scurried across the snow-shrouded cement walk, finally pulling up against the siding of the garage. Adair signaled again. The message was simple: *I'll raise the garage door, then you go in blasting.* Newbury gave the thumbs-up.

Adair put a shoulder to the outside wall of the garage and reached out his left arm, nudging open the side door. The solid-core door was shredded. It wobbled open, splinters flaking off in the cold. His guess was that there should be a light switch on the inside wall, mounted just to the right of the door-frame, and beside that, a button to operate the garage door. If he could get close enough to punch that but-ton, Newbury should have open season on their friend the assassin.

He eased a boot up on the cement stoop, crouch-ing as low to the ground as possible. The inner garage was impossibly dark. He felt naked and exposed, framed as he was in the doorway. He was facing into the empty space, barely able to breathe. He raised an arm over his head, touching the wall, and fingering his way up the Sheetrock. His fingers touched the light switch, then scrambled several inches to the right, but felt nothing.

The blast thundered through the night air. Adair started, shuffling his feet wildly, then spinning and firing at the rafters. His index finger held tight against the trigger, emptying the clip in a stream of fire and lead. The muzzle flashes lit up the garage in staccato squirts of luminosity. Empty shell casings danced at Adair's feet.

The Ford's tires exploded, and its rims sunk through the shredded rubber to the cement. St. John had had the garage window open and was working on silently punching out the screen when the lightning started. The spray of lead caught him across the back, whirling him against the wall. The SIG-Sauer was in his one good hand. He fell across the hood of the car, holding the gun outstretched in a firing posture. He fired impulsively, taking aim at nothing in particular.

One .40 caliber slug blew open Adair's throat, pushing him flat against the wall. Another peeled his face open from the left eye on over. Blood gurgled up his throat and foamed out through the open gash. He could no longer breathe. He crumbled to his knees and slumped over backward, pressing his head at an awkward angle against the wall. His cold dead eyes stared vacantly up at the exposed rafters.

St. John was aware only of the sudden quiet. The SIG-Sauer fell from his grip, clanking against the hood of the car where it fell. He could smell the acrid odor of burnt gunpowder. He could taste his own blood pooling in his upper lip. His head lay across his outstretched arm. For the briefest of moments an image of Megan flashed before his eyes. He wanted to believe that the love she'd shown him had made him a better man. He'd never have the chance to tell her good-bye, to hold her one last time and tell her he was sorry. He had almost escaped his old way of life. But, in the end, he would die the way he'd lived. And on some level that seemed only fair. He tried to focus on her, to hold her face in his mind's eye. Then she was gone, and the world turned black.

Newbury's corpse was slumped on the ground at the corner of the garage, blood hemorrhaging from the stump between his shoulders where his head used to sit. The Uzi dangled from his shoulder, swaying slightly in the kicking wind. He'd felt nothing. Death had come instantly and from out of nowhere.

Several minutes passed. There was no sound save the whistle of the wind and Grace's sobs from the rear of the garage. After an intense period of absolute stillness, there was a small, careful movement on the front porch of the house.

Naked except for the peach-colored towel tied around his waist, Dean held the .30-06 Winchester Model 70 at his side. He was shaking, both from the cold and from trauma.

The front door opened a crack, and Wyatt stuck his head out.

"Dad?" Wyatt whispered.

"Get in the house, son." Dean's voice was trembling. "And take this," he said, handing the hunting rifle to Wyatt. To his horror, as he'd scrounged through the closet, desperate for ammo, a single .30-06 shell had rattled out of the Winchester box and into his hand. One bullet. One shot. And by some miracle, he'd made that one pull of the trigger count.

He approached the garage barefoot, his toes and ankles numb in the snow. Bending at the waist, he put out a hand and touched the dead man on the shoulder. Newbury was sticky with gore. Dean saw that the man's head was missing. He backpedaled in the snow, suddenly dizzy. Then he convulsed and vomited between his feet.

Wyatt had on a pair of unlaced Reeboks and a hooded jogging top. He crossed the patio from the back door, honing in on his mother's sobs. He eased inside the garage, stepping past Adair's body in the dark. He opened the access panel and reset the breaker switch. The house lit up instantly. He moved past the door and hit the garage light. He nearly jumped out of his skin at the bloody corpse at his feet. He found his mother and helped her inside. He grabbed a blanket off the nearest bed and went outside to put it around his father. Then he hurried inside and waited at the door for the police.

At the first sign of sirens and flashing lights, Watkins started the van, keeping its lights off. He backed into a driveway on Eberhard Street, and then slipped into the night.

50

UNITED FLIGHT 0214 WAS NOT DIRECT. THAT was the one detail that gave them the upper hand. Flight 0214 had lifted off out of Buffalo, and would make stops in Richmond and Detroit before sailing on into Chicago. Their Learjet, on the other hand, had made a nonstop trip from a private airstrip in New York to O'Hare.

The team was made up of Eamon Desmond, Porter, Carmichael, and Lewis. R'mel had remained behind to deal with Megan Durant and Joel Benjamin. The Learjet landed at O'Hare without incident. Surprisingly, the weather was better in Chicago than farther east.

They had a good hour's jump on Weaver. She would simply walk right into their arms. Desmond passed out photocopies of the picture of Weaver to each member of his team. He told them to watch for the obvious disguises: a wig, a different hair color, a ball cap, a hood. He also told them to watch for anyone walking quickly with their head down, or being extra careful not to make eye contact. She was on the run, he said, and she'd be on the lookout. She'd be suspicious of anyone and anything. Don't spook her. Don't give her a reason to bolt.

Two of them would be stationed at the gate where 0214 was scheduled to dock. The other two would loiter near the outside doors. But if they didn't catch her early, she'd be tough to find. They had radios and were instructed to keep in close contact. If they saw something, or *thought* they saw something, they were to send up a flare. Then they were to pounce. They had the strictest orders to kill first and ask questions second.

Brooke was asleep when the plane crossed over into Michigan. She'd wanted to stay spry and alert, to keep her guard up, but the day had sapped her strength and her stamina, and she'd eventually dozed off. The in-flight meal on the tray in front of her had gone untouched save for a bite or two of the week-old salad. She slept with her head against the window.

The Boeing skipped through a patch of turbulence. Brooke awoke, momentarily disoriented. She sat up in her seat and smiled at the woman next to her. She rubbed her eyes with the heel of her hand until the world came back into focus. It was a blissful few seconds, during which the past day was forgotten. Then her mind recoiled, and the gravity of where she was and where she was going hit her like a wave of cold water.

The woman next to her leaned over and said, "We're over Lake Erie."

Brooke glanced out the window but saw little else other than the smear of snow and clouds and infinite gray in the sunless sky.

"We'll be coming down into Detroit any minute now," the woman added.

"Good."

The woman returned to the magazine opened in her lap.

Detroit. Richmond. Brooke hadn't anticipated the broken route. She'd have much preferred a direct path from Buffalo to Chicago O'Hare. But once in the air, there hadn't been a thing in the world she could do about it. If Stott's people knew she had the tape and had somehow figured out where she was headed, they might be on their way to Chicago now to head her off. Could they beat her? Just the consideration caused a chill of dread to walk up her spine.

What were the odds?

She shifted in her seat, suddenly uncomfortable and anxious and itchy to walk about, to breathe fresh air and to know who was after her and who wasn't. If this flight had been a straight shot, she would have been on the ground in Illinois by now.

The captain spoke over the intercom, announcing their approach into Detroit-Metro Airport. They would begin their descent momentarily. She was probably just being paranoid anyway. Okay, so say they've heard the message on the machine and know she has the tape. And go as far as to say they follow the trail to her parents' house in Syracuse. She didn't tell Mom, Dad, or Wyatt where she was headed or why. So, that would be the end of the trail. Right?

Her mind simply wouldn't let it go. A piece of the puzzle was missing. It was like an itch in the middle of her back, a fraction of an inch out of reach.

51

TRAFFIC THINNED AS THE DODGE PICKUP EDGED out of the city. R'mel watched his speedometer, keeping within the posted speed limit. It would certainly not be the best of times to get pulled over. He watched his mirrors. The old six-cylinder rumbled beneath the hood, pulling him farther into the night.

Snow thickened on the windshield. The wipers should have been replaced a decade ago. They pushed the snow from side to side, streaking the glass. His fanny pack was on the seat beside him. He found a pack of cigarettes and stuck one between his thin lips. The cab quickly clouded. He lowered his window a couple of inches. Periodically he'd glance through the rear window at the camper shell. All had been quiet back there. If those two died before he got them on down the road, it would simply save him some busy work at the end of the line. He turned up the radio and tapped some ash out the window.

The Boeing taxied up to the gate at Detroit-Metro. Fewer than a dozen passengers deplaned. The woman seated next to Brooke Weaver removed her seat belt and walked toward the lavatory.

Brooke pressed her head against the seat. She looked out over the wing. Lights from inside the terminal outlined the maintenance workers taking care of the plane. She blinked, staring off in the darkness over the runways. She'd never been to Detroit.

She estimated that it should take less than an hour in the air to reach O'Hare. What exactly would she say to Jefferson Peel? She'd considered the question during the drive from Syracuse to Buffalo. The only thing she could really tell him was the truth. What else was there? She was going there for only one reason: to tell him what had happened to his parents on the fateful day in California so many years ago, why they had died, and who was responsible. He deserved to be the first to know. And he deserved to have the opportunity to watch the tape alone in private. Then the truth would be known. The rest was up to him.

Peel was the CEO of Peel Consulting, a company his grandfather founded. They now had offices in Chicago, Orlando, San Francisco, Europe, Hong Kong, and Australia. He was a very busy man. Until that moment she hadn't considered whether he'd even be in town. It was coming up on Christmas, and it was likely that his family might be out of the city or even out of the country for the holiday. A pang of anxiety sprung up and her stomach tightened. Even if he were in town, it would not be a minor task getting in to see him or even getting a message to him. So getting to Chicago was only half the battle.

Boarding passengers moved up and down the aisle, stuffing luggage into the overhead compartments and under their seats. Brooke ignored them. The activity in the aisle reminded her about her backpack she'd stowed under her seat. For the time being, that backpack contained her lifeline, and she—

The credit card!

Brooke sat bolt upright in her seat, the blood draining from her face. *That's how they'll find me,* she thought. *My MasterCard. I paid for this flight with my MasterCard!* If they knew about her, they'd track every transaction she or any of her family made. And that's how they would know she was headed to Chicago. And now they knew her exact point of entry. They'd be waiting for her. She'd never have a chance. She and her backpack would disappear like Amelia Earhart and her plane.

A small cluster of flight attendants were talking near the door to the jetway. They'd been on the ground over ten minutes now, and she feared that the door was about to be pulled shut and locked so that they could get back in the air. She bent down and grabbed her backpack from beneath her seat. Her neighbor returned from the lavatory, and Brooke burst out of her seat and apologized when she bumped into the woman. The woman said something she didn't catch. Brooke shouldered her pack, then hurried down the aisle.

The flight attendants all gave her a look, but Brooke was out the door like a shot. She followed the jetway up into the gate. The terminal was crowded. She worked her way through the masses, her mind cluttered with new plans and new scenarios.

There was no ignoring the sensation in her gut. It was the feeling that she'd just gotten off a plane that was about to crash. The plane wasn't going down, but she'd very likely dodged a bullet nonetheless. Her flesh rippled with goose bumps. That sensation told her a lot. It was like an angel tapping her on the shoulder.

She could look for a seat on a flight with another airline, but that would require another credit card transaction, which would once again put them on her tail. But she still needed to get out of Detroit. Chicago was a five-hour drive. Car rentals would require the credit card. She'd never been to Detroit, or Illinois, for that matter. When she didn't show up on the United flight at O'Hare, they'd check all other flights and the bus stations. The longer she delayed, the more time they'd have to spread out and wait.

She needed to get moving. She needed to think on her feet, and to think two steps ahead of her adversaries. Whatever they might be expecting, she had to do something unpredictable. They'd be watching for anything and everything. Right now they were waiting for her plane to land in Chicago. So for the time being, that put her at least one step ahead. If she ever got a step behind, she was dead.

52

UNITED FLIGHT 0214 HAD BEEN ON THE GROUND for twenty-five minutes. It had come into O'Hare on time, and the passengers had flooded out into the terminal. When the last of the stragglers deplaned, Carmichael approached the gate agent and made an inquiry. The gate agent grudgingly agreed to check whether anyone was left onboard. Three minutes later, the agent came out, shaking her head.

"That's it," she said.

Carmichael thanked her and reported to Desmond. Desmond was standing next to a support column, eating from a small bag of peanuts. He made no physical response to her news. The Weaver girl had not been on the plane. She had to have caught their scent. Perhaps she'd deplaned and they'd simply missed her. Perhaps she'd hurried off deep inside the departing crowd. No, they'd watched for that. She wasn't on the plane when it landed. Whether or not she'd been on the plane at all was another question. But she wasn't in Chicago, or else she'd come by other means.

Had she switched flights during one of the stops?

Had she deplaned during one of the stops and jumped on a bus? Or rented a car? They'd come to an awkward junction. O'Hare was one of the busiest airports in the world. No way could they check every inbound flight. It was enough of a job to watch one gate, let alone dozens. That was too big a waste of manpower and time, but there was another choice, a more efficient use of both. Whether she came by land, air, or sea, Brooke Weaver was coming to find Jefferson Peel. They'd find Peel first. And let her come to them.

Desmond radioed Porter and Lewis. They met up next to an enormous span of towering windows that looked out onto the outside world. A hundred feet away a series of escalators delivered travelers to the airport's various levels. Carmichael had finally shed the brown wig and looked professional with her trim blond hair, jeans, and sports coat. Porter and Lewis looked pensive. They didn't care for Eamon Desmond. He was Stott's crony, and just the thought of Stott spooked them. Thinking of him gave them the sensation of walking down creaky wooden stairs into a musty, pitch-black basement at two in the morning; nothing pleasant could come from such a situation. Neither Desmond nor Stott bothered Carmichael. And Albertwood simply gave her the creeps. She made sure to rarely be alone with her employer. She was all-business, but gross was gross.

"She wasn't on the plane," Desmond said, working a sliver of peanut from between two teeth with his tongue.

"What if we missed her?" Porter said.

Desmond ignored him. "The last flights of the

day are coming and going. If she's coming through O'Hare tonight, we'll never pick her out of the crowd. She might have caught a connecting flight somewhere. Or she might have hopped off at a stopover, and may be coming the rest of the way by ground. She may be on to us. Whatever the case, we're wasting our time here. Porter, you'll stay behind, just in case she happens to wander in. And we may need you for air support. The general aviation hangars around here should give you plenty to choose from."

Porter crossed his arms over his chest and nodded.

"We'll take two cars out of here. Lewis and I will take the lead. Carmichael, you'll follow."

Carmichael nodded, pleased with the prospect of having her own space for a change. Lewis's expression sunk. Time alone in a car with Desmond was not high on his list.

At the Hertz desk, Carmichael presented fake Canadian papers and rented separate cars for her and her husband. Desmond and Lewis waited outside. Lewis lit a cigarette and stared off away from his new partner. Carmichael came through the door and pitched a key to Desmond. He in turn pitched the key to Lewis.

"You'll drive," he said.

Lewis shrugged and discarded the cigarette.

They found their respective forms of transportation and proceeded out of the rental lot. They had agreed to meet up at a Texaco station five miles west of the airport. They had an errand to run first.

Carmichael was in a gold Toyota Camry. Desmond

and Lewis had been dealt a white GMC Yukon. Both vehicles proceeded to long-term parking. Separately, they wound their way slowly through the parking lot.

The Camry was the first to stop. Carmichael turned out her headlights, and hurried on foot to a row of parked cars. The gold Camry she approached was not as well maintained as her rental. She whipped a flathead screwdriver from a coat pocket and quickly removed the Illinois plates. In just over a minute, the highjacked plates replaced the rental's plates. She turned out of the lot and disappeared down the highway.

The GMC followed suit. It took them an extra ten minutes to spot a parked vehicle in the long-term parking that matched theirs. Desmond removed the rental's plates while Lewis stood between parked cars and worked his flathead like a goon in a chop shop. By 9:45 P.M. they were on the highway.

A bedside lamp blinked on in the upstairs bedroom, and David Hayweather reached to answer the phone. He'd been deep asleep, and it took a few seconds for his mind to determine what planet he was on, that he was in bed with his wife, and that the telephone beside his head was ringing. He answered the phone in a gruff tone.

"Hello?" His mind was clouded, more asleep than awake. His wife, Clara, had rolled over, facing away from him. She buried her face in her pillow. She was a mother of two and had tucked her little ones in bed hours ago. Now it was well after ten at night.

David set the receiver on the bulge of his stomach and patted his wife on the hip.

"Babe, it's for you," he said, already nearly zonked out again.

There was no response from her side of the bed.

"Come on, Babe, take the phone."

Clara mumbled something into the pillow. Finally, she felt around for the receiver, then put it to her head.

". . . ullow," she mumbled, her voice muffled by the fluff of the pillow. *"Uhh? . . . "*

Clara Hayweather slowly pivoted onto her back, her eyes still shut tight. Then they ever-so-slowly opened, staring up at the ceiling. *"Brooke?"* she said. "Brooke Weaver? Sugar, you have *any idea* what time it is? Where in the world *are* you?"

David Hayweather was already snoring.

Clara sat up, a poof of tangled hair crowning her face. "Where? *Detroit?* What are you—sure, I'm listening. Hold on, hold on—slow down, Sugar. Let me get a pen and paper." She squinted her eyes against the light and leaned across her husband to open the drawer in the bedside table.

"Okay, Brooke, now slow down and tell me what's going on." Clara Hayweather listened carefully. Her eyes were slowly adjusting to the light in the room. She scribbled on the pad of paper on her lap. Suddenly she straightened rather abruptly. *"Who? You want me to contact who?"*

53

DAVID HAYWEATHER WAS DRESSED IN HIS TERRY cloth robe, standing barefoot at the front door to his house. His trim haircut stuck out at all angles, and he was bleary-eyed. The baby was asleep, but the three-year-old had come wandering out of her bedroom, dressed in pink pajamas, her golden-blond hair pulled back in a scrunchy. She rubbed at her eyes as she wobbled sleepily down the hallway to the front door and wrapped her tiny arms around David's left leg.

"Where's Momma?" She could barely hold her eyes open.

Hayweather had one hand on the doorknob, and the other was atop his daughter's head. He was looking out across the front lawn, waiting for the garage to open. When it did, light from within spilled out at oblong angles onto the snowy driveway. Clara's red Accord slowly backed out, easing down the drive and backing into the street. Clara waved at them. David waved back for himself and his daughter, and then closed the door and locked it. The car's headlight disappeared into the night.

They had met on the first day of class, their

freshman year at Harvard. The class was A Survey of the History of Western Civilization. It was a required course and couldn't have been more unbearable. Clara Hodgson stumbled into class late, and because prompter students had quickly taken all the seats in the rear of the classroom, she'd been forced to take an empty desk up front near the lectern. She sat beside a pretty blond-haired girl named Brooke Weaver.

Their backgrounds differed, as did their interests, but they clicked just the same and remained good friends throughout the four years of undergraduate studies in Cambridge. Not long after graduation, Clara married David Hayweather, a med student from Wheaton, Illinois. He was attending school in Boston. They moved back to his hometown after he completed his residency.

Her life had truly flourished in the five years since graduation from Harvard. David had a thriving upscale practice in Wheaton. The children, both girls, were beautiful. The house was less than two years old, mostly brick, with high gables and a large garage. They both drove new cars. Clara didn't work. Besides the kids, her schedule was filled with charity work. Chicago society was rife with fund-raising, and she'd found herself neck-deep in it ten to twelve months out of the year.

The fund-raising was a great source of pride for her, and she'd excelled at it. David's practice generated an enormous income; they'd never be in want of money. So there was not much reason for her to find a full-time job that would drag her away from home and force her to stick the kids into day care. Over the past couple of years, in the letters she and Brooke had exchanged, she had mentioned her involvement in the community.

One pet project in particular she'd mentioned was a small school in a suburb of Chicago called the Nash School for the Deaf. NSD specialized in speech therapy for children who were either completely deaf or severely hearing impaired. In the past decade the underpaid faculty at NSD had made quite a splash in the world of speech therapy. Children from across the country had been referred to them, as well as a handful from Europe. The school was a nonprofit organization, which relied heavily on support from medical organizations as well as independent donors.

Her headlights cut a path through the dreary late-night fog as she headed across the city to the home of Dr. Eucinda Omheimer. The snow seemed to have finally blown past them, heading on east, but had left low-hanging clouds in its wake. The morning sun would likely burn off most of it, but sundown meant hazardous road conditions. She turned on the car radio. It was set to an easy-listening station.

It had been nice to hear her old friend's voice again. Had it really been a year since they'd last spoken? It seemed impossible, but there was no denying the frantic edge to Brooke's voice. She was in a world of trouble and had asked her for help. Brooke had been fairly brief and guarded on the phone. Clara couldn't even begin to guess the severity of the situation, but after hearing her friend so distraught, she didn't hesitate to jump out of bed and take action.

And she would have never dreamed that something she'd mentioned in one of her letters to Brooke would come back to her in such dramatic fashion.

But Brooke had been specific and unflinching. She knew what she needed, and Clara wasn't about to deny her friend this one crucial favor.

She turned through an intersection into a neighborhood of modest homes. She could barely make out the street signs in the fog. Dr. Omheimer's home was on down just half a block on the left. As the Accord sped down the two-lane avenue, Clara could see that the porch light was on. She parked in the short driveway behind Dr. Omheimer's ancient car. She unbuckled her seat belt and grabbed her purse from the passenger's seat. She had called ahead. Dr. Omheimer slept only four or five hours a night, spending most of her off hours either with her nose in a book or cooking. She was rotund and jolly, and impossible to upset. She'd told Clara to come on over.

Brooke had been fairly vague on the phone. But one thing she'd been very clear about was the fact that Clara had the connections that just might save her life.

The road was an elongated horseshoe that rose gradually for several miles, and then took a sudden dip, came within a few hundred feet of Lake Michigan, then curved around and away, returning you in the general direction that you'd come.

Just beyond the sudden dip in the road an iron fence began. They followed the flow of the road for a quarter mile, then cut in and out through a lovely piece of wooded acreage, then reappeared to meet the road just before the road curved away from the water.

Behind the fence stood an enormous home, a twelve-thousand-square-foot fortress constructed mostly of river stone. The front lawn was bordered by woodland on either side, and the back lawn gave onto a small inlet of Lake Michigan. The estate was entirely enclosed by the iron fencing save for the natural barrier of the lake. The gate at the end of the drive functioned electronically, and was monitored by closed-circuit camera. This was the home of Jefferson Peel and his family.

The Camry parked back up the road a ways, above the rise in the hill. Carmichael killed her headlights, but because of the cold, left the engine running. She picked up her radio. "Echo-One. I'm ready and waiting," she said.

Desmond and Lewis cruised on down the lane, descending the easy slope, which leveled off and swept past the Peel estate. They continued on, following the liberal curve of the road, eventually heading back the way they'd come. Much of the acreage that filled the inside of the horseshoe was wooded. A few hundred feet beyond the sweep of the curve, Lewis pulled off the road and gently steered in among the trees. The traction was less forgiving here, and the tires began to spin in the mushy blanket of snow and pine needles.

Desmond gave the word, and the GMC eased to a halt. The sudden darkness and silence were abrupt. They moved through the trees. The snow was only ankle deep. It was just less than a quarter-mile walk to the far edge of the horseshoe. When they resurfaced, they were careful to stay in the shadows. It was a cold night. Clouds of breath rose from their faces.

Desmond raised the night-vision field glasses to his face, bracing against a tree to keep his arm steady.

Lewis spoke into his radio. "Echo-Three, you read?" He spoke in a low, controlled tone.

"Roger."

"We have visual, over," he said.

"Roger that," Carmichael said. "All clear from this end."

It was after 11 P.M. From their vantage point, few lights were visible inside the house, but enough to suggest that not much was going on. There could be lights left on all night for security, or just to keep from stubbing your toes when you got up for a drink of water, or to use the bathroom, or to grab a snack in the kitchen. For the moment, the night-vision field glasses didn't offer much more than the naked eye was capable of seeing. Desmond held them at his side, thinking through his options. If it kept up like this, it would certainly be a long night.

Desmond was certain that the Weaver girl would try to make a go of it—and probably tonight. It occurred to him that she might wait until morning, and confront Peel at work. She might suspect a stakeout, and the arrival of nightfall most likely had her spooked. If she made a run at the Peel estate tonight, it would all be over, quick and easy. If she tried an end run at Peel's office in the light of day, she'd never make it across the parking lot. And if she did get to Peel with the tape, that would simply mean that a bigger mess would have to be made.

54

STATE HIGHWAY 7 BECAME US 23, AND BY
midnight, R'mel had found his way to Stockbridge,
Massachusetts. The drive had taken longer than he
expected, and he still had over an hour to go. The
AM radio was driving him mad; the only stations
he'd managed to dial up were phone-in shows, back-
woods preachers, and country music. He listened to
the rantings of fire-and-brimstone preachers for three
hundred miles.

By midnight, the gas gauge was needling into the
red zone. He exited at Stockbridge, pulling the Dodge
pickup into a twenty-four-hour Sunoco station.
Through the glass, he could see a black woman sitting
on a stool behind the counter. He pumped in thirty dollars' worth of regular unleaded, and crossed the rutted
and patched pavement to pay. He slipped down an aisle
and grabbed a handful of candy bars, then grabbed a
bottled Diet Dr Pepper from the cooler along the wall.

The attendant never made eye contact. She clearly
wished she were somewhere else, *any*where else but
wasting her time pulling in five bucks an hour. R'mel
was certain he'd never seen a more obese human

being. He dumped his items onto the counter. He cast a glance at the folds around her waist and shoved the candy bars aside.

"Just the soda and the gas," he said.

It was at least another hour to Pittsfield. Onota Lake was not far from there. He hoped to be done with this mess by around 2 A.M. He hurried out across the pavement, circling around the rear of the truck. He unlocked the door to the camper shell, twisted the latch, and lifted it up on its pneumatic arms. Both of the detainees were still in there, bound from head to foot in mover's blankets and duct tape. The girl was petite, but the Benjamin character had enough size to him to require quite a bit of extra digging. R'mel frowned. He dreaded the work ahead of him. He considered whether to dig separate graves, or to just dig one but make it extra big. Neither option sounded promising.

Desmond had drugged the girl again; he had in fact given her double the dose from earlier. She'd be out for at least several more hours. But he figured Benjamin had likely already shaken it off. Neither of them were moving. R'mel lowered the door and locked the latch.

Ten miles down the road, the heater went out. He pulled the Dodge off to the side of the highway and found that the heater fuse beneath the dash had blown. It was too freaking cold to roar down the road at seventy mph without the heater blowing on him. He scrounged through the glove box but found nothing. He didn't want to backtrack to Stockbridge, and wasn't sure how much farther he'd have to continue on until he found another all-night station. For the moment he'd have to grin and bear it.

The drive in the cold made him dread digging the graves even more. *Perhaps,* he thought, *I'll just let Benjamin dig the graves himself. Yes. That way he can make some use of himself before he dies.*

The idea warmed him slightly.

They took turns. One would keep the watch, staying in the shadows of the trees across the road from the Peel estate, while the other spent a half an hour warming up in the GMC. Desmond was sitting in the driver's seat, nearly thawed, when Lewis's voice crackled over the radio.

"A fog light came on above the garage," Lewis said. "Looks like some activity."

Desmond was on his radio in an instant. "Can you see anyone?"

"Not yet . . . *wait,*" Lewis said.

"What? What? What do you see?"

"There are headlights. Headlights coming up the driveway from around the side of the house."

A silver Infiniti sedan approached the iron gate, and when it was within fifty feet, the gate separated at the center and slowly spread apart. Lewis could just hear the soft whirring of the gate's motor. The car passed through and turned onto the street. Its headlights glowed in the fog and lightly falling snow. It appeared to Lewis like a mythic creature abandoning its cave.

"It's a silver sedan," Lewis said into his radio. He had taken refuge behind a massive walnut tree. He pressed against the tree, its bark grating at his face. "Heading your way, Echo-Three."

"Could you see a face?" Desmond yelled.

"No. No. The view was pretty obscured. But the small glimpse I got looked like a man," Lewis remarked.

Peel! Desmond screamed in his own head. But could he be sure?

"Echo-Three, do you have a visual?" Desmond said.

"Affirmative," Carmichael said. "Silver Infiniti has just passed my position, and I am pursuing."

"I'm on my way," Desmond said. "Echo-Four, maintain your position. Keep watch while we check this guy out."

Lewis raised his arm to the tree and rested his forehead against his hand. Desmond was leaving him out there to freeze to death. His toes and fingers were numb, and it wasn't going to get any better. A gust of wind ripped through the trees, dumping clumps of snow on his shoulders and down the neck of his coat. His nose felt like wood. He hated Desmond. And he hated Stott.

Carmichael maintained a safe distance behind the Infiniti. She updated Desmond on her position, and within a few minutes she saw their headlights appear in her rearview mirror.

"Don't spook him," Desmond's voice said over her radio. "Let him lead us to her."

"Roger that," Carmichael said.

A new spark of life shot through Desmond. He focused his eyes dead ahead. If it *was* Jefferson Peel in that car, where else would he be going alone at 12:30 A.M. on a Saturday morning? Had Brooke Weaver managed to contact him? If so, where from and how? Had she indeed flown into O'Hare? How else could she have made it into Chicago so quickly? It seemed impossible.

But where else would he be going? They were already seven miles from his home and heading onto US 41, which was also Lake Shore Drive. He hadn't gotten out for a simple errand. He wasn't after milk or eggs or batteries for the television remote control. He was driving with a purpose. He was going to meet the girl.

And they had him in their sights.

Desmond smiled to himself. *Finally*, he thought. Finally they had her. And better yet, they would nab the two of them at once. That was a lovely thought. Desmond squeezed his fingers around the steering wheel. Mr. Stott had entrusted him with much responsibility. And here he was, finally, coming through the ordeal victorious. Mr. Stott would reward him greatly. That was Stott's way, to punish severely when it was called for, and to reward generously for a job very well done.

Fanciful notions danced in his head. What might Mr. Stott offer him as compensation for salvaging the consortium in the face of certain disaster? A villa in Greece, perhaps? His own office in Hong Kong? Perhaps a Lamborghini, or a few million dollars in a Swiss account? Or perhaps he'd be given his choice from all the above. Ah, yes! He'd given so many years of his life in service to Stott, and it was time for those years to be handsomely rewarded. Suddenly hot with adrenaline and anticipation, Desmond pressed the gas pedal, goosing the Yukon into the left lane, swishing past the Toyota Camry. Carmichael watched him pass. *Better you than me*, she thought.

Desmond keyed his handheld radio. "Echo-Two, do you read me?"

Static crackled for a few seconds, then Porter answered, "Roger that."

"We need you airborne, Echo-Two."

"Roger that."

"Follow Interstate Ninety southeast from O'Hare, until you reach Highway Forty. You should be on top of us by then. The rabbit is running."

"Roger. Echo-Two out."

Porter had exited the terminal area and now walked quickly across the windblown tarmac. The general aviation section of O'Hare was packed with privately owned and leased hangars. Most of the hangars housed fixed-wing aircraft. Some of the aircraft were staged outside the hangar doors, likely due to space restrictions, though a few were in the process of preparing for flights tonight. He'd seen a few helicopters staged outside a hangar as they had descended in the Lear.

He reached the hangar and saw only one chopper, a red and yellow Enstrom, sitting out on the tarmac. A man in grease-stained work coveralls shut the engine cowling and walked toward the side door of the hangar. Porter stole behind the corner of the sheet-metal building, and waited.

After a minute or two, a mechanic wearing coveralls appeared at the door, followed by the pilot, dressed in a heavy down vest and a baseball cap. They talked hurriedly, all the while pointing at the helicopter. Then they shook hands, and Porter heard the mechanic wish the pilot a good flight. The mechanic disappeared inside and shut the door behind him. The pilot headed for his machine.

There was a sharp northerly wind slicing across

the airfield. The pilot opened the Enstrom's right-side door and paused, patting his vest for a pack of cigarettes. He didn't hear the footsteps approaching. The suppressor on the barrel of the Glock touched just behind his right ear, but he saw and heard nothing. He was dead before even a single thought had time to formulate in his brain.

Porter caught the man under the arms and hefted him into the rear seat of the Enstrom. The bird was fueled and ready to go. Porter couldn't have asked for more. Where this nut had been heading at this hour of the morning, Porter could only imagine, but he'd clearly been anxious to get the machine in the air. Porter buckled in, and within seconds the rotors were buzzing overhead. The machine lifted off the ground, and he headed southeast, as instructed.

55

THE INFINITI SLOWED, SIGNALED LEFT AT A **T** IN the road, and headed down into the parking area of the marina. Its taillights blinked in the shifting fog as the luxury car eased over a series of speed bumps.

Desmond nearly wet his pants. Peel was heading toward the water. They couldn't get too close, not yet. The marina was quiet and dark except for a few lampposts that lined the parking area and dotted the mooring docks. They turned left at the T. The other car momentarily slipped out of sight behind a red brick structure, then flickered back into view, farther down the slope near the dock.

A question buzzed through Desmond's mind: was the girl here at the marina, or would he have to travel by water to meet her? If the girl was nearby, it would make easy work of disposing their bodies.

He radioed Carmichael, and they parked near each other along the outside perimeter of the parking area. He then radioed Porter, updating their location. Porter had found a laminated folding map of Illinois and quickly plotted his flight path to the marina. He'd be there in a matter of minutes.

Desmond nudged his door shut and motioned for Carmichael to follow him. They each carried 9mm Berettas. Except for the lampposts along its perimeter, the sloping parking area was dark. They came upon the parked Infiniti sedan. Its lights were off and it was abandoned.

The dark silhouette of a lone figure was walking hastily toward the dock. Even from this distance and in the dark, they could tell by the posture, size, and gait that it was male. Desmond was nearly salivating. Water lapped against the pilings beneath the dock, and against the boats themselves.

It wasn't a poor-man's dock, Desmond noted. These were yachts. Millions of dollars bobbing on the water. Fiberglass and wood and brass. Rich boys' toys.

The silhouetted figure stopped suddenly near a branch of the dock, and appeared to turn their way. Desmond yanked Carmichael by the arm, pulling her into the shadows. Had he seen them? There was no way to be sure. If they spooked him now, he might bolt, and then things might get complicated. But Peel hesitated for only a moment, then returned to his business.

He branched off to the right, disappearing between two vessels whose well-polished hulls stood proudly out of the water. A light winked on in the cabin of one of the boats. Desmond motioned for Carmichael to hold tight, and then he crossed to the far side of the walk for a better look.

The growl of a motor starting split the stillness of the night. Desmond looked suddenly frantic. He could hear the distinct sound of a propeller gurgling just beneath the surface of the water. Floodlights shone down on the dock. Desmond was careful to stay out of the light. The motor revved.

His radio crackled. "Do you see him?" It was Carmichael's voice.

"No."

The motor engaged, and suddenly the cabin cruiser began to ease away from its slip. Desmond sprinted across the wooden planks, but the boat moved too quickly. By the time he'd reached the water's edge, the boat was out of reach. Carmichael approached at a hurried jog, her cheeks and nose rosy from the cold.

Desmond whipped out his radio. "Echo Two, you read?"

"Roger, Echo-One, I hear you," Porter said.

The boat was pushing into deeper waters, quickly throttling up, and getting smaller by the second. If they didn't act fast, they'd lose him in the night. Shifting pillars of fog coasted across the water.

A stiff gust rustled the collar of Desmond's coat. "The rabbit is on the water. He's heading hard east. Can you find Fontane Marina?"

The Enstrom helicopter was still flying over the mainland. Porter flicked on an overhead light and grabbed for the laminated map. "Yeah, yeah, I got it," he said, stabbing the map with his index finger.

"He's in what looks like a thirty-foot cabin cruiser of some kind," Desmond said as the warning lights on the boat faded farther from view. "Right now he's maybe a quarter mile from shore, heading east."

"Roger."

The Enstrom blew out over the water, and Porter

banked to the southeast. He dropped in altitude. Desmond saw the lights of the chopper. "Echo-Two, I see you," he said. "He should be coming into your field of view at any moment."

"I've got 'em," Porter said as the boat's light passed beneath him. "I'm on top of him."

By now, the boat was beyond the view of the shore. They darted back toward the cars. Desmond ran on ahead of the woman. He passed the Infiniti, paying it little mind. Carmichael followed on his heels.

The chopper touched down in a grassy area a hundred feet from where they had parked. Desmond yelled instructions to Carmichael over the howl of the rotors. She nodded, then backed away and headed to her car. Desmond climbed into the helicopter, and within seconds the machine lifted off the grass and headed out over the water.

Carmichael sped through the T in the road, and turned back the way they'd come. Her orders were to return to the Peel estate and pick up Lewis. Once there, they were to wait, watch, and listen.

The cabin cruiser was more than a mile out by the time the chopper roared past overhead. There wasn't much they could do at the moment but keep the boat in sight. They would follow him and watch. The boat then turned north, heading upstate.

Desmond had to smile. Peel was an idiot, he thought. The dope hadn't expected a helicopter. He was in open water now, and he'd never shake the chopper. There was simply nowhere to run and nowhere to hide.

Minutes later, the Infiniti's trunk lid opened slowly, and a man dressed in a navy turtleneck sweater and an L.L. Bean hooded coat climbed out, shut the trunk lid, and unlocked the driver's side door. Jefferson Peel started the car and pulled out of the marina. He drove north on Lake Shore Drive until he hit Solidarity Drive.

He piloted the car with great caution, watching in every direction for anyone who might be following him. Traffic was light. He followed Solidarity Drive through the gate to Chicago Merrill C. Meigs Field. His headlights washed across a series of modest-size hangars until he spotted a green Range Rover parked up ahead on the tarmac in front of a hangar. Jefferson Peel honked twice—two sharp blasts of the horn. The side door opened. A man stuck his head out for a second, then ducked back inside.

Peel waited, and suddenly the big hangar door began to retract. The man appeared in the lighted expanse within, and waved him in. Peel drove the car inside.

At the touch of a button, a motor somewhere in the ceiling engaged, and the big door swung back down. The two men embraced but didn't waste time.

"Let's hurry," Isaac Rosenblatt said to his friend.

The plane was fueled and ready, and was awaiting them on the asphalt apron outside. Isaac Rosenblatt was one of Jeff Peel's oldest and dearest friends, and quite a wealthy man himself. Peel hadn't hesitated to call him, even at such a late and inconvenient hour. Peel owned two planes himself, a Cessna Piper Cub and a Learjet he used for business travel. But the phone call he had received barely an hour ago had convinced him that someone might follow him from his home, and that it would be safer to utilize some other resource for his flight out of Chicago. He'd phoned Isaac immediately.

They boarded Rosenblatt's Learjet. Isaac Rosenblatt settled into the cockpit, preparing for takeoff.

Peel's nerves were rattled. The past hour had shaken him deeply. At first he'd not known whether the phone call to his house could be taken seriously, but the cars that had followed him to the marina had quickly convinced him of the gravity of the situation. The face that greeted him in the passenger compartment of the Learjet was unfamiliar. But when Dr. Eucinda Omheimer had spoken with him on the phone less than sixty minutes ago, she assured him that the woman making this flight with him was trustworthy. Jeff Peel respected no one in the world more than Dr. Omheimer. His daughter had been born deaf, and he and his wife had feared she'd never be able to live a productive life. But thanks solely to Dr. Omheimer, his little Lydia was now ten years old and making huge strides in her communication skills. He would trust Dr. Eucinda Omheimer with his life.

So it was without reservation that he took a seat on the Learjet next to Clara Hayweather.

56

THE TAILGATE SLAMMED DOWN AGAINST ITS hinges, and R'mel raised the camper shell's door until its pneumatic arms caught. It was colder in northern Massachusetts than it had been in New York, and he didn't plan on staying out in the night air any longer than necessary. He grabbed Joel by the foot and, hauling him out of the bed of the Dodge, let him fall hard to the ground.

The thump jarred Joel's head, sending streaks of pain through his skull. It knocked the breath out of him. Wherever this was that they'd ended up, they'd traveled for hours. Joel was exhausted and ached from head to toe. He was starving and feeling dehydrated.

R'mel left the truck running. The job shouldn't take too long, and he was deathly afraid of not being able to restart the Dodge out here in the middle of nowhere. The engine chugged, and noxious exhaust puffed from the tailpipe. He snatched his Gerber knife from his belt, whipped out the blade, and knelt over Joel. He ran the blade under each strip of duct tape, and peeled each strip from around the quilted movers' blanket. Then he stood and gave the blanket a solid tug.

Joel rolled out onto the cold ground. Without the movers' blanket, the world was suddenly a very cold place. His wrists and ankles were still bound, the blindfold still covered his eyes, and a strip of duct tape still covered his mouth.

R'mel, Glock in hand, reached down and removed the blindfold and the tape. Joel gasped for breath, sucking in cold night air, filling his lungs.

"You will keep your mouth shut and you will listen carefully," R'mel snapped, pointing the gun at Joel's head. "Understand?"

In the weak moonlight it was difficult to see anything. Joel's eyes had yet to adjust to having any light at all. But he nodded just the same.

"I'm going to free your hands and feet, and you stand. If you try to run, I will shoot you. Understand?"

Joel was staring up at the snow falling from the night sky. He nodded.

R'mel ran the blade through the bindings.

Standing slowly, Joel rubbed the raw flesh of his wrists. They were situated between a forest and an enormous gouge in the earth that Joel surmised was some sort of rock quarry. The night was gray and cloudy, and there was a dusting of snow on the ground. He turned his face toward the Dodge and spotted what appeared to be a second victim bound by restraints in the bed of the truck.

"Walk toward those trees," R'mel ordered.

They moved into the edge of the forest, crunching through underbrush. When they were nearly fifty yards deep in the foliage, R'mel commanded him to stop. R'mel was holding a spade-shaped shovel with one hand, the Glock in the other. He marked off a six-foot-by-four-foot rectangle by dragging his heel in the snow. Then he dropped the shovel at Joel's feet.

"Dig!" he said.

Joel gave the shovel a bewildered look, then glanced up at R'mel. "Huh?"

"Dig."

"But . . . I don't—"

"Dig! Or I'll kill you now!"

Joel bent at the waist and picked up the shovel. He stepped up to the box outlined in the snow. He hesitated. A brutal squall blew in from the north and rattled through the trees. It felt as though the hide might peel off Joel's face. He was miserably cold. But he feared the gun more than the cold. The shovel took a bite of frozen earth, the metal spade ringing as it glanced off stones hidden just beneath the snow and soil.

"Why'd you bring me all the way out here?"

R'mel ignored him. He fetched a cigarette from a pocket, lit a match, and cupped it in his hands against the wind.

Joel dug. Progress was slow. His hands began to blister from gripping the wooden handle.

The drive from New York had worn R'mel down. It was all he could do to keep his eyes open. He cleared the snow from a small patch of ground and sat with his elbows resting on his knees. His eyes grew heavy as he watched the man dig his own grave. The occasional clanging of the shovel against unearthed rocks kept him at attention.

Even with the repetitive strokes of the shovel

keeping his body in motion, the wind and the cold sapped whatever heat Joel worked to generate. He could no longer feel his fingers. He tasted the blood on his lips. It was no mystery to him that he was preparing his own grave. His and the faceless chap in the back of the pickup truck. Every bite of dirt he removed with the spade shovel was another few inches deeper his final resting place became. He swung the blade and it sank into the soil, the metal ringing out against an embedded stone. Every downward stroke sent vibrations up the wooden handle to be absorbed by his arms. He was laboring to produce his deathbed, and feeling every second of the work. The muscles of his shoulders and chest were on fire. He was panting now; his lungs felt like bags of white-hot coals. Just the physical effort of—

Joel paused, halting the shovel in the air, mid-swing. Out of the corner of his eye, he took notice of something interesting: the man was nodding off. R'mel had slumped slightly forward, his elbows on his knees, and his head pitched forward between his thighs. Joel's heart raced. He glanced at the shovel in his frozen hands. He could see the gun dangling loosely, resting against R'mel's leg.

Joel tried to swallow but could produce no saliva. He pivoted delicately in the loose dirt where he'd been working. The man was a good eight feet away. One false move, one poorly placed step on the crusty forest floor, and he would wake suddenly and put a bullet through him.

He took one careful step. Then another.

He'd come within five feet of the man. A small snore escaped R'mel's nose.

Joel moved closer.

R'mel snored louder, then stirred for a moment in his sleep. Joel prayed for just another thirty seconds. His grip tightened around the wooden handle of the spade. He eyed its rounded blade. Then he wondered, *Should I put the blade through his throat or slam it to the side of his head?*

It was a question he'd never dreamed would pass through his brain.

But the thought didn't have time to linger.

His next step crunched down on a brittle tree branch hidden beneath the snow and leaves. The branch cruckled and popped, snapping crisp and bright and loud. Joel's heart stopped.

R'mel jerked his head up, his eyes clear and wide.

But the farming tool had already begun its arc. Joel held it in a two-fisted grip, both hands welded to the last six inches of the wooden handle. R'mel's brain registered what was happening, but the message didn't reach his hands in time to form a defense. The chipped, rounded metal spoon connected just beneath his jawline. It went three inches deep for the entire width of his throat.

R'mel could do nothing but fall on his back and clutch his opened throat with both hands. Blood spouted up between his interlaced fingers. He floundered and bucked on the ground. His 9mm Glock fell to the snow.

Joel dove for the gun. Then he stumbled backward, away from the man who was turning the snow red. R'mel lifted his head a few inches, just enough to lock eyes with Joel, conveying a look of shock and disbelief and horror. Joel hesitated for only a second, then raised the Glock and pumped half a dozen rounds into him.

R'mel lay still.

Joel dropped the shovel and stumbled backward in exhaustion. He turned and staggered through the woods toward the clearing. He emerged from the trees and spotted the Dodge. The engine had died. He climbed inside. The idiot had left the lights on. When the engine sputtered out during their jaunt into the woods, the headlights drained the battery. He turned the key but got nothing.

He slammed the door shut and scrambled to the back of the truck. If the guy in the back was alive, he had to get him help. They would both need food and water and someplace warm and dry to spend the night. Joel clambered onto the tailgate. He shimmied into the bed of the truck and labored to peel the duct tape from around the blanket. When he could, he tugged a portion of the blanket down until he was able to expose the face. His heart stuck in his throat.

It couldn't be possible. But there was no doubt. None at all.

He'd been digging the grave for himself and Megan.

57

AFTER FORTY-FIVE MINUTES OF BEATING A
northerly path up Lake Michigan, the cabin cruiser
cut its engine. The boat was two miles from shore.
The cabin lights winked out. And the boat just sat
there, a dark mass swaying in the waves.

Desmond pressed his face against the window of
the chopper. Something was wrong. The chopper
made a wide arc, circling around and putting its spotlight on the vessel below them.

Desmond spoke into his headset, "What's he
doing?" He shot a look at Porter.

Porter shrugged, struggling to keep control of the
Enstrom against the tug of a stubborn gale. "Has he
cut his engine? Looks like he's drifting."

Yes, Desmond thought. *That's exactly what he's
doing. But why?*

The vessel was now moving with the tug of the
current, as if no one was at the wheel. It was not a
good night for a pleasure cruise. Not a good night to
be out on the water. And there was certainly no reason to be this far out from shore. It was well after
1 A.M., and Jefferson Peel had taken his boat out into

the stormy waters of Lake Michigan and cut the power to the engines for no discernible reason.

A sickening feeling began to swell in Desmond's gut. Something was definitely not right. He motioned for Porter to take the chopper in low to the water. He wanted to get a closer look. There was nowhere to land, but they could put the spotlight on the vessel to try to find out what was going on. Had Peel spotted them and decided to play dead in the water? Would he wait until they'd left the area before he continued on? If Peel was out here to meet with the girl, what could he hope to accomplish by floating aimlessly? There wasn't another vessel in sight for as far as the eye could see. This entire excursion seemed almost to have been a purposeless exercise—

Bile rose in Desmond's throat. How could he have been so *stupid*? His arms and legs felt suddenly numb. Then in a noxious blast of lucidity, he realized the truth: they'd been lured by bait, and they'd bit down fully and completely. Even without having yet seen the final physical confirmation, the truth was plain and clear.

The boat listed in the water, waves crashing against the polished wood hull, spraying onto the cabin and the deck. It looked like a giant's toy against the vastness of the great lake.

"Bring her down close!" Desmond shouted, a fierce anxiety growing quickly in his chest.

Porter fought the controls. The Enstrom tossed in the wind, shuddering and wobbling. It was hard enough trying to keep the machine upright and steady, let alone hold in tight in the vicinity with the boat. And it spooked the crap out of Porter to hold the chopper so close to the angry black waves.

Suddenly, the cabin lights winked on and a flood-lamp mounted on the outside of the cabin illuminated the deck.

"Wait! Hold it steady," Desmond yelled. "Hold the spotlight on the deck!"

Just then, the cabin door tossed open in the wind, and a figure emerged, clad in a rain slicker and a boating cap. He grabbed hold of the railing, struggling to work his way to the forward deck.

Peel? Desmond mused. *What is he* doing?

The chopper reeled, its tail being jostled by a crosswind.

The man wearing the rain slicker braced against the metal railing and looked up at the helicopter. Desmond stared down, waiting breathlessly. Then the man jerked off his boating cap.

Desmond's stomach dropped. He clinched his fists, barely able to contain his rage. *"NO!"* They'd been duped. Wanting desperately to do something, but knowing all actions would be in vain, all he could do was slam the side of his fist against the Plexiglas, and shout again, *"NO!"*

The man standing on the deck was of Chinese descent. His name was Yong Chi, and he was the Pecls' groundskeeper. Yong waved his arm at the chopper, smiling brightly in the face of the strong gale, which whipped at his Fu Manchu mustache. He stabbed his fist into the air defiantly. He held an expression of pure delight. He released his grip on the railing and raised both arms high above his head, gesturing. The gestures were clearly not meant to be congenial. Then he flung his boating cap toward the chopper, and the wind from the rotors sent it sailing out across the water until it disappeared in the black waves.

Desmond lost all feeling below the neck. They'd followed the wrong man halfway across Lake Michigan. How would he explain that to Mr. Stott?

Yong Chi dipped back inside the cabin and fired the engine. Its warning lights sprang to life, highlighting the water ahead, and he pointed the bow due south.

Porter glanced at Desmond, awaiting a command. Desmond simply sat there, facing out across the blackness of the deep night. Then a desperate thought pounded across the arid landscape of his mind. *The car! The car!*

"Echo-Three!" he screamed into the handheld radio. He wasn't even sure the radio could reach them at this distance, especially in this storm. But he screamed into the radio nonetheless. "Echo-Three! Return, I repeat, Return to the marina! Peel was in the *car!*" He then slammed the radio to the floor of the chopper and pounded his fist to the seat. He muttered, "The car. He was in the car." He put his head back and closed his eyes. Porter pulled back on the controls, now aware of where they needed to go, without being told.

But Desmond knew there was nothing left at the marina to find. Peel was gone.

He was gone, and they'd never find him in time. They wouldn't find him at all. Not until it was too late. His face went slack. He was defeated. He'd lost Peel. He'd lost the girl. He'd lost the tape. He would not be returning to Belize. There was nothing for him there. If he went back to the island, Stott would have him butchered, and then feed his bloody carcass to the dogs.

58

THOUGH JEFF PEEL DIDN'T REMEMBER, THEY'D
actually met once before. Clara Hayweather described the occasion—a fund-raiser for the Nash
School for the Blind—during the short flight to Detroit. But Peel encountered too many faces in his line
of work to recall a suburban housewife/fund-raiser
he'd met in passing nearly two years ago.

The Learjet bounced through the cold front. Clara
conveyed all that she knew. Her friend's name was
Brooke Weaver, she explained. They'd attended Harvard together, and Brooke had gone into journalism.
For the last several years she'd worked for NBC News.
Peel listened intently, nodding occasionally, and asked a
periodic question. Brooke had woken her several hours
ago, frantic and scared to death, Clara said. She hadn't
gone into details on the phone, saying mostly that she
remembered a mention of Jefferson Peel from one of
Clara's letters. It was a matter of life and death that she
be put in immediate contact with Mr. Peel, Brooke had
said. Tonight, in fact. The only explanation she offered
was that it involved the truth behind the deaths of Senator Peel and his wife.

Clara Hayweather had an acquaintance with Dr. Eucinda Omheimer, a close friend to the Peel family. Dr. Omheimer had reached Jefferson Peel at home. Brooke had given Clara very specific instructions, which she'd passed on to Dr. Omheimer, who then passed them on to Peel himself.

For the moment, the value of this meeting was tantalizingly vague. Jeff Peel knew only that a woman name Brooke Weaver was in danger, that she needed to meet with him immediately, that she had insisted that Clara Hayweather come along with him, and that he might learn vital information regarding the deaths of his parents.

The intercom hissed, and Isaac Rosenblatt's husky voice said, "Buckle up, folks. We'll be landing in about three minutes."

The landing gear skipped on the asphalt strip and rolled to a stop on a narrow apron next to a large painted-blue hangar. It was a private airstrip that Rosenblatt used on occasion. He had phoned ahead, and a taxi was waiting outside the chain-link fence.

As Peel and Clara deplaned, Rosenblatt shook his hand, and said, "Good luck."

"I won't forget this," Peel said.

Rosenblatt just smiled, and patted his friend on the shoulder. "I'll be here waiting."

The taxi sped them northeast on Edsel Ford Freeway. Near Gross Pointe, they turned west, passing Harper Woods. Clara had scribbled Brooke's instructions on a piece of scrap paper. She read off the directions to the taxi driver one line at a time. They followed State Highway 102 due west for six or seven miles.

"It's the Hazel Park Motel," she said from the backseat.

The driver nodded, glancing in the rearview mirror. "Sure, I know the place."

The taxi veered off the highway, and slowed. The Hazel Park Motel was a quaint little stopover, with a green-shingle roof and a clean red brick facade. It was three stacked levels of rooms. Clara had a room number scribbled on the scrap of paper.

Peel paid the driver and leafed off a substantial tip. "We were never here, and you never saw us," he said to the man behind the wheel.

The driver gawked at the hundred-dollar bill. "Never *where?*"

"Good man," Peel said.

The taxi sped off down Highway 102 toward Detroit.

"Two forty-four," Clara said as they hurried across the slush-spattered parking lot. They found a flight of stairs leading to the second floor of rooms. "Room two forty-four should be all the way down the right side, and directly around the corner."

And there it was.

Jeff Peel and Clara Hayweather exchanged nervous glances, then he reached out and knocked twice on the door. There was no answer for a long moment. They could sense someone watching them.

There was the sound of the bolt turning, then the metallic scrape of the chain sliding from its bracket. The door opened just a crack, then slowly wider. Peel and Clara stared at the young woman standing in the light of the doorway.

"You made it," Brooke said with a weary half-smile.

It was a five-mile hike, in the snow, against the driving wind, at night. Joel was carrying his grown daughter in his arms. He'd bundled her in the blankets they'd been bound in during the long drive. He'd walked the five miles, carrying her the entire way. His legs felt like jelly. He'd lost touch with his extremities several miles back. Pure self-will was the only force capable of keeping him in forward motion, but he had his daughter in his arms, and if he could just manage to keep her alive, it would be enough.

Megan was breathing, and her pulse seemed strong, both good signs. But this extreme cold couldn't be a good thing for her. She needed warmth, solid food, and plenty of clean water to drink. He figured they were both severely dehydrated.

Over the next ridge, he spotted the outline of a farmhouse on down the road, perhaps a mile or more. He could hold on for another mile, easily. Easily. When he got closer, he saw that there were no lights on in the farmhouse. There was a large, somewhat decrepit barn in back.

The house stood a few hundred feet off the dirt road, connected to it by a meandering gravel strip. A rust-eaten mailbox sat atop a wooden post at the head of the driveway. Peeling letters on the mailbox spelled out the name GERRARD.

Joel mounted the front steps and gently lay Megan on the porch. He rang the doorbell, and then clanked the iron doorknocker a dozen or more times. There were no sounds from within, and no lights shone. The Gerrards had likely gone to spend Christmas with family. Joel couldn't help but indulge himself in a small grin, because he also would be spending Christmas with family.

He found a woodpile around back, hurled a piece of firewood through a bedroom window, and carefully cleared away the jagged shards around the edges. He went through headfirst. Easing from room to room, he crossed to the front door and carried Megan in out of the cold. He found the thermostat, and heard the furnace click on as he spun the dial.

Megan lay on her side on a heavy quilt in one of the bedrooms. Joel pulled back the bedspread, and tucked her in beneath the quilts and blankets. The house was already beginning to warm. They must have drugged her quite heavily, he thought. But she was breathing, and her pulse was still strong. She'd pull through.

The Gerrards owned a television but lived too far out in the sticks for cable, and there was no dish outside or on the roof. He adjusted the rabbit ears and managed to pick up the all-night news on ABC. He turned on a light in the kitchen, and put on a pot of coffee. There was food in the cupboard, and he filled a plate.

He sat in a rocking chair in front of the TV and watched the news through dense static interference. The muscles of his arms and legs were bruised and achy. Nothing a good night's sleep couldn't go a long way toward mending. There was a news report about a shooting in Syracuse. Joel leaned forward and turned up the volume a hair. It had happened at a residence on the outskirts of the city. Three men were dead. Each of them had been armed. The residents of the house had been home at the time of the shooting, but none of them had been harmed. Police weren't releasing many details at this time. Joel sat back in the rocker. *Syracuse*, he thought. *Syracuse*. Something in his gut spoke to him, telling him, unequivocally, that the man who'd attacked him at the Waldorf was one of the dead in Syracuse. And that same small voice told him that the man had been an important part of Megan's life. If this proved true, she would need her father now more than ever.

He finished his meal and set the plate on the floor beside the rocker. He put his head back, and TV light flickered on his face. Sleep washed over him without a moment's hesitation.

59

Saturday morning

THE FIRST LIGHT OF DAWN PIERCED THE STAND
of trees on the east side of the Hazel Park Motel. The
snow had stopped. The wind was still brisk. Though
daylight had only broken within the past half an
hour, the highway had already swelled with com-
muters heading into the city. Birds huddled in their
nests, and a lone fox bounded through the field on
the far side of the parking lot.

Clara Hayweather was fast asleep, balled in a
fetal position beneath the thin blanket of one of the
twin beds in room 244. Bundled snugly in the other
bed was Brooke. She'd finally slithered between the
sheets less than two hours earlier, and had slumbered
restlessly in that time. She woke with a start every
twenty minutes or so, her internal defense mechanism still on high alert. For the moment, though, she
was out cold, her chest rising with every breath.

Jefferson Peel was seated on the floor between
the beds. He had yet to sleep. And he had no plans to
sleep, at least for the foreseeable future. He had too

much ahead of him this day to care about rest. He'd sleep once his parents' deaths were avenged.

He was currently on his third viewing of the videotape. Tears had come and gone. The face of Vice President James Ettinger transfixed him, and he hung on every word. What he was hearing seemed utterly impossible. But Ettinger spelled out the details. Those names—Bertrum Stott, Julius Albertwood, H. Glen Shelby, Clifton Yates—they were names he was plenty familiar with, some more than others. But Clifton Yates, especially.

President Clifton Yates. The most powerful man in the world. The man who'd welcomed him to the White House on numerous occasions in the past six years. A man who'd shaken his hand, and smiled, and looked deep in his eyes with the warmth and sincerity of a dear and intimate friend. This man was a liar and a thief and a murderer. He would fall hard. His administration would crash in a burning heap, flames jutting to the sky, his name forever linked with shame. And it would happen today.

Brooke had told Peel about her boss, Darla Donovan, and the others from work, and the explosion at Darla's apartment building. She'd done a brave thing coming here, putting herself at risk so that he could learn the truth of what had really happened on that California highway on that day so many years ago. He would not forget it. Not ever. She'd also explained how frightened she still was, for herself and for her family. He promised to take care of them. And he would.

On the screen, Ettinger concluded, and the tape began to rewind in the VCR.

The morning was growing bright and alive outside. Jeff Peel hadn't slept in twenty-four hours, but he'd never felt more energized in his entire forty-three years on earth.

Peel needed to make a call but wanted to let the women sleep. He pulled on his coat and closed the door behind him. He stepped out of the room and shut the door. He pulled his cell phone from his coat and stopped near an ice machine to dial. There were many arrangements to make, and many plans to lay out.

It was time to set things into motion. It was time for the world to know the truth. It was time to bring the leader of the Free World to his knees.

60

WITHIN THE HOUR, ISAAC ROSENBLATT GREETED his old friend with a tall cup of hot coffee. The sky was clearing. Jeff Peel boarded the Learjet and sipped from his beverage. He sat up front in the cockpit with his friend.

"You ready?" Rosenblatt said as they taxied to the head of the runway.

Peel nodded. "I've never been more ready for anything in my life."

They lifted up out of Detroit, banked over the water, and headed south. Rosenblatt estimated their flight time to be less than an hour.

A taxi was waiting outside for Clara. It would deliver her to a major airport, where she'd catch a flight home, in a first-class seat, courtesy of Jefferson Peel.

A half hour later, a second Learjet taxied onto the same strip of runway and ripped into the sky. Brooke had settled into a plush leather seat and gazed out the window as the city faded into the landscape behind them. She was exhausted and bleary-eyed, but relieved to have gotten this far.

Peel had made arrangements for her and her family to be safeguarded until further notice. It was a huge relief to feel somewhat protected again.

With the relief came a new wave of sorrow. Her friends and colleagues were dead. Gone forever. Her life would not and could not ever be the same. For one, she'd never go back to NBC. At the moment, who could say that she'd even stay in journalism? There were more peaceful ways to spend your life and make a living. It was time to date someone, to *love* someone. Right now, though, her memories of the past couple of days would be hard to shake. She looked out the window at the world passing beneath her, allowing herself to get lost in the endless gray and blue. And then she fell asleep.

From Reagan National Airport, he took a taxi into the heart of D.C. He was greeted at the front doors of the CNN Washington, D.C., bureau by familiar faces. They shook hands, and a popular television anchor ushered him up the elevators to the studios.

The anchor showed Peel into his office, and locked the door. Peel told him what he wanted to do, and presented the infamous videotape. A secretary knocked at the door a few minutes later and offered them fresh coffee and pastries. The anchor tore into a jelly doughnut, but Peel ignored the food. The meeting lasted ten minutes, then the door to the office was flung open, and they rushed Peel to makeup to get him camera-ready.

The anchor rushed into the control room, videotape in hand. "Get this queued up, sports fans!" he said, handing the tape to the producer on duty. "And prepare to interrupt our current broadcast!"

Taken aback, the producer put her hands on her hips and shot him a look. "Do you have any idea what our current broadcast *is?*"

"Indeed I do!"

61

EVERY MAJOR MEDIA OUTLET WAS THERE TO GET a piece of the action. They ranged from CNN to Fox News, from MSNBC to the Associated Press. Even C-Span showed up with a camera. They battled for turf in the limited space allotted for news organizations. For the moment, it was the biggest story anyone had been a part of in several decades.

The cameras rolled. Reporters bunched shoulder to shoulder, their microphones at the ready for when the service was over. The same group had mashed inside the cathedral for the funeral service an hour earlier. And now, at the graveside service, this would be their last chance to get all the tears and wailing on tape and to get good shots of the widow dressed in black. They wanted shots of the Ettinger children; that would look great on the front page and on the evening news. The media circus salivated at the sight of the casket.

The earth beneath their feet was hard. As hard as earth can be without being bedrock. The temperature had dipped below zero again, and the windchill did nothing but add to the overall misery. Snow flicked against the polished brass and cherry of Ettinger's casket, peppering the American flag, which a formation of uniformed Marines had draped over the rounded lid.

The president opened his mouth and croaked out an anecdote from some years ago, an incident from their first campaign. His face was gray. The bags beneath his eyes had grown and even darkened in the past two or three days. Secret Service agents stood behind dark glasses, only a few paces off his heels.

The widow, cloaked in black, her face behind a veil, heard nothing. The wind whistled in her ears. Her children stood on either side, hands in hers. Stoic young faces, pink from the cold. Bradey stared numbly as flakes melted on the brass handles of the box that held his dad. Jude could taste the salt of her tears.

Yates chose his words with care.

"Not only have I lost my vice president—a gifted public servant and man of the people, but most of all, I've lost a friend, a confidant. This is a bitter pill to swallow. Friends, true friends, are never replaced. Others may come in time, added to those already dear to our hearts. The void left by one who has departed is never filled, and the void left by Jim Ettinger is great, indeed."

Eloise Ettinger, mother of both James and Nelson, listened from her wheelchair, tubes ran from her nose and from beneath layers of insulation to monitors on a metal cart to one side. Nelson Ettinger stood a step behind his mother and his sister-in-law, his hands deep in the pockets of his coat.

A minister closed the graveside service with a

generic prayer, and a few of the closer acquaintances skirted by to offer Miriam their condolences. Yates approached and took her hands in his. He leaned in close, speaking private words inches from one ear. She thanked him, and then he was quickly ushered away in a cluster of Secret Service.

Unlike many women married to politicians, she had not wed for money or power. She was *born* to money, and money by its very nature, produces power. She'd married for love. And had stayed in love, even through the turmoil that comes with a life lived in the public eye. Only James knew why he'd married her. She could not speak for him. He'd taken his heart to the grave.

Elaine collected Bradey and Jude and led them off toward the limousine. They wove among the endless white tombstones that made up Arlington National Cemetery.

For a short moment, Miriam was alone with her husband at his final resting place. She plucked her leather gloves off with her teeth, folded them, and set them on the American flag. She knelt at the head of the casket and spread her hands against the polished cherry.

Wind whistled through the cavity between the bulky casket and the hollowed-out patch of earth below it. The fabric of the big green canopy overhead whipped and flapped in the numbing breeze. Soon, Miriam could barely feel her fingers. Most of her body seemed frozen. But that was just as well. Let me freeze, she thought. She brushed her cheek against the hard wood, as if brushing against his chest. If she could, she'd go with him. Arm in arm.

Car engines fired in the near distance. Flashbulbs popped. She glanced up at the morons with the cameras and microphones. The carnival had already begun.

It was time to go. But this would be her last moment with him above ground. She could smell the fresh odor of disturbed dirt circulating in the opened chasm at her feet. Miriam said her good-byes and pressed her lips to the cherry lid. Then she rose and pulled on her gloves.

A glance to the east and she saw the limo idling at the curb, Elaine and the kids inside in the warmth. She started slowly toward it. Twenty or thirty feet from the limo, she paused and turned for a last look. The grounds crew had already removed the flag and were in the process of lowering the box into the hole.

Clifton Yates put his back against the seat and took a long breath. An aide handed him a bottle of water. He unscrewed the cap and took a sip. He loosened the tie around his collar. Chief of Staff Russ Vetris was seated next to him.

"How'd I do?" Yates asked, then sucked down half the water in the bottle.

"You won them over, as always," Vetris said.

They watched the endless rows of headstones pass outside the tinted windows as the limousine wound through Arlington Cemetery. Hundreds of cars had lined either side of the narrow roadway. Cameras snapped pictures of the sleek black limousine that carried the president past them.

Vetris was making notes in his day planner.

"Philbrick looked kinda shaky up there, don't you

think?" Yates said. Anthony Philbrick had taken his place beside the president during the funeral service. He'd made a short statement, sharing a few memories of James Ettinger, then segued into a homily on how the country could use this tragedy to pull together. His words at the graveside service had been a variation of the same speech.

"He'll loosen up," Vetris said without looking up. "We threw him in the deep water right off the bat."

Yates nodded, then glanced out the tinted window at the passing throng.

A cell phone rang, and everyone checked their coats. It was Vetris's phone. He dug it out of his coat, and answered it.

The president had his back against the plush leather, his eyes closed. It wouldn't have taken much to doze off. The five hours of sleep last night just hadn't cut the mustard.

A look of utter perplexity flushed over Vetris's face. He snapped the phone shut and barked at one of the aides riding with them, "The TV! Turn it on!"

Yates raised his head. He opened his eyes and watched the sudden commotion. A television set was mounted in the wooden console between two seats. A small receiver mounted on the outside of the car picked up satellite signals.

The aide fumbled with the small buttons beneath the TV screen.

"CNN!" Vetris barked. "Turn up the volume!"

The aide surfed through the channels, finally stopping on CNN. He cranked the volume several notches.

The president stared at the small screen.

The face of Jefferson Peel looked out at them from the TV screen. He was in the process of addressing the camera: ". . . that their deaths occurred under the most suspicious of circumstances. Just last night I came into possession of a piece of evidence that irrefutably proves that their deaths were no accident at all. You, the American people, will now see for yourselves, with your own eyes, that among those responsible for the deaths of Senator Lyndon Peel and his wife, Deborah, was none other than President Clifton Yates.

"This sounds shocking, I know, but the footage you are about to view will strip away any doubt that exists. The following taped statement was recorded in the hours preceding the murder of James Ettinger."

The live feed featuring the face of Peel was immediately replaced by a slightly grainy video recording. And suddenly there he was, Ettinger, dressed in a bathrobe, facing the camera in a poorly lit room. He cleared his throat, and began to speak:

> *"Hello. My name is James Highfield Ettinger, vice president of the United States. Today is the seventeenth of December. By the time anyone views this tape, I will have resigned from office . . ."*

Russ Vetris turned slowly to face the president. But he had nothing to say. No words would form in his throat. The shock was too absolute and sudden. The silence in the car was deafening.

All the blood had drained from the president's face. His vision wavered. There was a buzzing sound somewhere deep in his ears, and he thought he might be having a heart attack. He prayed that he was, and that he would die right here and right now. Because what lay ahead of him was too horrific to even imagine. The aides did their best not to make eye contact with the president.

With Ettinger's voice in the background, Yates put his face in his hands. He, along with everyone else in the limousine, knew full well at that moment that his presidency was over.

62

JOEL WOKE WITH HIS CHIN TOUCHING HIS chest. He'd slept later than he'd planned. The morning light was full and bright in the house. He blinked the sleep out of his eyes, only to see Megan standing in front of him.

Her eyes were fixed on him, cautious but strangely unafraid. He just sat there staring at her, his tongue waiting for his brain to send a signal.

"I have no idea where I am," she said. "What's going on?"

Joel wanted badly to rush forward and hold her, to comfort her and set her mind at ease. Joel said, "I wish I understood it all myself."

"I don't understand. How did I get here?"

"It looks like you got mixed up with some very dangerous people."

Megan eased closer.

"But you're safe now."

Megan stood frozen, studying the man before her. They both stood staring at each other. The look in his eyes was gentle and loving, familiar.

"Is it really you?" she asked.

Joel smiled, but said nothing.

Megan watched him uncertainly.

He said, "When you were seven, you found a small porcelain panda bear while playing in a neighbor's yard. Your mother washed the dirt from it in the sink. That panda was your prized possession."

Megan took an unconscious step forward, her eyes widening.

"You kept it on the windowsill in your bedroom. One day you knocked it off the windowsill and it broke into three or four pieces on the floor. You cried all afternoon until I got home to fix it. I glued it back together. Then you climbed onto my lap and smiled up at me. I've never forgotten that smile. It was the most beautiful thing I've ever seen."

Her eyes moistened, then welled up, tears finally spilling down one cheek and then the other. Her lower lip began to tremble.

He continued, "You hugged my neck and kissed me on the cheek, and that made me feel like the greatest superhero on earth. Do you remember what you named that little panda?"

Megan put her face in her hands. Tears seeped through her fingers. She nodded her head. "Yes," she said. "Randolph. I named him Randolph. He was my best friend." She raised her head. Her eyes sparkled with tears. "I'd forgotten about him."

Joel smiled. "I never forgot that bear. Because he made my baby girl so happy."

Megan approached him on unsteady legs. Her lips quivered as she parted them to speak. *"Daddy."*

"Sweetheart."

"It *is* you," she said.

Joel rushed forward and embraced her, enveloping her in his arms. Megan sobbed, pressing her face to his chest.

"I've missed you so much," she said.

"You have no idea how much I love you, Megan. I've loved you since the minute you were born."

"I would've tried to find you," she said. "But things with Mom were complicated."

"Shhh. I know . . . I know. Don't worry about what's already done."

Megan pulled away from him for a moment, a perplexed look on her face. "How . . . how'd we get here?"

"I'm not altogether certain. The past few days have been a blur." Joel described his sighting of her at the airport. He told about the events at the Waldorf, and the man who attacked him. He told her about the story on the news of the three men involved in a shooting in Syracuse, and of his suspicion of a connection between it all.

"Was it . . . Olin?" she asked, tearing up again.

"That's not a name I know. And I'd rather not speculate. But someone attacked me in my hotel room, and he claimed to be a part of your life," Joel said.

The realization of it settled upon her with the weight of lead. "Olin's dead, isn't he?"

"It's possible that he is. I'm sorry, Megan."

She clung to him once more, threading her arms around his midsection.

"But if it was him, he was involved with some terrible people. The people responsible for us being here. These people tried to kill us, and it is very likely they are responsible for his death."

It was then that the seed of doubt, planted on that night in London when she and Olin first met, blossomed forth. From the very beginning, a voice somewhere deep inside had warned her that Olin St. John was not the person he claimed to be. He'd been handsome, and rich, and he'd been so loving to her; none of that could be denied. But on some level, she'd always known something was amiss. Sometimes it's easier to deny than accept. Now she felt like a fool. Like a stubborn fool. She'd fallen so hard for Olin. He'd stepped into her life at a moment when she needed him most. So it had been so easy to paint him with a glossy veneer, and to accept him for who he said he was. Her family had disintegrated when she was so young that her foundation had been swept out from under her. And in truth, that's what Olin St. John represented. Something solid she could call her own.

Megan sobbed, her knees buckling.

Joel held her, cradling her in his arms. He had so many things to ask her, so many things to tell her. But they would all have to wait. First, there would have to be healing. And healing came only with time and patience and love. For now, it was enough just to hold her again.

63

July

THE PRIVATE AIRSTRIP WAS A STRAIGHT BLACK line of asphalt that ran for several hundred yards atop the high-mountain plateau. The Learjet had dropped through the clouds and glided through the towering mountains of Montana. The Weavers had never seen such country.

A blue Jeep was waiting at the small log building that served incoming aircraft. A good-looking young man dressed in a zippered jacket, heavy boots and jeans, who introduced himself as Kyle, helped them into the Jeep, and they headed off down a rough-and-tumble mountain road.

The cabin was seven miles from the airstrip, up near the clouds and God. It was a beautiful structure, made of logs but very modern in its architecture and amenities. Dean elbowed his wife when he spotted a TV dish on the red-tin roof. They pulled through a circle drive, and the Jeep came to a stop. Kyle showed them inside.

The cabin sat at the very lip of Glacier National

Park. They moved through the rooms and spotted a sliding glass door along the back wall. Grace opened it and stepped onto a broad deck overlooking a large mountain lake. The perimeter of the lake was outlined by a cathedral of jagged, snow-covered mountain peaks. It was breathtaking.

Kyle came up beside her.

"Ma'am," he said. "Brooke tends to take long hikes around this time of day." He turned so that Dean could hear him. "She's gone for hours at a time. There's a cell phone here, and her number is written on a pad of paper on the kitchen table. She takes the phone with her."

"Thank you," she said with a tired smile.

"My number is on there as well," he said. "Call me if you folks need anything. I'm available twenty-four seven."

From the front door, they watched the Jeep wind back down the mountain pass. The entire trip had been arranged and furnished by Jefferson Peel. The private jet and mountain cabin were both his. He owed much to their daughter, he had explained, and this was just one small way in which he could say thank you. Peel had attended Wyatt's funeral, the second week of February. It was now the middle of summer, and the events of those frozen months seemed like only a bad dream.

Brooke had left her job. Exactly what she'd do next was still up in the air. She'd chosen to take some time off, just to think and clear her head. Peel had offered her the use of his Montana cabin on an indefinite basis. As far as he was concerned, she could stay there for the next decade. He rarely used it. Kyle was his hired hand, and her parents and even Peel himself had no inkling of the fact that Kyle and Brooke had grown quite "close."

Both Weavers were standing out on the deck. Up here the air was unimaginably clean. The sun was almost directly overhead, reflected in the lake below. Though they'd spoken nearly every week to Brooke on the phone, they hadn't seen her in months. So much had gone on that Brooke explained she needed time to recover, to reorganize her life and her mind. They understood that she needed space. They planned to spend the week with her, to enjoy the mountains and the solitude. Getting away from upstate New York was good for them. Everything at home reminded them of Wyatt.

Dean put his arm around his wife's shoulders and kissed her cheek, and together they waited for their daughter.

Brooke sat perched on a boulder at the edge of the lake, with her arms around her knees. A stiff breeze disturbed the surface of the water, and blew her hair across her face.

Lately, she spent most of her daylight hours near the lake. Part of her considered living out here for good. But sooner or later, she knew, she'd need people again. For now though, she would simply take her time, enjoy the purity of the great outdoors, then ease back into the stream of the life she was born to be a part of.

A half a year had passed since the events of December turned her life upside down. It seemed like yesterday, yet it also seemed like years ago. And, more than anything, it seemed like the whole crazy rush of events had happened to somebody else. Many of her wounds were gradually beginning to heal, though her emotions remained raw. Sitting there, her thoughts went to Darla and the other members of the team. Her eyes misted. There was nothing fair or just or logical about what had happened, and she refused to diminish the memories of her friends. She'd spent the majority of her adult life with them, and she'd loved them like family. Then had come the news of Terri's murder. She couldn't deflect the horrid feelings of guilt, taking on herself absolute responsibility for her best friend's death.

And, of course, there was Wyatt. He had stayed strong right up to the end. But his body had simply given out on him. If there was one thing among the tragic circumstances of the past six months she could be thankful for, it was that she'd been at his side when he passed away. She'd held one hand and her mother had held the other, and they clung to him as he made the transition from this life to the next.

A cardinal alighted on a nearby branch of a tree only a few yards to her right and flitted its wings. She took it as a sign that Wyatt and her friends had made it safely to the other side.

The criminal prosecution of the president and his henchmen had dominated the news as well as much of the public discourse. Dozens of indictments had been handed down. In the wake of Yates's fall from grace, Anthony Philbrick had reluctantly taken the oath of office. Much speculation had revolved around whether Philbrick might grant Yates a pardon. But he hadn't. Yates would go down hard, and he would likely spend many of his golden years far away from the life of luxury he'd come to know. They had found Julius Albertwood in his wheelchair in his penthouse with a bullet in his head. The wound had been self-inflicted. The CIA was working on Bertrum Stott. He was not an American citizen and lived outside of the country. Government and media experts highly doubted that anyone could touch him.

Brooke herself had become something of a media darling, and that attention had drained her physically and emotionally. She hadn't asked for any of it. It was probably a splendid time to be in the news business, but to her, nothing could have seemed less appealing.

From the cabin she'd watched minimal TV. She'd again watched as Ettinger spilled the terrible truth about the most powerful man on the planet. But she couldn't take it for long. She'd had enough television to last a lifetime. For many weeks, she'd holed up in the cabin, shutting out the world and the way it had so ungraciously intruded upon her life. As summer arrived, the cloud around her slowly began to lift, buoying her spirits.

The afternoon sun was reflected in the water. She glanced at her watch. Her parents had probably arrived by now. She wondered what they'd thought of Kyle.

She smiled into the breeze. The mountains were magnificent. All in all, she was happy. Time would heal her wounds. Seasons would change. And most importantly, life would go on.

ATRIA BOOKS
PROUDLY PRESENTS

HIT AND RUN

CASEY MORETON

Available from Atria Books in trade paperback

Turn the page for a preview of
Hit and Run. . . .

Chapter 1

EVERYTHING WAS FINE UNTIL 3:00 A.M., MONDAY. THEY
had encountered surprisingly little traffic on the
drive from New York, most likely because of the
storm that had assaulted much of the East Coast that
evening. The rain had mostly tapered off by midnight, leaving in its place occasional patchy fog. Nick
Calevetti was at the wheel of Steven Adler's 1967
Ford Mustang, his lead foot hurtling them along at
ninety miles an hour. Steven had fallen asleep, his
head against the window, exhausted after two days of
Nick's whirlwind tour of Manhattan. With the road
to themselves, they would be in Boston in less than
an hour. They were making good time.

The fog worsened. For stretches at a time Nick
could hardly see the road at all. The headlights weren't
much help. But he never let off the gas. If they had his
Porsche, he thought with a grin, he'd be doing 110,
easy, fog or no fog. Steven's old Mustang could move,
but nothing like the Porsche.

The Mustang entered a fog bank and the road disappeared—no white lines, no nothing. Nick pursed his
lips and held the wheel steady. He could have been

driving off the edge of the earth and not known it. The fog was like a wall. He glanced at the speedometer and then accelerated, fearless. There was just a quick flash of color from out of nowhere, and something slammed into the front of the car, thumping first against the hood, then smashing into the windshield on the passenger side, reducing it to a web of a million sparkling diamonds. The impact was sudden and solid, sending an abrupt shudder through the car. Nick grabbed at the wheel with both hands, jerking it wildly. Tires squealing, the car crossed two lanes of traffic. Again, Nick jerked the wheel and again overcompensated. This reaction was so drastic, given the speed of the car, that the driver-side tires actually lifted off the ground for a moment, and the car nearly flipped.

Steven was thrown against the dash. He hadn't had even a split-second to react, to brace himself with his hands, and his head was forced into the windshield.

Partially out of reflex and partially out of desperation, Nick blindly thrust a foot at the brake pedal, but there was no traction on the wet asphalt. The car went into a full spin. It careened helplessly, skimming across the glasslike asphalt surface. Its momentum carried it nearly seventy feet down the interstate before it began to gradually slow, finally gaining some purchase on some loose gravel on the shoulder. The rear end swung around in a wide arc. When the car finally skidded to a full stop, it rocked on its springs for a few seconds, then settled. It sat at an angle, facing back in the direction from which it had traveled. Its rear driver-side tire was hanging off the shoulder onto wet grass, just two feet shy of a steep embankment.

Lightning flashed in the distance, muted by drifting ribbons of fog.

Steven had been tossed back, falling between the bucket seats, arms flailing, head snapping back as he screamed. Nick's entire upper body had been pressed against the steering wheel, then thrown back into his seat with tremendous force. He still gripped the wheel, an unconscious reflex. His eyes were wide with horror.

When at last all movement had ceased, they remained perfectly still, afraid to move, afraid to breathe.

Steven moaned.

There was blood everywhere. Nick glanced between the seats.

"Steven?"

Another moan.

"Man . . . you okay?" Nick had spatters of blood on his hands. Blood on the steering wheel. On the dash. He glanced all around. There was even a blood pattern on the ceiling of the car. Nick started trembling. He held his hands out in front of his face. Steven's legs were twisted about. Nick turned in his seat and put a hand on Steven's thigh.

"Steven!" Nick called out. It was dark in the backseat. Nick fumbled with the knobs and switches along the dash, groping for the control for the dome light. The dim light blinked on. There was more blood than he had imagined. His heart raced.

Nick threw open his door and fumbled to push the seat forward. His fingers were slick and clumsy. The mechanism that controlled the seat was stubborn, and it took him nearly half a minute to finally spring the seat forward so that he could access the backseat and get to Steven. He ducked his head, leaning inside. He braced himself on his knees. Steven had his arms crossed over his face. The pained moans were more frequent now, and longer. Nick's hands were trembling uncontrollably. His throat ached where the steering wheel had caught him under the chin. It was hard to swallow. There was also noticeable pain along the contour of his collarbone. But he had to ignore all of that, at least for the moment.

"Steven!"

Steven managed to unravel his legs. He raised his hands, and Nick got a better look at the damage. Steven's forehead was opened up. His face was covered in blood. "I'm . . . all right," Steven managed to say in barely a whisper. "I'm all right."

"Dude . . . your *head*!" Nick said.

"I know, I feel it. At least it's still attached."

The meat of the forehead was split open, a gash about two inches wide. His nose was bleeding as well.

"Can you move your neck?"

Steven coughed, a thick, throaty cough. "Not sure. Think so."

"Can you get up?"

"Haven't tried. Everything hurts."

Nick piled himself into the backseat, getting an arm around Steven's shoulders. "Careful, man. Let's get you sitting up at least."

Steven got into an upright sitting position without complication. There were numerous aches and pains, and lots of blood, but everything appeared to function normally. With the possible exception of his nose, nothing seemed to be broken. The gash in his forehead felt like a piece of hot metal. He gently probed all around it with a fingertip, hoping it didn't look as bad as it felt.

Nick was trying to catch his breath. He had been fueled by adrenaline for the past few minutes and he couldn't get himself to settle down. It felt like he'd taken a shot to the throat by a work boot. But he could breathe fine. His voice sounded a little hoarse but not too bad. His neck was stiffening, and that would likely worsen in the coming hours.

"What happened?" Steven said finally, leaning up slightly, massaging the back of his head.

"Man . . . I just . . ." Nick shook his head. "Everything's a blur, man."

"Was there another car?"

The fog had dissipated somewhat, and visibility had now increased to maybe a hundred feet. But it was still dark out, the light of the moon shrouded by weather conditions, and all the talking and sudden heavy breathing had fogged the windows even more. Nick raised his head and glanced around. Events had transpired so quickly and dramatically that his mind had become focused solely on survival and thankfulness that both he and Steven were alive. "Another car?"

"Who hit us?"

From where they sat, Nick couldn't see anything beyond the obscured glass. He shook his head. "We hit fog, man. That's what I remember. It was like somebody turned out the lights, and then . . . I don't know."

Steven glanced at his friend. Then he looked over the seats toward the dash and the windshield. "That my blood?"

Nick nodded. "All yours, as far as I can tell."

Steven, still overwhelmed at the sight of the car's

upholstery lacquered by his own life-giving blood, noticed the damage to the windshield. "My head tagged the windshield. I wasn't belted in."

"Me neither."

"Serves us right."

"Whatever."

"Look at that. The glass is destroyed." Steven shook his head slowly in awe. "How did I not shatter my skull?"

Nick didn't respond.

"Looks like somebody went at it with a Louisville Slugger!" He glanced back at Nick. "You're telling me my *head* did that, and I'm still sitting here alive, with a scratch above my eyes, talking to you? No way."

The car engine had died. They sat in silence for a long moment.

"Where are we?" Steven asked.

"On I-90. About an hour outside Boston."

"Slide out," Steven said. "I want to get a look at the car."

The early morning air of late spring was cool. Steven shivered.

The passenger-side headlight was smashed so all that remained was a shark's mouth of glass teeth framing the inside of the metal cavity. The glass shards glowed in the light of the remaining headlamp. The quarter-panel had come loose and was nowhere in sight. The grille was busted, half—maybe more—gone, chunks of plastic here and there on the ground and along the edge of the bumper. The hood had taken a shot. The front edge had curled under, and the top had a severe dip, like a three-hundred-pound man had repeatedly parked his rump there. And then there was the windshield, bubbled inward and sagging. Steven leaned forward slightly, extending a hand, gently probing a finger at the glass. Moonlight refracted off the countless individual fragments.

"Something hit us," Steven said. They were standing shoulder to shoulder, their silhouettes set aglow by the lone functioning headlight.

Nick stood still, staring at the damaged Mustang. He didn't blink for a long time.

Steven crouched down in front of the busted headlight, leaning in close for a better look. Then he shook his head, and stood. "Too dark. I've got a flashlight in the trunk." He pulled his key from the ignition and rounded the rear of the car, quickly popping the trunk lid. He returned carrying an inexpensive plastic flashlight, unscrewing one end to make sure it had batteries. He tested it, shining the light in his face.

Nick watched him work, his mind on rewind, desperately thinking back, backpedaling through the past ten minutes, trying to remember what had happened, hoping to get a mental fix on what they had collided with.

Nick had his hands buried in his armpits, standing safely away from the traffic lanes. The sounds of the collision still rang in his ears. He could still see the flash of color, still feel the impact, still feel the unexpected shock of it. He stood with one foot on wet grass, one foot on the edge of the shoulder. "You think it's still drivable?" he said.

Steven's back was to him. He had crouched with the flashlight, inspecting the damage. "Probably," he said. "We can hopefully at least get it home. I'd hate to leave it out here overnight."

"I don't understand what happened," Nick said, mainly to himself.

"This definitely wasn't metal on metal," Steven said, playing the light up the fold in the hood. "I would have lost more paint, for one thing." He drew in close to the busted headlight. Something caught his attention. He held the flashlight under his chin, moving his nose to within inches of the remains of the headlamp. There were spatters of blood on the jagged shards of glass, and a snatch of some kind of cloth. Even in the poor lighting he could tell it was denim. He stared hard. His mind blanked. He opened his mouth to call Nick, but words failed to rise from his throat.

Now it was more obvious. The blood spatters were not just visible on and around the remains of the headlamp but also along the exposed chrome of the bumper. He stood, the cone of white light falling across the hood of the car. More blood. And on the windshield, the most blood of all. A cold chill slithered up his spine, up the back of his neck.

"Nick," he said, his tone thick and dry. He looked over his shoulder, Nick several steps back, as if he were making a subtle effort to withdraw from the scene. "Nick . . .what did you hit?"

Nick shook his head.

Steven rubbed a hand along the stubble of his chin. He stood and looked over the roof of the car into the darkness beyond. He shut the open door, then walked directly out in front of the car, light from the single headlight gradually dimming on the back of his T-shirt. He felt sick to his stomach, with a headache to rival his all-time worst.

Steven began to slowly trace the path of the skid. The embankment to his left was a severe and sudden drop. If the Mustang hadn't stopped at the exact moment it did, they would have tumbled into the darkness below, where they could have been trapped for hours or days. He shined the flashlight down the slope, but the light was too weak to illuminate more than fifteen or twenty feet at a time. He turned and saw Nick following reluctantly at a distance.

Steven flashed back a couple of hours to their departure from Manhattan. Nick had had a few beers earlier that evening at the Yankee game, and a glass or two of wine at his favorite restaurant in midtown before they hit the road. On the way to the car, he had snatched the keys out of Steven's hand and darted for the driver's side. The argument didn't last long. Nick could be aggressive—frighteningly aggressive. He didn't lose many battles. And he hadn't lost that one. Steven had relented and grabbed them each a coffee-to-go on the way out of the city. Nick had seemed fine, in control of all his faculties, at least in Steven's judgment. Now he questioned that judgment. And his view of Nick was suddenly very suspect.

"See anything?" Nick said, catching up now.

Together they watched the beam from the flashlight pass over the wet grass of the embankment. It was too dark and still too foggy to make out anything beyond the range of the flashlight. The silhouettes of trees were vaguely visible on the horizon, and Steven thought he could hear water flowing somewhere nearby, most likely in the form of a stream of unknown size. To his knowledge, the Atlantic was several miles south.

"I've hit deer before," Steven said. "They can tear up a car in a hurry."

Nick nodded.

"But I found this in the headlight." Steven held out the small scrap of denim.

Nick examined it closely, his anxiety level elevating with every breath.

Steven rested the flashlight on his shoulder, panning it back and forth across the gloom. "Nick," he said, still focused on the gloom and the darkness that enveloped the slope of the embankment. "How many deer you know that wear denim?"

The question hung in the air. Then silence fell between them.

Finally, Nick dropped the swath of fabric at his feet. The tumblers were falling into place in his brain, and he had reached a conclusion. It was time to act, time to be decisive. He stepped in front of Steven so that his back was to the slope of the embankment. He stood nose-to-nose with his friend, squaring his shoulders.

"Whatever it is you're thinking, Steven, put it away. Just shut your brain and forget it. We hit a deer, man. Plain and simple. The car knocked it off the road and it ran off to die somewhere in the woods far from here. Okay? Got that? Your car hit Bambi, Steven. End of story. Don't make this complicated. Let's get in the car and get home." Nick offered a mild grin, and he placed a hand on Steven's shoulder.

"What about that denim?"

Nick, glaring deep into his eyes, said slowly and definitively, "I don't know what you're talking about."

"Please get out of my way," Steven said.

"No."

"We have to be sure . . ."

"Of what?"

Another silence filled the moment. It was clear that a lot was going on behind Steven's eyes. An eternity passed before he blinked. A great debate raged in his mind. He let out a long breath, then he nodded. "Fine," he sighed, and lowered the flashlight to his side.

Then they heard the moan.

Nick had already turned back toward the Mustang. He froze.

Steven looked at him.

"That was the wind," Nick snapped, unconvincingly.

"Shut up."

The next moan was lower but of longer duration and greater intensity. The haunting sound carried up the grassy slope of the embankment to them.

"Oh my God," Steven said, stunned. He took a step onto the damp grass.

Nick grabbed a fistful of shirt and jerked Steven to him. "*Walk away!*"

Steven couldn't believe what he was hearing. "Are you insane? Someone is down there!"

"Listen to me!" Nick's face was taut with desperation, his eyes wide, threatening. "If we don't leave now, we're in a world of trouble. Don't get involved!"

Steven stiff-armed him, freeing himself with a powerful, defiant shove. "Get out of my *way*!" And down he went, fool-hardily hurling himself down the precarious slope of the embankment. And in the same breath, Nick reacted, leaping, arms outstretched, tackling Steven, taking him hard to the ground, both of them rolling and tumbling, limbs flailing, grunting and groaning as they bumped and thrashed and struggled against one another.

Steven got to his feet and put a foot in Nick's chest, knocking him on his back. Nick grunted, scurried to his feet. The flashlight had fallen free during the tussle down the embankment. Steven spotted its diffused glow in a patch of flattened grass. Both men dived for it.

Steven struck him with an elbow under the chin. Nick fell back, sliding on his side a few feet down the slope, clutching a hand at his throat. He coughed and gagged, twisting up onto his knees.

Steven had the flashlight in hand. For the moment, he disregarded Nick. He stood still, listened, arms at his sides.

The moan came from nearby.

The flashlight panned, weak light cutting through the gloom.

Steven took a step forward. "Where . . . where are you?" He heard slight movement. He redirected the beam of light.

Nick was still on the ground, on his hands and knees, his head turned in the direction of the sounds of life emanating from the darkness.

Steven proceeded forward. "Hello?"

"*Heeeere . . .*"

Steven froze. He stopped breathing, his heart in his throat. His eyes cut in every direction but saw nothing. "Say again," he called out.

The only response was an intense, chill-raising moan.

Nick got to his feet, and approached.

Steven took cautious steps, moving deliberately down the slick terrain. "I can't see you."

"*Here . . .*"

"Over there," Nick said, pointing to the right of where Steven stood.

The beam of light shifted slightly, peeling away the veil of night to uncover a human form. Steven rushed forward. He stopped suddenly. An adult male lay facedown in the ankle-deep grass and weeds. Steven swallowed hard. Something inside him understood that from this moment on things would only get worse. He approached with caution, as if the body were a viper preparing to strike. He had no idea what to do, but he had to do something fast.

He turned. "Nick! HE'S ALIVE!"

Nick approached.

"Your cell phone!" Steven said. "Call 911, hurry!"

Nick stared past his friend to the man on the ground.

"Did you hear me?"

Nick just stared, mud and grass on his face and hands. His words came out monotone, "Leave him."

The man on the ground was now making constant guttural sounds, grotesque moans that chilled Steven to the bone.

"How can you say that?" Steven said.

"Leave him, Steven. You don't want to be a part of this."

"He's dying!" Steven yelled, his pulse racing. "Make the call!"

Nick shook his head. Then he began slowly backing away.

Dumbfounded, Steven returned his full attention to the man on the ground. He reached down and tugged at one shoulder, rolling the body faceup. He recoiled at what he saw. The person before him was a male, perhaps forty years of age, with a scraggly partial beard and untrimmed hair. He wore a jeans jacket over a stained white T-shirt and olive green cargo pants. The man's face had taken quite a shot. The nose was pushed to one side, with teeth forced through his lower lip. His face was smeared with blood. One eye was half open, the other swollen shut.

"Hold on, man," Steven said, his voice shaky. "We're gonna get you help. Just hold on." The man mumbled something Steven couldn't understand. "What's your name?" Steven said.

No response.

He worked a hand under the man's backside, feeling for a wallet. The back pocket of the cargo pants was buttoned. His nervous fingers felt fat and clumsy. Finally he managed to twist the button through the buttonhole. The wallet was a cheap nylon trifold with a Velcro fastener. Blinking away tears, barely able to focus, he peeled the wallet open, fumbling it to the ground once or twice. He held the light on the man's license. The name was Ronald Calther. The face in the photo was clean-shaven with a half smile.

"Okay, Ronald, everything is going to be fine. Just stay with me. Just stay awake and keep breathing. Can you hear me? Do you understand?"

Calther managed a slight nod. The one eye appeared to find Steven.

"My name's Steven Adler, Ronald. I know you're hurting, but I'll have an ambulance here in no time, and they'll get you patched up. Just focus on me, all right?"

Another, shorter nod.

Calther was badly broken. His legs were twisted,

folded in directions they weren't designed to bend, his pants torn and bloody. It didn't take a medical examiner to see that one arm was dislocated, the way it hung loose from the socket, the shoulder severely crushed. Steven didn't want to even speculate at the internal damage. His only goals for the moment were to get his hands on Nick's cell phone, get an ambulance dispatched, and keep Ronald Calther as comfortable as possible until the flashing lights could arrive.

Speaking of Nick, he was nowhere to be seen. Steven pivoted in the muddy slop and glanced up the high embankment, watching, waiting, and fuming inside. *That selfish idiot,* he thought.

He was hesitant to move Calther. The man was in no shape to be jostled around. There were almost certainly spinal injuries. His neck might be broken. Steven hated to keep him down where it was dark and damp, but he was very reluctant to shift his broken body any more than he already had. The best he could hope to do for now was to keep him warm, awake, alert, and distracted from the misery that had befallen him on such a godforsaken night.

He called out to Nick. The Mustang was just beyond view, though he thought he could possibly make out the distant glow of the one headlight. He kept a hand on Calther's chest, his feet shifting on the flattened grass where he was crouched.

No sign of Nick.

"NICK!"

Seconds passed. At last a dark silhouette emerged at the crest of the embankment. Steven waved a hand in the air, signaling for assistance. "COME ON! 911! HURRY!"

For the longest time, Nick did not move a muscle. His silhouette remained steadfast, as if anchored where he stood, midway between the Mustang and Steven. Again, Steven waved a hand. Then, thinking that perhaps his friend had lost sight of him, he hoisted the flashlight over his head, waving it from side to side.

"MAKE THE CALL! THEN GIVE ME A HAND!"

Finally, Nick turned toward the car.

Steven let out a long breath. He bent over Calther's body. "You breathing all right? Need some water? I've got a bottle of water in the car, I think."

Calther managed to move the index finger on one hand. He groaned, his face greasy with mud. Steven put his face in his hands and shook his head, thankful Calther had survived the collision, but praying that the paramedics would make it in time. Nick had already wasted valuable minutes.

A full minute passed. Then another.

"Comeoncomeoncomeon," Steven said under his breath.

He stared down at Calther, the guilt inside him building. Calther was staring back, with that one half-opened eye. The visual exchange lasted for several long seconds, until Calther at last broke eye contact and actually appeared to be looking past Steven's shoulder. Steven followed his gaze, turning to see what might have caught his attention. He was startled to see Nick standing there, nearly right behind him, towering over them, his eyes fully focused on the man on the ground.

With his left hand, Nick held a firm grip on the tire tool from the trunk of the Mustang. It was eighteen inches long, made of solid iron. One end was designed to loosen the lug nuts that held the tires on, with the other end slightly angled and tapered at the very end for use in removing the hubcaps. Nick held it just above the tapered end.

Steven put two and two together a fraction of a second too late.

"No!"

Nick was quick. He clocked Steven in the side of the head with the heel of his shoe. Steven saw stars but not in the sky. The force of the blow spun him away from Calther. The heel had caught him in the jaw. His body twisted and he was down on his knees, and then he went facedown into the muck.

Nick Calevetti lunged forward, raising the tire tool high over his head and bringing it down hard and swift, striking Calther in the skull with deadly precision.

Whack!

The first blow rang out with a grotesque crack. The sound was like the splitting of a ripe coconut. Calther groaned.

Nick swung a second time, with even greater ferocity.

Whack!

Steven brought his head around, his double vision slowly clearing so that he could refocus. He heard the sounds of Nick grunting as he continued the assault. Silhouetted against the gloomy backdrop, the arm came down again and again, blow after blow, the tire tool wielded like a weapon of destruction, each strike wringing ever more life from Ronald Calther.

Whack! Whack!

Nick stood in a stance with his legs spread as he

bent at the waist. Blood splattered in the darkness. Calther's body flinched every time the tool made contact with his head, until at last his brain simply died, ending all communication with his nerve endings.

Struggling to his feet, Steven staggered in the general direction of Ronald Calther. Steven dropped to his knees, kneeling beside the body. The moaning and groaning had ceased. He felt for a pulse. There was none. Calther had stopped breathing.

Steven wheeled around, still on his knees.

Nick had taken a half step back.

"He's . . . *dead*," Steven said, short of breath. "You . . . you killed him!"

Nick shook his head. "No, my friend, a car hit him. Accidents happen."

Steven got to his feet, staggered to Nick, clutched his shirt. *"Why?"*

Nick pushed him aside. "You still don't get it. My license has been revoked for six months, and I'm on probation. I have alcohol in my system, and plenty of it. The penal system would crucify me, man! They'd lick their chops, seeing a rich kid like me coming down the pike!"

"You didn't have to do this!"

"What do *you* know?"

"I know you killed a man tonight!"

They locked eyes for an instant; then Nick glanced down at the tire tool still dangling from one hand. Suddenly he took several steps away, reared his arm back, and then with all his might flung the tire tool into the black void of the night. He then turned to Steven and smirked. "No I didn't."